IT DIDN'T START WITH WATERGATE

VICTOR LASKY

IT DIDN'T

START WITH

WATERGATE

THE DIAL PRESS   New York   1977

Manufactured in the United States of America

Seventh printing

Library of Congress Cataloging in Publication Data

Lasky, Victor.
It didn't start with Watergate.

Includes index.
1. Watergate Affair, 1972– 2. Corruption
(in politics)—United States. 3. United States—Politics
and government—1945– 4. United States—Politics
and government—1933–1945. 5. Press and politics—United
States. I. Title.
JK2249.L37   364.1′32′0973   77–4298
ISBN 0–8037–3857–9

TO MY WIFE

Hatred of Walpole was almost the only feeling which was common to them. On this one point, therefore, they concentrated their whole strength. With gross ignorance, or gross dishonesty, they represented the Minister as the main grievance of the state. His dismissal, his punishment, would prove the certain cure for all the evils which the nation suffered. What was to be done after his fall, how misgovernment was to be prevented in future, were questions to which there were as many answers as there were noisy and ill-informed members of the Opposition. The only cry in which all could join was "Down with Walpole!"

—MACAULAY

IT DIDN'T START WITH WATERGATE

1

SOME DAY WHEN THE PASSIONS AROUSED
by Watergate begin to subside—as perhaps they have already
begun to do—objective historians may well begin to ask themselves just what all the furor was about.

And this has become a matter of major concern for those who
have never made any bones about their hatred of Richard M.
Nixon. Thus former Representative Jerome R. Waldie, the California Democrat who had loudly participated in the impeachment proceedings, thought that President Ford's pardon of the
former President was "a mistake in terms of timing because it
denied history an element of truth" about what crimes actually
were committed.

"I don't think there are many doubts now," said Waldie, "but
I'm worried about what historians will say fifty or one hundred
years from now. I'm worried that they will not be as aware as we
are of his complicity . . ."

But complicity in what? Precisely what is Nixon accused of
doing, if he actually did it, that his predecessors didn't do many
times over? The break-in and wiretapping at the Watergate? Just
how different was that from the bugging of Barry Goldwater's
apartment during the 1964 presidential campaign?

Granted that two wrongs don't make a right; but in law and
politics, two wrongs can make a respectable precedent. And
despite its well-publicized excesses, Watergate had numerous
though less-publicized precedents in previous administrations.
Tapping of phones under Nixon? Why, that was a way of life
under John F. Kennedy. The use of the Internal Revenue Service
to harass political opponents? Why, one of the more fascinating
things to come to light in Watergate's wake was the revelation
that the Kennedy régime had subjected Nixon to annoying tax
audits.

In many ways Watergate can be considered a media event. For
without its demonstrated hostility to Nixon particularly, and

right-of-center Republicans generally, Watergate would not have been blown up into hysterical proportions. The fact is that Democratic scandals of comparable, if not greater, significance were permitted to glide by without any of the overwhelming and unrelenting attention later paid Watergate by a press which, in its lust for *machismo,* sought to disembowel a hated President. At the same time every effort was made to redress the American political balance leftward, after its rightist drift. The aim of these partisans in nonpartisan clothing was retroactively to "win" the 1972 election. And, for the most part, they succeeded.

The eagerness of much of the media to commit regicide was freely conceded by Waldie. He noted that the press "disliked Nixon intensely," and he doubted whether the President would have been forced out of office "if the press had not desired it."

In contrast, according to Waldie, the press coverage of Nelson Rockefeller's nomination as Vice President was "abominable." Contending that Rocky's alleged involvement in "criminal acts" while serving as governor was treated "gently" by the media, Waldie insisted that the leading newspapers in the nation—*The New York Times,* the Los Angeles *Times,* the Washington *Post,* among others—wanted him confirmed, hence the laying off.

Whatever the merits of Waldie's argument, Nixon was banished into self-imposed exile, a broken man, while Rockefeller was confirmed as Vice President, a heartbeat away from the presidency itself. Whether Rockefeller, as governor of the Empire State, committed "crimes" is most arguable. But Waldie believes he did, as he believes Nixon did.

Less arguable is the thesis that never before in the history of the Republic has any man, in high office or out, been so thoroughly investigated as was Nixon. He was stripped and humiliated in public; his innermost thoughts as recorded on tapes were transcribed for a nation of voyeurs; and his income and expenditures down to the last penny were spread before every nit-picking tax lawyer. Even his psyche was probed without letup and amateur analysts questioned his sanity.

Finally, after resisting a merciless campaign of hatred and ridicule the likes of which had never before been leveled against any previous President, Nixon buckled. Unable to lead the nation at a time of burgeoning crises, some of which were the direct result of his weakened presidency, he resigned, the first Chief Executive in the nation's history to do so. The predominantly liberal media had helped bring down a President. The fourth estate had never before felt so powerful.

But was all this necessarily good for the nation?

Former Senator J. William Fulbright, for one, didn't think so. The Arkansas Democrat, who until his retirement from the Senate in 1974 headed the Foreign Relations Committee, considers the role of the press in Watergate disturbing.

In fact, as a writer for *The New York Times Magazine* put it, Fulbright "sounds almost like Julie Nixon Eisenhower as he criticizes the press." The writer, Daniel Yergin, quoted the former senator as having said:

> The Watergate was ballooned up into an enormous issue. People like those two reporters who uncovered it for the *Washington Post* and the *Post* itself—they were sort of like Christopher Columbus —they had discovered a whole new world. People made reputations overnight discovering some new scandal. They're still doing it, they just love it. The papers are devoted almost altogether to stories of this kind. . . . No one really approved of wiretapping, going back fifty years, but we all knew it was going on, and all accepted it—and a lot of other practices. In their minds people don't approve of covert CIA activities, and yet the majority of people say we've got to do it because the others are doing it."*

Fulbright, incidentally, would have settled for a Senate censure of Nixon, believing that act alone would have been enough to discipline what he described as an "arrogant" administration. But with the pressures being exerted without letup by a rampaging media, that was not to be. Instead we witnessed not only the political assassination of a President but the near-destruction of the prestige of the presidency itself—with great damage to the nation both at home and abroad. The consequences will be felt for generations to come.

That Watergate has been blown up out of all proportion to the realities—becoming a veritable "teapot in a tempest," to reverse the phrase—is the guiding thesis of the chapters that follow. As is the fact that Adam and Eve did not tryst at the Watergate. Original and subsequent sin were around a long time before Nixon was sworn into office. And political transgressions did not cease with the banishment of Nixon to San

---

*Daniel Yergin, "Fulbright's Last Frustration," *The New York Times Magazine*, Nov. 24, 1974.

Clemente. Now we know that while Jimmy Carter was jetting around during the 1976 primaries preaching goodness, honesty, compassion, and all the virtues of "born-again" Christianity, his minions were resorting to that most ancient of political evils— buying votes. And with federal funds yet. Jimmy's boys got caught, but most of the media couldn't have cared less. The first scandal of the Carter campaign was quickly and conveniently forgotten after the Democratic standardbearer conceded publicly that it was all so embarrassing.

"Watergate," of course, has become a catch-all for a variety of political sins, real and imagined. And all of it flowed from the break-in at the headquarters of the Democratic National Committee which was largely the result of poor judgment and amateurish stupidity on the part of the participants. Rarely has there been a more inane caper. Everything went wrong—as if by design. The walkie-talkies malfunctioned; the lock-picker had difficulty picking locks; and the burglars bugged the wrong phones, cut themselves on broken glass, and practically invited discovery. When apprehended, they were found to possess incriminating address books as well as large sums of currency easily traceable to the Nixon reelection effort. It was almost as if they had been deliberately dropping clues.

The extraordinary thing about the inane caper was that leading Democrats and at least one prominent journalist knew well in advance that something of the sort was in the works. As for the Democrats, they took no extra precautions to guard against the break-in. In fact they chortled with glee when the event finally took place. Of course, publicly, they viewed it with excessive alarm.

And while the break-in and wiretapping cannot be condoned, even if their fruits were almost nil, the so-called cover up and obstruction of justice can easily be explained in terms of human and natural reactions. They were not the "crimes of the century" as trumpeted by a gleeful media. For, in the final analysis, the "Great Conspiracy" consisted of a series of hastily contrived, last-minute actions aimed at figuring a way out of a mess whose origins to this day remain obscure.

All of which is not to say that Nixon did not help contribute to his own destruction. He blundered in the handling of the problems created by the break-in. He now concedes they were "errors of judgment." At first he did not take the episode seriously.

After all, political skulduggery, including wiretapping, had been practiced on him during his many campaigns. As he viewed it, it was all part of the game. What he had not counted on was the ferocity of an unforgiving media.

In the final analysis, therefore, Richard Nixon was less the sinner than he was sinned against. Or as Chancellor W. Allen Wallis of the University of Rochester put it, "The reaction by journalists and politicians to the Watergate break-in has been morally even more corrupt than the Watergate activities themselves."

There is probably no greater evidence of that corruption than the deliberate ignoring by much of the media and such political luminaries as Senator Sam Ervin of the numerous political excesses—some of which make Watergate look like penny-ante stuff—committed by Nixon's predecessors. But unlike Nixon, none of his predecessors in the Oval Office ever faced the remotest possibility of impeachment. Most of them were secure in the knowledge that majorities of their own party controlled the Congress; and they all presided during periods when the nation's capital was not in the mood to eviscerate itself—as was the case during the Nixon years. Moreover none of them was naïve enough to install taping systems which constantly recorded the most confidential of conversations. More importantly, none ever squandered his political power so ineptly. If Richard Nixon was guilty of anything at all, it was his inability to hold on to the overwhelming mandate given him by the American people in 1972.

The hypocrisy so evident in much of the bewailing of Watergate was noted by none other than Alexander Solzhenitsyn. Even before he left the Soviet Union, the Nobel Prize-winning author referred to the "dense hypocrisy characteristic of today's American political life," and, most notably, "of the Senate leaders with their distorted view of the discordant Watergate affair.

"Without in any way defending Nixon or the Republican party, how can one not be amazed at the hypocritical, clamorous rage displayed by the Democrats? Has American politics not been full of mutual deceit and cases of misconduct during previous election campaigns, except, perhaps, that they were not on such a high level of electronic technology and remained happily undiscovered?"

Never were truer words written.

So, did the Good Guys really win? Were there actually any Good Guys in all of this? Did Watergate produce a new race of heroes? The record, alas, as revealed in the following pages, shows few heroes but many hypocrites.

2

BEING HUMAN, ALL PRESIDENTS HAVE had their character flaws, Richard Nixon most definitely not excepted. But in the emotions engendered during the Watergate period, previous presidents were eulogized to an incredible degree in order to point out Nixon's deficiencies. This trend was carried to a ludicrous extreme when *The New Yorker* asked prominent persons "to tell us their reactions" to the famous (or infamous) edited transcripts of the tape recordings made by Nixon as President.

"I've read about half the transcripts, and the contrast with the Johnson White House is enormous," intoned Joseph A. Califano, Jr., who had been special assistant to President Johnson. "I think it's an utterly amoral discussion. . . . It really is a group of amoral people saving their own skins. . . . It's not really comparable to anything that happened to Johnson."

"What struck me first was the squalor of the Nixon White House," commented Arthur Schlesinger, Jr., the in-house and still functioning apologist for the Kennedy administration. "Nixon was always proud of his historic firsts, and this beats all his predecessors in sleaziness."

Apparently Schlesinger and Califano didn't have the faintest idea of what really went on behind the scenes in the administrations they so loyally and unquestioningly served. Schlesinger, for example, couldn't possibly have known about the numerous party girls sharing the President's bed. There were of course other, "nicer" young ladies who dallied in the delights of Camelot while Jackie was away—and she was away frequently. And a few aides close to the dashing young President were aware of how JFK would while away those precious moments between crises. But not apparently Schlesinger, who in none of his adulatory writings ever portrayed JFK for what he was—an activist President beyond Warren G. Harding's wildest hopes and dreams.

In any case Schlesinger and Califano have been unduly modest about the legacies both John Fitzgerald Kennedy and Lyndon Baines Johnson bequeathed to Richard Milhous Nixon. The fact remains that the whole truth was not fully served by their predictably pompous reactions to the Nixon tapes.

For there was little that was done during the Nixon administration of an offending nature that had not been done by preceding administrations, sometimes in spades. As Vermont Royster observed, "The harsh fact is that almost every single action of the Watergate perpetrators—wiretapping, spying on political enemies, covering up political malfeasance—has its antecedent example somewhere in recent history." The editor-emeritus of the *Wall Street Journal* also noted that "from Roosevelt to Nixon, Presidents at times concealed what they were doing and sometimes even lied to the country." And while not excusing Nixon, there can be little doubt that he was subjected to a scrutiny that no other President was ever subjected to or, most likely, ever will be again.

Apparently referring to his good friend John Kennedy, Joseph Alsop once wrote, "I myself have seen a felony being cheerfully compounded by a President of the United States, whose loss was one of the greatest losses of my life. It was vastly to his own advantage but equally to the advantage of this country. I laughed and said nothing."

Let's read that again. A felony—that is, a criminal act—was "compounded" by a President. That does not necessarily mean that the President committed the original crime. But it could mean that, for a consideration (perhaps to protect his administration) he agreed not to prosecute or punish a wrongdoer—in other words, a cover up of some presumably evil deed. Which, of course, was so funny that Alsop laughed and said nothing. What wasn't funny is the fact that Joe could have opened himself up to prosecution on a charge of obstructing justice in failing to report such criminal behavior. Fortunately for him, the statute of limitations undoubtedly applies in his case.

Whatever else can be said of Nixon, there was one thing he did not do in his five and a half years in office. As far as the record shows, he did not discuss the pros and cons of murdering foreign leaders who had aroused his ire. This is precisely what Kennedy did in a conversation with George Smathers, then a senator from Florida.

That conversation was recounted by Smathers in an oral history interview recorded on March 31, 1964, for the Kennedy Library.* The transcript reads:

> We had further conversation of assassination of Fidel Castro, what would be the reaction, how would the people react, would the people be gratified. I'm sure he [Kennedy] had his own ideas about it, but he was picking my brain. . . . As I recollect, he was just throwing out a great barrage of questions—he was certain it could be accomplished. . . . But the question was whether or not it would accomplish that which he wanted it to, whether or not the reaction throughout South America would be good or bad. And I talked with him about it and, frankly, at this particular time I felt, and I later on learned that he did, that I wasn't so much for the idea of assassination, particularly when it could be pinned on the United States.

Of course this and other revelations concerning the involvement of the Kennedy brothers—Jack and Bobby—in assassination discussions sent their defenders up the wall. Truly furious was Frank Mankiewicz, who publicly assailed Nelson Rockefeller as a "liar" for daring to suggest that such discussions occurred in the Kennedy White House. How Mankiewicz could have any direct knowledge of what transpired during the Kennedy years is difficult to comprehend simply because he was not in Camelot's inner circle. He did not become Robert Kennedy's press aide until several years after JFK's untimely death.

But that did not prevent Mankiewicz from going after William Safire who, in his column in *The New York Times* made the point that, as President, Nixon never ordered the murder of a fellow chief of state. Safire's implication was that Kennedy may well have done so. And that led Mankiewicz to write a lengthy rebuttal for the Washington *Post,* in which he contended that "Safire's column is representative of a well-orchestrated campaign on the part of die-hard believers in Nixon's innocence to make us forget the hard-earned lessons of Watergate by encouraging us to believe that all recent Presidents shared Nixon's genuinely and uniquely low moral standards."

It was, of course, an intemperate remark. True, Safire had been a speechwriter for Nixon; but he was far from being a "die-hard"

---

*As reported in Richard J. Walton, *Cold War and Counterrevolution: The Foreign Policy of John F. Kennedy* (New York: Viking, 1972) pp. 47–48.

believer in "Nixon's innocence." Moreover the reference to a "well-orchestrated campaign" was strictly a figment of an over-worked imagination. That Mankiewicz was carrying a heavy work load was evidenced by the fact that in a short period of time he had written several books portraying Nixon as the arch villain of all time; had traveled to Cuba, where he interviewed Castro at length for a friendly film documentary; and had co-authored another book based on his Cuban experiences in which Fidel most definitely is not portrayed as villainous. At the same time he appointed himself the chief defender of the Kennedy name and honor, even though he conceded he did not know all the facts.

Like Mankiewicz, Schlesinger was also fit to be tied by the assassination revelations. But Artie was more temperate in his defense of the Kennedys. He didn't go around calling people "liars" for saying there's evidence linking anti-Castro plotting to the Kennedys. Obviously he was not too certain as to just what the facts were. In an article in the *Wall Street Journal* Schlesinger noted that just prior to the Bay of Pigs he had sat in on many "top secret White House meetings" dealing with that upcoming fiasco, but that not once had the subject of bumping off Castro ever come up. This was indeed a remarkable confession on the part of the author of the "definitive" book on the Kennedy years, a Pulitzer Prize winner yet. For it demonstrated that Schlesinger never really knew what went on in the top echelons of the White House. One reason for that, as Dean Rusk once suggested in another context, was that everyone knew—from Kennedy down—that Artie was a blabbermouth. And the word went out from the Oval Office not to tell Schlesinger anything of consequence lest such information should become public knowledge among the Georgetown set that very night.

The die-hard loyalty of such Kennedy mythmakers was truly something to behold. According to the likes of Mankiewicz and Schlesinger, the Kennedys rarely, if ever, did anything wrong. Even when it was firmly established, for example, that Robert Kennedy directed the FBI to place a wiretap on Dr. Martin Luther King, Jr., Mankiewicz came up with an explanation fully exonerating his former employer. Mankiewicz did not deny the tap. He conceded that Kennedy did approve "one wiretap on the office of Martin Luther King," but only one. Which is somewhat like saying that the young lady was only a little bit pregnant.* But, wrote Mankiewicz, "the purpose was to attempt to prove or disprove a charge—by FBI Director J. Edgar Hoover—that a secret Communist was working for King. The results were negative. . . ."

The implication was that Robert Kennedy was the innocent dupe of the malevolent Hoover; and that as Attorney General he rarely, if ever, authorized the use of wiretaps.

A more reliable account as to why the King inquiry was launched has been provided by one of JFK's best friends, Charles Bartlett. In his column for the Washington *Star* Bartlett recently disclosed that the inquiry was authorized "in a spirit of anxiety" over Dr. King's associations. "The Kennedy brothers were initially puzzled over King's intentions. He appeared to have links that reached into both the Rockefeller and Communist camps. Uncertain whether he was conspiring to overthrow the country or the Kennedy Administration, they readily assented to Hoover's plans for close scrutiny."

The Kennedys' penchant for wiretapping has lately been documented by more official bodies. The Rockefeller Commission on CIA Activities Within the United States, for example, reported that a newsman had been wiretapped by the CIA in 1962—with no authority in law—"apparently with the knowledge and consent of Attorney General Kennedy." The Kennedy mythmakers said nothing about the revelation. And these were the same people who called for or helped fashion an article of impeachment when it was revealed that Nixon had approved the wiretapping of newsmen.

And talk about sleaziness! In conversations with Benjamin C. Bradlee, President Kennedy would sound out his journalist-friend on the possibility of obtaining and publishing information damaging to JFK's political adversaries—Bradlee who as executive editor of the Washington *Post*, which claims to have had much to do with saving the Constitution from Richard Nixon's depredations, apparently was not overly concerned about such matters when they involved his presidential buddy.**

---

*What Mankiewicz did not say (perhaps he did not know) was that that "one wiretap" remained in place for more than eighteen months, until removed in April 1965.
**Bradlee's diary recollections of his talks with JFK are contained in his extremely revealing book, *Conversations with Kennedy* (New York: W. W. Norton,

For, as Bradlee discloses with little disapproval, wiretapping, prying into tax returns, election fraud, misuse of federal agencies —all of these, he admits in effect, were practiced and/or discussed in his presence by President Kennedy. Occasionally Kennedy had FBI Director Hoover over for lunch, and a little dirt for dessert. "Boy, the dirt he has on those Senators," the President once said, shaking his head. And what apparently amused Kennedy more than anything else were Hoover's revelations about which whores his former Senate colleagues were then patronizing. On one occasion the director showed JFK a photograph of a German girl who had been involved with Bobby Baker—"a really beautiful woman," sighed the President.*

There was another reason for the President's buttering up of Hoover. As he undoubtedly suspected, the director had also been keeping a file on him going back to his days as a young World War II naval intelligence officer, at which time he had been carrying on with a comely foreigner suspected of having pro-Nazi sympathies. Which apparently was one of the reasons, if not the main one, why JFK on his election resisted strong liberal pressure to oust the director. Not even a President could know what was in a file kept under lock and key in Hoover's private office.

Thanks to Bradlee, too, we have now learned that Kennedy's private conversation was most uninhibited. His scatalogical references made Nixon's sound like a Boy Scout's. Fortunately (or unfortunately) for history, "Benjy"—as the President liked to call his buddy—was there to record the just-between-us-boys observations of a Chief Executive who, thanks to his speechwriters (and they were among the best), has gone down in history as an elegant, witty phrasemaker.

Now, it turns out, there was a different Kennedy hidden from public view—one whose "excesses of language," as Bradlee concedes, were "generally protected" by the press. In other words the readers of *Newsweek*, of which Bradlee was then Washington

---

1975). The "real" Kennedy emerges from the pages of this instant bestseller. Commenting on excerpts published in advance in *Playboy*, columnist Safire wrote in *The New York Times:* "Nowhere in these early selections from the Kennedy transcripts is there the idealistic uplift and intellectual stimulus that we have been led to associate with the late President."

*Early in 1975 the Washington *Post* precipitated a scandal by charging that the FBI keeps files on the private lives of elected officials. The executive editor had been aware of that for more than a decade.

bureau chief, were never made privy to the kind of language JFK generally used in normal, private conversation. Years later, though, *Newsweek*—like that other weekly publication—relished publishing Nixon's expletives, even those he sought to delete.

In this connection it is amusing to recall the numerous articles published by the Washington *Post* following the release of the Nixon transcripts. Various aides of former presidents were asked to contrast the moral tone in the Oval Office, when they sat near the throne, with that revealed by the tape-recorded, off-the-cuff behavior of Nixon. Almost without exception the aides to Roosevelt, Truman, Eisenhower, Kennedy, and Johnson (yes, Johnson!) found Nixon lacking; and none more so than Pierre Salinger. JFK's press secretary could hardly believe Nixon's language, nor the unseemly subjects he discussed. One could almost visualize Pierre's well-padded cheeks crimsoning in horror as he valiantly read on.

Salinger was also perturbed by the marked informality in the way subordinates spoke to Nixon. In Kennedy's day, wrote Salinger, he was always addressed as "sir" or "Mr. President." Now, suppose circumstances were reversed, with the transcripts revealing that Nixon's aides had called him "sir" and "Mr. President" in every sentence they uttered; the very same critics undoubtedly would have condemned the imperial manner of the Nixon White House, while applauding Kennedy's informality with his staff.

There were a few newsmen, however, who failed to be smitten by JFK's charms. One of them, the veteran Richard Wilson of the Cowles publications, was described by the young President as "the biggest S.O.B." in the press corps. Once JFK referred to Wilson in naval code as a "Charlie-Uncle-Nan-Tare." A puzzled Jackie demanded to know what exactly was "a Charlie-Uncle-Nan-Tare, for heaven's sake," but Kennedy didn't tell her.

Unlike Nixon, Kennedy generally relaxed with members of the fourth estate. A more uptight Nixon viewed the press corps as consisting mainly of liberal ideologues out to get him. And he wasn't too far wrong. But Kennedy, a frustrated sometime journalist himself, felt like one of the boys. And he frequently talked like one. Thus while seeking the presidential nomination in early 1960, he confided to a few *Newsweek* staffers how he intended to run in the forthcoming primaries: "Well, I'm going to fucking well take Ohio, for openers."*

That line did not appear in print in 1960. Nor did many other eye-opening remarks made by Kennedy. One such was transmitted to *Time*'s home office by a correspondent traveling with the pre-presidential Kennedy. Describing a weekend in Boston on a sultry summer day, the senator was quoted as having said, "It was so hot that even the niggers went to the beach." Of course *Time* ignored the remark in its published coverage. Yet the people's right to know anything and everything won out some years later, when Spiro Agnew made what he thought to be a jocular reference to a "fat Jap" traveling in the press corps.

Which was one of the reasons Nixon was assailed for having named him as his Vice President. But now we learn that Kennedy often referred to the man he selected as his Vice President as a "riverboat gambler." And when the scandals involving Bobby Baker (and indirectly LBJ) erupted, Kennedy was as unperturbed as was Nixon when Watergate first came to his attention. "Kennedy," writes Bradlee, "was unwilling to knock Baker, saying, 'I thought of him primarily as a rogue, not a crook. He was always telling me he knew where he could get me the cutest little girls, but he never did.' "

The fascinating thing about the Bradlee book is that the author professes to find nothing but charm in Jack despite repeated instances of vindictiveness and crudity. As when Kennedy urged Bradlee to get *Newsweek* to really give the business to Arthur Krock, the Pulitzer Prize-winning columnist of *The New York Times,* a man then in his late seventies who had written the introduction to Kennedy's college thesis, later published as the book *Why England Slept.* Annoyed by Krock's well-reasoned criticism of his presidency, Kennedy suggested that Bradlee "bust it off in old Arthur. He can't take it, and when you go after him he folds." But *Newsweek* treated Krock with somewhat more restraint, and Kennedy, annoyed, felt the magazine had not "tucked it to Arty" enough.

When Bradlee mentioned that *Newsweek* was planning to do a story on then Governor Rockefeller, the President suggested, "You ought to cut Rocky's ass open a little this week." Years later

---

*This is the way the JFK statement appeared in the *Playboy* version of the Bradlee book. When the book was published, the word "fucking" became "God-damn." Rather than deleting, the editors substituted.

a young man named Donald Segretti was cutting up adversaries for the Nixon reelection effort. Now we learn that JFK sought to make *Newsweek* his Segretti.

Kennedy asked whether *Newsweek* intended to look into Rockefeller's war record. He was particularly anxious to find out where the governor had been while Kennedy was commanding that famous PT boat in Japanese-infested Pacific waters—as if he didn't know. "Where was old Nels when you and I were dodging bullets in the Solomon Islands?" he wondered out loud. "How old was he? He must have been 31 or 32. Why don't you look into that?"*

"It is interesting," comments Bradlee, "how often Kennedy referred to the war records of political opponents." In this connection the President often mentioned Hubert Humphrey and Edward J. McCormack, Jr., the then Speaker's nephew, who had the temerity to contest baby brother Teddy in the 1962 Democratic primary for the Senate seat from Massachusetts. "When are you going to send one of your ace reporters to look into Eddie's record?" Kennedy asked Bradlee. Then Kennedy launched into an analysis of what he said was that record; namely, that McCormack had resigned his navy commission the very day he graduated from the Naval Academy, claiming a medical disability. "Half of it was nerves and half of it was a bad back, and he's been drawing a sixty percent disability ever since up until six months ago." The President then suggested that Bradlee talk to his aide David Powers, who had even more information.

As far as is known, Bradlee never used the Kennedy information on McCormack. Had he done so, he undoubtedly would have been challenged as to its accuracy. For the record shows that McCormack did not resign his commission when he graduated from Annapolis in 1946. Instead he served for three years in the navy, much of that time as a gunnery officer on a destroyer. In 1949 he severely hurt his back when he fell off a turret. He was then discharged from active duty.

The question still remains how Kennedy was aware that McCormack had been drawing disability allowances for his injury. One can only surmise how the President obtained this sup-

---

*Rockefeller, born July 8, 1908, was thirty-three years old when the Japanese attacked at Pearl Harbor. In *Who's Who in America* he is listed as Coordinator of Inter-American Affairs during the war years 1940–44, and as Assistant Secretary of State in 1945–46.

posedly confidential information from the files of the Veterans Administration, information to which he, even as President, was not entitled by law.

But the best-kept secret of the Kennedy administration is only hinted at in the Bradlee book. And that was the President's predilection for pretty girls. Kennedy's exploits would have put Warren Harding to shame. How he could find time for all those extracurricular activities, even during crises, has to be one of the wonders of Camelot. Perhaps his hyperactivity was stimulated by the shots of "speed" he frequently was given by the notorious Dr. Max Jacobson of New York. At any rate, according to *Time,* JFK in 1962 confided to British Prime Minister Harold Macmillan and Foreign Minister R. A. Butler that "if he went too long without a woman, he suffered headaches."

Even more significant was the way Kennedy managed to carry on without a single breath of scandal reaching the public prints. It wasn't because the boys with the ballpoint pens weren't aware of what was going on. Many of them were.

The media that wept copious tears about how Nixon degraded his office could never work up any moral indignation about the "moral stain" brought to the White House by one of its heroes. This was what *The New Republic* many years later meant, in another context, when it noted with sorrow that relations between JFK and the press had indeed been too "chummy."

President Kennedy's public image clashed mightily with his private life. The public image, presented through an all-too-willing media, was that of the good husband, the kind family man, and the perfect father. Camelot was never sullied by stories of what really was going on behind the scenes, the sybaritic, hedonistic life led by a President who felt he could do anything and get away with it.

As columnist Earl Wilson put it in his book *Show Business Laid Bare,** JFK would probably have approved of the contention that he was "the sexiest, swingingest President of the century, and not have thought it disrespectful." Wilson estimates that the President's "score card, if he kept one, would probably have run into dozens, even possibly hundreds." And not just celebrated actresses or socialities either, reports Wilson. His conquests in-

---

*(New York: G. P. Putnam's Sons, 1974).

cluded "stewardesses, secretaries, models and those strange creatures who like to offer their bodies to Big Names."

The Wilson book is the best source of information on this subject. My own sources during the Kennedy era were Secret Service agents assigned to guard the President. On an off-the-record basis they expressed concern about "Lancer's" (JFK's code name) dalliances with women he hardly knew. It wasn't so much that they were prudish. What concerned them were the security problems involved. One agent even wondered aloud whether the Russians might not be tempted to "plant a broad" in the President's bedroom. But there was little the agents could do about it.

It was the FBI, not the Secret Service, that determined the President was "making out" with a young woman who, between appointments in the White House bedroom, was also keeping company with Mafia hoods Sam ("Momo") Giancana and John Roselli, both of whom—since all the recent unwelcome publicity also involving their CIA connections—have been dispatched gangland-style to meet their maker. And it was Edgar Hoover himself who went to the White House to warn the President in a private session that a continuance of his secret relations with Judith Campbell (more currently Mrs. Exner) could only lead to political disaster. It had been a romance that flourished for several years after Senator Kennedy first spotted the comely Judith at a party in Las Vegas. As Mrs. Exner now remembers the President, he was "a warm, extraordinarily energetic and inquisitive man," who "was fascinated by Hollywood gossip and (by) who was sleeping with whom among the stars." Apparently the leader of the Free World never let Judith in on any state secrets such as the plots to waste Castro which her other boyfriends were supposed to be carrying out for the CIA.

But because of Hoover's warning JFK's relationship with Judith was terminated. And not too soon, either. For as Edwin A. Roberts, Jr., lately put it in the *National Observer:* "If his friendship with Judith Campbell Exner, who was also a friend of two Mafia leaders, hired by the CIA to kill Castro, had become public knowledge, it is safe to say that Kennedy's political career would have been over. He certainly would not have been renominated and perhaps he would have been forced to resign." Thus Judith Exner has become another romantic figure, to be remembered along with Arthur Schlesinger, Jr., Ted Sorensen, Pierre Salinger, and so many other fondly recalled names from the fabulous epoch of Camelot.

Another more tragic figure involved romantically with JFK was Mary Pinchot Meyer, a Washington artist and socialite. A year after Kennedy's assassination Mrs. Meyer was shot to death while walking along the old canal towpath in Georgetown. A twenty-five-year-old District man was arrested and tried for the death, but was acquitted.

Mrs. Meyer had once been married to a prominent CIA official, Cord Meyer, Jr. Before their divorce in 1956 the Meyers had lived in McLean, Virginia, where Ethel and Robert Kennedy were next-door neighbors. Following the divorce, Mary, then thirty-six, moved to a Georgetown townhouse around the corner from her sister, Mrs. Benjamin Bradlee (yes, Benjy was her brother-in-law), and Senator John F. Kennedy. Her closest friends at the time were the Truitts, Ann and James. Ann was a sculptor and Mary's confidante; Jim Truitt was then a vice president of the Washington *Post.* *

It was the Truitts in whom Mary Meyer confided about her affair with Kennedy. And Truitt, an old *Time-Life* correspondent, began keeping notes of what Mary told him. Many years later Truitt showed his notes to and was interviewed by the *National Enquirer.* The ensuing story was a sensational one indeed.**

Suffice it to say that the romance lasted from January 1962 to

---

*Truitt, who had been a former assistant to publisher Philip Graham until he died by his own hand, was let go from the newspaper in late 1970. Because of that position Truitt obviously knew a lot about the paper's dirty linen. So the management sought to make certain he wouldn't talk by agreeing to pay him off in exchange for his silence. Legal hush money?

On December 23, 1970, Frederick S. Beebe, then chairman of the board of the Washington Post Company, sent Truitt a letter, stating he had instructed "Bob Thome to send you a check for $35,000 as full payment in connection with the termination of your employment. . . ." Beebe, however, added this astonishing caveat: "As I am sure you understand from our recent discussions, this payment is premised upon the assurance you have given that you will not in the future write anything for publication about your experiences as an employe at the Post that is in any way derogatory of the Company, Phil or the Graham family."

**So sensational in fact that it could not be ignored by the Washington *Post.* A front-page story, written by Don Oberdorfer while Bradlee was vacationing in the Virgin Islands, told of JFK's two-year love affair with Mrs. Meyer. But other newspapers and the network news shows generally shunned the yarn. However *New Times* was later to explore the subject in great detail in a troubling article by Phillip Nobile and Ron Rosenbaum entitled "The Mysterious Murder of JFK's Mistress."

November 1963, when JFK was murdered. According to Truitt, the President would entertain his lady love in his living quarters several times a week during the twenty-three-month period. The two would "usually have drinks and dinner alone or sometimes with one of his aides. Then the aides would excuse themselves and leave."

Truitt's notes record an episode on the night of July 16, 1962, when Mary turned JFK on with marijuana which Truitt said later he had provided for the occasion. At first JFK didn't feel anything, but then he began to laugh and reputedly told Mary: "We're having a White House conference on narcotics here in two weeks." After the third joint JFK said, "No more. Suppose the Russians did something now."

Following Mary's death, her diary was uncovered by her sister, Tony Bradlee, who turned it over to James Angleton, then chief of CIA counterintelligence. An old friend of Mary Meyer, Angleton has since been vague as to what happened to the diary. According to Truitt, however, the document was taken to CIA headquarters, where it was destroyed.

JFK's fascination with Mary Meyer was alluded to by Bradlee in *Conversations with Kennedy*. In one passage Bradlee quotes the President as commenting after a White House dance in February 1962 on "the overall appeal of the daughter of Prince Paul of Yugoslavia and Mary Meyer. 'Mary would be rough to live with,' Kennedy noted, not for the first time. And I agreed, not for the first time."

Kennedy apparently was able to keep any number of romances going at the same time. Thus, according to Earl Wilson, the President had also been having a torrid romance with Marilyn Monroe for about a year before she died. It was a story which the columnist decided to disclose in order to "set the record straight," because Norman Mailer, in his book on the actress, dwelled mainly on Marilyn's friendship with Robert Kennedy.

Another authority is Sidney Skolsky, the Hollywood columnist, who wound up his memoirs by apologizing for having failed to report at the time that JFK had climbed into the sack with Miss Monroe.* Then followed this significant observation: "I confess that I still find it grim to speculate on what might have happened to me if I had tried to write about this romance in my column when it first came to my attention."

Don't Get Me Wrong—I Love Hollywood (New York: G. P. Putnam's Sons, 1975).

Monroe's death in August 1962 shook up the White House—
and every effort was made to downplay the relationships of Marilyn with the Kennedy brothers. For example Bobby had been in
Los Angeles the weekend of Marilyn's death. In fact women at
a card party next door to her home claimed they saw the Attorney General "and a man with a doctor's bag" enter her house the
day she died. Yet Peter Lawford, then Kennedy's brother-in-law,
insisted that RFK was not in California that weekend. This despite the fact that two newspapers reported him as being there.*

Perhaps more significant is the fact that much of the official
material relating to the Monroe death has disappeared. The complete file was removed from the records of the Los Angeles
Police Department and a top police official—now dead—is suspected of having pulled the file in order to curry favor with
Attorney General Kennedy. The official had had hopes of succeeding Hoover as FBI director. Also missing were the records
of Marilyn's long-distance phone calls. According to Slatzer,
many of the calls just prior to her death had been to Robert
Kennedy. And her last call apparently went to Lawford. The
actor himself told Earl Wilson that Marilyn's last words, as she
slipped into unconsciousness, were: "Say goodby to Pat [Pat
Kennedy Lawford], say goodby to the President, and say goodby
to yourself because you're a nice guy."

Her death was officially listed as a "probable suicide." Slatzer,
who thinks otherwise, has called for a new inquiry. But whatever
did happen in the troubling case, the truth is that there had
indeed been a massive cover up, one designed to protect the
Kennedys by hiding their relationships with the actress. And
while those relationships were common gossip in press circles at
the time, no major newspaper or television network appeared
interested enough to delve into the story.

Almost a similar state of affairs occurred seven years later
when Senator Edward M. Kennedy drove a car carrying a young
lady named Mary Jo Kopechne off a bridge at Chappaquiddick.

---

*Unanswered, and troubling, questions about the Monroe death are raised in an
extraordinary book, *The Life and Curious Death of Marilyn Monroe*, by Robert
F. Slatzer, who claims to have been one of the actress's former husbands (New
York: Pinnacle House, 1974). The reviews were few and far between. But Norman
Mailer, who had written at length about Bobby's romance with Marilyn, commented: "Slatzer's book really presents such a massive amount of evidence of the
possibility of a murder that you're left with the feeling that it's going to be harder
now to prove that she did commit suicide. . . ."

From the start it was obvious that "Teddy" was not telling the truth about the incident, which involved the girl's death by drowning. A report by the inquest judge also characterized the senator's driving of the car as probably "criminal." And that report doubted Kennedy's testimony on where he and the girl were headed when the accident took place.

Yet the newspapers and networks dropped the story after reporting the senator's convoluted explanation of what had happened that dark night in July 1969. It was an explanation devised at an amazing gathering at Hyannisport of the Camelot hierarchy come together to put a gloss over the events at Chappaquiddick. Fortunately for Kennedy, there was no tape recorder in his living room at the compound to record what must have been a remarkable discussion on how to circumvent the law.

In the wake of Watergate, however, several publications, including the Boston *Globe* and the Sunday Magazine of *The New York Times*, did publish belated accounts suggesting that Kennedy had not been fully responsive about Chappaquiddick. Which, of course, was a polite way of calling him a liar. Nevertheless, once the senator announced he was removing himself as a possible 1976 presidential contender, the matter was dropped. The stark fact remains that Kennedy emerged from an apparent negligent homicide with nothing more than a slap on the hand.

Ironically Kennedy was the first major politician to get interested in Watergate. Using the staff of his Subcommittee on Administrative Practices and Procedures, he launched his own private inquiry into the financing of the break-in. And then he sought—successfully, as it turned out—to convince the Senate Democratic leadership to pursue the investigation more thoroughly. Obviously Kennedy thought he had enough experience to tell a cover up when he saw one.

3

FOR SHEER SLEAZINESS IN POLITICS LIT-
tle can compare with the tactics employed in the relentless and
humorless drive of the clan Kennedy to win control of the White
House. And no one was more aware of this than Hubert Humphrey, who also sought the 1960 Democratic nomination for President. For, as Theodore White put it, the Kennedy organization
"clubbed" the senator from Minnesota into defeat.

At one point during the West Virginia primary Humphrey was
so angered by the campaign of smear and innuendo being waged
against him that he accused both Jack and Bobby Kennedy of
being guilty of "cheap, low-down gutter politics." He referred to
Jack as "the spoiled candidate" and to his brother, as "that young,
emotional, juvenile Bobby."

The Kennedys even brought in a surrogate to do their dirty
work in West Virginia. In a state with a high percentage of war
veterans, Franklin Delano Roosevelt, Jr., extolled Kennedy as
"the only wounded veteran" running for President. Which, of
course, could be considered hot stuff down in the land of cricks
and hollers. But then Roosevelt added something new to his
spiel. "There's another candidate in your primary," he said.
"He's a good Democrat, but I don't know where he was in World
War II."

The implication was quite clear: while JFK was courageously
defending the nation out there in the Pacific—and getting
wounded in the process—Hubert Humphrey was hiding out in
the hills somewhere.*

The next day the Washington *Star* editorially assailed the
Roosevelt statement as "a new low in dirty politics." Which indeed it was, the newspaper noting that Humphrey, married and

---

*Actually Kennedy was not wounded. An old back injury, aggravated by his
PT-109 disaster, plus a bout with malaria, brought him home from the Pacific.

the father of three children, had sought to enlist in the navy but had been rejected for a physical disability.

Kennedy not only failed to repudiate Roosevelt, but he issued an above-the-battle statement: "I have not discussed the matter and I am not going to. Mr. Roosevelt is down here making his speeches. I'm making mine."

One would have thought that common decency would have prevented still another attack on Humphrey. But no, FDR, Jr., revived the issue, this time not only blasting Humphrey as a "draft dodger" but reciting what he described as Hubert's efforts to obtain draft deferments during World War II.

Finally, after this blow was struck in his behalf, Kennedy issued a statement disapproving the injection of Humphrey's war record, or lack of one, into the campaign. But at an election rally later that night Kennedy insisted that no one had made "a greater contribution to the discussion of the issues" than Franklin Roosevelt, Jr.

All of which constituted a classic case of having your cake and eating it too.

Years later when questioned about his smearing of Humphrey, FDR told Jerry Tallmer of the *New York Post:* "The only thing I can say *publicly* about this is that it was based on so-called reliable information which was made available to me; and that it was used in the heat of the closing days of a vital and decisive primary; and that when I found it was unwarranted I went to Mr. Humphrey and not only ate crow but asked for his forgiveness."

Privately, however, he admitted that the "so-called reliable information" about Humphrey had come to him in dossier form from Robert Kennedy. "And Bobby left me holding the bag," he added bitterly.

The real inspiration for the unappetizing attack on Humphrey's patriotism was obviously Jack Kennedy, if we are to believe Ben Bradlee. Almost two years after he had bested the Minnesotan in the 1960 primaries, Bradlee noted in his diary, Kennedy's mind was still on Humphrey's war record, or lack of one.

The West Virginia primary had been, as one Charleston newspaper described it, "one of the worst name-calling campaigns in the history of presidential politics." And it ended amidst charges that the Kennedy forces had engaged in vote-buying on a massive scale. "One of the most corrupt elections in county history," said another paper.

Whereupon the FBI conducted an intensive investigation and filed a report of nearly 200 pages with the Justice Department. After Drew Pearson reported that an indictment of Bobby Kennedy was in the offing, Jack Kennedy demanded to know whether the Eisenhower administration intended to use the FBI as "a political weapon." The matter was dropped when the administration decided against opening itself to accusations of political persecution. JFK had shrewdly nipped a potential crisis in the bud.

"Dirty tricks" also played a role in the Wisconsin primary. As in West Virginia, the Kennedys had dragged out the hobgoblin of James Hoffa with which to scare the wits out of the rubes. Bobby, particularly, horrified audiences with the "news" that the Teamsters leader was prepared to spend "at least $2,000,000" to keep "my brother, the Senator" out of the White House. The implication, of course, was that Hoffa was in cahoots with Humphrey.

The former mayor of Minneapolis could hardly contain his anger. "You're looking at a man who has fought the rackets all his life," roared Humphrey. "And I did so before some of the people who are doing all the talking about rackets were dry behind the ears. Whoever is responsible deserves to have a spanking. And I said spanking because it applies to juveniles."

Sixteen years later Humphrey was still angry. Writing about the Kennedy campaign in the 1960 primaries, and its wholesale buying of votes in West Virginia, the Minnesotan noted in his memoirs:* "As a professional politician, I was able to accept and indeed respect the efficacy of the Kennedy campaign. But underneath the beautiful exterior, there was an element of ruthlessness and toughness that I had trouble either accepting or forgetting."

Another of Bobby's "dirty tricks"—one that kicked back in his face—concerned his planting a story that Jackie Robinson, the first Black to break into organized baseball, had joined Humphrey's entourage only because he received a fat fee.

As Robinson explained at the time, "When I inquired as to who had put out such a story, a Milwaukee newspaperman replied that Senator Kennedy's brother, Robert, had told him personally that I had been paid to join Humphrey's camp. I want to empha-

*The Education of a Public Man: My Life and Politics (New York: Doubleday, 1976).

size what I told that reporter: Whoever originated such a story is a liar."

Robert Kennedy did not respond. Months later during the fall campaign, however, he tried to have the last word. Appearing on the Barry Gray radio show in New York, he unloosed a sharp personal attack on Robinson, then supporting Nixon. He quoted extensively from a dossier which he said had been compiled by his investigators. Typical of the charges leveled by Bobby was the claim that Chock Full o' Nuts, which employed Robinson as personnel director, was owned by a reactionary Republican.

Robinson, listening at home, replied immediately. After noting that his employer was a registered member of the Liberal party, who had contributed to the Humphrey campaign, Robinson said: "If the younger Kennedy is going to resort to lies, then I can see what kind of campaign this is going to be. I don't see where my company has anything at all to do with his brother's having had breakfast with the White Citizens' Councils and the racist Governor of Alabama."

The significance of this episode is that, by his own admission, Robert Kennedy had used investigators to dig up "dirt" on his brother's opponents. Actually most of the intelligence operations were supervised by the candidate's father, Joseph P. Kennedy, who was not adverse to the uses of political blackmail. "Going back to 1960," wrote Professor John P. Roche many years later, "in both the primaries and the general election the late Joseph P. Kennedy had an intelligence network that put the FBI to shame."

But what is most interesting in retrospect is the fact that most liberals—and the media, for that matter—couldn't have cared less. Yet during the Nixon years they raised bloody Cain when it was disclosed that the Nixon White House had used a private investigator named Anthony Ulasewicz to check into such incidents as Ted Kennedy's peculiar conduct at Chappaquiddick. And no publication was more outraged about this delving into the private lives of the celebrated than the Washington *Post*. Beginning in 1976, however, the *Post* began publishing a series of exclusives about the sexual habits of certain members of Congress including, of course, the then powerful Wayne Hays of Ohio. Hays, who incidentally was strong for the impeachment of Nixon, was caught in a compromising situation by two young reporters assigned by Bradlee. The resulting scandal led to Hays's eventual retirement from Congress.

But probably the "dirtiest trick" of all in 1960 was the manner in which the Kennedys manipulated the "religious issue" for their political benefit. In effect the Kennedys used anti-Catholicism to win votes. In the closing days of the Wisconsin primary, for example, vicious anti-Catholic pamphlets were circulated widely throughout certain areas of the state. They were mailed in the many thousands to Catholic homes and, as Marquis Childs reported at the time, "often to individuals in care of the local chapter of the Knights of Columbus. While they seem to have originated with the lunatic fringe, the effect is naturally to create sympathy for Kennedy. . . . And this may well be true not only among Kennedy's fellow Catholics in Wisconsin but among others who have all along felt the injustice of discriminating against a candidate for the Presidency because of his religion."

Poor Humphrey and his aides knew immediately that some Machiavellian force was giving them the business. They believed that the mailings constituted a deceitful exercise in reverse psychology aimed at enraging Catholic voters against Humphrey.

And they were right.

The Humphrey organization publicly demanded that the U.S. Postal System trace the source of the literature. But that was not to be. Only later was it determined who had unloosed the bigoted material. It turned out that the source was none other than one of Bobby's hatchet men, a mysterious figure named Paul Corbin, whose exotic background consisted of a former membership in the Communist party and later an outspoken admiration for Senator Joe McCarthy.

As *National Review* later reported: "Corbin was involved in an anonymous mailing of virulently anti-Catholic literature to Catholics from a mail drop across the line in Minnesota, with such success that many of them, with a sort of negative Pavlovian reflex, voted for Kennedy."

It is significant that only *National Review* came up with this extraordinary story. None of the big Establishment newspapers, which were to have a field day exposing political chicanery during the Nixon years, seemed to be interested. And yet the exploits of Corbin were far more detrimental to the opposition than the later pranks of Donald Segretti, which in the main were more childish than serious. Needless to say, Segretti served time in the slammer while Corbin—at the Kennedys' suggestion—was named an assistant to the Democratic National Chairman and later placed on the payroll of the Joseph P. Kennedy, Jr., Foundation.

Corbin's activities in Wisconsin had the desired effect. Among other things Catholic Republicans by the many thousands crossed over party lines to register their protest against the "hate" literature flooding the state. This crossover was analyzed in detail over the CBS Television network by pollster Elmo Roper. John Kennedy, according to his chief aide Theodore Sorensen, "was so angry at Roper's telecast that he wrote a letter of protest to the network."

Actually Kennedy did more than just write. According to David Wise's carefully researched book, *The Politics of Lying,** the candidate personally telephoned CBS President Frank Stanton.

"Jack called from the airport in Fort Wayne," Stanton was quoted. "His voice was very strident. He objected to the CBS analysis of the primary vote in Wisconsin and said that we had raised the religious issue."

Stanton agreed, but he noted that it wasn't "something we invented. The papers are commenting on the religious issue, too."

"But," said Kennedy, "this is different. You're licensed."

Stanton was further outraged, he told Wise, when he learned that Kennedy had told a CBS correspondent, "Wait till I'm President—I'll cut Stanton's balls off."

The candidate's brother, Bobby, had been particularly incensed by the reporting of one CBS correspondent. The correspondent had reported from Wisconsin that the Catholic vote in that state was being taken for granted by the Kennedy forces. When this came to Bobby's attention, he went into an uncontrollable rage, sought out the correspondent, and denounced him as a "Stevenson Jew."

Only Jack Kennedy's quick intervention prevented the story of Bobby's use of an ethnic slur from hitting the nation's front pages. He got Bobby to apologize to the correspondent. One of the newsmen who had witnessed the imbroglio was William Lawrence of *The New York Times.* A good friend of the Kennedys, Lawrence did not file anything on it. Other politicians probably would not have been as fortunate.

---

*(New York: Random House, 1973).

But not all of the dirty tricks were committed by the Kennedy forces. Kennedy himself was a victim. One of the dirtiest and most decidedly illegal tricks was the burglaries of the Manhattan offices of physicians who had been treating the youthful candidate. The break-ins occurred prior to the 1960 Democratic National Convention. Many years later one of the physicians, Dr. Eugene J. Cohen, observed, "It was all done in a style similar to the burglary of the offices of Ellsberg's doctor."

Dr. Cohen also said it was obvious that the burglars were after the Kennedy files.

That same weekend there was another break-in at the offices of Dr. Janet G. Travell, who had been treating Kennedy's bad back. As Dr. Cohen noted, "It didn't take [the police] long to put two and two together. They asked who our patients were and when both of us came up with Kennedy, it was obvious what it was all about."

In recalling the two burglaries, *The New York Times* noted on May 4, 1973: "Mr. Kennedy's health had been an issue before and during the 1960 campaign with his Democratic opponents circulating reports that he suffered from Addison's disease."

Actually rumors about Kennedy's health had been circulating for many years. In 1954, for example, *Time* disclosed that the senator had Addison's Disease, an incurable but controllable deficiency of adrenal secretions. Five years later Fletcher Knebel reported in the Des Moines *Register* that a "whispering campaign aimed at discrediting Senator Kennedy as a Presidential candidate has gained increasing momentum in recent weeks. The whisperers have been stating as a fact that Kennedy has Addison's disease. So virulent is the power of gossip that even Governor Edmund G. [Pat] Brown of California was impelled to ask Kennedy personally about it. In an interview Kennedy said there is no basis to the rumor. He said he has tried in vain to learn the source."

According to his biographer, James MacGregor Burns, JFK had an "adrenal insufficiency" which some doctors could conceivably diagnose "as a mild case of Addison's Disease."

But exactly what information was obtained during the break-ins at the doctors' offices and exactly how that information was used, if indeed it was, was never established. Outside of a routine police investigation no one really probed in depth. If the Kennedy people were alarmed, they did not show it publicly. Perhaps it was because that was the sort of thing one simply expected in politics. And no one knew that better than John Kennedy and his associates, to whom "information" about the opposition was a way of life.

Ironically it was Kennedy who brought the issue of health to the fore. Just prior to the Democratic Convention he declared that the presidency demanded "the strength and health and vigor of young men." This immediately was interpreted as a slap at his rival for the nomination, Lyndon Johnson, who had suffered a massive heart attack five years earlier.

Some weeks before, a rumor had swept the Texas Democratic Convention about LBJ's having suffered another heart attack. Johnson said he had reason to believe the rumor had been launched by the Kennedy camp and was designed to make his health a major issue at the national convention. "It was that little bastard Bobby," LBJ told intimates.

The Johnson camp soon retaliated. At a press conference John Connally, then a Fort Worth lawyer, announced that the rumors about Jack Kennedy were true—namely, that the young Bostonian suffered from Addison's Disease. And India Edwards chimed in with the observation that Kennedy was the only man "offering himself for President who has been absent eight months in one year because of illness," a reference to the senator's illness in 1954, when he underwent surgery for a spinal disc condition. She threw in the claim that because of Addison's Disease, Kennedy was completely dependent on cortisone.

None of the reporters present asked where the Johnson people had obtained what after all was presumably confidential medical information.

Johnson himself assured a group of reporters that he knew as a fact that Kennedy was so stricken with Addison's Disease that the young senator "looked like a spavined hunchback." Kennedy wasn't overly happy with the remark, but he let it pass.

Twelve years later, during the 1972 campaign, burglars broke into the office of Nixon's personal physician and looked at the President's medical file. Dr. John Lungren, who had last examined Nixon in 1969, reported that records had been disturbed by intruders, who took nothing although cash was in plain view.

"I don't believe that any of the records were missing, but the papers were out of their chronological order and obviously scrutinized," Lungren said. "There is the supposition that they might have been photographed."

According to Lungren, the papers in the manila envelope file dated back to Nixon's days as Vice President and constituted "his complete medical record." But he doubted whether the records could have been of any value to the burglars, since "every examination I've ever given him showed him to be in perfect health."

According to the Long Beach (Calif.) *Independent-Press Telegram,* which broke the story, sources within the FBI indicated the Bureau felt the documents had been either photographed or hand-copied.

Apparently the burglars found nothing useful, for the issue of Nixon's health never arose during the 1972 campaign. Which is not to imply that his Democratic opponent, George McGovern, may have had anything to do with the break-in. What appears more likely, according to FBI sources, is that members of one of those left-wing guerrilla groups so prolific in California may have engineered the caper on their own as part of their ceaseless campaign to "get" the man they hated most in public life.

The story of the Lungren break-in received sparse attention in the nation's press and television networks when it finally broke in May of 1973. None of the big newspapers or networks, then pursuing Watergate with a vengeance, deigned to relegate any of their investigatory resources to solving the break-in. They had become far more interested in the burglary of the office of the psychiatrist who had treated Daniel J. Ellsberg, the man who had pilfered and publicized the Pentagon Papers. And the argument was that, even if the break-in was conceived as in the interests of national security, the end did not justify the illegal means.

But the press failed to object to a transgression of its own when in September 1973—at the very height of Watergate—the *New York Post* reproduced medical records which had been stolen from the files of St. Luke's Hospital. The records pertained to the illness of District Attorney Frank S. Hogan, who was then running for reelection. They indicated that Hogan was far more seriously ill than had been previously acknowledged.

Nevertheless the documents had been stolen, and Robert Spitzler, managing editor of the *Post,* refused to discuss how or from whom his newspaper had obtained them. But he defended the publication of the material, saying, "It was incumbent on us to print the truth. Lies were told for a month. The overriding consideration was the public's right to know."

The article provoked a protest from the New York County Medical Society's Board of Censors, which oversees medical ethics. The group questioned how a newspaper could have approved such a violation of the confidential doctor-patient relationship after it had so angrily criticized the attempted burglary of Ellsberg's psychiatric files.

No one, incidentally, went to jail for the violation of Hogan's civil rights. No one was even arrested for the crime.

4

ADLAI STEVENSON, IT MUST BE RECALLED, was also in the race for the 1960 presidential nomination. His legions consisted largely of intellectuals, students, and folks with a penchant for joining such organizations as Americans for Democratic Action and the American Civil Liberties Union. In short Adlai still had the heart of much of what was liberal America.

All of which was troubling to the Kennedy clan. For many liberals were still uncertain about Jack. They remembered him as being equivocal, at best, about "McCarthyism." And they were outraged by the excesses attributed to both Jack's father and brother. Adlai himself had been quoted as saying that "the amount of money being spent" by the Kennedys "is phenomenal, probably the highest amount spent on a campaign in history." Stevenson also described Kennedy as being "somewhat arrogant."

Stevenson's forces were making their numbers felt in Los Angeles, where the Democratic Convention was being held. They were everywhere, buttonholing delegates, getting on television, and giving the impression that, somehow, Adlai would beat the odds and succeed in obtaining his third nomination for the presidency.

Though the Kennedy forces felt they had the nomination in the bag, they knew that anything could happen, particularly at a volatile convention. They feared a gang-up on the part of their three remaining rivals, Stevenson, Lyndon Johnson, and Stuart Symington.

Stevenson's headquarters were located in a soon-to-be-abandoned loft building on Pershing Square in downtown Los Angeles, across the park from the Biltmore Hotel. Security was virtually nil as people roamed at will throughout the five floors of the ramshackle edifice. Direct telephone lines connected the Stevenson people with their trailer truck parked outside Convention Hall at the Sports Arena.

On July 12, 1960, *The New York Times* published this short dispatch:

> Los Angeles, July 11 (UPI)—A spokesman for the Stevenson for President Campaign Committee said tonight that its telephone lines at the Democratic National Convention had been tapped.
>
> John Sharon said he was so informed by a security officer for the Democratic National Committee.
>
> He told reporters that the officer said that the Stevenson lines from inside the sports area to a trailer outside, and one from the trailer to hotel headquarters, both had been tapped.
>
> Mr. Sharon would not speculate on who might have tapped the lines.

But others working for Stevenson were not as reticent. They stated quite flatly that they suspected the wiretapping was the work of Kennedy "goons." And during the convention proceedings themselves, as Ted White reported in *The Making of the President 1960*, several Stevenson leaders stated "that the Kennedy walkie-talkies were powerful and sensitive enough to monitor their own more primitive radio communications with the [convention] floor."

But who—to use the vernacular made popular by John Dean at a later date—had "screwed" whom back at the Democratic Convention?

Apparently the Kennedys had been done a major injustice in the light of what has since been revealed. It turns out that they themselves were victimized by a "dirty trick" of monumental proportions.

What occurred at the 1960 convention was a con job on the part of Adlai's people which fooled many delegates and journalists, including me.

And the man responsible for the con job was David Garth, a chubby-faced, cigar-smoking New Yorker who has since become more renowned as a media consultant for numerous Democratic candidates.

Garth had joined the Stevenson team in early 1960, when he became chairman of a New York committee to draft Adlai for the nomination. At the convention itself Garth orchestrated a "spontaneous" series of demonstrations for Stevenson which, as *The Village Voice* later noted, "came surprisingly close to knocking John Kennedy out of the presidential box." Whether Kennedy actually was in that much danger can be argued. But few observers at the scene can dispute the fact that Stevenson's troops came mighty close to disrupting the proceedings. Among other things Adlai's people had perfected the ancient political art of forging convention tickets in order to pack the galleries at the Sports Arena.

Many years later in an interview with Jack Newfield published in *New York*, Dave Garth boasted about another caper he had pulled off in Los Angeles:

"We had put a tap on the Kennedy phone lines into the Amphitheater. And then we put out a statement accusing the Kennedy people of putting a tap on the Stevenson phones. Bobby ran into me in a parking lot, and boy, was he angry."*

In telling of this choice piece of *chutzpah,* Garth voiced pride rather than guilt, according to Newfield. The interview took place in mid-1970, at a time when Watergate was still only the name of a plush apartment-office complex on the banks of the Potomac. In other words it was before wiretapping in a political context had taken on more notorious connotations.

The irony of ironies came less than a year after the Los Angeles convention, when Garth was named chairman of New York's Fair Campaign Practices Committee, an organization devoted to combatting "dirty tricks" in politics. Since then, as a political consultant, this self-confessed wiretapper has represented such clients as Mayor John Lindsay, Senator Adlai Stevenson, Jr., of Illinois, Senator John Tunney of California, former Governor Jack Gilligan of Ohio, Governor Brendan Byrne of New Jersey, Mayor Tom Bradley of Los Angeles, Congressman Richard Ottinger of New York, and Governor Hugh Carey of New York. And, needless to say, all of these Democratic worthies—Garth represents mainly Democrats of the liberal persuasion—have commented with horror on the evils of Watergate.

In the presidential race itself, the epic battle between Kennedy and Nixon, the Democratic candidate employed the same tactics that he had tried out against Humphrey in the primaries. There was a new wrinkle, however. This time Kennedy implied that Nixon, of all people, was somehow soft on commu-

---

*The Kennedy high command in order to discourage such efforts had announced that their elaborate communications setup was decidedly "spy-proof." They were wrong. The Stevenson people were privy to their phone conversations.

nism. This was because Harry Bridges, the left-wing boss of West Coast longshoremen, had announced he would vote Republican that year because, he claimed, JFK was a foe of labor.

"It's an interesting fact," Kennedy trumpeted, "that neither the Teamsters Union nor the Longshoremen's Union dominated by Mr. Bridges is supporting me in this campaign and that both unions are opposing me. . . . I want to get the crooks and the Communists out of the union movement, like Mr. Bridges. . . ."

Thus the belated champion of liberalism made the point that Nixon was being supported by "crooks and Communists." And no one in the media, which constantly is on the lookout for intemperate political remarks, seemed to care—or even notice.

Like a broken record Kennedy kept coming back to Hoffa, contending among other things that the Justice Department had not "carried out the laws in the case of Mr. Hoffa with vigor." Of course everyone knew that Justice was headed by one of Nixon's oldest political friends, William P. Rogers. "In my judgment," JFK added, "an effective Attorney General with the present laws on the books could remove Mr. Hoffa from office"—and presumably put him behind bars. (Years later during Nixon's second try for the presidency, the Republican candidate also called for an "effective Attorney General," contending that Lyndon Johnson's chief law officer Ramsey Clark was soft on crime.)

Following his primary victory in West Virginia, Jack Kennedy had stated that he believed "we have now buried the religious issue" once and for all.

But it was a short burial. The issue was soon revived by the Kennedy forces. Even the liberal *Commonweal* wondered whether the issue wasn't being kept alive by the Kennedys "to take advantage of the natural resentment many Catholics feel when the so-called religious issue is raised."

And once again vast amounts of anti-Catholic literature were flooding the country. Down in South Carolina the Greenville *News* noted that much of the bigoted material originated in the North. "The origin of this material makes us all the more curious as to just who is mainly responsible for its distribution. . . . The question is: Who is making the most use of the religious issue, and for or against whom?"

It was a good question. Of course almost everyone including Nixon knew the answer. Try as he might, Nixon could not keep the issue out of the campaign. His opponent kept bringing it up.

And there was no way to stop him. After all, it was one of the biggest things Kennedy had going for him.

The outright cynicism implicit in keeping the issue alive was demonstrated when Bobby, as campaign manager, accused the Republicans of spending over $1 million to distribute anti-Catholic propaganda. Following the campaign, this allegation was checked out by the Fair Campaign Practices Committee, which found it to be without foundation.

The religious ploy paid off. In the end a massive swing of Catholic voters to Kennedy was the biggest factor in his election. According to George Gallup, the Catholic vote for the Democrats leaped to 78 percent in 1960, a 27-point jump from 1956. Which was a major reason Kennedy took lopsided majorities in the big cities.

"One thing is certain," pollster Elmo Roper observed in the *Saturday Review*. "If there was a net victim of religious prejudice it was Nixon more than Kennedy."

And Boston's Richard Cardinal Cushing, following the election, nominated Nixon as "Good Will Man of the Year," explaining that "during the recent campaign which tested and taxed all his powers, physical and mental, he never exploited the religious or any other issue that would tend to divide the American people."

During the campaign Nixon had been the target of other low-level tactics. In Black districts in the North handbills and posters were distributed reproducing a racist convenant in Nixon's deed to his Washington home. The covenant barred future sale of the property to any Negro or "Armenians, Jews, Hebrews and Syrians." What was not mentioned was the fact that when Nixon purchased the house, such covenants had been outlawed by the Supreme Court for three years. At the same time Nixon was being pictured as "integrationist" in the South. There Democrats were circulating in white communities leaflets which displayed the Vice President in friendly poses with Black people. The caption read: "Vice President Richard M. Nixon has been an NAACP member for over ten years!"

There had been one major effort to link the Republican party with a group of Protestant clergymen who were seriously concerned about whether a Catholic President could resist pressures from the Pope. Whether wiretapping was involved in this effort, as alleged by one of the supposed participants, is a big question that has yet to be resolved. What is now known, however, is that the Kennedy forces authorized acts of surveillance and espionage aimed at the clergymen, including a former Republican congressman.

The central figure in all of this was Carmine Bellino, a former FBI specialist in accounting with close ties to the Kennedy family. In 1947 following thirteen years of government service, Bellino shared an office with Robert A. Maheu in Washington. The rent was paid in part by the Central Intelligence Agency, so that —as Maheu was to testify many years later—"I would be available to them as situations arose."* The testimony was given in Los Angeles in connection with Maheu's $17.3 million defamation suit against Howard Hughes, for whom he had once worked.

Whether Bellino did any work for the CIA in this period was not disclosed at the trial. But he did have wide experience in congressional investigations. Bellino had worked for the Senate Select Committee investigating labor racketeering when Robert Kennedy was its chief counsel. And Bobby described Bellino as "the best investigator in America."

Later Bellino worked for Bobby, when he managed his brother's presidential campaign. He carried out various intelligence assignments, utilizing the services of former FBI and CIA agents as well as private investigators. Bellino reported directly to Bobby.

Among those who worked for Bellino were John W. Leon, a Washington private eye; Edward Murray Jones, a former congressional investigator; Oliver W. Angelone, a former FBI agent; and John Joseph Frank, a former FBI and CIA agent. During the campaign Joseph Shimon, then an inspector in the Washington Police Department, had been requested to cooperate in a plan which, according to his sworn affidavit, involved the installation of eavesdropping devices in hotel rooms occupied by Republicans.

In 1962 Leon, Angelone, Frank, and Shimon were indicted in a wiretapping case in which a lawyer for the El Paso Natural Gas

---

*One of those "situations," as it turned out, led to Maheu's hiring of Mafia leaders Roselli and Giancana in the CIA plot to assassinate Castro. Prior to that the CIA enlisted Maheu to arrange the production of a pornographic film purporting to show Indonesian President Sukarno engaging in sexual relations with a woman in Moscow. The object of the bogus film was to arouse Sukarno's anger against the Soviet government by arranging for its circulation in Indonesia, presumably under Soviet auspices. However the film was never shown as planned.

Company, in Washington for a Federal Power Commission hearing, found an electronic bug under a coffee table in his suite at the Mayflower Hotel. All four were later convicted.

But no one at the time of the "Mayflower Case," as it was then billed in the press, linked the defendants to Bellino, for whom they had carried out assignments during the 1960 campaign. The main reason, of course, was that they had been working under cover for the Kennedy campaign and few knew of the relationship. Disclosure of the Bellino connection could have been dreadfully embarrassing, for by this time Bellino was serving as a special White House consultant handling sensitive behind-the-scenes investigations for the new President. Among other things he was asked by both Kennedys to check into their wives' excessive spending habits to determine whether someone wasn't stealing them blind.

But mostly Bellino's activities resembled those of the White House "plumbers" of the Nixon era. Years later it was disclosed that, at President Kennedy's personal direction, Bellino had obtained from the Internal Revenue Service the tax returns of numerous citizens. Exactly what was done with this supposedly confidential data can only be surmised. What is known is that Kennedy often delighted in telling friends just how much—or how little—billionaires like John Paul Getty and H. L. Hunt were paying in federal taxes. Needless to say, this was information which not even a President was entitled to know.

Bellino maintained his intimate connections with the Kennedy family after the President's death. Having been let go by the Johnson White House, he turned up as chief investigator for the Senate Subcommittee on Practices and Procedures, chaired by Senator Edward M. Kennedy. In 1973 he was named chief investigator for the Select Senate Watergate Committee, headed by Sam Ervin. For Bellino it was like old times—once again he was going after Nixon. And then all hell broke loose.

On July 24, 1973, during the Watergate hearings, Republican National Chairman George Bush released three sworn affidavits suggesting that Bellino had recruited spies to help defeat Nixon in the 1960 presidential campaign.

Bellino flatly denied the charges.

One of the affidavits was signed by John Leon, who claimed he had been retained by Bellino in 1960 to "infiltrate the operations" of Albert B. ("Ab") Hermann, a longtime employee of the Republican National Committee. After failing to "penetrate the office operations" of the national committee, Leon swore that he was instructed by Bellino to place Hermann "under physical surveillance." He said he had watched Hermann's office with field glasses and used "an electric device known as 'the big ear' aimed at Mr. Hermann's window."

Among those who assisted him in the surveillance "on two or three nights each" were John Frank and Eddie Jones. The Leon affidavit also said that Jones had described himself as "the world's greatest wiretapper," Jones boasting that under Bellino's supervision he had successfully tapped James Hoffa's telephones in Tampa, Florida.

"During long conversations with me," Leon went on, "Ed Jones stated that he had tapped the telephones of three ministers in the Mayflower Hotel in the fall of 1960. According to Jones, Carmine Bellino suspected that these ministers were responsible for some of the anti-Catholic, anti-Kennedy literature that was distributed during the 1960 campaign. Ed Jones told me he could not spend much time with me on surveillance because he had several good wiretaps going for Bellino."

Leon also said that following one of the televised 1960 debates between Kennedy and Nixon, he had a discussion with John Frank, Oliver Angelone, and another investigator whose name he could not recall. "There was agreement that Mr. Kennedy was extremely well prepared for points raised by Mr. Nixon—that he 'had the debate all wrapped up.' Angelone remarked 'Jonesy really did his job well this time.' "

The Leon affidavit added: "Although I did not participate in installation of eavesdropping devices and did not tap telephone lines for Carmine Bellino during the 1960 campaign, I am confident that Ed Jones and Oliver Angelone successfully bugged the Nixon space or tapped his phones prior to the television debate."

But Jones denied he had ever engaged in bugging or wiretapping "against Republican party officials." In a sworn affidavit, however, he did concede that while working for Bellino he had participated "in two surveillance efforts prior to the 1960 presidential election. Although I could not identify the subjects of these surveillances, I assume they were Republican officials or supporters. Two or three teams and cars were used in the surveillance and other members of the team had the responsibility of identification of the subject. I recall that Bellino was present on one or both surveillances."

According to Jones, "one of the surveillances was at National Airport, where we attempted to pick up an individual coming to Washington. The other surveillance effort involved an individual with offices in the vicinity of 19th and M Streets, N.W., Washington, D.C."

The third affidavit released by George Bush was signed by Joseph Shimon, a retired Washington police inspector, who claimed that during the 1960 campaign he had been approached by Oliver Angelone to help him gain access to the top two floors of the Wardman Park Hotel (now the Sheraton Park) that Nixon planned to occupy, for the purpose of installing eavesdropping devices. At the time Angelone explained he was working for Bellino. But Shimon declined the offer because, as he explained, "I did not desire to jeopardize my status in the Metropolitan Police Department." (Later Shimon became a defendant in the "Mayflower Case.")

Angelone, whose conviction in the Mayflower Case was reversed in the U.S. Court of Appeals on grounds he had been granted immunity for testifying before a grand jury, denied he ever appealed to Shimon for any such help. But he conceded that in the course of the 1960 campaign Bellino had asked him to try to find out at what hotel a certain individual, whose name he could not remember, was staying. It was possible, he said, that he might have asked Shimon to assist him in getting the registration card of this person. Angelone's recollection was that the individual in whom Bellino was interested had registered at the Wardman Park.

Bellino, the center of the controversy, came out fighting. He accused Bush of seeking "to distract me from carrying out what I consider one of the most important assignments of my life."

In a later statement he denied any partisan motives in his activities as chief investigator of the Watergate Committee. He claimed that he had even campaigned for Nixon when he ran for Vice President in 1952.

But Bellino's "nonpartisanship" was called into question when it was disclosed that he had paid for a full-page advertisement in the Elizabeth, New Jersey, *Daily Journal* of October 29, 1968, which attacked Nixon for allegedly accepting Hoffa's support in 1960. The ad urged readers to vote for Humphrey and Muskie. The truth is that, whatever his feelings toward Nixon may have been back in the early fifties, Bellino's dislike of the Republican candidate in later years was most intense. This may have been the result of his long and intimate relationship with the Kennedys.

Nevertheless Bellino flatly and unequivocally denied ever having asked Leon or anyone else to undertake any wiretapping or electronic surveillance at any time.

But he did admit complicity in the physical surveillance of certain individuals. His purpose was to determine the source of certain literature believed to be anti-Catholic. He did remember sending his two sons along with someone, possibly Jones, out to National Airport to tail a former congressman named O. K. Armstrong who, Bellino had learned, would be arriving on a certain flight. How he obtained this information he did not say. But he did say that he had been asked by Bobby Kennedy to determine whether Armstrong, a member of the editorial staff of the *Reader's Digest*, would make contact with other Republicans while in Washington.

Jones and the two Bellino boys lost the former congressman at the airport. Somehow Bellino learned that Armstrong was going to attend a meeting of Protestant ministers at the Mayflower Hotel, at which the chief speaker was to be the Reverend Norman Vincent Peale. "In this connection," said Bellino, "I was in the lobby observing those entering to determine whether anyone of interest was participating." Bellino added that he may have reported to Bobby Kennedy on what he saw. But he denied Leon's allegation that several of the clergymen's rooms had been wiretapped at his behest.

Bellino said that, in line with Bobby Kennedy's request, he was attempting to determine whether Armstrong was going to meet with Republican leaders while in Washington. As it happened, after the Mayflower meeting was over, Armstrong did confer with "Ab" Hermann about prospective speaking engagements.

Bellino could not recall whether he ever asked John Leon to do any work for him during the 1960 campaign. But he was quite certain that he had never authorized any surveillance of Hermann at that time, as contended by Leon.

Bellino did concede knowing Leon, but in another connection. He said that Leon's firm, Allied Investigating Services, had done some work for his firm in the fifties. And Bellino had also known Eddie Jones. This was when Bobby Kennedy hired Jones as an investigator for the Senate Rackets Committee. At the time, Bellino recalled, the hiring caused a "bit of a flap" because Jones had been indicted in New York in the late forties in a wiretapping case. Nevertheless Bellino used Jones in Detroit in connection with the investigation of Hoffa and other Teamster leaders.

As for Angelone, Bellino said, all that former FBI agent did for him during the campaign was to locate a hotel registration card, presumably that of O. K. Armstrong.

Needless to say, Armstrong was absolutely flabbergasted many years later when he learned that he had been the subject of a surveillance directed by Bellino. He did recall, however, flying to Washington to attend a private meeting of clergymen and laymen pledged to support Nixon. The meeting, which was held at the Mayflower Hotel, was addressed by Peale and others.

"At the close of one of the afternoon speeches," Armstrong recalled, "someone on the stage drew back the curtain, and discovered a man sitting on the floor, with a tape recorder in his hands. Apparently he had recorded every word said at the meeting, for the media next day had verbatim reports of Dr. Peale's speech and of my remarks. . . ."

"I have discussed this with Mr. Bellino," Armstrong went on, "and he could not recall who selected my name for shadowing, who was at the airport and why, except that 'we wanted to find out what the Republicans were doing.' His memory was also faulty as to why Dr. Peale was shadowed, and as to who obtained a copy of Peale's speech the day before it was delivered."

There was no way for anyone to have obtained an advance copy of the Peale speech, according to Armstrong. As he wrote to a Senate investigator, "There was no copy, or manuscript, of Dr. Peale's speech." The fact was that "he spoke extemporaneously. . . . The quotes in the papers next day were from the tape recordings made by the man hidden behind the curtain of the meeting room—planted, likely, by Bellino himself. Bellino's statement that they had a copy of Dr. Peale's speech is completely false."

Also false, according to Armstrong, was the interpretation that the quotes released to the press without Dr. Peale's permission were anti-Catholic. The well-played story that one of Nixon's most prominent religious supporters was a "bigot" did enormous damage to the Republican cause. According to Armstrong, the entire Bellino caper was a prime example of a "dirty trick."

Following the publication of the Bush charges against Bellino, Chairman Ervin appointed a subcommittee to look into them. He named as its head Herman Talmadge, Democrat of Georgia, and as other members Daniel K. Inouye, Democrat of Hawaii, and Edward Gurney, Republican of Florida.

For the most part the subcommittee conducted its investigation of Bellino in half-hearted fashion. It was a chore that had to be done and it was done as quickly as possible.

Unfortunately there was no way to interrogate the principal witness against Bellino. For John Leon had died just days before Bush made public his signed affidavit.

Nevertheless the inquiry produced some interesting sidelights. One was a letter to Leon from Robert Kennedy dated November 17, 1960:

> I have been advised of the help which you extended in Senator Kennedy's campaign. I just want you to know how much I appreciate your interest and efforts in my brother's behalf.
>
> Thank you again, and I hope I will have a chance to see you in the near future.

Apparently the Kennedys relied on Leon for another investigative service. In a letter to his Washington attorney Arthur G. Lambert, dated October 5, 1967, Leon wrote that he had been asked on July 6, 1961, by James M. McInerney, an attorney representing both President Kennedy and his brother,

> to run a Polygraph [lie-detector] examination on a personal friend of Bobby Kennedy, Paul Corbin. Mr. Corbin was slated for a high position in the Kennedy Administration, and the FBI had come up with information that associated him with the Communist party.
>
> This was a very unusual request, coming from the Attorney General, asking me to clear a man that his own FBI had indicated was a member of the Communist party. I made a very careful examination of the man, and forwarded a report on my tests, which clearly were to some extent in contradiction to FBI reports.

The Leon letter also recited much of the material contained in his later affidavit. Though he made no reference to Bellino, he wrote of his surveillance of Hermann and of Ed Jones's statement to him that he was tapping the telephones of clergymen at the Mayflower. In addition, according to the letter, Leon and Frank had "confided" that they had been "recruited for the campaign of the late President Kennedy to 'black bag' some hotel rooms in the Mayflower Hotel," tasks "they had performed gratuitously."*

---

*"Black-bagging" is the vernacular for illegal break-ins and burglaries committed by law enforcement agencies. The FBI, for example, had special teams trained

Some of these statements had turned up as early as December 21, 1965, when John Leon was interviewed by Bernard Fensterwald, then chief counsel to a Senate Subcommittee looking into wiretapping. Based on the notes he took at the interview, Fensterwald did recall that Leon may have told him that Bellino had asked Leon to do political surveillance; that Leon said he would do physical surveillance but could not handle electronic work; and that it was Jones who undertook the electronic work. However this information was not brought out at the open hearings because, said Fensterwald, Chairman Edward V. Long of Missouri thought the thrust of his investigation should be concentrated more on industrial and marital bugging than on political. A more likely reason was that Long did not want to tangle with a fellow Democratic senator, Robert F. Kennedy of New York.

Among the handwritten notes made by Fensterwald during his interview with Leon was this reference: "Jones was supposed to get a job when RFK gets in." The record shows that, following JFK's election in 1960, Jones was employed as an investigator by the Immigration and Naturalization Service. After 1967 he was assigned to the Philippines. Also working for the government is Angelone. Since 1964 he has been an investigative officer in the New York offices of the General Services Administration.

At the very least it was firmly established by even the desultory investigation conducted by the Talmadge subcommittee that Bellino had initiated and even participated in the surveillance of political opponents. Normally it would be assumed that such a belated disclosure would have horrified the members of a Senate committee looking into such political excesses.

Instead the chairman of the Watergate Committee, the sainted Sam Ervin, fully exonerated Bellino and described him as "a faithful public servant of exemplary character."

---

and equipped for such assignments. Usually "black bag jobs" were performed to obtain diplomatic materials such as codebooks at foreign embassies or in underworld haunts. Another target has been radical groups of all sorts. The Trotskyite Socialist Workers party, along with the Ku Klux Klan, were repeatedly victimized by FBI break-ins, as were Arab groups suspected of harboring anti-Jewish terrorists.

5

P R O B A B L Y   T H E   U L T I M A T E   ''D I R T Y   T R I C K''
—far more consequential than anything that was said to have
occurred in Watergate—was the theft of the 1960 election. For
this was an outright repudiation of the will of the American
people.

During that long election night in November 1960 when the
final votes cast by more than 69 million Americans (then the
largest turnout in U.S. history) were being counted, the identity
of the victor was uncertain. Finally everything appeared to hang
on Illinois. According to Ben Bradlee, Jack Kennedy placed a call
to Richard Daley. And it was from the lips of the Chicago mayor
that Kennedy for the first time heard those rapturous words,
"Mr. President."

"Mr. President," Daley told Kennedy, "with a little bit of luck
and the help of a few close friends, you're going to carry Illinois."

And that is how Kennedy knew he had it made. He could now
retire after a long, exasperating night fully aware that "Der
Mare," whom he and his family had cultivated for many years,
would come through for him—as he most decidedly did. Though
Bradlee had "often wondered about (Daley's) statement," the
Washington *Post* executive didn't think it mattered too much
since someone had once told him that the Republicans "could
well have stolen as many votes in Southern Illinois as Daley
might have stolen in Cook County." In other words, to quote the
phrase made popular during Watergate, everybody does it. Years
later, however, Nixon's associates were to go to jail for political
crimes. Kennedy's kept getting reelected mayor of Chicago.

"That the Daley-controlled wards in Chicago supplied the
10,000 votes to put over the Kennedy-Johnson ticket can hardly
be questioned," conceded the pro-Kennedy columnist Marquis
Childs thirteen years later. And he felt that "in hindsight it might
have been better (for Nixon) to have faced up to the frauds of
1960." But there is nothing in the record to indicate that Childs

himself suggested any such thing at the time of Kennedy's razor-thin victory over Nixon. In fact had Nixon contested the election, as he was then being strongly urged to do, he undoubtedly would have been bitterly assailed by liberals like Childs as a sore loser and much worse.

Even Ted White has been forced to admit that perhaps enough votes were stolen in Texas and Illinois to have won the presidency for Kennedy. In his new book *Breach of Faith,** which is about Nixon's downfall, he states: "Democratic vote-stealing had definitely taken place on a massive scale in Illinois and Texas (where 100,000 big-city votes were simply disqualified); and on a lesser scale elsewhere."

Whether Kennedy himself was directly involved in any of the electoral skulduggery that produced his slim victory has never been established. What has been established, however, is that not only was he aware of what was going on but he approved of it. Talk about impeachable offenses!

That there was skulduggery aplenty is clear from the record. An avalanche of Democratic votes in Cook County, held back until they were needed, allowed Kennedy to offset losses downstate and win a ballot-thin 8,585-vote plurality in Illinois. Daley's powerful machine employed virtually every big-city trick to bolster the vote. These included the usual spoiling of Republican ballots; the voting of floaters and tombstones; and the tallying of "votes" of those who had once lived on streets bulldozed out of existence by urban renewal.

Until recently it was Daley who was given the major credit (or blame) for having helped Kennedy swing the election. But now it develops that Mafia chief Sam "Momo" Giancana may also have played a decisive role. Giancana, who had awesome political power in Chicago and its environs, had often boasted to Judith Campbell, the young lady whose charms he had shared with Kennedy, that he used that power to elect Kennedy. "Listen, honey," he told Judith, "if it wasn't for me, your boyfriend wouldn't even be in the White House." All of which puzzled the young lady in question, since as she later chronicled, her Mafia friend was always knocking the Kennedy family. Among other things Giancana, who ought to have known, described Joseph P. Kennedy as "one of the biggest crooks who ever lived." Yet for some reason Giancana gave orders to the "boys" to assure Ken-

---

*(New York: Atheneum, 1975).

nedy's victory over Nixon. Which may be one of the reasons why, despite some FBI harassment, the strong-arm man led a somewhat charmed life during the Kennedy years. Another reason, of course, was his involvement with the CIA in the Kennedy-endorsed plot to "snuff" Castro.

Without exception Chicago's newspapers took the position that, as the *Tribune* then put it, "the election of November 8 [1960] was characterized by such gross and palpable fraud as to justify the conclusion that (Nixon) was deprived of victory."

Vote frauds in behalf of the Democratic ticket were performed on an even grander scale in Texas, where Lyndon Johnson—JFK's runningmate—ruled the roost. Every phase of the state's election machinery from precinct tally clerk to the State Board of Canvassers was in the hands of Organization (read LBJ) Democrats. So, considering the long, traditional history of vote-stealing in the Lone Star State, what happened in 1960 was not too surprising. The stuffing of ballot boxes reached a new high; dozens of election machines in Republican precincts jammed mysteriously; and tens of thousands of ballots disappeared overnight. According to an eye-opening series of articles published in the *New York Herald-Tribune*, a minimum of 100,000 votes tallied for the Kennedy-Johnson ticket never existed in the first place. Yet despite all this the ticket finally carried Texas by a slim margin of 46,000 votes.

Look magazine ran an article entitled "How to Steal an Election," which annoyed Kennedy. And no wonder. For it said: "For the first time, many thousands of Americans suddenly realized that elections can be stolen. They only half-believed it before 1960, as part of our historical lore. . . . Many, many thousands of voters and civic minded people in several leading states no longer take the easygoing attitude toward election frauds."

And in a foreword to Neal R. Pierce's *The People's President*, published in 1968, *New York Times* columnist Tom Wicker observed:

> A shift of only 4,480 popular votes from Kennedy to Nixon in Illinois, where there were *highly plausible charges of fraud* [emphasis added] and 4,491 in Missouri would have given neither man an electoral majority and thrown the decision into the House of Representatives. If an additional 1,148 votes had been counted for Nixon in New Mexico, 58 from Hawaii, and 1,247 in Nevada, he would have won an outright majority in the electoral college.

Wicker added: "Any experienced reporter or politician knows that the few votes can easily be 'swung' in any state by fraud or honest error."

That the 1960 election results were more the product of fraud than honest error was the position taken by J. Edgar Hoover. And the FBI director made no bones about saying so to such close friends as Philip Hochstein, then editor of the Newark (N.J.) *Star-Ledger.*

Hochstein happened to be visiting Hoover the day after President-elect Kennedy had announced Hoover's reappointment. As Hochstein recalled, Hoover was not too happy. When the editor offered him congratulations on being reappointed, Hoover launched into a denunciation of "election frauds" and exclaimed that, as far as he was concerned, Kennedy "is not the President-elect." Then Hoover complained that he had not been "permitted" to investigate the election frauds which had led to the theft of the election from Nixon.

Hochstein asked who was preventing him from launching such a full-scale probe, and Hoover replied: "Ike and Nixon."

Between themselves President Eisenhower and Vice President Nixon had decided that, despite the closeness of the election and the obvious irregularities that had occurred, the nation's welfare at a time of great troubles abroad demanded that a new President be inaugurated without a controversy that would divide the country.

That this was the case can be seen from what happened after the *New York Herald-Tribune* began publishing a series of articles which contended that the election had indeed been "stolen." The articles were written by Earl Mazo, who reported the mechanics of the gigantic rip-off after first-hand investigations in Illinois and Texas. Twelve pieces in all were scheduled for publication. After four of them appeared, Nixon—then serving in his final weeks as Vice President—asked Mazo to come over to see him.

Mazo, of course, had been aware that Nixon was being besieged by outraged Republicans to contest the election. He also knew that Nixon's office was being inundated with great amounts of new evidence concerning "irregularities" in several states. Mazo therefore expected the Vice President to tell him that he had decided to contest the election, as well as ask for a federally supervised probe of the chicanery that had cost him the election.

But that was not what Nixon had in mind. Much to Mazo's

amazement the Vice President asked the correspondent if it were possible for the *Herald-Tribune* to cease publishing the articles. Since he felt the conversation was of high historical import, Mazo put down all the details in a memorandum for his personal files as soon as he returned to his office.

In his memorandum, Mazo noted:

> Right off, as we shook hands, Nixon said, "Earl, those are interesting articles you are writing—but no one steals the presidency of the United States."
>
> I thought he might be kidding. But never was a man more deadly serious. We chatted for an hour or two about the campaign, the odd vote patterns in various places, and this and that. Then, continent-by-continent, he enumerated potential international crises that could be dealt with only by the President of a united country, and not a nation torn by the kind of partisan bitterness and chaos that inevitably would result from an official challenge of the election result.

At one point in the lengthy conversation, Nixon said: "Our country can't afford the agony of a Constitutional crisis—and I damn well will not be a party to creating one just to become President or anything else."

Because of Nixon's request the *Herald-Tribune* canceled the remainder of the Mazo series.

Offers of money and lawyers to mount a challenge against the 1960 results continued to flood in, however. Leonard W. Hall, who had co-managed the Nixon campaign, recalls how Admiral Lewis Strauss, former head of the Atomic Energy Commission, said, "Len, you get the lawyers. Don't worry about the money for legal fees. We'll get that."

Hall carried that message to Nixon. But Nixon said no, explaining the terrible damage that would be done to the American image abroad should he challenge the election.

Nixon also telephoned the editors of the Chicago *Daily News* and Chicago *Tribune*—Basil L. Walters and Don Maxwell respectively—and pleaded with them successfully to end their editorial campaigns demanding a recount of the Cook County vote. Thus Nixon quickly dampened a rapidly growing movement that might easily have produced what he feared most—a "constitutional crisis" that could have led to the paralysis of the presidency at a time of great global unrest.

John Kennedy, at that time, was not too certain whether he

was really "in" as President. The papers were full of reports that the Republicans might contest his election and that a lot of money was being raised for that purpose. Kennedy then did what he always did best. He decided to meet with the man he had so narrowly (though questionably) beaten. Through the good offices of former President Hoover a meeting was arranged. Kennedy flew from Palm Beach to Key Biscayne, where Nixon was vacationing. According to Nixon, after exchanging pleasantries, Kennedy said, "Well, it's hard to tell who won the election at this point." Nixon said that, though the verdict was close, the final result had been pretty well determined. Kennedy, breathing much easier, then knew there would be no contest of his claim to the presidency.

Later the President-elect went to the White House to confer with outgoing President Eisenhower who, as aide Ted Sorensen reported in his book *Kennedy*, "had regarded Kennedy with disdain in the campaign and who had apparently delayed their first meeting until it was clear no recount could change the voters' verdict . . ."*

Added Sorensen: "Eisenhower and Nixon, merely by meeting with Kennedy, were patriotically recognizing the certainty of his election, and thus helping to put an end to the bitter charges of fraud, the demands for recounts and the threats of Southern independent electors."

Probably the most interesting thing about 1960 was the general unwillingness of the media to pursue allegations that the election had been "stolen" by the Democrats. Only a handful of newspapers (and they were generally of the Republican persuasion) were excited enough to look into a story that could easily have developed into one about "the biggest political crime of the century," far greater in its import than Watergate.

By and large the great organs of Eastern opinion, most specifically *The New York Times* and the Washington *Post*, played down the story. As for the television networks, they were too enraptured with the pictorial possibilities inherent in a glamor-

---

*(New York: Harper & Row, 1965), p. 231. Ike's negative attitude toward his successor did not improve much during Kennedy's occupancy of the White House. Ike thought JFK "extremely over-rated" and could not understand his popularity. Ike's feelings about Bobby Kennedy were expressed in a letter dated March 26, 1968: "It is difficult for me to see a single qualification that the man has for the presidency. I think he is shallow, vain and untrustworthy—on top of which he is indecisive. Yet his attraction for many people is extraordinary. . . ."

ous new administration, one attuned to the requirements of a medium geared to show business. Besides, most of the top television personalities had made little secret of their favoring Kennedy over Nixon in the first place. And some of them had gone out of their way to aid Kennedy whenever they could. Thus during the first televised "debate" between Kennedy and Nixon a question was asked by one of the newsmen-panelists which, though of little substantive value, was to plague the Vice President all through the campaign.

The question was put by Sandor Vanocur, an outspoken admirer of Kennedy. The NBC correspondent, who had been making a practice of needling JFK's political foes, noted that Eisenhower had been "asked to give one example of a major idea of yours that he adopted. His reply was, and I am quoting, 'If you give me a week, I might think of one.' Now, that was a month ago, sir, and the President hasn't brought it up since, and I am wondering, sir, if you can clarify . . ."

The day Eisenhower made the remark he phoned Nixon to express his anger toward the way it was being interpreted by the press. As Nixon wrote later, Eisenhower "pointed out he was simply being facetious and yet they played it straight and wrote it seriously. I could only reply to Vanocur's question in the same vein, but I am sure that to millions of unsophisticated televiewers, this question had been most effective in raising a doubt in their minds with regard to one of my strongest campaign themes and assets—my experience as Vice President."

What Nixon did not learn until later was that during at least one debate, he was dealing with a stacked deck. One of the newsmen-panelists had been in touch with Kennedy's managers. Questions which the Kennedy camp wanted asked of Nixon were phoned to the newsman, who had no qualms about asking them.

At the same time Kennedy's advisers had unusual facilities for determining what kind of questions were likely to be asked of the senator. As the Washington *Star* reported, "In all four debates, the Senator was not asked a single substantive question that had not been covered in the briefing." As a result JFK was rarely at a loss for words.

Little was left to chance. Kennedy's managers had also taken the precaution of having one of their agents travel constantly with the Vice President. Whenever Nixon opened his mouth, whether it be in formal speeches or off-the-cuff remarks, tape recordings would be made and transmitted to the Democratic candidate. Kennedy spent considerable time, prior to each debate, listening to these tapes. His managers later claimed they helped put JFK in a properly aggressive mood.

There were other times during the campaign when Nixon never knew what hit him. Kennedy, for example, made a big issue of the supposed decline of American prestige abroad during the Eisenhower-Nixon years. Nixon responded by contending that U.S. prestige was at an all-time high. Kennedy then challenged the Republican administration to make public surveys on the subject carried out overseas by the United States Information Agency (USIA). Nixon countered that these public opinion polls were classified as confidential—which, in fact, they were.

That didn't prevent the Kennedy camp from arranging for their theft from the supposedly secret files of the USIA and transmittal to Kennedy himself. As Ted Sorensen later reported,

> The polls strongly backed the Senator's position and made Nixon's claims about them look like deliberate misinformation. To avoid charges that he had improperly obtained classified material, Kennedy turned the polls over to *The New York Times,* who immediately printed them without mention of how they had been acquired, and the Senator was then free to quote them as official proof of our plummeting prestige.

Needless to say, this "dirty trick"—then considered only a bit of "upmanship"—did Kennedy no harm. Indeed it helped eke out his eyelash victory in a down-to-the-wire finish. Of course as President, Kennedy was not overly anxious to release USIA "prestige" polls taken during his administration.

6

In the late summer of 1963 Richard Nixon telephoned to thank me for having sent him a pre-publication copy of my new book *J.F.K.: The Man and the Myth,* a critical look at the life and record of the man who had bested him for the presidency.

At the time Nixon lived in New York. He had come to the Big Apple to seek his fortune after having been trounced in his 1962 race for the governorship of California.

"That's quite a book," the former Vice President told me. "I've just finished it and, frankly, I never knew what bastards those Kennedys were."

The remark puzzled me (and, for that matter, still does). Was it possible that Nixon never really knew what he was up against when he ran for President in 1960?

"Those fellows sure know how to play rough," Nixon went on.

And I couldn't have agreed more. For that very morning I had received a call from a Washington friend warning that the Kennedys were out to "get" me for having written that antagonistic book about the President. The friend, a staff member of the Senate Internal Security Subcommittee, reported that two of "Bobby's boys" had been around looking for derogatory material about me in the files. They made one mistake, however, when they signed an official request for the material. But more of this later.

I told Nixon about the call. He didn't seem overly surprised. He said he had had similar problems with the Kennedys. Specifically, on his return to California following his 1960 defeat, the man who lost the presidency by a handful of votes found himself being audited by the Internal Revenue Service. As did Robert H. Finch, one of his 1960 campaign managers. The experience wasn't too pleasant for either Nixon or Finch, involving as it did a time-consuming search for documents of all kinds, but in the end their tax returns were found to be in order.

Nixon said that others involved in his presidential campaign had had similar experiences. "Oh, what the hell," he said, "it's all part of the game, I guess."

The Kennedys had long had an interest in the Internal Revenue Service. For one thing the family was often harassed during the Truman years for allegedly failing to pay its proper share of taxes. Joseph P. Kennedy, the paterfamilias, had always blamed Truman for his woes. And now, following Jack's election to the White House, the Kennedys felt that at long last the IRS was theirs.

In fact the very first day he took over as Kennedy's new IRS commissioner in 1961, Mortimer Caplin received a call from a White House aide who said "it was the President's wish" that he immediately dismiss Donald Bacon as regional commissioner in Boston. Bacon, the White House aide reported, was a "holdover Republican" who was creating tax difficulties for any number of good, loyal Massachusetts Democrats. Caplin, who had taught law at the University of Virginia before becoming the nation's chief tax collector, thought there was something nonkosher about the request. He checked into the Democrats being investigated in the Bay State and found that they indeed were having tax problems, but justifiably. Whereupon, according to Caplin, he notified the President that he intended to retain the "holdover Republican" in his job.

Caplin never did identify the aide who had called him with the President's request. Apparently it was Carmine Bellino, who from the moment Kennedy entered the White House was interested in developing tax information with which to destroy the "political enemies" of the new administration.

Bellino had been named special consultant to the President. Few around the White House ever knew what he was up to. Those who did usually referred to him as a "troubleshooter." But in post-Watergate terms he could more accurately be described as a "hatchet man."

And assisting Bellino in developing tax information against Kennedy's "enemies" was none other than Mortimer Caplin—a fact which emerged during the course of the Senate Watergate hearings.

The disclosure came about following the testimony of John Dean, former counsel to President Nixon, that the White House had sought to use the IRS to attack the administration's political enemies.

This was denied by John Ehrlichman, who cited a Senate debate published in the April 16, 1970, *Congressional Record* to demonstrate that procedures safeguarding the privacy of tax returns were much stricter under Nixon than under Kennedy in 1961.

"Six days after [Kennedy's] inauguration," Ehrlichman testified, Bellino "called on the commissioner of Internal Revenue and undertook inspection of many, many tax returns for days at a time."

Ehrlichman also noted that from Nixon's inauguration up to the time of the 1970 Senate debate, the White House had made only nine written requests to the IRS for permission to view tax records. This contrasted sharply with the Kennedy administration, during which Bellino viewed tax records without written requests.

Caplin was not immediately available for comment regarding Ehrlichman's allegations. However the *Congressional Record* for April 16, 1970, did contain a memorandum from JFK's IRS commissioner stating that on January 26, 1961—six days after the inauguration—Bellino had shown up at his office to request "permission to inspect our files" on an individual whose name had been excised from the memo "and others."

"Although we had no precedent to guide us," the Caplin memo went on, "we decided that Mr. Bellino, in his capacity as a representative of the President, could inspect our files without a written request."

Bellino's response to the Ehrlichman revelations was that he had every legal right to examine tax returns as part of an official Justice Department investigation of labor racketeering, with particular emphasis on the Teamsters and its then chief, Jimmy Hoffa. After all, Bellino added, having been active in the Senate probe of labor racketeering in the fifties, he was probably the one person most familiar with the subject in the new administration. And that is why, he said, the President authorized him to check certain tax returns.

But the fact remains that Bellino was not part of the Justice Department. He was a White House "consultant," the same title later given to E. Howard Hunt during the Nixon years.

As far as the Watergate hearings were concerned, the matter raised by Ehrlichman was left hanging. Sam Ervin, who had become a folk hero exposing the malefactions of the Nixon administration, wanted no part of looking into the excesses of the past—particularly the Democratic past.

What we now know, thanks again to Ben Bradlee, was the enormous interest shown by President Kennedy in other people's tax returns. For example Kennedy "stunned" Bradlee at the dinner table one night by revealing that J. Paul Getty, reputedly the richest man in the world, had paid exactly $500 in income taxes the previous year, while H. L. Hunt, the oil tycoon, forked over only $22,000 to IRS.

Bradlee, needless to say, did not think it politic to inquire how or why the President happened to be carrying such precise data in his head. Obviously Kennedy had made some effort to acquire the information, planning to make some practical use of it. Exactly what he had in mind we probably will never know. A month later he was dead.

But Bradlee did ask the President just how much Daniel Ludwig, the shipbuilding magnate, had paid in tax. Bradlee had been cruising with Kennedy when they noticed that a yacht owned by Ludwig had failed to turn out its crew to salute the President, a fact which seemed to annoy Kennedy. (Talk about the Imperial presidency!)

Kennedy smiled at Bradlee's question but didn't bite. He pointed out that "all this tax information was secret, and it was probably illegal for him to know or at least for him to tell me." But Bradlee pressed on, suggesting that JFK leak IRS data on rich men's returns in order to get a tax reform bill through the Congress.

"Maybe after 1964," replied Kennedy.

Much has been made of the practice of the IRS during the Nixon years of urging special investigations of student protesters, Black militants, outright subversives, and anyone who was financing them.

But the practice of using the IRS for political purposes did not start with Nixon. In the fall of 1961, at the behest of the Kennedy brothers, the targets were mainly tax-exempt right-wing groups whose cries of outrage were patently ignored by liberal groups which normally favor the right to dissent. In some cases liberal groups actively promoted the harassment, if not destruction, of ultra-conservative voices which the media had labeled "kooky." Undoubtedly some of them were. But none of the organizations harassed by the Kennedys advocated bomb-throwing, rioting, or outright revolution.

The campaign to crush right-wing dissent had its origins in a twenty-four-page memorandum written by Victor Reuther of the United Automobile Workers. Transmitted to Robert Kennedy, the memorandum urged the use of federal agencies to head off and dry up conservative critics of the administration. The Attorney General liked it so much that he circulated copies to key members of the administration and sympathetic congressmen.

Reuther, a longtime mover and shaker in liberal causes (including, believe it or not, civil liberties), began his repressive document by noting that President Kennedy had made several speeches attacking the "radical right" as a pernicious influence in American politics. He argued that such talk was not good enough. What was needed was governmental action. And he named as targets a host of organizations and individuals. Included were such groups as the John Birch Society, Dr. Fred Schwarz's Christian Anti-Communist Crusade, and H. L. Hunt's "Life Lines." Individuals named by Reuther included the Reverend Billy James Hargis, and Senators Strom Thurmond and Barry Goldwater, among many others.

Concerning these ideological misfits the Reuther memorandum said: "What are needed are deliberate policies and programs to contain the radical right from further expansion and in the long run to reduce it to its historic role of the impotent lunatic fringe . . . they must never be permitted to become so strong as to obstruct action needed for democratic survival and success."

Reuther then suggested various punitive measures, including the placing of the right-wing dissenters on the Attorney General's list of subversive organizations. "The mere act of indicating that an investigation will be made will certainly bring home to many people something they have never considered—the subversive character of these organizations and their similarity to the listed groups on the left."

Reuther also proposed that "the flow of big money to the radical right should be dammed to the extent possible," urging that such organizations as the William Volker Fund, Dr. George Benson's National Education Program, and the Christian Anti-Communist Crusade should be deprived of their tax-exempt status. "Prompt revocation in a few cases might scare off a substantial part of the big money now flowing into these tax-exempt organizations." Moreover there was "the big question whether

Schwarz, Hargis, etc., are themselves complying with the tax laws." Reuther said there was enough evidence to justify "the most complete check on these various means of financing the radical right."

Though the existence of the memorandum was known to the Washington press corps, the interest was minimal. In fact I was the first to "break" the story in my North American Newspaper Alliance column. No one, outside of a few of those affected by this would-be assault on the Constitution and the freedoms of the American people, really cared. No Senate committee was created to look into the matter. As always it was a case of whose ox was gored.

President Kennedy soon mouthed the Reuther line. In reply to a question at a press conference, he said that the federal government ought to be concerned if tax-exempt money was being diverted to nonexempt purposes. This was a reference to the law which sets strict limitations on the direct political activities that may be engaged in by tax-exempt organizations.

According to a staff report prepared for the Joint Committee on Internal Revenue Taxation,* this comment was followed up by an inquiry to Mitchell Rogovin, then assistant to the IRS commissioner, from John Siegenthaler, then an assistant to Attorney General Kennedy. Siegenthaler, a former investigative reporter, asked about the tax-exempt status of four or five organizations generally considered to be right-wing, according to the report. That information was quickly supplied.

Rogovin himself supplied a list of eighteen organizations for investigation, the names of which he claimed to have gathered from articles in *Time* and *Newsweek*.** An audit of most of them was begun almost immediately. At the same time the regional IRS commissioners in New York and San Francisco were ordered to launch examinations of "six large corporate taxpayers" who were alleged to be financial backers of "extremist groups."

At this early stage the program appeared to be focused entirely on right-wing organizations. Concern was expressed about this

---

*Investigation of the Special Service Staff of the Internal Revenue Service, Prepared for the Joint Committee on Internal Revenue Taxation By Its Staff, June 5, 1975 (Washington, D.C.: Government Printing Office, 1975).
**On leaving government, Rogovin became one of Washington's better-known civil liberties lawyers. He represented various individuals and organizations in legal actions stemming from alleged harassment during the Nixon administration, but was forced to withdraw as general counsel of Common Cause and the Institute for Policy Studies (a leftist think tank) when—surprisingly—he agreed to act as outside counsel for the beleaguered CIA in 1975.

pronounced ideological bias. Rogovin therefore sent over a list of what he described as "alleged left of center" organizations for investigation. Since he had difficulty obtaining the names of such organizations, Rogovin thinks he may have asked the FBI for help.

Mortimer Caplin, who was then Commissioner of Internal Revenue, made reports on the progress of the investigation of "ideological organizations" not only to his superior in the Treasury Department, Undersecretary Henry Fowler, but also to Myer Feldman, a member of the White House staff, and to Attorney General Kennedy.

By the summer of 1963 the investigation apparently dwindled to a state of complete inactivity—so much so that there were renewed demands for action on the part of liberal spokesmen. Senator Maurine Neuberger, for example, speaking before the AFL-CIO's Committee on Political Education, demanded the cancelation of tax exemptions of conservative organizations, including the most scholarly. "It is painfully clear," the Oregon Democrat said, "that the tax service has simply not done the job Congress gave it, to rout out the propagandists from the bona fide educators."

On July 5, 1963, Feldman, then deputy special counsel to the President, requested a report from Caplin on the progress of the investigation. By this time the revocation of the exempt status of two right-wing organizations had been recommended and another had been warned that the IRS intended to revoke its exemption.

Apparently that wasn't good enough for the White House. For President Kennedy himself got on the phone and told Caplin that he wanted the IRS "to go ahead with (an) aggressive program—on both sides of center." By this time JFK had become terribly annoyed with left-wingers who were badgering him not only for his anti-Castro activities but for his intervention in Vietnam.

Caplin later told congressional investigators that he thought Kennedy had called him "because Mr. Feldman might have thought that the Service was dragging its feet and was not aggressive enough."

Within the week Rogovin met with Feldman at the White House. The purpose was to bring the White House up to date on the anti-extremist program. At another meeting a month later, Feldman suggested the deletion of two organizations—one left-wing and one right-wing—from the list under study. This was promptly arranged.

At about the same time Rogovin met with Robert Kennedy to brief the Attorney General on the status of the project. Kennedy recommended "expediting" the investigation of one right-wing group. This too was done. The group's tax-exempt status was subsequently lifted.

A task force which was set up following these various meetings finally recommended revocation of the exempt status of fifteen organizations, all but one of which could be described as right-wing.

The irony is that the IRS witch-hunt, particularly as it was concentrated against right-wing dissenters, was applauded by the very same people who later were to raise unshirted hell when the Nixon administration sought to use the same techniques to "contain"—in Reuther's word—the Black Panthers, the Weathermen, and other violence-prone New Left groups.

The Kennedy administration also decided to go after its right-wing critics in the broadcast media. Reuther had noted the increasing use of conservative commentaries on the airwaves. And his memorandum suggested that the IRS be instructed to check into the business sponsorship of these programs. Observing that the broadcasts invariably lambasted Kennedy and his "liberal" policies, Reuther also proposed that the Federal Communications Commission conduct an investigation "into the extent of the practice of giving free time to the radical right," as well as the possibility of taking "measures to encourage stations to assign comparable time for an opposing point of view on a free basis." In other words Reuther wanted the FCC to enforce the "fairness doctrine" against right-wing commentators.

The fairness of the FCC's "fairness doctrine" came under strong attack in early 1975 with the disclosure that the Kennedy and Johnson administrations had used the rule to stifle radio attacks during the 1964 presidential campaign.

The disclosure was contained in *The Good Guys, the Bad Guys and the First Amendment,* written by Fred W. Friendly—Edward R. Murrow Professor at the Columbia Graduate School of Journalism, a Ford Foundation adviser, and former president of CBS News.*

---

*An excerpt from the book was published as an article in *The New York Times Magazine,* March 30, 1975. The book itself was published by Random House in 1976.

Friendly focused on the 1969 Supreme Court decision which upheld the right of the FCC to order a broadcaster to grant reply time to a person or group claiming to have suffered from a broadcast. Digging into the tangled background of the case, Friendly discovered that the decision was "tainted."

What had happened back in the New Frontier was this, according to Friendly: Since "Kennedy and the Democratic National Committee believed that the Republicans might nominate Goldwater and that the right-wing radio commentators who supported him could damage the President's chances for re-election," the White House "decided to see if the fairness doctrine could again be used, this time for partisan political purposes."

According to Friendly, the Democrats created and maintained professionally staffed organizations that monitored stations carrying right-wing commentary and then demanded time for reply. The White House was particularly anxious to blunt broadcasters critical of such administration goals as the nuclear test ban treaty. These demands for equal time, which stations would have to provide gratis, were regarded by most of their executives as harassments they'd rather avoid. This many of them did, either by dropping the commentaries or by censoring them.

It was a conspiracy, pure and simple; one which was aimed at curbing free expression. And, according to Friendly, it led right to the door of the Oval Office. For directing the campaign aimed at curbing dissent was none other than Kenneth P. O'Donnell who, as White House appointments secretary, troubleshooter, and expediter, was considered to be Kennedy's political right-hand.* At a meeting in the Fish Room O'Donnell instructed Wayne Phillips, a former *New York Times* reporter then working for the Housing and Home Finance Agency, to check whether the fairness doctrine could be used in behalf of the President's reelection campaign. Whereupon Phillips hired Wesley McCune, a specialist who kept track of right-wingers and their organizations, to monitor commentators. As a result of McCune's efforts the Democrats were able to reply quickly to hundreds of broadcasts—for free.

The success of this venture convinced the Democratic National Committee that it had a good thing going. Not only was the DNC getting a lot of free time, but its covert campaign—as one

---

*Years later President Nixon's appointments secretary, Dwight Chapin, hired a college chum, Donald Segretti, to play silly pranks on the Democrats. But Chapin, unlike O'Donnell, got caught at it.

of its former officials told Friendly—succeeded in inhibiting many right-wing stations. A "confidential" DNC memorandum put it this way:

> The right-wingers operate on a strictly cash basis and it is for this reason that they are carried by so many small stations. Were our efforts to be continued on a year-round basis, we would find that many of these stations would consider the broadcast of these programs bothersome and burdensome (especially if they are ultimately required to give us free time) and would start dropping the programs from their broadcast schedule.

So the DNC decided to expand. It retained the public relations firm of Ruder & Finn, which in turn set up a phony committee, seemingly divorced from the Democratic party but actually financed by it. This was done through a system of "laundering" party funds for the purpose of deception.

The phony committee was supposedly bipartisan. It was given a fancy title—The National Council for Civic Responsibility. Selected as its head was a liberal Republican, Arthur Larson, who had served as director of the United States Information Agency under Eisenhower. Larson, who was sincerely alarmed at what he considered the growing influence of "radical reactionary organizations" (talk about name calling), apparently was not aware that the National Council was an undercover parapolitical operation of the Democratic party.

At least Larson gave that impression on the eve of the 1964 election. Asked whether his organization was involved with any political party, Larson said: "No, this is completely divorced from political parties because neither President Johnson nor General Eisenhower nor anybody connected with the political campaign was aware that this organization was about to be formed."

Of course Larson now knows better.

Several hundred distinguished Americans gladly gave their names as sponsors of the new supposedly nonpartisan group. They included Marion B. Folsom, former member of the Eisenhower cabinet; General J. Lawton Collins, former army chief of staff; Detlev Bronk, president of Rockefeller Institute; Erwin Griswold, dean of Harvard Law School; Robert B. Meyner, former Democratic governor of New Jersey; and Ralph McGill, publisher of the Atlanta *Constitution*.

The National Council for Civic Responsibility had been formed too quickly to obtain a tax-exempt status. So the Democrats ar-

ranged to combine it with the Public Affairs Institute headed by
H. Dewey Anderson. This was a pre-Nader type of "citizen's
lobby," more or less defunct, which had one charm from the
Democrats' viewpoint—it had tax exemption. Thus the National
Council was permitted to solicit tax-deductible contributions.
The biggest donation, however, was a fat $50,000 check from the
Democratic National Committee. Later the DNC sent over addi-
tional thousands of dollars in cash.

According to Friendly, Dewey Anderson had been contacted
by James H. Rowe, a Washington lawyer closely associated with
Democratic presidents from Roosevelt to Johnson. Rowe asked
Anderson to meet privately at the offices of the Democratic Na-
tional Committee with Chairman John Bailey and Treasurer
Richard Maguire, an old JFK hand from Massachusetts.

"We got the money and you got the tax exemption and we
need you to fight these right-wing radio extremists," Anderson
recalls Bailey and Rowe telling him. Anderson was only too
happy to cooperate. *Voilà.* What had been known as the National
Council for Civic Responsibility became the National Committee
for Civic Responsibility of the Public Affairs Institute. The tax-
exempt status, of course, meant not only that contributions could
be written off but that the taxpayer, in the final analysis, was
paying for a partisan political effort.

Needless to say, this amounted to a political dirty trick of gigantic proportions—and one that violated a law which, incidentally,
had been introduced in 1954 by none other than then Senator
Lyndon Johnson.

But prior to Watergate, dirty tricks were an accepted practice
in political life and no one paid too much attention. The National
Committee obtained considerable media coverage. Only one reporter, Jack Anderson, exposed the fact that the Civic Responsibility group had been covertly financed with Democratic funds;
but this was four months after the election, and no one seemed
to care. Once LBJ was elected, the Democrats lost interest in
subsidizing a campaign to expose the villainous right-wingers
who, only months before, had constituted such a potent threat to
American freedom. These "sleazy and seamy activities," as
Dewey Anderson more recently described them, went
thoroughly unnoticed by the same news media which years later
were to go ape over every sordid Watergate detail.

Larson himself feels sheepish about his participation in this
pre-Watergate-type activity. "The whole thing was not my idea,"

he told Friendly, "but let's face it, we decided to use radio and the fairness doctrine to harass the extreme right. In the light of Watergate, it was wrong. We felt the ends justified the means. They never do. I guess I was like a babe in the woods."

An estimated $200,000 in tax-exempt funds was raised by the Larson group. To counteract right-wing broadcasts, the national committee produced its own series of radio programs, described by Friendly as "as shrill as those they were designed to counter." The researcher was a free-lance writer, Fred Cook, who was paid by Ruder & Finn. In addition Cook was subsidized by the Democratic National Committee to write a book on the 1964 Republican candidate for President entitled *Goldwater: Extremist of the Right.** Also at the behest of Wayne Phillips, now an official at the Democratic National Committee, Cook wrote an article for *The Nation* entitled "Hate Groups of the Air," about right-wing extremists supposedly dominating the airwaves. Much of the research for *The Nation* article was provided by Wesley McCune.

The Reverend Billy James Hargis, who bought time on stations for his daily "Christian Crusade" broadcasts, taped a two-minute reply to Cook, terming him a "professional mudslinger" for his Goldwater book as well as his article for *The Nation*. In addition Hargis accused Cook of dishonesty, of falsifying stories, and of having written a book defending Alger Hiss. In so doing, Hargis provided an inexact account of how Cook came to lose his job at the *New York World-Telegram & Sun* in 1959.

One of the stations carrying the Hargis broadcast was WGCB, located in Red Lion, Pennsylvania. Cook demanded that the station grant him equal time to reply. The tiny station refused, saying in effect that if Cook wanted to broadcast over its facilities he would have to pay for the time. Cook then took the matter to the FCC, which ruled in his favor under the fairness doctrine. Eventually the matter went to the Supreme Court, which upheld the ruling. The Red Lion case became historic because, as Fred Friendly pointed out, the court's unanimous ruling established "the power of government to intervene directly in the content of broadcasting."

---

*By coincidence Fred Cook sat behind me on the rewrite battery of the now defunct *New York World-Telegram & Sun*. Also by coincidence, as Fred Friendly noted in his *Times* article, the technique used to bring out the Cook book was "similar to Laurence Rockefeller's financing of the Victor Lasky book critical of former Supreme Court Justice Arthur Goldberg." With one difference, however. At the time I did not know that Laurence Rockefeller was my patron.

But, as Friendly also noted, Cook did not bring his action against WGCB simply as "an offended private citizen." Cook was a participant in White House efforts to suppress right-wing voices —a fact not known either by the FCC or the Supreme Court when the Red Lion case was being adjudicated.

Henry Geller, the FCC general counsel who wrote the decision upholding Cook's right of reply, termed the startling information uncovered by Friendly "alarming," and said he would have written the rules differently had he known how the Red Lion case came about.

Billy James Hargis, whose stations began dropping him "by the dozens" because of the organized requests for free time, observed: "I had said all along that there was a campaign by the White House to get me, but no one in the press would listen to me or believe me."

And there is no doubt, as Friendly quotes a former Ruder & Finn executive who handled the clandestine White House operation, that "if we did in 1974 what we did in 1964, we'd be answering questions before some Congressional Committee"—and, it could be added, probably before old "Maximum John."

"But," as columnist William F. Buckley, Jr., observed, "one hopes that the liberal moralist on night-duty for the Establishment will take the time to express an appropriate shame and contrition over the hypocrisy, deception, and unlawfulness of the Democratic Creeps of ten years ago."

That will be the day.

7

IT IS A CURIOUS FACT THOUGH ONE THAT many observers still refuse to accept, that in many of the offenses that occurred in the Watergate era John Kennedy clearly anticipated Richard Nixon. Kennedy, too, talked about "getting" his enemies. "Don't get mad, get even," was the well-known watchword along the New Frontier. And people who worked for the Kennedys formed a cadre of "do-anything-for-the-boss" loyalists—an "Irish Mafia," as they were called, antedating the clumsier "German Mafia" that attained such disrepute under Nixon.

Kennedy and his top aides, in particular, liked to think of themselves as being "tough" and "hardnosed," terms that were considered compliments in the Camelot era. Thus at the height of the 1962 steel crisis Kennedy told Ben Bradlee that the major companies "fucked us, and we've got to fuck them." (Kennedy's use of the four-letter word and its declensions so popular among the young was most prolific.)

Like the two presidents who succeeded him, Kennedy was obsessed with the press. What made his obsession so ludicrous, however, was that, better than most other chief executives, he had won over a media which for the most part was entranced with his grace and style. And even today, because of the trauma of his untimely death, a mythic glow protects his memory. Or as Joe Flaherty put it in *The Village Voice,* "When one thinks of Kennedy's sins, the transgressions are muted by memories of his elan."

Kennedy was expert at "using" the media. Most revealing was a memo found in his handwriting at the Kennedy Library in Waltham, Massachusetts. Dated October 22, 1962, the memo concerned the Cuban missile crisis. Addressed to his staff, it read: "Is there a plan to brief and brainwash key press within twelve hours or so?" There followed a list of those to be "brainwashed": *The*

New York Times, Walter Lippmann, Marquis Childs, Joseph Alsop, and "key bureau chiefs."*

The harsh fact remains that Kennedy hated to be criticized and, on occasion, he would, like Nixon after him, let off steam by voicing bravura threats of retaliation. In his book *The Politics of Lying* David Wise tells the little-known story of how Kennedy, displeased with an NBC-TV news treatment of his handling of the steel crisis, phoned FCC Chairman Newton Minow, saying: "Did you see that goddamn thing on Huntley-Brinkley? I thought they were supposed to be our friends. I want you to do something about that. You do something about that."

Fortunately, Minow did nothing. Instead he phoned Ken O'Donnell the next day to say, "Just tell the President he's very lucky he has an FCC chairman who doesn't do what the President tells him."

On another occasion a Fischetti cartoon caused an explosion in the President's suite at the Carlyle Hotel in New York. Published on the front page of the *New York Herald-Tribune*, it pictured press secretary Pierre Salinger, just returned from Moscow, as telling Kennedy, "Mr. Khrushchev said he liked your style in the steel crisis."

At 7:30 A.M. the phone rang in the hotel room occupied by Dave Wise, the *Tribune*'s White House correspondent. "I just wanted you to know the President's reaction to this morning's *Herald-Tribune*," Salinger told a startled Wise. "The fucking *Herald-Tribune* is at it again." And, Salinger added, the President would very much appreciate it if Wise would personally so inform his publisher John Hay Whitney. Which Wise did, much to "Jock" Whitney's discomfiture.

Back in Washington later a still steaming Kennedy ordered the cancelation of all twenty-two White House subscriptions to the *Herald-Tribune*. And Salinger let it be known that the President had a dramatic purpose in mind—namely, to call attention to the double standard employed by the "once-respected" *Trib* in its free-wheeling coverage of the Democratic scandals involving Billy Sol Estes, while taking a more nonchalant approach toward

---

*The memo was among nearly 100,000 Kennedy papers made public in January 1974. Some years later when staff members of the Senate Intelligence Committee visited the Library, according to William Safire, "suspicious gaps were discovered in the telephone logs of the President's calls. Nor was there any record of a private telephone, installed in a tiny room just off the Oval Office, where Kennedy made private calls outside the White House switchboard."

a then current Senate probe into alleged hanky-panky of Eisenhower administration figures. "And those bastards didn't have a line on it," Kennedy told Bradlee. "We read enough shit. We just don't have to read that particular brand."

The banning of the *Tribune* backfired. Even normally friendly sources noted that the President not only canceled his own subscription, but twenty-one others, leaving the impression that he was deciding the reading habits of his associates. "President Kennedy," observed the late Robert G. Spivack, "grimly believes in the right to dissent. In fact, he will tell you what you can dissent about."

Later the White House leaked the story that the *Trib*'s banishment was actually the work of an "overzealous" aide rather than the President's, but that hardly squares with accounts of the incident published by insiders Schlesinger, Sorensen, and Bradlee. The truth is Kennedy despised the *Herald-Tribune*, believing that its publisher was keeping it alive in order to help Rockefeller's presidential chances in 1964.

Obviously Kennedy was no stranger to the concept of an enemies list—or what he less elegantly called a "shit list"—and surprisingly, of all people, Ben Bradlee once found himself on it. "Benjy" felt Kennedy's icy scorn after he talked too freely to Fletcher Knebel, who was writing a piece entitled "Kennedy vs. The Press" for *Look* magazine. In the piece Bradlee was quoted as saying of the Kennedy brothers, "It's almost impossible to write a story they like. Even if a story is quite favorable to their side, they'll find one paragraph to quibble with."

That did it. For several months Benjy lived in virtual purgatory. No longer did he hear from the President. No longer was he invited over to the White House for dinner and those oh-so-intimate conversations. He knew he had done the unpardonable —he had criticized the Kennedys. Finally from out of the blue Kennedy called. The "exile" was over. And once again Benjy was a happy man.

Despite his closeness to JFK, Bradlee is convinced to this day that he had been wiretapped by the Kennedys. "My God," he told me, "they wiretapped practically everyone else in this town."*

---

*My conversation with Bradlee took place outside the Watergate apartments, where we both lived, the weekend following Nixon's resignation. I had begun the chat by remarking, "Well, you finally did it. You 'got' the President." Bradlee countered by saying I was wrong. "Nixon did it to himself," he said.

And Bradlee knew what he was talking about. The Kennedys' predilection for listening in on other people's private conversations constituted seminal work in this field. They established a record in the number of wiretaps, both authorized and unauthorized, that has yet to be equaled. Not even the Nixon administration topped them.

In fact Kennedy delighted in joking about this. Again we turn to Bradlee for the evidence. It seems that during the steel crisis, the President toasted Attorney General Kennedy at a dinner party. In so doing he referred to a phone conversation he had had with Thomas F. Patton of Republic Steel.

Patton had complained that Bobby was wiretapping steel executives and harassing them through the IRS. The President assured Patton that the Attorney General would never do any such thing.

"And, of course," the President said in closing, "Patton was right."

At that point Bobby rose and yelled in mock anger, "They were mean to my brother. They can't do that to my brother."

Which, of course, meant that the administration—with the President's knowledge and approval—had indeed been harassing executives who had the temerity to raise steel prices. In view of Bradlee's later preoccupation with presidential abuses of power, it is instructive to note that the future executive editor of the Washington *Post* apparently saw nothing wrong with such behavior. For one thing he did not expose these serious violations of civil liberties. In fact even now Benjy appears to treat the whole episode in a humorous vein.

Not everyone in the press corps was amused by such goings-on. Hanson Baldwin, for one, shook up the Oval Office by denouncing Kennedy (in an article in the April 1963 issue of *Atlantic*) for using intimidation as a weapon. Baldwin, then military affairs analyst of *The New York Times,* charged that "the blatant methods used by the Administration and its tampering with the news deserve considerably more criticism and discussion than they have received."

Kennedy told Bradlee that the reason for Baldwin's disenchantment was that, in some article, he had committed a "major security violation" which, in turn, had led to a "massive FBI investigation." Significantly Bradlee did nothing to sound the tocsin about this obvious violation of the First Amendment. Of course in years to come Bradlee was to become more vigilant about such violations.

What the President apparently did not tell Benjy, however, was the fact that his brother had ordered the FBI to wiretap both Baldwin and his secretary, not only at their *New York Times* offices but at their homes. Or that a year before, in 1961, a tap had been placed on one of Bradlee's colleagues, Lloyd Norman, then *Newsweek*'s Pentagon correspondent.

Bradlee, of course, had suspected that a lot of this sort of thing was going on, but it wasn't until a decade later that he learned the full extent of Kennedy wiretapping.

Also among those wiretapped was French-born Professor Bernard Fall of Howard University, who had written numerous books on Indochina and had reportedly maintained close contact with representatives of North Vietnam.

Another was Robert Amory, Jr., a top CIA official who was a close friend of the President. The allegation at the time was that Amory was friendly with an East European diplomat believed to be an undercover intelligence agent.

Most of these taps may have been said to have a "national security" purpose, but a number could hardly be so described. Within months of his becoming Attorney General, for example, Robert Kennedy authorized FBI wiretaps in a wide-ranging investigation of sugar lobbying in behalf of the Dominican Republic and other countries. Among six individuals whose phones were tapped was Christine Gallagher, then chief clerk of the House Agriculture Committee and secretary to Committee Chairman Harold Cooley of North Carolina. A bug was placed in the New York hotel room where Cooley was to meet foreign officials, and Robert Kennedy received FBI reports on information so obtained. Also tapped were three officials of the Agriculture Department, as well as the law firm of Surrey & Karasik, which represented Dominican sugar interests. The investigation went on for over a year but never produced an indictment.

And following the 1964 publication of a seventy-one-page pamphlet, *The Strange Death of Marilyn Monroe*, which suggested that the death of the actress was not the result of suicide but of murder, its right-wing author Frank A. Capell was subjected to a wiretap authorized by Kennedy's successor as Attorney General, Nicholas D. Katzenbach. Needless to say, this could hardly have been considered a "national security" matter.

As Richard Nixon was later to note, JFK initiated far more taps than he did (as many as 100, said Nixon), and Kennedy didn't even have a war on his hands.

Electronic surveillance was ordered by the Kennedys during the searing controversy over Moise Tshombe and his efforts to have the copper-rich Katanga Province secede from what then was the former Belgian Congo. The Kennedys opposed secession, and the issue became a hot one as Republican critics claimed the President was involving himself in something that was none of his business.

Carl T. Rowan, then in the State Department, recalled recently a speech he delivered in Philadelphia

> that turned out to be ultra-controversial because I talked about the large amounts of money being spent to sway U.S. congressmen and others by Tshombe's U.S. lobbyist, Michel Streulens. It has never been revealed how I could make the charges with such confidence. The simple fact is that the State Department had regular access to Streulens's bank records and knew on whom he was spending his substantial expense account.
>
> Furthermore, there were daily reports on what Streulens and Tshombe said to each other via telex. I assumed—correctly—that someone in our government was monitoring.
>
> This inside information gave the Kennedy Administration and the State Department considerable advantage in the bruising domestic debate that raged for months.

Apparently Rowan has had second thoughts about all of this. For, in a recent column, he asked:

"Did 'national security' justify some bank giving the government, without subpoena or other process of law, records of Streulens's expenditures? Did some overriding national interest justify the monitoring of Streulens's telex messages? Answers to those questions will not come easy to many Americans."

Hanson Baldwin's article in the *Atlantic* was an important one. Typically it was generally overlooked in the age of Camelot. Though he did not describe his own unpleasant experiences with the FBI, he did say that the free-wheeling use of federal cops to investigate leaks had grown to menacing proportions. He claimed that some of the most respected reporters in Washington had experienced "the treatment," which included FBI visits to their homes, tapping of their phones, shadowing of reporters, investigations of their friendships, and other forms of intimidation. "In all these cases the newsmen concerned have told the FBI in effect that their sources were their business," Baldwin reported. ". . . These investigations have ranged throughout the Pentagon, the State Department, and other executive branches of government. And Mr. Kennedy has been the first President to send the FBI into the Pentagon, superseding the services' own investigative and internal security agencies."

At the same time Kennedy had no compunction about trying to get correspondents fired by calling their publishers. He did this in the case of David Halberstam, whose reports on Vietnam to *The New York Times* infuriated the President. As far as can be determined, this was another of JFK's "historic firsts."

For the most part the media allowed this extraordinary state of affairs to continue with little criticism. The Bradlees and others, who years later were to take the lead in bringing down a President for abusing his powers, said nothing—at least publicly—about such abuses when committed by the Kennedys.

Exactly how much wiretapping went on within the White House itself has never been fully determined. But apparently it was widespread. Years later when Watergate broke wide open, Brigadier General Godfrey McHugh, Kennedy's air force aide, was quoted by Betty Beale as saying: "When I was in the White House, my phone was bugged all the time. Everybody's was. The FBI men would even come to the office and play back something I said on the phone and ask if it wasn't classified. I would tell them, 'No, I was discussing a story that had already appeared in the newspaper.' A few days later they would be back to ask about another comment—because they didn't keep up with the number of newspapers we had to read."

The Kennedys' use of the FBI to do their dirty work extended to the flap over steel prices in the spring of 1962. FBI agents were dispatched in the middle of the night to interview reporters on their published accounts of interviews with steel executives. Max Lerner found the episode "distasteful" and smacking of a "police operation," while the Richmond (Va.) *Times-Dispatch* described it as an "indefensible abuse of personal power by a hired public servant"—meaning Bobby Kennedy.

Bobby, of course, was the enforcer in his brother's administration. He was the tough guy, who had few compunctions about using threats to silence political opponents. There was the occasion he called in Earl Mazo of the *New York Herald-Tribune*.

Mazo had written a series of articles about Texas's wheeler-dealer Billie Sol Estes and his financially profitable, though questionable, ties with the New Frontier.

According to Mazo, Bobby "blew his stack" in denouncing him. On his desk Bobby had placed a thick folder conspicuously marked with Mazo's name. It was obvious that the Justice Department had collected quite a file on the maverick newsman, who happened to have been born in Poland. The atmosphere was one of intimidation. And, as Mazo recalled, "Bobby's so-called 'lecture,' as it has been described, was in reality a childish outburst. He was so enraged over our coverage of the Estes scandal that I expected at any moment he would throw himself to the floor, screaming and bawling for his way. Instead, he paced back and forth, storming and complaining. It was something to see!" (That was the week, incidentally, when President Kennedy banned Mazo's newspaper from the White House.)

Extraordinary measures were taken by the Kennedys in order to whip press critics into line. Representative Bob Wilson, a California Republican, told his fellow solons at the time, "I know of one instance where a publisher was invited to the White House where he was wined and dined . . . and then was asked to go down the street to the Department of Justice, where he had a conference with the President's brother. The conference had to do with a possible anti-trust violation. So, the orders soon went out—and we have this on good authority—that the critical columnists and newspapermen on this particular paper were to let up on their criticism of the New Frontier."

Wilson also reported that other newsmen who were critical of the administration were offered "very cozy and very attractive jobs. One columnist told me that he was offered a very exciting job in the State Department. He turned it down. Shortly thereafter his income-tax returns were being checked."

Another who suddenly began having difficulties with the IRS was columnist Jim Bishop. "They started about the time Robert Kennedy became the Attorney General. I wrote a story and said he acted as though the rest of us were working on his old man's plantation. After that, audits."

Likewise Walter Winchell's taxes received a fine-tooth combing after the Broadway columnist had given unshirted hell to both JFK and RFK. As Winchell told me at the time, "The Kennedys are out to 'get' me." The columnist said he had never before had that much trouble with the IRS, even when Truman, whom he had attacked just as vigorously, had been President.

This writer, too, had aroused Bobby's fury for having written *J.F.K.: The Man and the Myth.* After the book zoomed to number one on the bestseller lists, it was disclosed that federal officials had launched an investigation of me. Apparently President Kennedy himself took a more tolerant view of the book. As he told *Time-Life* correspondent Hugh Sidey at the time, "I read the whole thing and found it fascinating."

Bobby did not find the book fascinating. And he sought to cover up a highly improper, if not illegal, investigation of me. At first, in a letter to then Senator Kenneth Keating of New York, the Attorney General emphatically denied he had ever authorized any such investigation. Only later—after evidence had been produced—did he concede that "overzealous" officials had undertaken the probe, but without his approval. As it turned out, these officials had served under Bobby as Senate investigators. Both were known to have a penchant for wiretapping and, following the 1960 election, had been placed on the payroll of the Immigration and Naturalization Service. What Keating had also established at the time was that the FBI had originally been asked to conduct the investigation but that Hoover emphatically refused to involve the Bureau in what was, as the director put it, strictly a "political vendetta."

The "overzealous" snoopers had as one of their chores the task of trying to link me with subversive activities. To this end they scoured government dossiers looking for any kind of dirt. But they blundered when they signed an official request for such information from the Senate Internal Security Subcommittee. Whereupon one of the subcommittee's employees—an old friend —phoned to warn me that Bobby's boys were poking around the files.

The files contained nothing. But that did not stop the Attorney General from unloosing a campaign of vilification. All of a sudden several Democratic chairmen in Western states publicly accused me of being an ex-Communist, while Democratic National Chairman John Bailey described me as a "Birchite." Thus the executive wing of government, under the Kennedys, used its enormous power in an attempt to defame one of its critics.

In retrospect what made the entire episode even more significant was the total lack of interest shown by the same liberal press which was to become outraged—and quite properly so—by the Nixon administration's misuse of the FBI in conducting a field investigation of Daniel Schorr. Such newspapers as the Washington *Post* and *The New York Times* couldn't have cared less about the violations of the civil liberties of an anti-Kennedy author. No teams of investigative reporters were assigned to dig into what appeared to be an insidious attack on the First Amendment. Likewise not one word of protest emanated from the usually vigilant American Civil Liberties Union.

If anything, liberal publicists like James Wechsler treated the episode as a joke. In his *New York Post* column on October 15, 1963, Wechsler noted that Governor Rockefeller, in an Indiana speech, had condemned the Kennedys for seeking to harass me. "After diligent inquiry," wrote Wechsler, "it becomes my harsh duty to inform author Victor Lasky and his publishers that he is in no danger of prosecution, or any other form of federal harassment. It is also my gratuitous counsel that he cease transmitting the delusion of danger to Governor Rockefeller and his ghosts."

I had never transmitted anything to Rockefeller—the only major figure, incidentally, who at the time perceived the dangers inherent in the New Frontier's efforts to throttle a critic.

Wechsler also derided my claim that Immigration officials had made inquiries of the Senate Internal Security Subcommittee for information in its files about me. "Lasky's lament raised certain intrinsic doubts," he wrote. "For one thing, he had been a 'friendly' witness before Mr. Eastland's subcommittee (and) it would hardly seem plausible that anyone would view the subcommittee files as a source of derogatory information about so staunch a guardian of the republic."

But "for one thing" I had never been a "friendly" witness before the Eastland Subcommittee. At the time I had testified only once before a Senate committee: representing the Freedom of the Press Committee of the Overseas Press Club of America, I criticized the Eisenhower administration for its refusal to permit American correspondents to travel to Communist China. (The committee, incidentally, was headed by Sam Ervin of North Carolina.)

"Nevertheless," Wechsler continued,

I have ascertained that a call was made. It was made by a zealous, lower-level agent in the Immigration Service who, having read of Mr. Lasky's ardent labors in the cause of super-patriotism in the press notices of his historic work, believed he might some day be a valuable informant in immigration cases.

This dedicated gumshoe called the subcommittee to ascertain where Lasky could be located in the event that his guidance were needed. He carefully recorded the data in his notebook. Out of this inquiry was born Lasky's tale of persecution which Governor Rockefeller so carelessly embraced in his Indiana speech, thereby giving this episode national attention.

And there you have it. It was all due to a "zealous, lower-level agent," who wanted my address in case he would need my services as a "valuable informant in immigration cases," presumably involving foreign-born Communists. Well, one of the few former members of the Young Communist League whom I personally knew at the time was James Wechsler. However, as far as I know, he was born in this country and was therefore presumably ineligible for deportation.

But the story demonstrates the lengths to which the Kennedy administration—or more specifically Robert Kennedy and his aides—went in seeking to cover up a blunder in dispatching gumshoes on the trail of a critic.

A month after the Wechsler column appeared, Robert Kennedy's press officer telephoned my publisher to relay the Attorney General's concern about the "blunder" committed by those "over-zealous" subordinates. The question raised was whether I would cease publicly voicing my accusations on the matter. I said I would, provided that I receive an official letter of apology.

A few days later John Kennedy was murdered. The issue immediately became inconsequential.

On June 12, 1971, J. Edgar Hoover informed me that Robert Kennedy had wiretapped my telephone for several weeks in the summer of 1963. The FBI had not done the job, he said. Rather it was done by "outside people," whom he did not identify. In other words, long before the Nixon administration, the Kennedys had their own "plumbers" operation going for them.

Some idea of how Robert Kennedy operated in these illegal enterprises has been provided by a Mafia "wireman" who claims to have worked for the Attorney General. He is Gerard M. Callahan, once described by the district attorney of Queens County as "a notorious criminal, highly publicized as the electronics expert of the underworld." Which he indeed was.

According to Callahan, he also worked for Attorney General Kennedy. An account of that work can be found in a little-publicized book which he wrote in collaboration with Paul S. Meskil, a top crime reporter for the *New York Daily News.** Here Callahan tells how he was first summoned to Washington in the late fifties to confer with Bobby Kennedy, then chief counsel of the Labor Rackets Committee. Kennedy was working on a bill to make unauthorized wiretaps a federal crime and he wanted to tap Callahan's expertise.

After Kennedy was appointed Attorney General, he would contact Callahan from time to time. But on one occasion he asked "Cheesebox"—as Callahan was known in the underworld—to perform a "wire" job so secret and sensitive that the Attorney General said he could not entrust it to the FBI.

What Kennedy wanted done, he explained over lunch in his New York hotel suite in early September 1963, was the wiretapping of the press corps during his brother's forthcoming visits to Newport, Rhode Island. The President was planning to join his family at Hammersmith Farm, the summer residence of Mr. and Mrs. Hugh D. Auchincloss, Jackie's mother and stepfather.

According to Callahan, Kennedy told him that the correspondents would be staying at the Newport Motor Inn and would be using a conference room as their headquarters. About twenty to thirty telephones would be installed and Kennedy wanted to know everything that was said on them. All Callahan would have to do was put in the taps. A friend would operate the recording equipment, which would be installed in a room near the motel.

Callahan agreed to do the job and Kennedy gave him "a substantial down payment" to cover the costs of equipment and expenses. But, as Callahan told Kennedy, "there was one small fly in the ointment. I was out on bail in a criminal case. My picture had appeared in many newspapers. My mug shots were on file in several police departments, the FBI, and the security offices of phone companies and racetracks all over the country, including Rhode Island. If I got collared in Newport, my New York bail would be revoked and I'd be thrown in the slammer."

"Well," Kennedy said, "try to be as inconspicuous as possible and if you get into trouble call me at this number and I'll take care of it."

Kennedy, according to Callahan, also told him that his friend

---

*Paul S. Meskil and Gerard M. Callahan, *Cheesebox* (Englewood Cliffs, N. J.: Prentice-Hall, 1974).

would contact him and, when the job was completed, pay him the rest of the money.

Two days later the friend did call. They made arrangements to meet in Jamestown, Rhode Island. The friend, a man in his early forties, introduced himself as "Jim." They then drove to Newport where that night Callahan went to work. After installing the taps on the cables leading into the press room, Callahan ran extension lines into a nearby house where "Jim" had installed his recording equipment. The tapes were ready to roll.

Callahan returned to New York. Later that September he received a call from "Jim" asking him to get back to Newport in order to remove the wiretap equipment. This done, "Jim" paid him the remainder of his fee for what Callahan described as "secret service to the Attorney General."

To this day Callahan says he does not know—or even care to know—just why Kennedy wanted the Newport taps or whether the President himself was aware of them. He just assumed that's the way politicians operate. Which is why Callahan wasn't surprised or shocked when nine years later he read about Watergate.

Another person who had good reason to believe that his private phone in his Senate offices had been wiretapped by the Kennedys was Kenneth Keating. This was back in 1962, when the New York Republican was warning that the Soviets were setting up an offensive missile site in Cuba. The Kennedy administration scoffed at the warning. The President himself said there was no such evidence. It took several months before he found it and we were eyeball to eyeball with the Soviet Union in a possible nuclear confrontation.

During this period I had several interviews with Keating. The interviews always took place in the hallway outside his offices. The political atmosphere was tense. The Kennedys were infuriated with Keating for revealing information they considered politically embarrassing. Keating talked to me in the hallway because, as he then told me, he had good reason to believe that the Kennedys were learning everything he was saying in the privacy of his office. And, as he later said, he was unquestionably put under surveillance on orders of Attorney General Kennedy without a court order.

Ironically Keating was beaten in his reelection try by none other than Robert Kennedy. It was a tough campaign, one of the toughest the Empire State had ever seen. A decade later, talking about that campaign with Mike Berlin of the *New York Post,* Keating made this observation: "I don't want to make any allegations against people who are no longer here to defend themselves, but political espionage didn't start with Watergate."

8

In the early summer of 1975 Senator Frank Church decided against holding open hearings on the subject of the Central Intelligence Agency's involvement in plots to assassinate foreign leaders.

His decision, as chairman of the Senate Select Committee on Intelligence investigating CIA malefactions, came as a complete surprise. For not long before, the Idaho Democrat had given every indication of being anxious to get to the bottom of the charges involving the CIA's role in assassinations. In fact when the Rockefeller Commission refused to make public its file on the subject, Church said, "The American people are entitled to know what their government has done—the good and the bad, the right and the wrong."

His resolve lasted only a few short weeks. Then he announced that he did not want "to hold up the whole sordid story and telecast it to every corner of the world." Hence the lid on public hearings of his committee.

What had happened to change the senator's mind?

According to Republican sources on the committee, the evidence that had been amassed behind closed doors demonstrated quite convincingly that the Kennedy brothers had been up to their ears in, at the very least, assassination talk. And airing of such distasteful information would not accrue to the political benefit of a politician who, besides being a loyal Kennedy Democrat, had made no secret of his own presidential ambitions. Obviously Church believed that demythologizing JFK—by publicizing the fact that the President had discussed murder in the Oval Office—would not do his political fortunes much good.

Which apparently is why this ardent advocate of the people's right to know anything and everything about their government suddenly had a change of heart. Obviously there were things the people were not entitled to know. And what appeared to be in the making in that summer was another of those cover ups for which Washington has become famous. This time, however, the cover up appeared to be aimed at protecting the reputations of John and Robert Kennedy.

Even those parts of the media which had always insisted on publicizing everything suddenly decided it wasn't absolutely necessary. Thus columnist Mary McGrory, while calling for public hearings on all the evil deeds performed by the CIA, added tellingly: "Assassination can be left out for the moment." For, as she had previously pointed out: "The unspoken threat in all this is that Church, a faithful ally of John Kennedy, might find himself in the end pointing a finger at the Democrats' beloved victim of assassination." And for Ms. Mary, who loved the Kennedys like her own, that would have been just too much.

But as evidence accumulated and was pieced together, it became obvious to all except those who refused to see that official encouragement of high-level plotting against foreign rulers reached its high point, not under Nixon or even Johnson, but under Kennedy. Indeed most of the data on this unsavory practice concerned the Kennedy years.

The temper of the Kennedy years fitted tough actions. The new President had made it clear in his Inaugural speech—"Ask not what your country can do for you . . ."—what kind of leader he expected to be: " . . . we shall pay any price, bear any burden, meet any hardship, support any friend, oppose any foe to assure the survival of the success of liberty. . . . In the long history of the world, only a few generations have been granted the role of defending freedom in its hour of maximum danger. I do not shrink from this responsibility—I welcome it."

Within weeks the new President was encouraging the largest military buildup in the nation's history, going much further than even Eisenhower. At the same time he gave the go-ahead to the Bay of Pigs invasion, a project which, though already under way under Eisenhower, had been halted pending Kennedy's approval. And when the invasion failed, largely because he got cold feet about using airpower to back up the anti-Castro forces on the beaches, Kennedy felt humiliated. As did brother Bobby, who became infuriated when Undersecretary of State Chester Bowles advised newsmen that he had opposed the venture but had been overruled by JFK. Poking Bowles in the chest, Bobby snarled, "So you advised against this operation. Well, as of now, you were all for it." When Bowles threatened to resign and speak out, rather than take another assignment, Bobby warned him, "We will destroy you." This was the same sort of warning Bobby delivered to Humphrey when the senator refused to support JFK's nomination. "I'm going to get you," Bobby shouted angrily.

It was in this kind of *macho* atmosphere that various plots to "depose" Castro were discussed. Angered by Fidel's victory over the U.S.-backed troops, the Kennedy brothers vowed to "get even" with the Cuban dictator. After the Bay of Pigs the President himself spurred the CIA into an immense covert war against Cuba. It required the services of thousands of men and cost as much as $100 million a year.*

At the same time the Kennedys covertly ordered several U.S. agencies to find some sure means of "eliminating" Castro. The CIA had been thinking along these lines for some time. In fact the Agency had, even under Eisenhower, worked with Mafia leaders Giancana and Roselli in devising plans to bump off Fidel.

Bobby Kennedy learned all this himself in the form of a detailed secret memorandum from J. Edgar Hoover dated May 1, 1961. The director informed the Attorney General of the CIA's dealings with Giancana and Roselli. The FBI had discovered the surprising connection in its own investigation of the two racket figures. Though the Hoover memorandum never mentioned the words "assassination" or "elimination" (the euphemism employed in spy circles), the director did refer to the CIA's relationships with the mobsters as "dirty business." According to sources quoted by *The New York Times*, Attorney General Kennedy jotted this note on top of the memorandum: "Have this followed up vigorously." The memo also bore his handwritten initials "R.F.K."

A year later Kennedy was given a more precise briefing on why the CIA was dealing with Mafiosi. Lawrence Houston, general counsel for the Agency from its founding in 1947, told the Attorney General about the planned effort to "dispose" of Castro. More recently Houston disclosed that the briefing did not seem to surprise Kennedy. In fact he "didn't seem very perturbed" about the plot, only about the CIA's use of organized crime. "If you are going to have anything to do with the Mafia," Kennedy said, "you come see me first."

As a result of this May 1962 meeting with Houston Kennedy gave Hoover further details on the CIA operation. The FBI chief

---

*For details of the covert war, see the article "The Kennedy Vendetta," by Taylor Branch and George Crile III, in *Harper's*, August 1975.

then wrote a "memorandum for the files," which thirteen years later was turned over to the Rockefeller Commission. In that memorandum Hoover had voiced concern that Giancana could "blackmail" the United States. Which, in fact, he attempted to do. But then he himself was "disposed of" in what appeared to be a gangland slaying in 1975.

It was in the summer of 1962 that Robert Kennedy contacted Major General Edward G. Lansdale and ordered him to begin work on a special CIA project to develop various options for "getting rid of" Fidel Castro. In an interview with the Washington *Star*, Lansdale emphasized that the Attorney General had not used the word "assassination." However, he added, there could be no doubt that "the project for disposing of Castro envisioned the whole spectrum of plans from overthrowing the Cuban leader to assassinating him."

Kennedy had gone to Lansdale, then special assistant to Secretary of Defense McNamara, because he and the President had lost faith in the CIA following the Bay of Pigs. And he couldn't have gone to a better man. In the late 1940s Lansdale had been an adviser to President Magsaysay of the Philippines, in which role he helped put down the Communist-led Huk rebellion. In the mid-fifties he served as a CIA political officer in Saigon, where he helped establish the Diem régime, and one of the men who admired and served under him in counter-insurgent work was none other than Daniel Ellsberg. Lansdale's colorful activities in South Vietnam captured the imagination of several major writers; he is believed to be the model for "Colonel Hillandale" in the novel *The Ugly American* and for "Pyle" in *The Quiet American*.

But there was no fiction about why Bobby went to Lansdale. The situation in the Caribbean was tense. There was growing concern in Washington about the increasing presence of Soviet military advisers in Cuba, as well as suspicion that they were installing an ICBM missile force on the island. Senator Keating had been sounding the alarm and the situation was most embarrassing for an administration already humiliated by the Bay of Pigs.

Lansdale knew all of this when he relayed Kennedy's orders directly to CIA official William K. Harvey—thus bypassing the Agency's chain of command, including the director himself, John A. McCone. Lansdale instructed Harvey to prepare "contingency" plans for disposing of Castro because he wanted to know whether the United States had the capabilities for such an operation.

Asked in 1975 by Washington *Star* reporter Jeremiah O'Leary if he checked on Harvey's progress in carrying out Bobby Kennedy's instructions, Lansdale said he did not keep abreast of the details. But, he added, he "was often in conversation with President Kennedy and his brother." At the time he was working on other plans for their consideration about how to cope with Cuban threats to the United States.

Meanwhile a special cabinet-level group had been set up by President Kennedy to direct anti-Cuban operations. Titled "Operation Mongoose," the group was headed by his brother. The name is revealing. A mongoose is a ferret-like mammal found in India. It is known for its ferocity in attacking and killing the most poisonous snakes.

Other members of the group included Secretary McNamara; CIA Director McCone; Secretary of State Rusk; and McGeorge Bundy, the President's national security adviser. The Rockefeller Commission obtained the minutes of an August 10, 1962, meeting of this group, whose official title was Special Group (Augmented), which clearly indicate that the subject of assassinating Castro was discussed. Robert Kennedy was not listed as being present at this meeting. And though the notion of killing Castro was dismissed, plans were subsequently made to do just that. As Bundy, now head of the Ford Foundation, was to tell reporters in 1975, Kennedy officials often discussed "how nice it would be if this or that leader" were not around.

As far as can be determined, there were two other meetings of the group planning Operation Mongoose. Former CIA chief McCone was to acknowledge that the group had "directed mischievous things against Castro, like infiltrating saboteurs, blowing up bridges and carrying on general confusion." These activities involved the Pentagon; U.S. navy ships, for example, were used to transport infiltrators (mainly of Cuban origin) to points close to the Cuban coast. Deeply involved in all of this was none other than Joseph Califano, then a Pentagon official, who later was to serve President Johnson and then as HEW Secretary under President Carter.

That Robert Kennedy (and hence his brother the President) well knew about the plot against Castro has been established beyond a reasonable doubt. This despite the pleas of Frank

Church not to hold the Kennedys responsible for all those plots gestated in their tenure since, as the senator put it, the CIA had acted like a "rogue elephant," that is, acted on its own with no responsible officials including the President aware of what the Agency was doing. Perhaps so; but highly unlikely. One of JFK's best friends, former Senator Smathers of Florida, told the Church Committee that President Kennedy had sought his reaction to a possible assassination plot against Castro early in 1962. And Rockefeller, after examining all the evidence, observed, "I think it's fair to say that no major undertakings were taken by the CIA without either knowledge and/or approval of the White House."

Rockefeller quickly came under fire for pointing the finger at the Kennedys. White House reporters asked whether President Ford was displeased with the Vice President for that reason. The White House response was "No!" As John Osborne reported in *The New Republic,* "On the face of it, the President had no right to be displeased and I'm told that he had no grounds to be. I'm also told to be very cautious indeed about absolving the Kennedys or falling in with the attempts of former Kennedy associates, notably Adam Walinsky and Frank Mankiewicz, to suggest that Ford apologists are deliberately smearing John and Robert Kennedy in order to get at Senator Edward Kennedy."

Without knowing all the facts, both Walinsky and Mankiewicz had been quick to deny that either Kennedy knew anything about the assassination plots. How they were so positive is puzzling, since Mankiewicz in that period was serving with the Peace Corps in Lima, Peru, and Walinsky was barely an adult. Nevertheless they actually claimed there was "no evidence" that the brothers "were 'involved' in any assassination in any way." At the same time they did not deny that anti-Castro plotting had taken place during the Kennedy years. And if such plotting had taken place, then President Kennedy most certainly should have known about it. To say that he didn't is just about as damaging as to say that he did.

The intended target, Castro, was well aware of who was out to "get" him. He has since claimed that his security police foiled many similar plots. These attempts prompted the Cuban leader to warn the Kennedy administration that it would find itself in danger if it continued. In an interview with Associated Press correspondent Daniel Harker in September 1963, Castro delivered this warning: "We are prepared to fight them and answer in kind. United States leaders should think that if they are aiding terrorist plans to eliminate Cuban leaders, they themselves will not be safe."

Two months later on November 22, 1963, the day John Kennedy was killed in Dallas, a high-ranking CIA official named Desmond Fitzgerald was meeting with a senior Cuban official named Rolando Cubela, whom the CIA had recruited as an important "asset" inside Cuba, but whom some believe was a double agent. Cubela, a Castro intimate, was given the CIA code name AM/LASH. By September 1963 AM/LASH was proposing an "inside job" against the Castro régime, including Fidel's assassination. And his talk about getting rid of the Cuban dictator was communicated to CIA headquarters on September 7, 1963. Later that evening Castro delivered his warning against any U.S. efforts to assassinate Cuban leaders via Harker.

Previously Fitzgerald had been introduced to Cubela as a "personal representative" of Attorney General Kennedy. On that occasion AM/LASH asked for an assassination weapon such as a high-powered rifle with telescopic sights. But no such rifle was immediately available. On November 22, 1963, Cubela was provided instead with a poison pen outfitted with a hypodermic needle. As a long-secret CIA report observed, "It is likely that at the very moment President Kennedy was shot, a CIA officer was meeting with a Cuban agent and giving him an assassination device for use against Castro."

Jack Anderson, who was the first to break the story of the anti-Castro plotting in January 1971, reported that Robert Kennedy was emotionally devastated by the possibility that the efforts he launched may well have led to the death of his beloved brother.

What was still puzzling, according to Senator Richard Schweiker of Pennsylvania, was the fact that the Warren Commission which investigated the Kennedy assassination had been told nothing about the CIA plotting, even though the late Allen Dulles, then the Agency's director, sat on the panel. Schweiker, who as a member of the Church Committee listened to all the witnesses on the subject, raised the possibility that the President had been killed in retaliation for his anti-Castro activities. He called for a new investigation of the President's death.

And President Johnson, shortly after taking office in 1963, discovered that, as he put it, "We had been operating a damned Murder Inc. in the Caribbean." That was how he phrased it— several months before his death—to Leo Janos, a former aide.

Janos, writing in the June 1973 issue of *Atlantic,* reported that LBJ had speculated that Kennedy's assassination may have been triggered by a vengeance-seeking Castro. Even more recently it was disclosed that Johnson believed that the assassin, Lee Harvey Oswald, may have been "influenced or directed" by the Castro government. As LBJ confided to Howard K. Smith, "I will tell you something that will rock you. Kennedy was trying to get Castro, but Castro got to him first."

The irony is that, if this was the case, the Johnson administration did everything possible to prevent the truth from coming out. The Warren Commission, formed at LBJ's urgent insistence, operated under severe handicaps. From the beginning it faced persistent White House pressures to dispel conspiracy rumors. And it had hardly been formed when Attorney General Katzenbach wrote each member to suggest that they publicize the FBI's findings that Oswald was the lone assassin.

Johnson also believed that his predecessor had given the go-ahead signal for the plots which led to the killings of the Dominican Republic's Generalissimo Rafael Trujillo on May 30, 1961, and of South Vietnam's President Ngo Dinh Diem on November 1, 1963.

What Johnson in effect was saying, in so-called backgrounders, was that Kennedy had been working both sides of the Caribbean, by plotting Castro's destruction as well as that of Castro's most bitter enemy Trujillo. Never before—or since—has there been an "Imperial presidency" in which the "disposal" of foreign leaders was so eagerly discussed and plotted.

As Franklin Roosevelt once supposedly said of Trujillo: "He's a son-of-a-bitch, but he's our son-of-a-bitch." The Caribbean strong-man had long been regarded as an ally of the United States. In fact Trujillo was an admirer of Kennedy; shortly before the 1960 election, his radio station had endorsed him for President. A broadcast over *La Voz Dominicana,* beamed to North America, described Kennedy as "a dynamic, angry young man who likes to call a spade a spade, a fighting man . . . aware of the dangerous Russian interference in the Caribbean. . . ."

Half a year later the "dynamic, angry young man" headed an administration which gave material support to Trujillo's enemies. Almost at the last minute the administration got cold feet about the plot involving Dominican army officers, and made an abortive effort to prevent the assassination. Apparently higher-ups in Washington, perhaps including the President, felt that a miscarriage of the plot would be too embarrassing, particularly on the heels of the Bay of Pigs. But it was too late. Forces unleashed by the administration could not be contained in the final hours.

Trujillo came to a bloody end on a lonely coastal road six weeks after the Bay of Pigs fiasco. He was speeding in a limousine toward San Cristobal, where he had planned a rendezvous with his twenty-year-old mistress. Suddenly a Chevrolet drew abreast. In it were four men laden with all types of small arms. Within minutes the Generalissimo was dead. The arms had been provided by American officials.

Ironically the whole story was published in convincing detail in the April 13, 1963, issue of *The New Republic*. But the article, written by Norman Gall, then a reporter for the San Juan *Star*, caused so little stir at the time that the editors of *The New Republic* had to be reminded of their considerable scoop fourteen years after the fact. On June 28, 1975, the liberal magazine reprinted its 1963 dispatch, with the suggestion that members of the Church Committee read it. In an accompanying up-date, it noted that the original draft of the piece had stated bluntly that "President Kennedy knew of and approved plans to bump off Trujillo," but that this reference had been deleted from the published version.

According to *The New Republic*, other publications—most notably *Time* and the *New York Post*—also knew the whole story but did not print it. The magazine disclosed that the original draft of the Gall article had first been submitted to *Post* columnist William Shannon, but that Shannon didn't buy it because, he said, the *Post* did not have an important enough audience. Instead Shannon passed the article along to *The New Republic*, suggesting that the reference to Kennedy be excised.* Which was precisely what was done, *The New Republic* today conceding that "relations between the press and President Kennedy, everyone now recognizes in retrospect, were too chummy."

If Kennedy had, in the words of *The New Republic*, indeed known "and approved plans to bump off Trujillo," he was in direct violation of the law. As were all others involved in the plot. For under the Criminal Code, it is an illegal act if anyone within

---

*Shannon, at present a columnist for *The New York Times*, now recalls that he thought back in 1963 that *The New Republic* was being excessively cautious in editing out the reference to Kennedy.

the United States "knowingly begins . . . or provides or prepares a means for or furnishes the money for, or takes part in, any military or naval expedition or enterprise to be carried on from thence against the territory or dominion of any foreign prince or state, or of any colony, district or people with whom the United States is at peace."

And the United States most definitely was "at peace" with the Dominican Republic, which, unlike Cuba, was considered a "friendly nation."

Violation of the statute is punishable by a $3,000 fine or imprisonment for not more than three years or both. By now, the statute of limitations probably protects the plotters.

Then there was the toppling of the government of President Miguel Ydigoras Fuentes of Guatemala. According to Ydigoras, it was President Kennedy who ordered the coup which overthrew him in March 1963. The reason, he claims, was that Kennedy had to find a "scapegoat" for his failure of the Bay of Pigs.

Now living in El Salvador, the former Guatemalan president claims that the attempt to terminate the Castro régime failed because of "the great indecisions of President Kennedy."

"As always," Ydigoras told an interviewer, "he had to find a scapegoat, and that scapegoat was Ydigoras Fuentes. It was through Kennedy's orders that my government was destroyed."

An ardent foe of Castro, Ydigoras had permitted the CIA to train hundreds of Cuban exiles as an invasion force within Guatemala.

But an even greater scandal of the Kennedy administration in terms of its dire consequences was the manner in which the highest officials of the government at the time, including the President, were involved in the conspiracy leading to the overthrow of South Vietnam's President Ngo Dinh Diem.

Once again Kennedy and his associates definitely violated the law by plotting a coup against a friendly government. And once again a Kennedy-approved conspiracy led to murder.

Diem's death, which Kennedy had not directly planned, was a tragedy not only for South Vietnam but for the United States as well. It was, as the *Wall Street Journal* has observed, "the worst single mistake of postwar foreign policy. It was this act more than anything else that bogged the U.S. down in Vietnam." For it left the young Southeast Asian nation leaderless and it led to the overwhelming involvement of American troops in an undeclared war (which many liberals later insisted was not only immoral but illegal) to save South Vietnam from falling to communism.

As President Johnson told reporters during a discussion of Vietnam in August 1967, "On instructions of ours we assassinated Diem and then, by God, I walked into it. It was too late and we went through one government after another."

In all, over 50,000 American boys died and several hundred thousand were wounded in what was to become the most unpopular war in the nation's history. It was a conflict which led one President to decide not to stand for reelection and, more indirectly, caused another to resign—the first ever to do so. For what has become known as "Watergate" had its origins in the emotional turmoil occasioned by that faraway jungle war. And, in a perverse way, it was the unraveling of Watergate which led to the destruction of a strong presidency which, in turn, led to the final weakening of the American resolve in Vietnam. Who in his right mind could ever have conceived that the antics of a Jeb Magruder and a G. Gordon Liddy could have ultimately resulted in such catastrophe?

Despite the efforts of Schlesinger and others to revise history, the fact is that Vietnam, in the final analysis, was Kennedy's war. But it was one for which he originally did not want to take the credit—or discredit. Thus without public announcement or even approval of the Congress, the President covertly authorized the dispatch of thousands of American troops to South Vietnam. Arriving without fanfare, they soon began to die. In many ways "Nam" was a measure of JFK's presumed *machismo*. In the backwash of his humiliation at the Bay of Pigs, he wanted to demonstrate to the "fucking Commies" that he could be tough, too. Having read Lansdale's report on Vietcong successes, he called upon the army to establish a tough, counter-guerrilla unit which became known as the Green Berets. Not only did Kennedy keep a beret on his desk in the Oval Office, but he took a personal interest in the equipment which was to be used to wipe out left-wing guerrillas. At the same time he authorized covert operations inside North Vietnam itself. They were not too successful.

All of this was carried on without the knowledge of the American people, through clever manipulation of the news and outright lying. At least that's the conclusion of a study prepared for the Senate Foreign Relations Committee in 1972. Chairman Fulbright, commenting on the study covering the Vietnam decisions of the Kennedy presidency, said: "Executive secrecy and dissembling during the early 1960's is reminiscent of Lord Palmerston's lack of candor with the British Parliament in initiating the Opium War of 1839."

And there was a great deal of dissembling on the part of the Kennedy administration about the coup that led to Diem's murder. The essential facts were reported at the time by the late Marguerite Higgins, but they were largely ignored until the publication of the secret documents now known as the Pentagon Papers and the recent uproar about the CIA.

Any objective reading of the Pentagon Papers would confirm that the Kennedy administration was not only aware of the conspiracy of the Saigon generals to oust Diem, but encouraged it. Kennedy himself approved a cable sent to Ambassador Henry Cabot Lodge in Saigon on August 24, 1963, ordering him to bring about Diem's overthrow. This was at the time when the authoritarian activities of Diem's brother and sister-in-law, the Ngo Dinh Nhus, were arousing concern particularly among correspondents stationed in Saigon. There were charges of corruption, Swiss bank accounts, and police brutality—all getting major attention in the American press. All of which further convinced the President that Diem and Nhu had to go, and the sooner the better.

The cable, written by Assistant Secretary of State Roger Hilsman, began by saying that the U.S. "cannot tolerate situation in which power lies in hands" of Nhu and his wife. The key paragraph went on to declare in the stuttering language of cable-ese:

"We wish give Diem reasonable opportunity to remove Nhus, but if he remains obdurate, then we are prepared to accept the obvious implication that we can no longer support Diem. You may also tell appropriate military commanders we will give them direct support in any interim period of breakdown central government mechanism."

The cable had been sent over the signature of Acting Secretary of State George W. Ball.

Ambassador Lodge, who received the message, told a congressional subcommittee in July 1975 that he thought the telegram "insane," adding that its instructions were countermanded eight days later.

But Ball, before the same group, defended the message. He said it had been brought to him by Hilsman and roving Ambassador Averill Harriman. After which he telephoned President

Kennedy, weekending in Hyannisport, "and he told me, 'If you and Secretary Rusk think it's the right thing to do, go ahead.' " Ball next called Rusk in New York, "and he wasn't too enthusiastic, but he agreed."

Lodge may now believe the August 24, 1963, cable was "insane," but the record shows that on August 29, 1963, he sent this message to Rusk: "We are launched on a course from which there is no respectable turning back: the overthrow of the Diem Government. There is no turning back in part because U.S. prestige is already committed to this end in large measure and will become more so as facts leak out. In a more fundamental sense, there is no turning back because there is no possibility, in my view, that the war can be won under a Diem administration. . . ."

Lodge, of course, denies that he at any time recommended the "disposal" of Diem. But others in the pro-coup faction, notably Hilsman, most definitely envisioned the possible liquidation of the South Vietnamese leader with greater equanimity. In a memo to Rusk dated August 30, 1963, Hilsman put it this way:

"We should encourage the coup group to fight the battle to the end and to destroy the palace if necessary to gain victory . . . unconditional surrender should be the terms for the Ngo family, since it will otherwise seek to outmaneuver both the coup forces and the U.S. If the family is taken alive, the Nhus should be banished to France . . . Diem should be treated as the generals wish."

The next day Rusk received another message from Lodge, reporting the collapse of the conspiracy because, as the ambassador put it, there was "neither the will nor the organization among the generals to accomplish anything." At the same time Lodge sent even more disturbing news. It seemed, he reported, that Diem's brother Nhu was secretly dealing with Hanoi and the Vietcong through the French and Polish ambassadors, both of whose governments were seeking a neutralist solution to the conflict. Whether or not this was true was never firmly established. But it is significant that talk of a "neutralist solution to the conflict" sent shock waves of anxiety throughout the Kennedy administration.

The administration did not know what to do next. "The U.S. found itself at the end of August, 1963, without a policy and with most of its bridges burned," a Pentagon official noted.

The National Security Council, in emergency session on August 31, could not reach a consensus. Hilsman, for example, argued forcefully against the United States acquiescing "to a strong Nhu-dominated government." He said such a course of action would be bad for the American image.

Disagreeing were Vice President Johnson, Rusk, and McNamara. According to minutes, Rusk said that U.S. policy should be based on two points—"that we will not pull out of Vietnam until the war is won, and that we will not run a coup." McNamara expressed approval of this view, as did Johnson, who added that he had great reservations about a coup, particularly since he had never really seen a "genuine alternative to Diem." He also said "we should stop playing cops and robbers and get back to talking straight to the (Saigon government) . . . and once again go about winning the war."

But that was more easily said than done. For the next five weeks the administration could come up with no real policy.

About this time the administration faced still another embarrassment. Madame Nhu, the glamorous "Tiger Lady" and hostess at Diem's state dinners, arrived from Europe where she had been warmly received. But in Washington her presence was greeted with outright dismay. Apparently constrained by guilt and shame over the as yet unexecuted conspiracy, the official bureaucracy, from Kennedy down, refused to greet her. However her presence was acknowledged by the State Department when it called a meeting of editors asking that stories about her be buried among the truss ads.

Meanwhile Kennedy began applying pressure by cutting off various kinds of economic aid to South Vietnam. Heartened by these developments, the Saigon generals once again began to plot Diem's downfall. And once again Washington was interested.

On October 6, 1963, the White House sent this message to Lodge: "While we do not wish to stimulate coup, we also do not wish to leave impression that U.S. would thwart a change of government or deny economic and military assistance to a new regime if it appeared capable of increasing effectiveness of military effort, ensuring popular support to win war and improving working relations with U.S."

At the same time the White House warned the ambassador and the CIA station chief "to preserve security" in their contacts with the conspirators in order to preserve "plausibility of denial." The major CIA operative in South Vietnam, Lieutenant Colonel

Lucien Conein, had been meeting secretly with such dissident generals as Duong Van Minh to discuss toppling Diem. Minh, who became known as "Big" Minh, had told Conein on October 5 that what the anti-Diemists wanted was "American assurances that the (United States) will not attempt to thwart" their plan.

On October 30, 1963, McGeorge Bundy cabled Lodge that "once a coup under responsible leadership has begun . . . it is in the interest of the U.S. Government that it should succeed."

Two days later, on November 1, 1963, the coup began. The hypocrisy of the American position is illustrated by a poignant excerpt from a cablegram from Lodge to the State Department. It reported the last telephone conversation between Lodge and President Diem:

DIEM: Some units have made a rebellion and I want to know what is the attitude of the U.S.?

LODGE: I do not feel well enough informed to be able to tell you. I have heard the shooting, but am not acquainted with all the facts. Also it is 4:30 A.M. in Washington and the U.S. Government cannot possibly have a view.

DIEM: But you must have some general ideas. After all, I am a Chief of State. I have tried to do my duty. I want to do now what duty and good sense require. I believe in duty above all.

LODGE: You have certainly done your duty. As I told you only this morning, I admire your courage and your great contributions to your country. No one can take away from you the credit for all you have done. Now I am worried about your physical safety. I have a report that those in charge of the current activity offer you and your brother safe conduct out of the country if you resign. Have you heard this?

DIEM: No. (And then after a pause) You have my telephone number.

LODGE: Yes. If I can do anything for your physical safety, please call me.

DIEM: I am trying to re-establish order.

But it was too late. While fighting was going on at the palace, Diem and his brother Nhu escaped through a secret tunnel and made their way to Cholon, the Chinese quarter. The next day they surrendered to several armored units. Soon afterward, hands cuffed behind them, they were shot to death in the back of an armored car.

President Kennedy was reported to be shocked and dismayed by the murders. But Madame Nhu, still in the United States, accused him of having incited the coup. Said the Tiger Lady: "If you have the Kennedy administration for an ally, you don't need any enemy."

"There could be no question," *Time* reported in its November 8, 1963, issue, "that the U.S. . . . had effectively encouraged the overthrow of the Diem regime." The magazine reminded its readers that "only a few weeks ago" President Kennedy, during a television interview with Walter Cronkite, "argued that the winning of the war against the Communist Viet Cong would probably require 'changes in policy, and perhaps in personnel' in the Diem Government."

Three weeks after the murders in Saigon there was the shocking murder in Dallas. And the Tiger Lady, bitter over the assassinations of her husband and her brother-in-law, commented that justice had been served. Speaking off-the-record to reporters at his Texas ranch shortly after he took over the presidency, Lyndon Johnson said that his predecessor's death could be considered "some kind of terrible retribution" for the deaths of Diem and Trujillo.

His U.S.-approved coup successful, "Big" Minh became chief of state of South Vietnam. But, proving ineffectual, he quit after three months, going into exile in Thailand. In 1968 Marshal Thieu, by now the president, permitted Minh to return to Saigon where he espoused a neutralist line. In the final hours of a non-Communist South Vietnam he was once again sworn in as the chief executive. But it was too late. The Communists refused to negotiate with him. Rather than put up any further resistance, "Big" Minh announced his country's unconditional surrender. Within hours Communist forces had penetrated the center of Saigon. Finally the war was over. The United States was deeply humiliated.

But questions created by the executions of Diem and his brother remain. From the beginning there was an attempt to cover up the complicity of the Kennedy administration. On his return to the United States in June 1964, for example, Ambassador Lodge told *The New York Times* that "the overthrow . . . of the Diem regime was a purely Vietnamese affair. We never participated in the planning. We never gave any advice. We had nothing whatever to do with it. . . . We had nothing to do with overthrowing the government, and it's—I shall always be loyal to President Kennedy's memory on this, because I carried out his policy. . . ."

But his successor in Saigon, Maxwell D. Taylor, viewed the episode somewhat differently. In the course of an NBC Television interview General Taylor said in 1971: "One of the most serious wrongs, in my judgment, was our connivance at the overthrow of President Diem. Because regardless of what you thought of President Diem, we had absolutely nothing but chaos which followed. And it was that chaos that I inherited—perhaps Homeric justice—in the year I was Ambassador."

Asked who in Washington had connived in the plot, Taylor said: "Well, obviously, it has to be approved by the President . . . I would be sure that no American ever wanted Diem assassinated, you understand. And it was certainly a terrible shock to President Kennedy when that developed. But the organization of coups and the execution of a coup is not like organizing a tea party; it's a very dangerous business.

"So I didn't think we had any right to be surprised when Diem and his brother were murdered."

President Nixon himself never had any doubt about who was behind the Diem murder. At a press conference on September 16, 1971, he said: "I would remind all concerned that the way we got into Vietnam was through overthrowing Diem and the complicity in the murder of Diem . . ."

Significantly Nixon's remarks were accepted without the usual fusillade of criticism. Even his detractors, many of whom had been enamored of the New Frontier, realized that Nixon was absolutely correct in his evaluation.

Nevertheless there was a ridiculous effort to gild the lily on this question during the Nixon years. Without Nixon's knowledge E. Howard Hunt, a retired CIA agent hired as a special consultant at the White House, forged a number of cables linking President Kennedy directly to Diem's assassination. And in hopes of promoting an article on the subject, Hunt showed some of the phony cables to William Lambert of *Life*.

In his appearance before the Ervin Committee, Hunt testified he had been asked to forge the documents by Charles Colson, then a senior White House aide. But Colson contended that Hunt might have "misunderstood something I said to him."

Why phony documents had to be manufactured is difficult to fathom, particularly since Hunt himself in his testimony noted that "on the basis of the accumulated evidence and the cable documentation," which he had obtained from the State Department, it was obvious that "the Kennedy Administration was implicitly if not explicitly responsible for the assassination of Diem."

Then, under questioning by Sam Dash, chief counsel of the Watergate Committee, Hunt made a sensational disclosure. He testified that, in his examination of the cable traffic between Washington and Saigon at the time of the coup, he had discovered that "certain cables had been abstracted from the files maintained by the Department of State in chronological fashion. . . ."

It was a disclosure which (perhaps not so surprisingly) was overlooked by a media usually on the search for sensations. But it did raise some interesting questions that, to this day, remain unanswered. Was a State Department inquiry launched as to who was responsible for the "abstracting"? If not, why not? Were the documents returned to the archives or are they considered permanently missing?

In all probability these crucial papers were destroyed. And one can only conjecture as to why this extraordinary act of "paper-burning" took place. The idea quite obviously was to cover up the role of certain highly placed Americans in the undermining and murder of a foreign leader.

Which is probably as vicious a piece of business as the forging of phony cables.

The pattern that emerges from all the illegal actions perpetrated by the Kennedy administration abroad casts great doubt on the thesis that such activities should be condoned on the grounds of "national security" and anti-communism. The two foreign leaders who wound up dead were themselves anti-Communists and American allies. The irony is that the Communist, Castro, who nearly plunged this country into a nuclear war with the Soviet Union, remains alive.

Still another irony: In 1975, while Castro was bitterly complaining (via Senator McGovern) that the United States had sought to kill him on numerous occasions, the French government expelled several of his "diplomats" on charges that they were involved with an Arab terrorist-assassination ring.

Finally the Senate Intelligence Committee unveiled its "Assassination Report." Given the committee's leadership, and particularly a chairman who was panting to obtain the Democratic nomination for President, it should have come as no surprise that the Report would engage in verbal gymnastics to cover the indelible trail of the "men of style" who ruled the nation in the early sixties. The report was thick with partisanship. It was protective of John Kennedy. And it overreached in its conclusions involving Eisenhower and Nixon.

Well, even by the material disclosed in the Report, it would appear that G. Gordon Liddy was a piker. Hit men. Mafiosi contacts. Kennedy and brother Bobby standing in the cabinet room "chewing out" a CIA official for "sitting on his ass and not doing anything about getting rid of Castro and the Castro regime." The committee record bristles with such talk as "get rid of," "knock off," "eliminate," and "slashing" the Cuban dictator. But, as Richard J. Walton has observed, because the committee was not able to find a "smoking gun," it "brought the accusation right to President John F. Kennedy's door" yet "did not open the door."

"In not quite accusing President Kennedy, the Committee was aided by another factor," wrote Walton on the Op-Ed page of *The New York Times*. "With Mr. Nixon, the press was in full cry, helping the public become convinced that President Nixon was guilty. But that has not been so with Mr. Kennedy."

Still, even the record could leave little doubt that the subject of assassination was discussed by or in the presence of Secretary of Defense McNamara, National Security Adviser Bundy, and Robert F. Kennedy, the President's alter ego. And the evidence also clearly indicates that the CIA was operating on the logical assumption that the President wanted Castro removed by any means necessary. Moreover there can be no argument that JFK knew what was going on. In his Oval Office conversation with Senator Smathers, the President had observed he was certain the Castro assassination could be accomplished. While all of this may not constitute a "smoking gun," as Richard Walton pointed out, it adds up to "a pretty solid case."

Unable totally to exonerate President Kennedy, the Church Committee relied on what during the Watergate era was to become known as the everybody-does-it contention. Thus, through the art of juxtaposition, the clearly more prominent connection of JFK with assassination plots was deliberately diluted by references to Eisenhower and Nixon.

According to the Report, the committee found evidence to permit "a reasonable inference that the plot to assassinate [Patrice] Lumumba [of the Congo] was authorized by President Eisenhower." Then came this caveat: "There is enough countervailing testimony by Eisenhower Administration officials and enough ambiguity and lack of clarity . . . to preclude the Committee from making a finding that the President intended an assassination effort against Lumumba." As it turned out, Lumumba was indeed killed in early 1961 by Congolese rivals. "It does not appear that the U.S. was in any way involved in the killing."

The "reasonable inference" was based on the uncorroborated testimony of Robert H. Johnson, who had been a notetaker at the only two NSC sessions at which Eisenhower was present during his entire administration. During one of those sessions, Johnson first testified: "President Eisenhower said something—I can no longer remember his words—that came across to me as an order for the assassination of Lumumba . . . there was no discussion; the meeting simply moved on." Later in his testimony, Johnson said: "I must confess that in thinking about the incident more recently I have had some doubts."

Needless to say, that kind of evidence is less than compelling, and certainly does not support any "reasonable inference"—particularly in view of the fact that all Eisenhower's top advisers flatly and angrily denied the Johnson story. Retired general Andrew J. Goodpaster, Ike's chief military adviser, informed Church that there had been no single instance "within my knowledge and memory" of an assassination "course of action" proposed to or by Eisenhower either in or outside NSC meetings. Similar testimony came from Gordon Gray, Ike's national security assistant.

Equally weak was the strained effort to drag Nixon into the committee Report. What better way to fuzz up damning evidence about the Kennedy administration than to haul in the name of the disgraced President? According to the Report, General René Schneider, commander in chief of Chile's army, was killed while resisting a kidnapping attempt in October 1970. The previous month Nixon had ordered the CIA "to play a direct role in organizing a military coup in Chile to prevent [Salvador] Allende's accession to the presidency." But even the Report acknowledges that there was no assassination plot. There was not even a coup attempt, for Allende had not yet assumed power. Schneider's death was totally unforeseen and unexpected, and there were no U.S. orders to "get rid" of him, as the Report itself concedes. More pointedly the general was not even a head of state, as were all others who were included in the committee's inquiry.

The use of covert actions and funds to prevent Allende's accession to power was hardly in the same league as putting out a contract on Castro with Mafia "hit men." Moreover, though

Church seemed to ignore the evidence, such covert actions had been begun under John Kennedy's directions. As former CIA Director McCone put it to *Fortune* writer Charles J. V. Murphy: "As early as 1962 President Kennedy had decided in the National Security Council that the Agency should see to it that Castro's agitators did not take Chile into the Communist camp under Allende's banner. In 1964, that decision was confirmed by President Johnson." Later Nixon was to disclose that Kennedy and Johnson had expended "approximately four million dollars on behalf of Mr. Allende's opponents and had prevented Mr. Allende from becoming President in the early sixties."*

But probably the committee's most closely guarded secret was President Kennedy's link, albeit indirect, to the Mafia. Nevertheless the secret was hinted at on page 129 of its Assassination Report. "Evidence before the Committee indicates that a close friend of President Kennedy had frequent contact with the President from the end of 1960 through mid-1962. FBI reports and testimony indicate the President's friend was also a close friend of John Roselli and Sam Giancana and saw them often during this same period." According to a footnote: "White House telephone logs show seventy instances of phone contact between the White House and the President's friend whose testimony confirms frequent phone contact with the President himself. Both the President's friend and Roselli testified that the friend did not know about either the (Castro) assassination operation or the wire tap case.** Giancana was killed before he was available for questioning."

And there the matter would have rested, had it not been for investigative reporters Dan Thomasson and Tim Wyngaard of Scripps-Howard, who discovered that "the President's friend" was a beautiful girl who divided her time between the leadership of the underworld and the President of the United States. Though their story was of Pulitzer Prize dimensions, it was not picked up elsewhere—until Church blundered. Angered by what he considered leaks from within the Intelligence Committee, he and Senator Gary Hart set up a plumbers' type operation seeking to discover the source, complete with threats of perjury

*None of which, incidentally, was disclosed by either Schlesinger or Sorensen in their adulatory accounts of the Kennedy years.
**The "wire tap case" involved Giancana, caught in the process of bugging a motel room occupied by an unfaithful girlfriend who had been carrying on with a Las Vegas comedian.

and warnings of lie-detector tests. One wonders, in retrospect, whether the senators would have been so concerned about leaks had the story involved Nixon.

By then Bill Safire was onto the story. The columnist accused the Church Committee of a "cover up" for neglecting to dwell at any length on the sex, age, professional experience, and gangland connections of Judith Campbell Exner. There no longer was any way of containing the story Church and his fellow senators (including some Republicans) had sought so desperately to bottle up.

"Why should Church do that?" asked Nicholas von Hoffman.

> A partisan inclination to keep the coffin lid shut so that we may believe in dead Democrats? Or a dread at what may go on in people's heads when they find out they have no heroes alive or dead? Church may have made the decision the lie must be preserved, not for votes, not for party advantage, but because he's scared we can't take it if we're told whatever the hell went on with the Kennedys.
>
> Can we take not knowing? It was always whispered that Kennedy's old man had gangster connections. And the son? Was he President or Hoodlum Prince? The question is out: Did Kennedy have the dignity of dying the victim of a madman or a political assassin or was Dallas just another gangland slaying?
>
> . . . Tell us, all you folks who've written so many, many books about those golden one thousand days when you all swarmed out of Harvard, Madison Avenue and Stamford, Connecticut, to electrify us with your good taste. Tell us again, please, but now put in about the gangsters and whatever else was corrupt, ruthless, cruel and illegal but which really happened. No more Camelot, please.

In faraway Austria Pierre Salinger told reporters that the Kennedy allegations were actually designed to wipe out Ted Kennedy's presidential chances, and he suggested that the stories were being spread by "supporters of former President Nixon . . . a case of sour grapes."

In San Clemente, meanwhile, Richard Nixon telephoned a friend to say that he was "terribly concerned" about the new revelations concerning John Kennedy. "They can only do further damage to the institution of the presidency itself," said the former President. There are some things, he suggested, that are better not known.

9

IN HIS BOOK ON THE "CURIOUS" DEATH OF
Marilyn Monroe, Robert Slatzer tells of reading sections of a
diary kept by the actress. There was one entry which read:
"Bobby told me today, 'I want to put that S.O.B. Jimmy Hoffa
into jail, no matter how I do it.' "

Well, Bobby finally accomplished what often appeared to be
the Kennedys' major aim in public life—"getting" Hoffa. The
Teamsters' leader had long headed the brothers' "enemies list."
For one thing Jack Kennedy had invariably made him a campaign issue. All through the 1960 campaign the future President
would frequently wonder out loud why a Republican administration had not put Hoffa into jail. Hoffa's civil liberties were of little
concern to the Kennedys and, for that matter, to most of their
supporters.

Hoffa first came into the lives of the Kennedys in the mid-fifties
during the course of the Senate hearings into labor racketeering.
Bobby was chief counsel of the committee headed by Senator
John McClellan of Arkansas. Almost from the beginning Bobby's
pursuit of Hoffa had all the hallmarks of a personal vendetta. The
Teamsters leader, unlike others questioned by Bobby, never relied on the Fifth Amendment, which would have permitted him
to refuse to answer questions on the grounds that his testimony
might tend to incriminate him. And this annoyed Bobby no end.

But even more annoying was the way the cocky labor leader
would beat Bobby down in any of their well-publicized arguments. Hoffa would deliberately go out of his way to irritate his
inquisitor. As he told me in his Washington office in August 1966,
"Oh, I used to love to bug the little bastard. Whenever Bobby
would get tangled up in one of his involved questions, I would
wink at him. That invariably got him. 'Mr. Chairman,' he'd shout,
'would you please instruct the witness to stop making faces at
me?' "

Hoffa laughed and laughed.

No doubt Hoffa's "smartass" tactics did infuriate Bobby. As Professor Monroe Freedman, writing on the subject of "Prosecutorial Ethics" in the *Georgetown Law Journal*, noted:

> From the day that James Hoffa told Robert Kennedy that he was nothing but a rich man's kid who never had to earn a nickel in his life, Hoffa was a marked man. When Kennedy became Attorney General, satisfying this grudge became the public policy of the United States, and Hoffa, along with Roy Cohn and perhaps other enemies from Kennedy's past, was singled out for special attention by United States Attorneys. This is, of course, the very antithesis of the rule of law, and serves to bring into sharp focus the ethical obligation of the prosecutor to refrain from abusing his power by prosecutions that are directed at individuals rather than at crimes.

Bobby had many "enemies." But none obsessed him more than James Riddle Hoffa, who had often humiliated him in public. There was to be no forgetting. And, inevitably, Bobby was to have the last laugh.

Hardly had the New Frontier been established on the banks of the Potomac when Robert Kennedy organized a special investigations unit within the Justice Department which had one major assignment—nailing Hoffa.

The new group in many respects resembled one that was to be organized under Richard Nixon in 1971—the so-called plumbers formed within the White House to concentrate on "getting" Daniel Ellsberg.

To head the "Get Hoffa" squad, the Attorney General named one of his old Senate investigators, former FBI agent Walter Sheridan. The squad, if anything, was a curiosity within the Department if only because Sheridan was not a lawyer. But Sheridan did have direct access to the Attorney General and, in the bureaucratic world of Washington, that meant clout with a capital C.

Probably the best analysis of this unprecedented group can be found in Victor Navasky's *Kennedy Justice*, a not unfriendly appraisal of Kennedy's tenure as Attorney General.* The "Get Hoffa" squad, wrote Navasky,

> was staffed by men whose experience for the most part was investigative rather than legal. . . . Its men were on twenty-four-hour call. It had constant access to, and the interest and wholehearted

---

*(New York: Atheneum, 1971), p. 404.

support, of the Attorney General. It had free access to the files of the McClellan Committee. It was in touch with grand juries throughout the country. It had an undercover air of mystery about it. Its *modus operandi* was cloak and dagger. . . . And unlike every other unit of the Justice Department, which is organized around subject areas of responsibility, the Sheridan unit's *raison d'être* seemed to be not a subject area but a target: Jimmy Hoffa. Its relations with the FBI were highly irregular in that it received little or no cooperation from the top, yet Sheridan, an ex-FBI man, had a degree of line cooperation in the field that was, in some respects, unparalleled. He actually coordinated FBI agents with his own men—told them where to go when, and they went. . . . Since Sheridan was, in a sense, intruding on FBI turf, the situation was highly irregular.

As Charles Shaffer, an eager squad member, said: "Some people say Kennedy was out to get Hoffa. Well, let me tell you, they are one hundred percent right. . . . And Bobby couldn't wait. He asked when was the earliest I could start. I said two calendar months. He said be here Monday. I said I couldn't possibly. I had cases to clean up, work, obligations, family. . . . He said a week from Monday and that was that."

Almost anything went in this frenzied effort, even the violations of the Teamsters boss's civil rights. A few journalists—they were few and far between—did perceive the menacing aspects of the anti-Hoffa crusade. Columnist Richard Starnes, for example, commented in *The New York World-Telegram & Sun:* "For all I know, Hoffa may be guilty of wholesale mopery. But is the Attorney General entitled to dedicate the immense power of the federal government to chucking him in jail? I've followed Hoffa's career with some passing interest, and all I can swear to of my own knowledge is that he makes lousy speeches. He may set fire to orphan asylums for kicks, but does this deprive him of the right to due process?"

And later on, writing in *The Village Voice,* Nat Hentoff recalled "Robert Kennedy's transmogrification of the grand jury system (in) his pursuit of Jimmy Hoffa in the manner of an eighteenth-century legal adviser to the czar."

The pursuit was relentless. "I knew where Hoffa was twenty-four hours a day," Sheridan bragged. Hoffa himself was convinced, as he told me, that he was being followed everywhere by FBI agents, that his phones were tapped, mail opened, and that electronic listening devices were beamed on him from half a mile away. Moreover, he claimed, FBI agents posed as bellhops, desk clerks, maids, and doormen at hotels where the Teamsters held their conventions. The IRS combed his tax returns as well as those of other union officials. And anyone who did business with them found themselves subjected to IRS inquisitions.

Most liberals, however, cheered when Hoffa finally was convicted on the kind of evidence which, if used against the likes of Dan Ellsberg, would have occasioned outraged protests on the part of the American Civil Liberties Union.

Robert Kennedy was so delighted with the guilty verdict that he threw a party for the "Get Hoffa" squad in Georgetown. His loyalists presented the Attorney General with a leather wallet embossed with the very words the jury foreman uttered when he announced the verdict.

The campaign to "get" Hoffa involved both infiltration of the Teamsters and use of a personal friend as a paid informer—the sort of things liberals are usually so up in arms against. The informer was Edward Grady Partin, whose twenty-year criminal record included everything from breaking and entering to rape. After making a deal with Sheridan, Partin was sprung from a Baton Rouge, Louisiana, cell, even though the FBI considered him highly unreliable. Following his release, Partin insinuated himself into Hoffa's entourage, becoming a bartender, errand boy, bag carrier, and general factotum, and all the time telling Bobby's boys what Hoffa was saying and doing.

Eventually Hoffa was found guilty on a charge of jury tampering. Partin's testimony, which proved critical in obtaining the conviction, included details of Hoffa's conversations with his attorney—conversations which Hoffa quite correctly believed were confidential and whose revelation by a paid government agent could arguably be seen as a violation of the Sixth Amendment's guarantee of right to counsel. Yet there was no public outcry at the time about the government's "shoddy" tactics, nor were there any frenzied shouts about our liberties being imperiled. Rather the predominant reaction was that a somewhat unsavory labor boss with Republican links had gotten his just due.

Even the Supreme Court, dominated by liberal justices, later upheld the conviction. With only Chief Justice Warren dissenting, the High Court rejected Hoffa's contention that Partin's presence in his camp was the human equivalent of an electronic bug. In his dissent, Warren noted:

"Here the Government reaches into the jailhouse to employ a

man who was himself facing indictments far more serious (and later including one for perjury) than the one confronting the man against whom he offered to inform. It employed him not for the purpose of testifying to something that had already happened, but, rather, for the purpose of infiltration, to see if crimes would in the future be committed. The Government in its zeal even assisted him in gaining a position from which he could be a witness to the confidential relationship of attorney and client engaged in the preparation of a criminal defense. And, for the dubious evidence thus obtained, the Government paid an enormous price. Certainly if a criminal defendant insinuated his informer into the prosecution's camp in this manner he would be guilty of obstructing justice. I cannot agree that what happened in this case is in keeping with the standards of justice in our federal system and I must, therefore, dissent."

Hoffa himself, commenting in November 1974, contended that Watergate was tame compared to what the "Get Hoffa" squad did to nail him.

Another aspect of the anti-Hoffa crusade is worth noting, particularly in view of Charles Colson's later plea of guilty to a charge of obstructing justice, in that he had sought to defame Ellsberg by releasing unfavorable publicity about a man under indictment. Robert Kennedy had absolutely no compunction about arranging for derogatory articles on Hoffa to be published in such national magazines as *Life,* and he authorized "background" papers to be covertly fed to certain favored reporters. Obviously such tactics constituted, as Victor Navasky noted, "potential interference with the rights of the accused and even of the not-yet-accused." For using such tactics in the Nixon years, Colson went to jail.

Similar sordid practices were engaged in by Kennedy against his old and bitter foe, Roy Cohn. This was a feud which went back to the days when both were young, anti-Communist, and rivals for the approval of the late Senator Joseph McCarthy. As Freedman had noted in the *Georgetown Law Journal,* from the moment Kennedy became Attorney General he singled out Cohn (along with Hoffa and others) for special attention by U.S. attorneys. After two trials on charges of obstruction and perjury in a stock fraud case, Cohn was acquitted.

Later it was disclosed that Cohn had been the subject of a "mail cover," a procedure whereby the Post Office scrutinizes the outside of envelopes to find out with whom certain individuals are corresponding. (In later years the Rockefeller Commission condemned the CIA for indulging in this practice.) At the same time it was disclosed that the Attorney General had been instrumental in placing another derogatory article in *Life*, entitled "Roy Cohn: Is He a Liar Under Oath?" Senator Edward V. Long, the Missouri Democrat who held hearings on the episode, said, "This thing smells to high heaven." And the Chicago *Tribune* said that the practice of an Attorney General in promoting prejudicial magazine pieces about individuals under federal indictment called for "the fullest kind of investigation by the responsible committees in Congress. It is one of the most serious charges ever made against a high officer of Government."

But by that time Kennedy was a U.S. senator, and he got away with it. The Democratic-controlled Senate committee was not interested in following through.

During his long, and eventually unsuccessful, battle to remain out of prison, Hoffa insisted that he had been consistently wiretapped and/or bugged by "Bobby's boys." But he could never prove it. The Attorney General himself emphatically denied any such activities. But there can be little doubt that, while he was with the McClellan Committee, Kennedy was not above using wiretaps. To him they were necessary weapons—and he got away with it. For few civil libertarians seemed to care when he would open hearings with transcripts and/or recordings of private telephone conversations. In his memoir *With Kennedy*, Pierre Salinger narrates with evident satisfaction how he, as one of Bobby's investigators, invaded a union official's home in Seattle without a warrant to search for missing Teamsters records. The story, which also involves the seduction of a maid, is funny, but it does raise a question as to the propriety or even legality of the tactics used by Bobby's people in the pursuit of evidence.

Kennedy's denial of wiretapping in the Hoffa case was not bought by all newsmen. Walter Trohan, the veteran Chicago *Tribune* correspondent who had close ties to both Lyndon Johnson and J. Edgar Hoover, stated flatly that Kennedy "set up an extensive wiretap group under his own command in the Department of Justice. The group was headed by three men. One of these was given a job in the Justice Department, a second was placed on the White House payroll of his brother, the late John F. Kennedy, and the third was put on the payroll of the Immigration and Naturalization Service."

In addition to wiretapping, a great deal of "bugging"—that is, eavesdropping with microphone-type listening devices—also occurred during the Kennedy years. Some of it came to light after Robert Kennedy had won election as senator. The revelations were to prove intensely embarrassing to Kennedy who, in seeking eventually to become his party's presidential standardbearer, was busily cultivating the liberal community which, for the most part, had a decided distaste for electronic surveillance.

Probably the most sensational case involved Fred B. Black, Jr., a former next-door neighbor of Lyndon Johnson and a business associate of LBJ's former "right-hand man" in the Senate, Bobby Baker. Black had been convicted in a tax evasion case. Things looked pretty black for Black, he told me, until one day the maid who was cleaning a hospitality suite he kept at the Sheraton-Carlton Hotel told him that several "repairmen" had come in and installed something near a lamp. Sure enough, it was a "bug." Black called his attorney.

This forced the Justice Department to move. On May 24, 1966, Solicitor General Thurgood Marshall filed a memorandum with the Supreme Court which disclosed that early in 1963, at about the time a Missouri grand jury was listening to evidence against Black, the FBI had "bugged" his hotel suite. Accounts of Black's conversations with his lawyers, among other things, were passed on to Justice officials. Other references in the taped conversations had to do with Lyndon Johnson. These too were passed on to Justice and presumably to Bobby himself; at least Johnson thought so. Eventually the Supreme Court vacated Black's conviction and ordered a new trial.

Kennedy's office issued a statement asserting that the senator had no knowledge of the "bugging" of Black's suite. In effect he placed the onus on the FBI.

Almost as if he were waiting for the opportunity, Hoover struck back by releasing documents proving that Kennedy had authorized all sorts of electronic surveillances in "both security and major criminal cases." In a letter to Congressman H. R. Gross, the FBI director had this to say:

> Mr. Kennedy, during his term of office, exhibited great interest in pursuing such matters and, while in different metropolitan areas, not only listened to the results of microphone surveillances [bugging] but raised questions relative to obtaining better equipment. He was briefed frequently by an FBI official regarding such matters. FBI usage of such devices, while always handled in a sparing, carefully controlled manner and, as indicated, only with

the specific authority of the Attorney General, was obviously increased at Mr. Kennedy's insistence while he was in office.

Kennedy continued to deny that he knew what was going on inside the FBI as Attorney General. But documents signed by Kennedy himself were there to dispute him. And then Edwyn Silberling, chief of Justice's Organized Crime section when Kennedy reigned supreme, told Les Whitten that despite his claim to the contrary, Bobby was well aware of FBI "bugging" practices. Silberling recalled a meeting at which Kennedy urged the FBI to use more "technical equipment" to smash the rackets. The meeting took place in the Attorney General's fifth-floor office. Among those present was Courtney Evans, the FBI's liaison with Kennedy. "Everybody at the meeting knew (Kennedy) was talking about electronic surveillance—parabolic microphones, spike microphones, bugs—that is micro-transmitters—the whole thing," said Silberling.

Observing the well-publicized contretemps between Kennedy and Hoover was Lyndon Johnson. And there could be no doubt that the President was savoring every moment of Bobby's discomfiture. LBJ's dislike of the junior senator was hardly any secret. For one thing, as he once informed Justice William O. Douglas, he had reason to believe his own phones had been tapped. This apparently had occurred during his vice presidency and LBJ held Bobby responsible.

At any rate in his January 1967 State of the Union message Johnson hit hard at all wiretapping and bugging, public and private, "except when the security of the nation itself is at stake." Sitting sphinxlike, Bobby Kennedy was the only person within range of the TV camera who did not applaud when LBJ denounced electronic "bugging" and "snooping." Of course LBJ's fixation on the subject did not deter him from ordering "snooping" on his own political opponents.

In the final weeks of his life Kennedy was again to be embarrassed by the wiretapping issue. He was then engaged in primary contests with Senator Eugene McCarthy and, with the 1968 Democratic presidential nomination at stake, they were going after each other hot and heavy. From out of the blue Drew Pearson broke the story that Kennedy, as Attorney General, had authorized the tapping of Martin Luther King's telephones. According to the columnist, Kennedy's reason for giving the go-ahead to the FBI was that the civil rights leader had been "in touch with various Communists and was being influenced by them."

Asked by newsmen for comment, Kennedy refused to confirm or deny the story. Instead he sought to evade questions. But he was put on the spot in a television debate with his rival when McCarthy asked Bobby whether or not he had ordered the tap on Dr. King, as disclosed by Pearson. Kennedy's response was that as the nation's chief law officer he had authorized wiretapping procedures in "national security" cases; but that, by law, he could not discuss any such cases. To the uninitiated it could have sounded like a denial.

The truth which Kennedy sought to evade, but which ultimately emerged, was that he had indeed approved the wiretapping of King as well as of other Black leaders. And the irony was that only weeks before his debate with McCarthy, Kennedy had chartered a plane to return King's body from Memphis, where the civil rights leader had been slain, to his home city of Atlanta. The episode had been well publicized, as was Kennedy's appearance at the funeral.

Before long Kennedy himself was dead. But his legacy lives on. As Nicholas von Hoffman put it in the Washington *Post* just as Watergate began to break wide open,

> Is the Watergate bugging any more of an affront to civil liberties than the Martin Luther King bugging? That was done under John Kennedy, and ordered by his brother, an Attorney General who was as savage in his own way as John Mitchell was in his. Can the Kennedy use of the FBI to intimidate the U.S. Steel Corp. into a price rollback be defended by anyone with a respect for our basic laws?

Except for mavericks like Von Hoffman, few liberals were overly concerned about the violations of the rights of a major steel corporation. Nor did many liberals rush to the defense of Otto F. Otepka when the State Department announced its intention to dismiss him as its chief security evaluations officer on charges he had given confidential documents to the Senate Internal Security Subcommittee. Otepka remained on the payroll, however, during a long series of appeals. In March 1969, after years of bitter struggle to preserve his honor as a dedicated civil servant, President Nixon appointed him to a $36,000-a-year job with the Subversive Activities Control Board.*

The Otepka case was a stunner, for it involved harassment, illegal bugging, wiretapping, personal surveillance, and perjured confessions. But liberal anger that time around was reserved for the victim of these governmental abuses, and not their perpetrators.

Otepka was a career official who had been subpoenaed to testify before the Senate subcommittee on certain laxities in the administration of the State Department's employee security program. A longtime expert in his field, Otepka gave his frank opinion on a high Kennedy appointee and refused to change his report. In so doing, he aroused the wrath of Robert Kennedy with whom he had previously discussed the case. From that moment he was a marked man.

Refusing to capitulate to all sorts of pressures, Otepka stood his ground. When State Department higher-ups flatly denied his allegations, Otepka produced documents from his files which effectively corroborated his testimony. As noted in the subcommittee's report: "Mr. Otepka furnished copies of the document . . . to illustrate security procedures and to prove that his superior had lied under oath to this subcommittee concerning security procedures . . . the State Department was trying to hide a new policy of phasing out effective security procedures. . . . Quite simply, Otepka and a small band of associates were in the way."

There began a campaign of persecution with few parallels in the annals of the civil service. Branded an "enemy" of the Kennedy administration, Otepka was demoted from his job, deprived of a portion of his staff, and moved out of his office. Ultimately he was placed under "criminal charges" on the extraordinary contention that by furnishing a Senate committee with data concerning lax State Department security practices, he himself had violated Department security practices.

A "Get Otepka" squad had done its dirty work. Consisting of State Department officials, the group included Elmer Dewey Hill, David I. Belisle, and John F. Reilly—the last a former Justice Department lawyer who got his job at State on the recommendation of Bobby's executive assistant.

Later it was learned that, on his arrival at State, Reilly had

---

*The full, authoritative account of this case is contained in *The Ordeal of Otto Otepka* by William J. Gill (New Rochelle, N.Y.: Arlington House, 1969).

been briefed about the nettling problem of "leaks" to Senate investigators. His mission was to stop them. As he was quoted as saying at the time, "I was sent over here to do a job and by God I'm going to do it."

And by God he certainly tried. The measures taken by the Kennedy "plumbers" included almost every form of illegality in the book, such as breaking into Otepka's office, cracking open his office safe, ransacking his trash bag, bugging his room, and wire-tapping his phones. But when questioned about all of this under oath, Reilly, Hill, and Belisle not only made broad categorical denials that they had ever done such things; they denied that they even knew about them.

However, when they learned the subcommittee had independent evidence of their crimes, the witnesses switched their story. Hill, playing much the same role as did John Dean in the Watergate controversy, testified as follows: "Mr. John F. Reilly, Deputy Assistant Secretary for Security, asked me to explore the possibility of arranging some way to eavesdrop on conversations taking place in Mr. Otepka's office. Mr. Reilly explained to me that he would only consider such a technique if other investigative methods failed. . . . That evening Mr. Schneider and I altered the existing wiring in the telephone in Mr. Otepka's office. We then established a circuit from Mr. Otepka's office to the Division of Technical Services Laboratory by making additional connections in the existing telephone wiring system. . . ." And he went on and on and on.

Reilly and Belisle eventually admitted that they had wire-tapped Otepka's phone as well as bugged his office. But they insisted that their previous denials under oath had been justified because "static" on the wire made their efforts "ineffective." Yet even this explanation was false. For Hill later admitted that he, Reilly, and Belisle had listened to about a dozen recordings made of Otepka's conversations. Hill also testified that he had given the recordings to an unidentified man who met him in a State Department corridor. But Reilly later testified he had no recollection of the recordings or even such conversations with Hill.

In the face of all this criminality, including lying under oath, the Justice Department under Kennedy refused to take any action such as prosecuting outright perjurers. And what was the liberal reaction? Zilch. The media couldn't have cared less; there were no cries for the incarceration of the culprits, impeachment or, at the very least, resignation.

What did happen to those worthies? Secretary of State Rusk, under whom all these shenanigans had taken place, forced the resignation of Elmer Dewey Hill, who was the first to tell all. But the Secretary was a lot more lenient with Belisle, who was not only kept at State but actually promoted. Reilly, the Howard Hunt of the pre-Watergate "plumbers," was permitted to resign without a blemish recorded in his file, and somehow the administration arranged for this wiretapper to be given a well-paying FCC job as a hearing examiner.

The big joke is that, in more recent testimony before a Senate subcommittee, Dean Rusk voiced strong feelings against some of the tactics employed by the Nixon administration in the name of national security. The former Secretary also flatly denied that he knew anything about eavesdropping or wiretapping of any State Department employees during the Kennedy or Johnson administrations. He said he would have quit as Secretary had such evil things been done.

But, as the Pulitzer Prize-winning correspondent for the Cowles newspapers, Clark Mollenhoff, pointed out, it was "a burst of self-righteousness totally out of character with (Rusk's) active role in the cover-up in the Otepka case. . . . Thousands of pages of testimony . . . on the infamous ordeal of Otepka demonstrate that the Secretary of State knew of the controversy over the illegal wiretapping and night entry of Otepka's safe. Rusk also took an active part in covering up for the individuals engaged in the shameful efforts to frame Otepka. . . ."

Mollenhoff accused Rusk of either having

> an exceedingly bad memory or (having) engaged in an intentional misrepresentation to the Congress. . . . Repetition of the documented story of Rusk's responsibility in the Otepka matter isn't intended to minimize crimes of Nixon administration officials. Rather, it demonstrates that lack of integrity in high places is not a characteristic unique to this administration.
>
> Incidentally, it also points up that important segments of the press and television were considerably less aggressive in dealing with such evidence of abuse of executive power when it was done by officials of the Kennedy and Johnson administrations.

Throughout Otepka's lengthy ordeal the major organs of the Eastern Establishment, most notably *The New York Times* and the Washington *Post*, treated him like some sort of leper who threatened the survival of democracy. The *Times* unloosed several bitter attacks on Otepka as being not only reprehensible but dangerous, observing on one occasion that "orderly procedures are essential if the vital division of power between the legislative and executive branches is not to be undermined. The use of 'underground' methods to obtain classified documents from lower-level officials is a dangerous departure from orderly procedures."

A decade later this very same newspaper won the Pulitzer Prize for receiving and publishing highly classified documents siphoned from the Pentagon; and it is the same newspaper which pounded the Nixon administration for doing to Ellsberg exactly what the Kennedy administration did to Otepka. When it had its own ideological chore to perform, the value of "orderly procedures" was somehow diminished. Obviously the *Times*'s logic was affected by the fact that Otepka was a political conservative, while Ellsberg was a man whose deeds conformed with the *Times*'s list to the left.

At the height of the controversy the Washington *Post* too charged that what Otepka did was "unlawful" and "unconscionable." The paper explained that "he gave classified information to someone not authorized to receive it . . . he had no authority to give it. . . . If any underling in the State Department were free at his own discretion to disclose confidential cables or if any agent of the Federal Bureau of Investigation could leak the contents of secret files whenever he felt like it, the executive branch of government would have no security at all."

The irony, of course, is that during its coverage of Watergate the *Post* relied on what it termed a high-level source within the government which it affectionately nicknamed "Deep Throat." And won a Pulitzer Prize for that coverage.

10

ON APRIL 1, 1975, GEORGE B. PARR, THE
Democratic boss of Duval County, Texas, was found dead in a
pasture of his south Texas ranch with a bullet wound in his head.
Though no note was found, a local justice of the peace ruled that
the death had been a suicide. Parr, a former millionaire oilman,
banker, and deputy sheriff, had been facing a prison term for
income tax evasion.

Except for a dispatch in *The New York Times* the story of Parr's
death received little attention in the nation's media. Yet his was
a name to remember, especially at a time of furor over electoral
shenanigans. For without George Berham Parr, Lyndon Baines
Johnson would not have become President of the United States.

The year was 1948. Johnson, an obscure congressman opposed
to President Truman's civil rights program and a supporter of
what he called "the anti-Communist Taft-Hartley labor bill," was
running for the Democratic Senate nomination in Texas. In those
days obtaining the Democratic nomination was tantamount to
election in the Lone Star State.

Johnson ran against the Dixiecrat governor Coke Stevenson
and several others. When the returns were in, the popular Stevenson had 71,000 more votes than Johnson but he lacked a majority in the crowded field. This necessitated a runoff. In the
runoff Johnson again trailed Stevenson—or so everyone thought.
But then Parr came into the picture.

To understand the significance of this, one must understand
the significance of Parr. This dapper little man with the cold
green eyes ruled three counties in southeast Texas with an iron
hand—Duval, Jim Wells, and Zapata. This oil-rich brush country
was an area inhabited largely by Mexican-Americans. Parr paid
their poll taxes, got them jobs, was generous with gifts to their
sick and needy, and voted them like cattle. Parr also collected
large payoffs from construction companies doing business in his

bailiwick, houses of ill repute and moonshine and gambling businesses. In 1936, he went to prison on an income tax rap.

Parr, who rarely appeared in public unless surrounded by tough, unshaven Mexican *pistoleros*, never let any of his "constituents" forget who was *El Jefe*. It literally was suicide to oppose him; and hardly anyone tried. As the *Times* noted, "Only Federal agents and Texas rangers ever successfully questioned his authority. Others who did took their lives in their hands. At least two men were shot to death by deputy sheriffs loyal to Parr." Other brutal deaths were associated with his volatile career.

The significance of all this lies in the fact that Parr favored Johnson in the 1948 runoff. Days after the polls had closed, a "correction" of the vote came in from Precinct 13 in the hamlet of Alice in Jim Wells County on the Mexican border. The "correction" gave Johnson 202 votes which local election officials claimed they had somehow previously overlooked. But it was enough to give Johnson the Democratic nomination by eighty-seven votes.

Parr had come through. The self-styled "Duke of Duval" had once again come up with enough votes to get his man in. And Coke Stevenson was furious.

"I was beaten by a stuffed ballot box," he told reporters. "And I can prove it."

Parr laughed and called Stevenson a poor loser. "In previous elections," *El Jefe* noted, "the district has gone for Stevenson with as much enthusiasm as it has gone against him in this year's Senate election. I never heard a complaint from him then about the bloc vote in Duval County."

Charging fraud, the governor appealed to the federal court for redress. His laywers produced evidence clearly demonstrating that "voters" from the graveyard and from across the border in Mexico had been recorded for Johnson. The lawyers also produced a couple of courageous Chicanos who testified that Parr had voted their names without their knowledge.

After hearing all the arguments, Judge T. Whitfield Davidson was moved to comment: "There has not one word of evidence been submitted [sic] to disprove this plaintiff's claim he has been robbed of a seat in the United States Senate."

At the same time Davidson issued an injunction denying Johnson a place on the ballot.

As a result there was great consternation among leading

Democrats in Washington. Not that the liberals or even Truman particularly loved Johnson. If anyone followed a Southern line, it was he. But they much preferred him to his more outspoken Dixiecrat opponent. Which is precisely what Truman told Johnson when the President barnstormed through Texas late in September.

Meanwhile Washington lawyer Abe Fortas took charge of the legal maneuvers to save Johnson's "election." In these he was capably assisted by none other than Joe Rauh, an ultra-liberal then most active in the affairs of Americans for Democratic Action. (In years to come, Rauh was to emerge as one of LBJ's more vociferous critics.)

One day after Judge Davidson reopened his hearing in Fort Worth, Fortas went to see Associate Justice Hugo Black, a former Ku Klux Klansman-turned-civil libertarian. It was their mutual interest in liberal causes which had made them good friends. They spent considerable time discussing Lyndon's election problem. And Fortas got what he wanted.

On September 28, 1948, Black issued an order staying the Davidson injunction. This meant that Johnson's name could appear on the November ballot. Black's order declared that the federal courts lacked jurisdiction over state elections. In effect Black had ruled that Johnson would be the next senator from Texas.

Adjourning his court, an angered Judge Davidson denounced the Black order as "unduly hasty and probably unlawful"—which it most certainly was. The judge noted, for example, that the Stevenson-Johnson controversy had involved a federal office. Then he pointed out that only four years previously, Justice Black had voted exactly the opposite when the High Court ruled that federal courts could indeed interfere to see that Negroes were not barred from voting in Texas primaries.

But the ball game was over.

Johnson, however, faced one more hurdle on his way to the Senate. So bitter were the protests of the Stevenson supporters that the Senate voted to look into the contested primary. But Senate investigators soon discovered that most of the ballots in Duval, Jim Wells, and Zapata counties—the "Duke's" bailiwick —had been destroyed. Who destroyed them? Well, according to Parr, some illiterate Mexican janitors must have thought they were trash ready to be burned.

The big Senate probe was over even before it began.

Meanwhile Truman was barnstorming Texas in what appeared

to be a forlorn pursuit of the presidency. When his train stopped at San Antonio, Parr got aboard to spend a half-hour with the President. Immediately there was speculation that Parr would get a presidential pardon for an old income tax conviction.

Truman, of course, was no stranger to stuffed ballots. In fact he could never have become President if he had not scraped victory out of the 1934 Senate primary in Missouri with the help of 50,000 fraudulent votes from Tom Pendergast's Kansas City machine. And years later when Boss Pendergast passed on to his just reward, Truman flew to the funeral. The President ignored the criticism. He knew it would soon blow over.

So pleased was Truman with Parr's good work on behalf of the team that, shortly after his election, he did reward the "Duke of Duval" with a pardon. And when Parr again was found guilty of income tax evasion, Fortas argued the case all the way to the Supreme Court and got the "Duke" off on a technicality.

Eventually a grateful Lyndon Johnson nominated Fortas as a justice on the Supreme Court.

Stevenson never forgot nor forgave. Not only had he made broadcasts urging his supporters to vote for Johnson's Republican opponent in the 1948 contest, but subsequently he backed LBJ's opponent in the 1954 election. In 1960, rather than support a ticket with Johnson on it, he supported Nixon in the presidential race.

"I am not a brass collar Democrat any more," he told an interviewer in 1964, sixteen years after the fateful contest with Lyndon Johnson. "I don't feel as kindly towards the Democrats as perhaps I should. This may sound like sour grapes, but when they put the stamp of approval on the way the office of U.S. Senator was lost to me. . . ."

The law finally caught up with Parr. In 1974 he was sentenced to ten years at hard labor and a fine of $14,000 for failing to list $287,000 in taxable income between 1966 and 1969. A year after this his appeal was rejected by the Court of Appeals. The "Duke of Duval" had run out of all his options. No longer did he have friends in high places who could come to his rescue. A week later he was found slumped over the steering wheel of his car, a bullet wound in his right temple. The man whose political power helped send Lyndon Johnson to the Senate in 1948 was dead.

So exhilarated was Lyndon Johnson on reaching the political mountaintop in 1948 that, according to one biographer, he told this story about his first Senate victory:

Little Manuel was sitting on a curbstone, crying bitter tears. Another Mexican, happening along, asked, "What's the trouble with you, Manuel?"

"My father was here last Saturday and he did not come to see me."

"But, Manuel, your father has been dead ten years."

"That's true," Manuel sobbed. "But he was here last Saturday and he voted for Lyndon Johnson, but he did not even come to see me."

The joke lost its humorous aspects for Johnson when, on taking his seat in the Senate, he began to be twitted as "Landslide Lyndon." It was a sobriquet which was to haunt him throughout his political career. And the fact that President Kennedy also called him "Landslide" in private conversation irritated LBJ no end. But there was little he could do about it. As Vice President, he could only grin and bear it.

As time passed, LBJ was to become even more irritated about rumors concerning his wealth. And he went out of his way to discourage newspaper stories about how he came to fortune. The fact remains, however, that when the tall, gangly Texan first went to Congress in the thirties, he was a poor boy, dirt-poor. But, after a lifetime in Washington, Johnson died leaving a fortune estimated at between $14 and $20 million. In other words the Johnsons had been among the wealthiest families ever to occupy the White House.

How Johnson managed to amass such great wealth without ever leaving government service still raises questions. In fact, it became a campaign issue during the 1964 presidential contest. A few publications did try to dig out the facts. But for the most part the media ignored the story. There was no Watergate press corps prying into LBJ's affairs.

It appears that the keystone of the Johnson fortune was the family ownership of radio-TV station KTBC in Austin, a communications combine which for a long time had a television monopoly in that city and environs. To what extent this monopoly enjoyed its extraordinary prosperity because of favorable rulings by the Federal Communications Commission, as Louis Kohlmeier wrote in the *Wall Street Journal,* would take "a subtle scientist to measure precisely." The question raised by Kohlmeier's Pulitzer Prize-winning articles in 1964 was how much Johnson's political prominence as Senate Majority Leader may have played in the FCC's exceptionally beneficent rulings. It was a good question but, needless to say, one that was never explored by any congressional body.

In December 1963, shortly after Johnson was sworn in as President, the FCC came through again for the Johnsons. This time the regulatory agency rejected an application by a community antenna television service which threatened KTBC's monopoly in Austin. And the question was raised whether the FCC, in making its decision, could not have been influenced by the knowledge that the President was involved. The Johnson response to what after all was a striking conflict-of-interest situation was to place all the broadcasting properties in the control of a blind trust. But the propriety of this arrangement was also questioned after disclosure that the trustee selected by the Johnsons was an old friend who visited them frequently at the White House.

Johnson's public utterances on his finances were few and far between. And when he did refer to them at two press conferences in April 1964 he was far from being candid. Thus, looking reporters in the eye, he could say, "I have no interest in any television any place." On another occasion he claimed, "I don't have any interest in government-regulated industries of any kind and never have had." Technically, of course, he was being accurate. The stock in the broadcast properties was held in the name of his wife and two daughters.

So sensitive was he about discussions of his finances that he sought to head off publication by *Life* of an article on the subject. Despite a personal appeal by the President, the editors went ahead with the piece, entitled "How LBJ's Family Amassed Its Fortune."

Written by investigative reporters Keith Wheeler and William Lambert, the article made clear their gut feeling that the public record did not necessarily reveal the entire story. Thus, in analyzing the family's numerous real estate deals, Wheeler and Lambert had this to say:

> Following the trail of some of these transactions resembles the action in a Western movie, where the cowboys ride off in a cloud of dust to the south, the herd stampedes northeastward, the Indians start to westward but, once out of sight, circle toward the north, the rustlers drift eastward and the cavalry, coming to the rescue, gets lost entirely—all over stony ground leaving little trace.

Needless to say, the article was written without the cooperation of the White House; nevertheless its authors placed the
Johnson assets at about $14 million. Several days later the White
House released an audit which put the figure at $3.5 million.
Again there was deception. For the lower figure was based on the
purchase price of the family's holdings and not the contemporary
market value.

Except for *Life,* the *Wall Street Journal,* and a few other publications, the media generally remained mum about the unseemly
growth of Johnson's wealth while in office. There was no spree
of digging or moralizing, with scores of bloodhound reporters on
the case, as there was to be when Nixon's finances—trifling as
compared with his predecessor's—became an issue.

The role of Bobby Baker in the building of the Johnson fortune
was never fully cleared up. The main reason, of course, was the
refusal of Senate Democrats to permit any probing of that curious relationship. Even President Kennedy had often wondered
out loud about how LBJ made his money. But Kennedy, as he
told Bradlee on October 22, 1963, was fairly certain Johnson had
not been "on the take since he was elected." Before that,
Kennedy told his friend, "I'm not so sure." At the same time, on
that day, Kennedy indirectly acknowledged that LBJ, while serving one heartbeat away from the presidency, had been improperly tooling around the country in Grumman corporate jets.

Exactly one month later John Kennedy's heart stopped beat-
ing, and the nation had a new President.

11

AS VICE PRESIDENT, LYNDON JOHNSON
felt he had good reason to fear the Kennedys. He was well aware
that they were spreading all kinds of stories about him behind his
back. The fact that the President would constantly refer to him
as "Landslide," in speaking to intimates, had reached him. And
causing Johnson extreme embarrassment was a published report
that at a party at Robert Kennedy's home—Hickory Hill—some
friends had given the Attorney General an LBJ voodoo doll in
which to stick pins. But there was little this proud Texan could
do but take it. He was, after all, completely beholden to the
young President whom he had once described as "looking like a
spavined hunchback."

In other words there was no love lost between the Kennedys
and Johnson. In fact the Vice President was convinced that the
President and his brother had been spreading the word that he
would be "dumped" from the ticket in 1964. And Johnson, as he
told his old crony Senator Thomas J. Dodd in October 1963, was
resigned to that embarrassing fate. His eyes brimming with tears,
Johnson told the Connecticut Democrat that the Kennedys were
"sadists."

In his conversation with Dodd Johnson also confided his
fear that he was being wiretapped, as well as being kept
under surveillance. Though he did not explain in detail, he
said he had "solid information" that "Bobby"—whom he invariably characterized as a "little bastard"—was keeping tabs
on everything he was doing for the purpose of "getting"
him.

Many of Lyndon's friends thought him slightly paranoid about
Bobby, but in view of later revelations the Vice President might
not have been too far off base in his suspicions. Johnson's mood
in this period was later summed up by a journalist who had

interviewed him at length. "During his Vice Presidential tenure," wrote Arnold Beichman,*

> Johnson's loyalties were surely tried. He had an unhappy idea that he was being followed, that his wires were tapped. What outsiders can only sense is how black were those days for him and the dark foreboding about his political future. What is now said in Washington—and which has not been publicly confirmed—is that, as soon as he became President, Johnson ordered an end to widespread wiretapping. With good reason, Johnson is for the right to privacy.

Johnson was absolutely convinced, for example, that it was the Justice Department which had leaked stories on the suspicious financial shenanigans of Robert G. (Bobby) Baker, the gangling South Carolinian who had served some hair-raising years as secretary to then Senate Majority Leader Johnson. It was during that period that Johnson had said of Baker, "I have two daughters. If I had a son, this would be the boy. . . . (He is) my strong right arm, the last man I see at night, the first one I see in the morning." In some quarters Baker was referred to as the "one hundred and first Senator."

In the fall of 1963 the scandal involving Baker broke wide open. A private suit had been filed in federal court charging that he had improperly used his influence in the Senate to obtain defense plant contracts for his vending machine firm. That unloosed a torrent of stories concerning other of Baker's financial wheeling-and-dealing, as well as sensational yarns concerning the preoccupation of some of the high and mighty with booze and broads.

Because of LBJ's once close ties to Baker, the Vice President's name was linked to the Senate aide's as soon as the case began to unravel. And immediately there was speculation that President Kennedy would use the scandal as an excuse for "dumping" LBJ from the 1964 ticket. The question arose at Kennedy's next-to-last press conference on October 31, 1963. When a reporter asked whether he wanted Johnson on the ticket and whether he expected "that he will be on," the President said quickly: "Yes to both questions."

But Kennedy seemed to be ambivalent on the subject. Speaking privately with his loyal secretary, Mrs. Evelyn Lincoln, the

---

*But as we shall see, LBJ's concern for the "right to privacy" was largely self-centered. As President he had no compunctions about ordering the wiretapping of whoever he considered *persona non grata*.

President indicated his intention of getting rid of Johnson. In her book *Kennedy and Johnson,* Mrs. Lincoln said she had asked the President who he intended to have as his runningmate.

"At this time," Kennedy replied unhesitatingly, "I am thinking about Governor Terry Sanford of North Carolina. But it will not be Lyndon."

But in talking with Bradlee, the President said that talk about dumping Lyndon from the ticket was "preposterous on the face of it. We've got to carry Texas in '64, and maybe Georgia." In other words the same Southern strategy that led JFK to pick LBJ as his runningmate in the first place.*

Still it was becoming painfully obvious that *l'affaire* Baker was shaping up as a major Republican issue against the Kennedy administration in the following year. At GOP urging, the Senate voted to investigate the case. Baker had resigned his post rather than respond to questions at an executive session of Senate leaders. And Johnson feared further political damage.

Then came Dallas—and Johnson inherited the presidency. The investigation into Baker's affairs continued in executive session, and for some weeks the new President waited for the other shoe to drop. For he knew exactly what was being testified to behind those closed Senate doors. And the testimony did not make LBJ look too good. So much so that some of LBJ's aides pleaded with him to repudiate Baker with a statement "to the effect that he had trusted and been fond of this young man and was sorry he had turned bad," according to Eric Goldman, one of those aides.

Johnson decided to say nothing. Was it because Baker knew too much?

Finally Johnson was forced to break his silence. The Senate Rules Committee, which had been conducting the investigation, made public some extraordinary testimony involving the new President. The sworn testimony came from a suburban Maryland insurance salesman, Don B. Reynolds, who claimed he had taken Baker into his firm as a vice president in order to exploit his political contacts. This was the way he made huge payoffs to Baker. Reynolds also testified that it was Baker who had asked him to sell a life insurance policy to Lyndon Johnson. This was

---

*Except for a last-minute decision to go all-out for Southern support, Kennedy would have selected Senator Stuart Symington in 1960, according to Clark Clifford, who recently told the St. Louis *Post-Dispatch* that on the night of his 1960 nomination, Kennedy promised the spot to Symington but withdrew the offer the next day. Such are the vagaries of history.

in 1957, two years after the then Majority Leader had suffered a massive heart attack. Reynolds arranged for a $100,000 policy, despite the fact that Johnson was considered to be in a high-risk category.

Not long afterward Reynolds received a call from Walter Jenkins, one of LBJ's top aides, who suggested it would be nice if Reynolds would purchase some advertising time on KTBC, the Austin television station owned by Mrs. Johnson. The implication was clear. Johnson was demanding a kickback on the broker's commission Reynolds had received on the Majority Leader's policy. Reynolds took the hint and bought the commercial spots for $1,208, which he later resold at a fraction of what they cost to a kitchenware manufacturer who had more need for them.

Two years later, according to Reynolds, Baker advised him it would also be nice if he would present Johnson with a certain kind of high-fidelity stereophonic phonograph. The $585 phonograph was promptly sent to the Johnson home, along with invoices listing Reynolds as the purchaser, the insurance man testified. And then in 1961, after becoming Vice President, Lyndon Johnson bought another $100,000 life insurance policy from Reynolds.

After Reynolds testified about Jenkins, the presidential aide hid in his White House office, refusing to take any calls from reporters. And LBJ, as usual when he was in trouble, turned to two lawyer-friends for advice on what to do next. Both Abe Fortas and Clark Clifford suggested that Jenkins turn down Republican suggestions that he appear before the Senate Rules Committee where he would undergo tough cross-examination. On their advice Jenkins dispatched an evasive memorandum which seemed to deny much of Reynolds's testimony.

All of which was recalled during the Watergate furor by Senator Carl Curtis, who had been the ranking Republican on the Senate committee that investigated the Baker case. As he told North Carolina Republicans on November 3, 1973: "The Committee needed the testimony of Walter Jenkins. Do you think we ever got it? We battled for months and never did get the testimony of Walter Jenkins. There were six Democrats and three Republicans on the Committee. Time and again our efforts to get the testimony of Walter Jenkins were thwarted by a straight party vote of six to three.

"On a couple of occasions, I took our fight to the Senate floor. I offered proposals whereby the Senate as a whole would instruct the Committee to subpoena a witness if three Senators made such a request. It was voted down. Who do you suppose opposed this effort? Who do you suppose was aligned with the coverup and concealing of evidence?

"Who do you suppose took the position that a Senate Committee couldn't even question one White House employee if he was a Democrat? Well, there were a lot of people opposing our efforts but included in that group were the guiding lights on the Democratic side of the present Senate Committee investigating the Watergate scandal. My, how times have changed!

". . . Where were these purists of the TV networks when Clark Clifford and Abe Fortas were conducting a coverup? Why were they so silent then?"

Reynolds, under oath, had also told several other shocking stories involving Johnson. He spoke of the time Baker opened a satchel full of paper money which he said was a $100,000 payoff to Johnson for pushing through a $7 billion TFX plane contract. So much pressure had been exerted to get the contract for Texas-based General Dynamics that Republicans called the TFX the "LBJ."

Another Reynolds story described how Johnson, making an official trip to the Far East as Vice President, drew $100,000 in counterpart funds while in Hong Kong. This is money earned by the U.S. government in foreign countries and can only be spent there. According to Reynolds, Johnson had spent all that money "in a period of twelve to fourteen hours buying gifts for people who were loaded."

The case of Baker and his highly placed friends actually would never have been broken had it not been for the untiring efforts of a little-known Republican senator from Delaware, John J. Williams. It was this soft-spoken former chicken-feed dealer who had persuaded Reynolds to talk in the first place. And Williams operated without a staff of investigators, funds, or power of subpoena.*

Even before the story broke into the headlines, Williams knew that his curiosity about the case had triggered someone pretty high up in Washington to "get" him. Strangers posing as Washington investigators were poking around his home town, asking

---

*The revealing story is told in an article by John Barron in the *Reader's Digest*, September 1965, entitled "The Case of Bobby Baker and the Courageous Senator."

questions about such things as the kind of farm subsidies the senator was collecting. Williams knew immediately that an effort was being made to prove he was benefitting from legislation he helped pass. But Williams remained unafraid and more determined than ever to pursue his inquiries into corruption in high places.

Then one night in February 1964 he met with an official in the Johnson administration who had something frightening to say. "I couldn't risk going to your office," he told Williams, "but I can't stomach what they're doing to you. Senator, your mail is being intercepted. Every letter you write to any federal official asking about the Baker case is immediately routed to a special handler. He sends the Senate Rules Committee copies of any information sent to you. Sometimes he even checks with the Committee before deciding whether your inquiry is to be answered at all. You'd better be careful about what you put in writing."

When Williams confirmed and then disclosed that his mail was indeed being watched by unauthorized persons, the Washington *Star* declared editorially: "The Senate should be totally outraged. Obviously someone high in the Executive Branch issued the instructions for this monitoring. Nothing of the sort, as far as anyone knows, has ever been done before. Who issued the order?"

Well, everyone knew who issued the order; but in those pre-Watergate days no one wanted to take the lead in fingering a President. Johnson had just taken office under tragic circumstances and most everyone wished him well, particularly his fellow Democrats controlling Congress, not a few of whom had had their own special relationships with Baker.

But that didn't deter Johnson from employing even the IRS in efforts to harass a courageous senator from Delaware who came to be called "the conscience of the Senate." For suddenly the IRS ordered Williams to produce all the records he had used to prepare a return he had submitted two years before. This meant the senator had to leave Washington and submit to a line-by-line audit by an IRS agent. It also meant that Williams had to curtail his personal investigation into Baker's tangled affairs. The payoff, incidentally, was that after all the auditing and time spent, the IRS determined that the government owed the senator money. But it was Williams's belief that had there been anything wrong in his tax return that information most certainly would have been passed on to Baker's highly placed friends.

Meanwhile, at the suggestion of his pals Fortas and Clifford,

Lyndon Johnson broke his silence. At an impromptu press conference LBJ himself brought up the newspaper stories about "an insurance policy that was written on my life some seven years ago, and I am still here." He did not refer to the television time purchased by Reynolds but did allude to the stereo by describing it first as "a gift . . . that an employee of mine [Baker] made to me and Mrs. Johnson" and then as a gift of "the Baker family." He noted that the Bakers and the Johnsons had frequently exchanged gifts. Baker, he claimed, "was an employee of the public and had no business pending before me and was asking for nothing, and so far as I know expected nothing in return any more than I did when I had presented him with gifts."

LBJ ended the discussion by saying he would not entertain any more questions on the subject. Thus reporters did not have the opportunity to ask the President why the invoice attached to the delivered set read: "Charge to Don Reynolds, 8484 Fenton Street, Silver Spring; shipped to Lyndon Johnson, 4931 30th Street NW, Washington, D.C., one stereo."

At later press conferences LBJ would not permit further probing into these areas. Even the persistent Clark Mollenhoff was cut off when he asked *verboten* questions. But the correspondent once received some sort of reply to a question. "How do you feel about the general ethical question that's been raised, relative to high government officials . . . who have an interest in government-regulated industries, such as television?" Mollenhoff asked.

LBJ, his face hardening, replied that he owned no stock in the Texas Broadcasting Company, that Lady Bird's stock was under the tight control of trustees. "I see no conflict in any way," he snarled.

And then came a White House blitz aimed at blackening Reynolds's reputation. "Persons within and close to the Johnson Administration," reported Cabell Philipps in *The New York Times*, "have attempted to use secret Government documents to impugn" the Reynolds testimony. Confidential files from the FBI and air force Intelligence containing derogatory information about Reynolds were shown to selected editors and newsmen, according to the *Times*. Reynolds, who had been an air force officer, had engaged in black market activities while overseas and other unethical conduct, according to the dossiers. Drew Pearson, who also had been shown the files, weighed in with a report, presumably based on FBI sources, describing Reynolds as a man who "has brought reckless charges in the past against people who crossed him, accusing them of being Communists and sex deviates."

But Reynolds had not accused LBJ of being a Communist or a pervert. His charges boiled down to the contention that Johnson, wittingly or unwittingly, had accepted kickbacks as Majority Leader. It was the kind of charge which, had it been proven in a court of law, could have resulted in a conviction. After all, lesser mortals in government, when found guilty of the same allegation, spent time in the slammer. At the very least accepting kickbacks most definitely was an impeachable offense.

Just as shocking, in the light of the holier-than-thou attitude taken by much of the media during Watergate, was the extraordinary nonchalance exhibited by newsmen and editors willing to peruse supposedly confidential investigative files containing raw, unevaluated gossip about an American citizen. There were very few words of protest about what after all was illegal behavior on the part of the White House. Eye-opening too was the questionable, if not illegal, misuse of the FBI which, on orders of the White House, launched a full field investigation of Reynolds.

Also misused on White House orders was the IRS. Full field investigations of Reynolds's friends and business associates were launched by chief counsel Sheldon Cohen, formerly a young law associate of Fortas. Reynolds himself, warned that his life might be in danger, later fled the country.

Meanwhile LBJ sought to divorce himself completely from Baker. He let the word get out that he was abandoning him. And, as was reported by Evans and Novak,* "This irritation with his former protégé was heightened by the President's deep concern over whether Attorney General Kennedy would use the Baker case against him in some way."

LBJ had good reason to be concerned. He well knew that Bobby was no friend of his and, in fact, resented that he had succeeded to the office won at the polls by his beloved brother. To the Kennedyites LBJ was a "usurper." Moreover Johnson did not know how much Bobby knew about him and what he intended to do with that information. As an Attorney General not beholden to him, Kennedy might proceed on certain investigations that could prove damaging to the new President.

---

*In *Lyndon B. Johnson: The Exercise of Power* by Rowland Evans and Robert Novak (New York: New American Library, 1966). Probably the best sourcebook on LBJ and his early years in the presidency.

Also giving LBJ nightmares was the fear that Baker, who knew so much, might spill the beans. And Baker was indeed indicating that he might do just that unless he were bailed out of his difficulties. The word went out to Democratic leaders that LBJ wanted a lid placed on the Senate probe of Baker's affairs then under way.

Of course there was still Senator Williams who, despite all sorts of threats and obstacles being hurled in his path, refused to lay off. But the threats had their effect on potential witnesses who had promised to tell all they knew about Baker. One important businessman, who previously had said he would provide evidence, told the senator, "I don't know what you're talking about, Senator. I never talked to you before in my life. I'm sorry, but I'm sure you understand."

The senator himself began to feel the heat of an angered LBJ. What he did not know was that the very night LBJ assumed the presidency, he had spoken to Abe Fortas about Williams. On that occasion the new President vowed to punish Williams. There was talk about turning the IRS loose on the Delaware maverick, perhaps getting enough on him to send the "bastard" to jail on an income tax rap. And if that wasn't feasible, the Democrats would flood the state with money to try to defeat the "sonofabitch" when he came up for reelection the next year.

All of which was done.

Also in the works was a campaign of character assassination. Williams was called a "crackpot" by Democratic members of the Rules Committee. Others said he just hated Democratic presidents, recalling his earlier relentless attacks on the Truman administration. Drew Pearson wanted to know why Williams had not been outraged by Eisenhower's acceptance of expensive gifts while serving in office. The Washington *Post* helped the LBJ cause by publishing a false, unchecked story alleging that the senator had been using hidden microphones in his office to record interviews.

On only one other occasion did LBJ publicly discuss Baker. That was during a television interview on March 15, 1964. Asked if he was still a friend of Baker's, the President said he hadn't seen or talked with him since he resigned from his Senate post. He denied that Baker had been his protégé. "He was there before I came to the Senate for ten years, doing a job substantially the same as he is doing now; he was elected by all the Senators

. . . including the Republican Senators." Which was not exactly telling it like it was.

As his former press secretary, George Reedy, later put it, "Johnson was really panicked. . . . He adopted this line that he hardly knew Baker, and I think he tried to convince himself the line was true. . . . Whatever Johnson tells you at any given moment he thinks is the truth. The first victim of the Johnson whopper is always Lyndon Baines Johnson."

Meanwhile Democratic leaders in the Senate began moving behind the scenes to bring the probe to a rapid conclusion. It was an election year and they did not want to provide the Republicans a juicy issue. By party-line votes the Democratic majority on the Rules Committee rejected Republican efforts to expand the scope and duration of the inquiry. The hearings were terminated on March 25.

On July 8 the panel's report was released. While the Democratic majority found Baker "guilty of many gross improprieties" in his numerous business dealings, its review of the insurance episode in effect exonerated Johnson. The Democrats denounced the President's accuser in these words: "It appears rather obvious that Reynolds in his effort to enjoy the limelight of this investigation was not reluctant to draw on his imagination and to add to his store of knowledge as time passed."

The Republicans felt otherwise. Their minority report observed that the investigation of the case had never been fully explored, noting for example that Jenkins had never been called to testify in person and be subjected to cross-examination.

Previously, on May 14, 1964, the Democratic majority in the full Senate voted to quash further hearings. In effect the Democrats had voted for a cover up. They wanted to make certain no White House witnesses were called to connect Baker's activities with those of his former boss. Seven times senators were given the opportunity of getting to the bottom of the scandal and all seven times the Democrats voted nay. Not all of them, to be sure, but enough to override the solid vote of the Republicans for an airing of the story which, many of them felt, could lead right into the Oval Office.

Among those who voted repeatedly for the cover up was Sam Ervin. Two other Democrats to appear on the Ervin Committee who voted to terminate the Baker hearings were Herman Talmadge of Georgia and Dan Inouye of Hawaii. Only in 1973 did Ervin, Talmadge, and Inoyue want to dig and dig and dig.

All of this was recalled nine years later, at the height of the Watergate hearings, by a Republican congressman from Illinois, Philip M. Crane, who made this pertinent observation: "I think it is fair to state that the American people have been subjected to a great deal of moralizing by certain members of the Senate Watergate Committee in connection with their television show. Now, mind you, moralizing has its place. However, selective indignation has no place in the pulpit."

Crane obviously was referring to such "extremist humbug"— in a Richmond, Virginia, newspaper's phrase—as Senator Sam's teary-eyed declaration that Watergate was worse than the Civil War, in which half a million Americans lost their lives.

Other Democrats who voted in behalf of the Baker cover up included Bayh of Indiana, Byrd of West Virginia, Cannon of Nevada, Church of Idaho, McGovern of South Dakota, Mansfield of Montana, Muskie of Maine, and Pastore of Rhode Island. Many of these worthies, needless to say, were later to be horrified by allegations of a cover up at Watergate.

After the Senate committee ended its Baker probe in July 1964, declaring that any further evidence on Baker would be "repetitious and cumulative," Lyndon Johnson knew that the worst was over. He then decided to resolve the other "Bobby problem." Among other things, Kennedy had decided he wanted to be named LBJ's runningmate at the upcoming national convention in Atlantic City. But LBJ wasn't buying.

LBJ suspected, and not without cause, that Kennedy was leading a cabal aimed at destroying his credibility as President. From the beginning he sought to ease Kennedy supporters out of his administration. After supposedly confidential information began to leak out of the White House, LBJ asked J. Edgar Hoover to discreetly determine the Kennedyites in his midst. According to *Time,* after one such FBI probe, Richard Goodwin—who had coined the phrase "the Great Society" for LBJ—decided to resign as a presidential speechwriter, accepting a job as senior fellow at Wesleyan University at half his White House pay. Johnson also ordered FBI name checks of all high officials in the Democratic National Committee. So phobic was LBJ about Bobby that once, when the Washington *Star* attacked him editorially, the President asked Hoover to determine whether there was any Kennedy money behind the paper. There wasn't.

On July 29, 1964, the two antagonists met in the Oval Office. Kennedy noticed immediately that LBJ had switched on his tape recorder. So he was relatively restrained when LBJ informed him there was no way that he could become the vice presidential candidate. Bobby did not argue. But he did say that the Kennedy family would not be overly happy if Sargent Shriver were selected as the number two man. Within the family, of course, there was a sense of priority and a brother-in-law was way down the list.

Then they discussed other possible jobs for Bobby. Would he be interested in an embassy in Rome, London, or Paris, or possibly another cabinet post? RFK said he was only interested in remaining as Attorney General. He had a number of important tasks that remained to be completed.

That brought the subject around to the forthcoming campaign and Bobby suggested that the Baker case might prove embarrassing. But Johnson said he didn't think so. For one thing he felt the Republicans wouldn't dare to make an issue of the case. He said too many Republicans themselves were vulnerable. And he named a few who had better keep their traps shut. The President implied he had the goods on them. Which was why the President thought the case was dead.

But the Baker case, though dying, was not yet buried. It became, as the Democrats had feared, a campaign issue. Not only did the Republicans keep screaming "whitewash," but their presidential standardbearer Barry Goldwater said: "Bobby Baker's affairs lead right straight into the White House."

At the same time Williams kept digging into the Baker cesspool and coming up with still more startling allegations of high-level wrongdoing. One of those allegations had to do with Baker's conspiring to channel an illegal payment of $25,000 from a construction millionaire working on government projects, Matthew McCloskey, into the 1960 Kennedy-Johnson campaign chest. Reynolds had sworn under oath that he had acted as the "bagman" in that transaction. His testimony was bolstered by copies of invoices and a canceled check.

The new allegations compelled the Senate to reopen the investigation. Through Fortas, LBJ was in close touch with leading Democratic senators. Two days of hearings were held in October. Then the hearings were suspended until *after* the election for lack of a quorum. Whereupon the chairman of the Rules Committee, Everett Jordan of North Carolina, left Washington to join Mrs. Johnson on her whistle-stop tour of the South.

All through that fall wave after wave of administration spokesmen invaded Delaware to belittle Williams as some sort of
cranky old eccentric. And then on the Saturday before the election, much to the amazement of accompanying correspondents,
LBJ himself turned up in a small Delaware town to plead for
Williams's defeat. "Give me men I can work with!" he bellowed.
It was an unscheduled, last-minute appearance in a state with
only three electoral votes. And Williams thought he might go
down to defeat.

But the people of Delaware voted independently. While they
gave LBJ an overwhelming vote, they also elected Williams to a
fourth term by 7,000 votes.

Still Williams's long ordeal was not yet over. He again had to
appear before the IRS to defend his tax returns. And a smear
campaign was launched to make the sixty-one-year-old senator
appear as a sanctimonious hypocrite.

Word had been leaked that Carole Tyler, Baker's confidential
secretary, was going to expose the senator's sex life. This was the
same woman who had repeatedly taken the Fifth Amendment
before the Rules Committee in order to avoid saying anything.

Finally Miss Tyler turned up at a Nashville press conference.
Reading from a typewritten statement, she said, "I wonder what
you would think if you knew that the principal instigator of the
Senate investigation was seen by me on July 6 at 6:30 A.M. with
a lady—not his wife—just after they finished breakfast. And just
think, this is the gentleman who has been criticizing the Senate
Rules Committee for not going into the so-called sex angle of the
Baker case.* I leave it to his conscience, if any, as to why he was
with this lady—not his wife—at such a time near a summer resort."

Asked to name the senator, Miss Tyler responded, "I think you
know who I mean."

Actually Miss Tyler had been telling the truth. She did, in fact,
see the senator with a lady not his wife. The lady happened to
be his granddaughter, whom he was accompanying to her home
following a weekend at the beach. But Williams refused to dig-
nify the attack by commenting on it at the time.

The Rules Committee issued a second "final" report. Origi-

_____
*Though the Baker case was replete with sex angles, the fact was that Senator
Williams never called on the Rules Committee to investigate them.

nally the draft of the report, leaked out to friendly reporters, contained innuendoes and insinuations about Williams's having withheld information and making false charges.

Williams angrily demanded of his fellow senators that they either put up or shut up. "Retract the charges or else repeat them in my presence," he declared on the Senate floor. The cover-up artists on the Rules Committee decided that discretion was the better part of valor. They deleted all the attacks on Williams. But they had definitely succeeded in circulating canards without assuming responsibility.

"I have plenty of time," Williams again warned. "And I am not about to be intimidated. In fact, my curiosity and determination grow as resistance intensifies."

Bobby Baker did not seem overly troubled. Having played ball with his friends in high places by taking the Fifth Amendment and saying nothing, he fully expected that, even if indicted, nothing would happen to him. He was to be proved wrong. Because of Williams's bulldog persistence, the Criminal Division of the Justice Department finally was forced to move. But the Criminal Division didn't get J. Edgar Hoover's cooperation. When the division requested that the FBI "wire" an informant who was about to confer with Baker, the director not only refused but reported the request to the President. Whereupon, without LBJ's knowledge, the Justice Department lawyers went to the Treasury Department's Bureau of Narcotics and got the help they sought.

These events were revealed in January 1967 when Baker finally went on trial, accused of seven counts of tax evasion, one count of theft, and one count of conspiracy to defraud the government. On January 17, 1967, Assistant FBI Director Cartha D. ("Deke") DeLoach was summoned to the White House by LBJ aide Marvin Watson. The President was "quite exercised," Watson reported, at the news that the Bureau of Narcotics had arranged for the "recording device." In an internal memo DeLoach reported that "Watson told me that the President wanted a complete rundown" on former Assistant Attorney General Herbert J. Miller, who had ordered the use of wiretaps and bugs in the Baker investigation.

The memo outlined Watson's request that the check on Miller and four Treasury officials be made "as discreetly as possible," and that the FBI reports on them "should specifically point out whether any of these individuals were close to Bobby Kennedy."

Moreover, according to the memo: "The President does not want any record made of this request. He wants the memoranda in question to be blind memoranda. He desires that they be as thorough as possible and wants this done on an expeditious basis."

DeLoach noted that the President should be told that "Jack Miller was formerly an Assistant AG under Bobby Kennedy and is now a law partner of former Bureau [Assistant Director] Courtney Evans," who had served as a liaison between the FBI and Attorney General Kennedy.* DeLoach concluded by saying that Evans's "lying defense of Kennedy" should be set forth, an apparent reference to public statements by Evans earlier that Kennedy had not known of FBI electronic surveillance of Martin Luther King, Jr.

In effect, therefore, the President through Watson had ordered the FBI to conduct an unusual investigation of another federal law enforcement agency for daring to poke around in the affairs of his former protégé. LBJ was absolutely certain that "Bobby's boys," still in the federal bureaucracy, were still out to "get" him. At the time, of course, Kennedy had become a senator and appeared to be mobilizing anti-LBJ sentiment for his own try at the presidency.

Meanwhile Baker, who had been found guilty, began a series of appeals that took several years. In January 1971 the man whom Johnson once considered to be like "a son" began serving a one-to-three year sentence in the federal penitentiary at Lewisburg. By that time Johnson was no longer in office. Baker was paroled in 1972, after serving seventeen months.

---

*Ironically one of Attorney Miller's more celebrated clients currently is Richard M. Nixon.

12

IT WAS LYNDON JOHNSON WHO ONCE UT-
tered the memorable obscenity about not feeling safe unless he
had a man's unmentionables in his pocket. As much as any other
President (and probably more) Lyndon Johnson devoted considerable effort to obtaining intimate information about his foes or
potential foes, which added up to quite a list. Except for his wife,
Lady Bird, he didn't trust a soul and, as he once said half-jokingly,
"Sometimes I'm not too sure about her."

As President, Johnson had no hesitation about using various
investigatory agencies to carry on political warfare against his
adversaries. In so doing, he emulated the man he had admired
most in political life, Franklin Delano Roosevelt. For FDR also
used (or misused) the FBI to dig up dirt on his enemies. On
several occasions FDR asked the FBI to call off investigations of
political allies and friends, most notably Undersecretary of State
Sumner Welles, who had been accused of homosexual activities.

All this and much more were contained in a secret memorandum prepared by an official of the FBI, William C. Sullivan. A
scholarly expert in counter-intelligence, Sullivan had written the
memorandum at the request of John Dean when he was still at
the White House. The document outlined political uses made of
the Bureau dating back to the New Deal. When Dean broke with
Nixon, he turned the Sullivan memo over to the Watergate Committee, along with a huge batch of materials. But the committee,
headed by Sam Ervin, decided to bury the memo and forget it.
Nevertheless portions were leaked and published in *Time*.

Its existence was confirmed by Ervin's deputy counsel Rufus L.
Edminsten, who said the reason the committee would not use
the memorandum as a basis of inquiry was because it contained
"personal cheap shots" based on undocumented recollections
and generally was "rather distasteful." Moreover, he claimed,
the document was "not based on any established facts."

Of course this was the same committee which had gone out of

its way to enliven its Nixon record with every piece of gossip and hearsay evidence it could find anywhere. But, all of a sudden, the Democrats controlling the committee decided against permitting "cheap shots" in a record already cluttered with them. Why? The reason is obvious. The Sullivan memorandum had centered its attention on the misdeeds of two Democrats, Franklin Roosevelt and Lyndon Johnson. And the main thrust of the Democrats was to "get" a Republican President. To do this successfully, it was essential to cover up the numerous improprieties of his predecessors with the result—*and for the purpose*—of isolating Nixon's sins and making them appear unique and unprecedented. In this they succeeded with a vengeance.

According to John Dean, the memorandum came into being as the result of a request by Nixon during the Watergate furor. Aware that the FBI had conducted political intelligence operations in Democratic administrations, Nixon asked Dean to obtain examples from Sullivan. And Sullivan, forced to resign from the FBI after a policy feud with Hoover, was only too happy to comply. To compile his memorandum, Sullivan used data from secret records listing presidential requests for political help going back to the days of FDR.

According to the memo, FDR used the G-men lavishly. Not only did he employ them to check out potential appointees, a perfectly legitimate function, but also to snoop into the private lives of his opponents on such issues as lend-lease, a hardly legitimate enterprise. On one occasion the President asked the Bureau to investigate an army colonel who had been acting as Mrs. Roosevelt's escort. "Mrs. Roosevelt would also make some unusual requests," Sullivan cryptically noted.

Sullivan had more to say about FDR's relations with the Bureau in a letter to a conference on "privacy in a free society."*

"Such a very great man as Franklin D. Roosevelt saw nothing wrong in asking the FBI to investigate those opposing his lend-lease policy—a purely political request," wrote Sullivan.

---

*Sullivan was supposed to appear in person but was prevented from doing so by a heart attack. However his letter was published in the final report of the annual Chief Justice Earl Warren Conference on Advocacy, held June 1974 at Cambridge, Mass. There were some fifty participants—law professors, an assistant district attorney from Manhattan, computer experts, diverse academics, law enforcement officials, members of Congress, journalists, judges (federal and state), and William Ruckelshaus, former acting director of the FBI. The rapporteur (a euphemism for secretary) was civil libertarian Nat Hentoff.

He also had us look into the activities of others who opposed our entrance into World War II just as later administrations had the FBI look into those opposing the conflict in Vietnam. It was a political request also when he instructed us to put a telephone tap, a microphone and a physical surveillance on an internationally known leader in his Administration.

It was done; the results he wanted secured and given to him. Certain records of this kind and others were not then or later put into the regular filing system. Rather, they were deliberately kept out of it. Electronic devices were used freely all through World War II, with a minimum of controls. President Roosevelt made requests of various kinds.

In other words the tactics associated with Watergate were first put to use by Roosevelt. The identity of the "internationally known leader" whom FDR had ordered wiretapped, bugged, and physically surveilled was not made known, though Sullivan would have most certainly named him had he been asked by the Watergate Committee.

From various pieces of evidence it could well have been Joseph P. Kennedy, then U.S. ambassador to Great Britain. Kennedy, an outspoken isolationist and unofficial leader of the anti-war forces, had thought very seriously of contesting FDR for the presidency. An early supporter of FDR and the New Deal's first chairman of the Securities and Exchange Commission, Kennedy was bitterly opposed to a third term for the President.

And Roosevelt was well aware of what his ambassador was saying, even privately. For one thing the British Secret Service had been tapping his London quarters and offices. As they suspected, Kennedy was taking a defeatist position regarding Britain in the war. After consulting with Winston Churchill and other cabinet members, the Secret Service arranged for a sheaf of tapped conversations in which Kennedy expressed critical opinions of FDR to reach the President.*

Early in 1940 Kennedy announced he would not seek the Democratic nomination. However he continued with his campaign to keep the United States out of a European war, which he felt was an abomination. In October 1940 he returned from London with the reported objective of working against Roosevelt. In fact there was more than talk that he was prepared to endorse the Republi-

---

*This is what Randolph Churchill told C. L. Sulzberger in Paris in January 1960. The story is contained in Sulzberger's *The Last of the Giants* (New York: Macmillan, 1970), pp. 629–630.

can candidate, Wendell Willkie. A report even circulated in Washington that Henry Luce had arranged for radio time for Kennedy's "I'm for Willkie" speech.

On his return to Washington Kennedy telephoned Roosevelt. As it happened, FDR was conferring with Speaker Sam Rayburn and a little-known congressman from Texas named Lyndon Johnson when the call came. As Johnson later recounted the President's end of the conversation to Arthur Krock, this was what was said:

"Ah, Joe, old friend, it is so good to hear your voice. Please come to the White House tonight for a little family dinner. I'm dying to talk to you."

Roosevelt then put down the phone and drew his forefinger, razor-fashion, across his throat.

Kennedy did dine at the White House that night. Before the meal was served, he had a chat with the President. Exactly what was said in that private meeting was never made known. But the next day Kennedy endorsed Roosevelt for a third term over a national radio hookup.

The speech caused astonishment among friends and foes alike. Krock, in his memoirs, said the Kennedy broadcast was "out of keeping, not only with the wholly opposite view he had been expressing privately (to me, among others), but with Kennedy's earned reputation as one of the most forthright men in public life." And William R. Castle, one of the major backers of the isolationist America First Committee, termed the speech a "stooge" job for Roosevelt, saying privately that some large financial consideration must have been involved—"Everyone in Boston knows that Kennedy is money mad."

The Castle thesis seems unlikely. Kennedy, while greedy, did have principles. And one of them was to prevent a war in which he quite candidly admitted he did not want his sons to get killed. Moreover he felt that, whether you liked it or not, Nazism indeed was the wave of the future. In his opinion the United States could never resolve the basic conflicts of Europe.

Which is pretty much what Kennedy told an interviewer for the Boston *Globe* following the election. Among other things he announced that he would lead a Keep-America-out-of-war crusade. "I'm willing to spend all I've got to keep us out of war," he said. "There's no sense in our getting in. We'd just be left holding the bag." As far as he was concerned, "Democracy is finished in

England." With labor leaders helping run the government, "national socialism is coming out of it." U.S. entry into the war would result in the same dread state of affairs here at home. Perhaps his greatest indiscretion was in discussing Eleanor Roosevelt. "She's always sending me a note to have some little Susie Glotz to tea at the Embassy."

At any rate the interview caused a storm both domestically and internationally. As a result Kennedy resigned as ambassador. His political career was virtually destroyed. From that point on he began to work to put one of his sons in the White House.

Unknown to most Americans and despite his statements to the contrary, Roosevelt had embarked on a carefully planned, mostly secret program to involve the United States in the war. He felt that Hitler and his Nazi régime were abominations which had to be destroyed. Thus FDR authorized the sale of weapons abroad over the objections of Congress and, not so incidentally, an American public then vigorously isolationist. And he helped to establish a joint Anglo-American intelligence network, sharing U.S. secrets with the British.

"The President said he wanted a war with Germany, but that he would not declare it," Churchill reported to his war cabinet after meeting with Roosevelt in the summer of 1941. "He would instead become more and more provocative. Mr. Roosevelt said he could look for an incident which would justify him in opening hostilities."

Convinced he would succeed in getting the United States into the conflict, Roosevelt began to map out war plans with Churchill through the offices of a man code-named Intrepid and an office called British Security Coordination. Intrepid (actually Sir William Stephenson, a Canadian-born inventor) worked out of offices on the thirty-sixth floor of Rockefeller Center in Manhattan, acting as coordinator between the two leaders, shuffling papers back and forth, and engineering the creation of a U.S. intelligence network that became the Office of Strategic Services (OSS) when war finally came.*

In his letter to the Earl Warren conference on privacy, William Sullivan made clear that many anti-libertarian things had been

---

*The story, based on Sir William's recollections as well as materials in the British archives, is told in William Stephenson's, *A Man Called Intrepid: The Secret War* (New York: Harcourt Brace Jovanovich, 1976).

done by the FBI, beginning in the late thirties, in the name of national security which should not now be condemned. He noted that

> in a pre-war atmosphere to be followed soon by World War II
> . . . we were all convinced we were fighting for the survival of our
> nation. The enemy was real. In this nation, with sabotage attempts
> and other problems facing it, the overall enemy consisted of Bun-
> dists and native fascists in support of the Axis powers, and their
> espionage agents. To be candid, the "right to privacy" was not at
> issue nor was it an impediment to solving cases. It mattered not
> whether electronic devices or other techniques were used. The
> issues were black and white and crystal clear. The methodology
> was pragmatic: will it work; will it get the necessary results? The
> primacy of civil liberties on occasions gave way to expediency.
> President Franklin D. Roosevelt posed no barrier to this method
> and, for me, this was no criticism of him at that perilous time.

Sullivan continued:

> The FBI security operations developed through a pre-war psy-
> chology which was quickly transformed into a war psychology. In
> a very real sense it has breathed, lived and worked within the
> framework of this war psychology ever since. World War II was
> followed by the Korean War which in turn was followed by the
> Vietnam conflict. Permeating our entire nation on the home front
> was the Cold War. Hence, just as a soldier on the field of battle did
> not consider it wrong to kill the enemy, so, too, on the home front
> it was not considered wrong in major cases to use extraordinary
> measures in security work. The same enemy was before both. Both
> had the same goal—vanquish the enemy. We did not consider this
> unlawful. . . .

What Sullivan did not say was that just prior to and during World War II most liberals, with a few significant exceptions, were wholeheartedly in support of any effort to throttle antiwar dissent. The fact that civil liberties were being openly and grossly violated led to very little criticism. In fact liberals applauded when, even before the United States entered the war, the Attorney General convened a grand jury to investigate the finances of the nation's leading antiwar organization, the America First Committee. During the war itself there were no liberal outcries when the Roosevelt administration impaneled a grand jury to bring the Chicago *Tribune,* and particularly its publisher, Colonel McCormick, to "justice" for publishing a story involving Japanese fleet movements.

Nor did the liberals protest when it became known that FDR had personally ordered the IRS to look into Charles A. Lindbergh's tax returns. Lindbergh, of course, had been taking a jaundiced view toward FDR's inching into the European conflict. But the IRS probe came only after Lindbergh refused a deal whereby he would become the nation's first Secretary of Air if only he would support the President's position of all aid to France and Britain "short of war."

Asked about the probe, Lindbergh told reporters he welcomed it. He said he thought it was a privilege to be an American and pay taxes. Moreover, he said, he always paid an extra 10 percent after calculating what he owed the government. The IRS probe, though annoying, came to naught.

Lindbergh campaigned against FDR's "short of war" measures on the ground that they were not steps toward peace, as the President was arguing. Rather the aviator contended that FDR was seeking to create incidents at sea that inevitably would drag the nation into war when he authorized Atlantic patrols, a "shoot-on-sight" policy, as well as having armed American merchant ships enter war zones. According to Lindbergh, this was "government by subterfuge" and one profoundly undemocratic, since the President refused to take the issue to Congress. Lindbergh repeatedly called for "open discussion, more legislative authority in foreign affairs, and limitations on the President's war making powers." These were the very arguments, as Wayne S. Cole noted with a touch of irony in a recent book,* that "liberal internationalists would use in attacking President Nixon thirty years later."

It was largely Lindbergh's effective assaults on what he termed misuse of presidential powers that led the Roosevelt administration to place the "Lone Eagle" and his antiwar associates on their enemies list. Lindbergh, of course, had made one ill-advised comment on what he termed Jewish "agitation" to involve the United States in the war. The remark set off an explosion which FDR exploited to a fare-thee-well. According to Cole, Roosevelt deliberately "used that tactic of identifying isolationists with Nazism to discredit Lindbergh." This, says Cole, was "fundamentally similar to" the tactics used by McCarthyites "in attacking liberal internationalists in the early 1950's."

---

*Wayne S. Cole, *Charles A. Lindbergh and the Battle Against American Intervention in World War II* (New York: Harcourt Brace Jovanovich, 1975).

Not all isolationists were reactionaries by any means. Quite a number were liberals, and even Socialists, whose pacifist beliefs could not be altered even though the potential enemy was Nazi Germany. One such was Norman Thomas, who had appeared with Lindbergh at a number of antiwar rallies around the country. The Socialist leader, who was embarrassed by Lindbergh's reference to Jews, said in his defense that the flier was "not as anti-Semitic as some who seize the opportunity to criticize him."

Thomas could well have been referring to FDR himself. For the President, though strongly backed by Jews throughout his political career, was given to anti-Semitic outbursts. Walter Trohan, the veteran Washington correspondent, tells of one episode involving Governor Herbert Lehman of New York.* The year was 1937, after FDR had proposed "packing" the Supreme Court. Lehman, though a stalwart New Dealer, spoke out against the proposal.

Roosevelt, who was at Hyde Park at the time, was asked what he had to say about Lehman's statement. He lost his smile and snapped: "What I have to say will have to be off the record."

The correspondents had no choice but to agree. But they were taken aback when the President thrust out his chin and sneered: "What else could you expect from a Jew?"**

But probably FDR's shabbiest act was his refusal to permit a German ship carrying nearly 1,000 Jewish refugees to unload its human cargo in the United States. This was in 1939. The refugees, who had also been refused entry into Cuba, were returned to Europe where many of them perished in the Nazi holocaust. Why did FDR turn these pitiful people back? The best answer seems to be that he was unwilling to buck American public opinion.

One of those who bitterly condemned FDR for turning back the refugees was Norman Thomas, who had been appearing at

---

*In his *Political Animals* (Garden City, N.Y.: Doubleday, 1975), p. 99.
**FDR's successor, Harry S Truman, also indulged in occasional anti-Semitic slurs. A 1946 entry in the diaries of Henry A. Wallace, recently unveiled by the University of Iowa, pictures an exasperated Truman trying to cope with Zionist pressures for an independent state of Israel. "President Truman expressed himself as being very much 'put out' with the Jews," wrote Wallace, then Secretary of Commerce, after a Cabinet luncheon. "He said that 'Jesus Christ couldn't please them when he was here on earth, so how could anyone expect that I would have any luck?' President Truman said he had no use for them and didn't care what happened to them." Of course, HST's anger cooled and in 1948, despite State Department opposition, he approved the founding of the new Jewish state.

America First rallies around the country. The antiwar movement was growing by leaps and bounds. It attracted adherents of varied opinions (including some who had been considered in the forefront of U.S. progressivism), such as William Benton, Harry Elmer Barnes, Charles A. Beard, Stuart Chase, Chester Bowles, John L. Lewis, John T. Flynn, and Oswald Garrison Villard. When Roosevelt announced his "shoot-on-sight" order (permitting U.S. vessels to fire on any hostile vessel), such luminaries as Philip C. Jessup, Edwin S. Corwin, Ray Lyman Wilbur, Charles A. Beard, and Igor Sikorsky signed a statement that called the new policy "a grave threat to the Constitutional powers of Congress and to the democratic principle of majority rule." The order stood.

FDR took the offensive, terming his critics, and particularly Lindbergh, "Copperheads." Thus, in effect, the President called them "traitors." Not only that but, according to Cole, he ordered the wiretapping of their telephones; and he asked that telegrams criticizing his defense policies be sent to the FBI director for investigation, and correspondence endorsing Lindbergh's opposition to U.S. ships acting as convoys be filed by the Secret Service. Rarely had any legitimate movement of American citizens, none of whom had any links to any foreign power, faced such official hostility, abuse, and repression. But most liberals couldn't have cared less. In fact they happily joined in the witch-hunt.

Immediately after Pearl Harbor the America First Committee went out of business. "No good purpose can now be served by considering what might have been," the committee stated. "We are at war . . . the primary objective is . . . victory." Numerous leaders and members joined the Roosevelt administration for the duration of the war. The head of America First, Richard Stewart, along with General Robert E. Wood, were soon serving in the armed forces, while Chester Bowles became head of the Office of Price Administration. However, though he volunteered, Lindbergh was not permitted to serve his country. Roosevelt was not having him back in the Air Corps unless he ate crow, apologizing for his antiwar views. This Lindbergh would not do.

Also sidelined for the war's duration was Joe Kennedy, who had wired his Commander-in-Chief: "Name the battlefront. I'm yours to command." The ambassador never heard from Roosevelt. So he devoted the war years to making money—and lots of it.

As Norman Thomas noted, the Lindbergh case was one of the

least attractive manifestations of FDR's penchant for personal vendetta—a startling example of a great leader indulging in petty revenge and, in the process, nearly depriving the nation of the services of a leading aviation expert. But Lindbergh felt it his duty to serve. Without permission of Washington he became a civilian consultant to aircraft manufacturers and, as such, was sent on missions to Europe and the Pacific area in behalf of the U.S. Air Corps. On one occasion while flight-testing a Republic "Thunderbolt" fighter, he nearly lost his life. And, though a civilian, he flew combat missions against the Japanese.

What the American Civil Liberties Union eventually would call "the worst single wholesale violation of civil rights of American citizens in our history" took place shortly after Pearl Harbor with Roosevelt's approval. Over 110,000 men, women, and children of Japanese ancestry—both citizens and aliens—were forced out of their homes, their properties expropriated, and evacuated to internment camps guarded by troops.

This extraordinary measure was taken as a result of pressures on the West Coast, where most of the Nisei lived. The fear was that the Japanese-Americans would engage in sabotage of vital installations. Doing most of the clamoring for the mass internments, unprecedented in American history, were such outspoken liberals as California's Governor Culbert L. Olson and Attorney General Earl Warren. Secretary of War Henry L. Stimson gave approval after he had concluded that "their racial characteristics are such that we cannot understand or trust even the citizen Japanese."

Roosevelt signed the evacuation order, a move supported by Congress a month later. And the United States, officially at war with an ideology based on concentration camps, had its own concentration camps. Except for the likes of a tiny handful of civil libertarians including Norman Thomas, the liberal community was largely silent. The big Establishment newspapers for the most part said nothing. Walter Lippmann, normally so zealous of individual liberties, supported the strong measures on the grounds that the Pacific Coast was officially a battle zone and no one had a constitutional right to "do business on a battlefield." His views were endorsed by Westbrook Pegler, who demanded that every Japanese should be under armed guard, "and to hell with habeas corpus until the danger is over."

Only a few congressmen tried to stem the tide of hysteria, the most notable being Senator Robert Taft. But the Ohio Republican's plea for sanity was drowned out by what amounted to frenzied appeals to anti-yellow racism. Significantly J. Edgar Hoover had also sought to prevent the administration from going overboard against the Japanese-Americans. In a memorandum to Attorney General Francis Biddle, the director warned that "the necessity for mass evacuation is based primarily upon public hysteria and political pressure rather than on factual data."

Roosevelt even flirted with the idea of interning German aliens. But there was a problem, his Attorney General told him: there were so many of them, perhaps 600,000. "And you're going to intern all of them?" Roosevelt asked. Not quite, replied Biddle. Roosevelt then said, "I don't care so much about the Italians. They are a lot of opera singers, but the Germans are different, they may be dangerous." Calmer heads prevailed, however, and there were no mass roundups as there had been of the Japanese. Perhaps, as some critics were to contend in years to come, racism did play a major role in determining who was to be interned.

In his biography of Roosevelt during the war years, James MacGregor Burns analyzes the President's peculiar ambivalence toward civil liberties.* The Williams College professor noted that "Roosevelt was not a strong civil libertarian. Like Jefferson in earlier days, he was all for civil liberties in general but easily found exceptions in particular."

According to Burns, Roosevelt told Biddle at a cabinet meeting that while civil liberties were okay for 99 percent of the American people, the Attorney General ought to bear down on the rest. "When Biddle pleaded that it was hard to get convictions, Roosevelt answered that when Lincoln's Attorney General would not proceed against Vallandigham, Lincoln declared martial law in that county and then had Vallandigham tried by a drumhead court-martial. Earlier he had treated Biddle's earnest support of civil liberties as a joking matter. . . ."

"Indeed," Burns continued, "Roosevelt seemed to enjoy shocking the shy Philadelphian. Once, when J. Edgar Hoover confessed to the President, in the Attorney General's presence, that an FBI agent had tried to tap the telephone wire of left-wing union leader Harry Bridges, and had been caught in the act,

---

*Roosevelt: The Soldier of Freedom 1940–1945 (New York: Harcourt Brace Jovanovich, 1970), pp. 216–217.

Roosevelt roared with laughter, slapped Hoover on the back, and shouted gleefully, 'By God, Edgar, that's the first time you've been caught with your pants down!' "

"To be sure," Burns contended, "Roosevelt's civil liberties derelictions were not numerous, but certainly the wartime White House was not dependably a source of strong and sustained support for civil liberties in specific situations."

Most assuredly not, but how certain can Professor Burns be about the number of derelictions under Roosevelt? By his own accounting they were indeed extensive. The tragedy that befell innocent Americans of Japanese descent violated every guarantee in the American Constitution. And only now, as a result of such revelations as the Sullivan memorandum, are we beginning to learn the extent to which FDR misused the FBI for political and/or personal purposes. As for wiretapping and "bugging," the record clearly demonstrates FDR's fondness for such illegal gathering of information.

In May 1973 at the height of the controversy over Watergate, Bob Considine asked John Roosevelt, the President's youngest son, what he thought about the scandal. John Roosevelt responded, "I can't understand all the commotion in this case. Hell, my father just about invented bugging. Had them spread all over, and thought nothing of it."

In retrospect, therefore, under the presidential impeachment standards that became so popular against President Nixon, Franklin Roosevelt could have been put on trial by the Senate for violating civil liberties in wholesale fashion; suborning illegalities by having antiwar and other political opponents wiretapped and "bugged"; and waging an undeclared war against Germany, Italy, and Japan, thus making a mockery of his own "neutrality" pledges written into law. In addition FDR repeatedly lied to the American people, as when he gave them "one more assurance. . . . Your boys are not going to be sent into any foreign wars."

Roosevelt's campaign to destroy the Supreme Court by "packing" it with rubber stamp justices would have been enough, in today's climate of opinion, to have justified impeachment proceedings. It was a blow against the independence of a coordinate branch unrivaled by any earlier or later President. According to Arthur Krock, FDR was even prepared to defy the High Court. This was in 1935, when the court was considering an act of Congress which, at Roosevelt's behest, had canceled the gold repayment clause in contracts both private and governmental. Fearing the act would be overturned, FDR composed a "fireside chat" to announce he would not comply, citing the Golden Rule, the Scriptures, and "the dictates of common sense"—but not the Constitution. As it turned out, the court narrowly upheld the act. FDR confided to an aide: "The nation will never know what a great treat it missed in not hearing the marvelous radio address."

But for sheer eyebrow-lifting arrogance there was the way in which FDR used his high office to assist his sons, James and Elliott, in efforts to make their fortunes. All anyone who wanted important favors from the administration had to do was take out insurance in a firm in which James was a partner. Thus Pan American Airways insured many of its new Pacific clippers with the Roosevelt company. As did the Columbia Broadcasting System, dependent for its life on government license. The Fox Theater Building in Los Angeles stood on land that required title insurance; Joe Schenck, a Fox official, was in the slammer at the time and seeking a federal pardon. The broker who had negotiated a $315,000 policy on the land was told that the Roosevelt company would take over this business. In all, according to an article in the *Saturday Evening Post,* James Roosevelt made over $1 million from his insurance company at the height of the depression.

Even more horrendous in his wheeling-and-dealing, always using his White House connections, was Elliott Roosevelt. On one occasion Elliott had his father talk by phone with the principal owner of the Atlantic and Pacific Tea Company, John Hartford, to suggest that a $200,000 loan to his son would be "appreciated." The A&P was then under attack by New Deal Congressman Wright Patman of Texas, who had been talking about hitting such chain store operations with more taxes.

So what's a businessman to do under these extraordinary circumstances? Well, Hartford did it. The next day he gave Elliott a check for $200,000 and accepted a block of radio stock as collateral. This was in 1939. Hartford, who knew that it was a bad loan, never did hear from Elliott again personally. But that was all right, as he later told a congressional committee, since he figured that by making the loan, he was "being taken off the hook."

In 1942 FDR asked Jesse Jones, the head of the Reconstruction Finance Corporation, to straighten out Elliott's financial problems. Jones met with Hartford and convinced him to accept a $4,000 settlement, writing off the $196,000 loss on his income tax returns. As part of the deal Hartford returned the radio stock.

Later it developed that the stock was worth around $1 million. The President sent the stock to Elliott's divorced second wife, half for herself and half in trust for the children.

As John T. Flynn noted in his antagonistic biography *The Roosevelt Myth*, "It is probable that in all the history of the government this was the first time that such a trick was turned by an American president and by one who exhibited himself before the people as the most righteous paragon of moral and political excellence that had ever occupied that office."

There was, of course, critical publicity about this unsavory episode; but there was no congressional or public outcry about its constituting such gross misuse of presidential influence as to warrant impeachment proceedings.

Which raises the question: How did FDR escape the indignation and rebellion against the inflation of presidential powers that eventually brought down Nixon?

For one thing, the nation was in an all-out war (one which some critics claimed FDR deliberately helped get us into in the first place), a tough, widespread conflict fought on various oceans and continents. And whatever else can be said of him, Franklin Roosevelt was a superb Commander-in-Chief, one whose vibrant voice inspired confidence at a crucial time.

Then, too, Roosevelt had a completely subservient Congress, one overwhelmingly controlled by his own party. Moreover he was a superb party leader as well as an expert at dispensing patronage in the right places.

FDR had also won over most of the Washington press corps. Except for a handful of "reactionaries" who worked for such papers as the Chicago *Tribune,* most of the reporters covering the White House considered the President to be beyond reproach. Anti-New Dealers among correspondents were actually shunned by their more numerous colleagues. On one occasion Roosevelt himself figuratively pinned an Iron Cross on an anti-war columnist. The message was clear to would-be dissenters.

But the main reason FDR got away with his assorted shenanigans was that most Americans, even if they had known of all of them, couldn't have cared less. They looked at the man's whole record and decided that getting out of the lingering economic depression was far more important to them than lofty debates about the misuse of presidential powers. Of course it could have been argued (as it was) that the New Deal was only succeeding in finally eradicating mass unemployment by plunging the nation into war. But for many Americans then eking out a meager existence, that at best was an academic argument. It was only later, with the nation reaching its greatest affluence in history in conditions of peace, that the American people could afford the luxury of driving a President out of office.

Despite the violent resentments and vitriolic attacks that he inspired, there was never any serious effort to oust Roosevelt from office. If anything, thanks to a clever and often unscrupulous propaganda campaign directed by the White House, his opponents were depicted as "appeasers," "Fascists," "economic royalists," and much worse. And the majority of Americans loved it, as they demonstrated when he permitted himself to be drafted for an unprecedented third term in 1940. FDR won easily, then repeating his triumph—a dying man—in 1944. And today, because historians like Arthur Schlesinger and James MacGregor Burns were so enamored of FDR's strong presidency, a monumental bibliography attests to his greatness.

But some intellectuals are having second thoughts. As Professor Philip Kurland, a constitutional scholar at the University of Chicago Law School, has observed: "When it is a President with what has come to be called 'charisma,' a Franklin Delano Roosevelt or a John Fitzgerald Kennedy, some of us have applauded the seizure of power by the President. When that office is occupied by one whose objectives are less to our tastes, we deplore the power that has become his to exercise."

Thus when Richard Nixon charged that his administration was being judged by a double standard, it could be argued that he was indulging in uncharacteristic understatement.

Of course FDR has all but joined the deities on Olympus. When the Nixon tapes were published, former FDR aides insisted that the level of discussion in their White House was far more elevated. According to James Rowe, Jr., for example, FDR ruled the White House with "undiluted charm"; and he added, "I cannot ever remember hearing him swear." Yet some of the conversations between FDR and his aides were hardly charming.

On April 30, 1943—according to contemporaneous notes taken by his administrative assistant (and later press secretary) Jonathan Daniels—there was a discussion of the Fair Employment Practices Committee, reluctantly set up by FDR under Negro pressure. Also present in the Oval Office were Marvin McIntyre, a secretary to the President, and Elmer Davis, director of the Office of War Information. FDR agreed to Daniels's suggestion that FEPC problems "be centered in McIntyre rather than have several people around town fooling with it."* Daniels also proposed that the matter be settled before President Edwin Barclay of Liberia arrived in Washington for a visit.

Which reminded Roosevelt of his trip to Liberia following the Casablanca conference. While there, the President said he had talked to some medical officers who were appalled by the venereal disease rate among our Negro troops.

"I suppose it must be ten or twelve percent," the President said to one of the officers.

"Ten or twelve!" said the officer. "It's seventy-five percent."

The same officer had told the President that the venereal disease rate among Liberians was 100 percent.

"I suppose," FDR added, "they all get it before they are grown, as I understand there is no such thing as chastity in Liberia after the age of five or six."

Whereupon Elmer Davis wondered about President Barclay's condition. After all, he was coming for a stay at the White House. Davis suggested that they could wash off the toilet seat with Lysol. Following the war, Davis became one of American liberalism's most powerful voices on radio.**

According to Daniels, the conversation shifted in content but not in bawdiness. Davis said he had been having a row with the War Department, which had been grabbing off much of the rubber supply. As a result there was a shortage of elastic and women were bitterly complaining that they weren't able to keep their pants up. Davis said that the OWI had suggested to the War Department that if the army kept its soldiers at home at night it wouldn't make any difference.

"Such is the conversation in the presidential office on occasion," wrote Daniels.

On July 29, 1943, another "charming" discussion was held in the Oval Office. Present, besides the President and Daniels, was Welch Pogue, chairman of the Civil Aeronautics Board. Roosevelt got right to the point. He wanted to talk about the airline situation. He said he had discussed with the British, when Chamberlain was prime minister, the development of the West Indies

---

*This story and others are told in Jonathan Daniels's, *White House Witness: 1942–1945* (Garden City, N.Y.: Doubleday, 1975).
**In 1976, Earl Butz was forced to resign as Gerald Ford's Secretary of Agriculture because he told an anti-Black joke in private.

—British, American, Dutch, and French. And the way to do it, he said, was through the tourist. In other words, he added, he wanted those islands to produce more than "sugar and niggers."

On January 13, 1944, Daniels conferred with FDR's press secretary Stephen Early about adverse publicity Harry Hopkins had been receiving in connection with allegations that he had received a "jeweled payoff" from Lord Beaverbrook for having helped push through a multibillion-dollar Lend-Lease program to assist the beleaguered British. The allegations, first published in the anti-administration Washington *Times-Herald,* were picked up by Republican leaders, who demanded an explanation. Hopkins, of course, was FDR's most intimate adviser. And his wife issued a denial. "I don't even own one emerald," she said. "It's a lie. I never owned an emerald and don't own one now." In what seemed to be a White House denial, Early himself spoke of "the malicious rumors and statements now being published by certain newspapers hostile to the Government and to certain officials of the Government."

But Early had a different story to tell Daniels that frosty January morning. "The trouble is to find a clean spot on Harry anywhere," he said. The Beaverbrook jewels couldn't be explained away because, while they weren't emeralds, they most certainly were diamonds. "I have seen them myself," Early went on. "Fortunately for Harry they were antique diamond clips which had been in Beaverbrook's family for some time. Harry didn't declare them and smuggled them into the country. He sent them over to [Assistant Secretary of the Treasury] Gaston and said he wanted a statement from them to the effect that they were declared for duty and what about it. They had them appraised and examined and established the fact that they were antique and, as such, not subject to duty."

Dirty tricks as practiced in Roosevelt's time were also described by Daniels. It seems that while Vice President Wallace was Secretary of Agriculture, he had written a number of letters indicating that he was receiving inspiration for government policies from the spirit world. As David Niles, a presidential troubleshooter, told the story to Daniels on August 3, 1943, the letters had fallen into Republican hands some time during the 1940 campaign when FDR was running against Wendell Willkie.

A medium who had been fired from Agriculture apparently stole the letters right out of Wallace's files. Roy Howard was offered them for publication; though a good Republican he turned them down. The letters finally were purchased by another publisher, Paul Block, who sent a reporter to confront Wallace with them. Niles added: "We were afraid that Wallace, being an honest guy, would say, 'Yes, I wrote them—so what?' "

"Morris Ernst," Niles went on, "did a good job. He was sent West to meet Wallace, who was coming to Chicago, to see to it that this reporter didn't get to Wallace. Every day the Democrats expected the story to break. I must have lost fifty pounds in three weeks. We went out and dug up some dirty stuff on Willkie, with photographs showing that Willkie's father had been buried in potter's field as a drunkard with whom Willkie would have nothing to do. Only after the presidential campaign began did he have his body moved to a decent part of the cemetery. We let the Republicans know that if they used the Wallace stuff, we were going to use the stuff on Willkie. The Wallace letters were never used, but they are still in the possession of the Republicans."

The various Roosevelt campaigns were rough indeed. Former GOP chairman John D.M. Hamilton contends, for example, that his office was bugged when he was campaign manager for Alfred Landon's presidential race in 1936. Hamilton claims that the bugging was ordered by FDR's Secretary of the Interior Harold Ickes, who was known to have a penchant for illegal eavesdropping. The bugging in Hamilton's office was quickly discovered by the GOP's security expert. "We never announced anything or made any public charges," Hamilton told the *National Observer*. "We just used that phone to leak out wrong information to the Democrats to make them look silly, and when we wanted to say anything private, we went to another phone."

Hamilton Fish, who served as a New York congressman from 1921 to 1945, was a Republican high on FDR's "enemies" list. Though a fellow Harvard man and fellow mid-Hudson politician, Fish was barred from the White House because, FDR believed, he had made a nasty remark about the President's mother. This Fish denies. But the fact remains that Fish was an opponent of the New Deal who had built a following around the country. And, as war clouds thickened, Fish was one of the more vociferous leaders of the antiwar movement.

Almost from the beginning of FDR's reign he found himself harassed because of his anti-New Deal views, says Fish. In a letter to *The New York Times* at the height of the Ervin hearings, Fish recalled "a telephone call from Senator Reed in the nineteen-thirties to tell me that my phone was being tapped, and so were those of many other Republican members of Congress. . . ."

Two weeks before the outbreak of World War II Fish attended an interparliamentary conference in Norway as chairman of a congressional group where, he says, he "was promptly spied upon by our own Government. Reports of my visits with British Foreign Secretary Lord Halifax and French Foreign Minister Georges Bonnet are now resting in the archives of the State Department."

"And speaking of 'enemies,'" Fish continued, "no one had more political enemies than the highly vindictive FDR. I was one of them, and for five years my income tax reports were minutely investigated (as were my wife's). That effort occupied at least half a dozen Internal Revenue agents and must have cost at least $50,000. The result: I got an $80 refund.

"You might ask why I didn't complain to Speaker Rayburn when I found out that my wires were being tapped. There is a simple answer: He would have told me that there was nothing I could do about it.

"And this sums up the situation. During all of the Roosevelt and most of the Johnson Administrations, the Democrats controlled Congress, so no matter what a Democratic President would do, there was no chance whatever of having an open investigation, much less one broadcast nationwide on television."

Roosevelt had also ordered the FBI to put taps on the home telephones of several of his own top advisers, including Hopkins and Tommy "The Cork" Corcoran. FDR suspected that Hopkins's wife was leaking anti-administration information to the Washington *Times-Herald,* published by the rabidly anti-New Deal Eleanor ("Cissy") Patterson. Needless to say, there was no love lost between the President and this lady. When Morris Ernst wrote him saying he was going to interview the publisher on behalf of his client Walter Winchell and proposed to "examine Cissy down to her undies," the President asked not to be present on that occasion—"I have a weak stomach." Mrs. Patterson, incidentally, believed that she was being wiretapped; but there is nothing in FBI records to indicate that, if true, the Bureau had anything to do with it.

When Truman became President in 1945, he instructed his military aide, Brigadier General Harry Vaughan, to deal directly with J. Edgar Hoover. As a result Vaughan began receiving transcripts of the taps on FDR's aides. According to Vaughan, he showed Truman a transcript of the tap on Corcoran. The new President was most unimpressed. In fact he was horrified when he glanced at one transcript which was mainly about Mrs. Corcoran making appointments with her hairdresser. "Well, I don't give a goddam whether Mrs. Corcoran gets her hair fixed or doesn't get her hair fixed," Truman told Vaughan. "What the hell is that crap?"

"It's a wiretap," Vaughan replied.

"Cut them all off," the President said angrily. "Tell the FBI we haven't got any time for that kind of shit."

But the tap on Corcoran was not cut off. For Corcoran's activities reportedly chagrined Truman on the grounds that they might "interfere with the proper administration of government." According to the Senate Intelligence Committee, "More than 175 reports overheard on this wiretap, which continued until 1948, were delivered to the Truman White House."

As the French say: The more things change, the more they remain the same.

13

In an editorial published on March 4, 1975—seven months after Richard Nixon left for his self-imposed "exile" in San Clemente—the Washington *Star* had this to say: "Watergate investigators who so diligently dug into misuse of government agencies by the Nixon Administration managed, either accidentally or deliberately, to overlook or play down flagrant abuses by previous administrations."

For the moment let us rest the role of the media itself in participating in what amounted to a massive cover up of the political excesses and abuses of power of presidents who preceded Nixon. Suffice it to say that when evidence of such transgressions occasionally turned up in the course of investigations conducted by the Watergate Committee, for example, the nation's leading newspapers and television networks, for the most part, decided to ignore them.

And, for the most part, they still do.

In the same editorial the *Star* also said, in connection with high-level misuse of the FBI for political purposes: "One of the worst White House offenders appears to have been Lyndon Johnson."

This was pretty much the expert judgment of William Sullivan, formerly number three man at the FBI, who offered to testify before the Watergate Committee on behalf of the Nixon administration in order to "draw a very clear contrast" between its relationship with the FBI and that of previous administrations. At the time Sullivan told John Dean that his documented testimony would place the Nixon administration in "a very favorable light."

But the Democratic-controlled committee wasn't buying. Chairman Ervin explained that his mandate was to investigate the 1972 election and nothing else. There was no way that committee Republicans (or at least two of them) could budge the Great Constitutionalist. They just didn't have the votes.

According to the Sullivan memorandum, Johnson went much further than FDR in misusing the FBI. He had no hesitation about using the Bureau for personal investigations. Thus when Don Reynolds testified about kickbacks extorted from him in connection with life insurance policies he had sold Johnson, the President called for a thorough investigation of the insurance salesman. Among other things LBJ wanted the FBI to determine whether the Republicans had given Reynolds $25,000 for "bribery purposes." After running a check, the FBI reported no. But the Bureau (as did other investigatory agencies) did turn up some embarrassing personal information about Reynolds which the White House leaked to friendly newsmen.

Johnson also ordered top FBI officials to get him anything and everything about his 1964 Republican opponent, because Goldwater was a major general in the air force reserve and, according to LBJ, had more "secrets" than "we have in the White House."

According to Sullivan, Johnson would rely on "devious and complex" ways to "ask the FBI for derogatory information of one type or another on Senators in his own Democratic Party who were opposing him. This information he would give to Republican Senator Dirksen, who would use it with telling effect."

While the memo did not go into detail as to the kind of FBI information LBJ had provided the Senate Minority Leader, all indications were that the targets of the Dirksen assaults were legislators who opposed the President on Vietnam. Needless to say, the President had every right to zero in on adversaries even within his own party. Questionable, however, was the use he made of supposedly confidential information obtained by the FBI. This was information he was not entitled to in the first place. Moreover it was intelligence which the FBI should never have gathered.

In retrospect it is ironic that LBJ, who did so much to manipulate the FBI for improper purposes, himself feared Hoover's power. "I would rather have him inside the tent pissing out than outside the tent pissing in," the President once said. And, according to the Sullivan memorandum, LBJ was constantly asking whether the FBI had a wiretap on his phone.

But where LBJ really went overboard in violating all the rules was in ordering the FBI to set up a special squad to be used personally by him at both the 1964 and 1968 Democratic National Conventions. "The cover would be that it was a security squad to be used against militants," wrote Sullivan. "Nothing of this scope had ever been done before or since to my memory." And that, of course, applies to the Nixon administration.

Heading the thirty-one member "special squad" at Atlantic City, where the 1964 convention was held, was Cartha "Deke" DeLoach, then the FBI's liaison with LBJ.

The major assignment of the FBI task force was to set up electronic surveillance of several civil rights leaders, including Dr. Martin Luther King. At LBJ's direction "bugs" and wiretaps were installed in the hotel suite occupied by King and in a storefront that was used as a headquarters by several civil rights groups. Also monitored by electronic devices were James Farmer, then national director of the Congress of Racial Equality and later a high Nixon official, and Mrs. Fannie Lou Hamer, another civil rights activist.

The information gathered by the surveillances was reported directly to Johnson by DeLoach, on a direct telephone line to the Oval Office specially installed to bypass the White House switchboard. The President was given information on these electronic surveillances on almost an hourly basis all during convention week. Johnson's appetite for such information was insatiable.

That information included the doings of Attorney General Kennedy, especially what he was saying to King and others in the civil rights movement. This also involved physical surveillance of those delegates friendly to the Kennedy family. At the time the President was fearful—with some justification—that Bobby might seek to stampede the delegates into supporting him for Vice President.

Nevertheless Dr. King's civil liberties—among other things his right to privacy—were most definitely violated by an Imperial presidency gone bananas.

It was particularly ironic that the 1964 wiretapping and bugging involved both King and Kennedy, since the latter, as Attorney General, had ordered an earlier tap on the civil rights leader because of allegations that a Soviet-connected Communist was in his entourage.

Another irony was that nine years later the Watergate Committee was fully apprised of these shocking violations of political morality by the Johnson administration. Yet Chairman Ervin refused to permit the release of a staff memorandum on the subject, on the spurious grounds that the committee had not been empowered to look into anything but the 1972 election. That supposedly ironbound rule did not prevent the committee from publicizing Nixon misdeeds of preceding years.

The long-buried memo finally surfaced when Ronald Kessler of the Washington *Post* learned of its existence. On January 26, 1975, the *Post* published details of the document, which had summarized a 1973 interview with the former agent in charge of the FBI's office in Atlantic City.

The former agent, Leo Clark, was quoted as saying that the FBI operation was designed to gather intelligence on potential violence or disruptions at the convention. But, he conceded, he had been instructed by DeLoach not to inform the Secret Service of the operation, even though it supposedly was in charge of protecting the President. Nor was he to discuss the electronic surveillance with the FBI's Newark office, which was supposed to have coordinated security at the convention.

And there were these additional details:

On instructions from DeLoach, Clark determined where Dr. King and Jim Farmer would be staying while attending the convention. Clark said he was also told to check the whereabouts of other civil rights leaders with surveillance in mind.

After learning that King would be stopping at the Claridge Hotel, Clark was instructed to survey the building to determine the feasibility of installing wiretaps as well as microphone (bug) surveillance. Clark then arranged with the hotel management to provide King with adjoining rooms 1901, 1902, and 1903. Prior to King's arrival these rooms were surveyed by two FBI technical men.

Clark reserved a room for himself, a floor below King's suite. He said his room was used to monitor transmissions of wiretaps and bugs from Dr. King's quarters, as well as from an Atlantic Avenue storefront used by CORE and other groups. Though Clark did not say so, obviously a break-in had been necessary to install the electronic equipment at the storefront.

The conversations were monitored on a twenty-four-hour basis by FBI agents as well as tape-recorded. The information was transmitted by telephone to DeLoach and two other agents at a control center on the second floor of the old Post Office Building. According to the committee memo, Clark recalled overhearing DeLoach speaking on the telephone to President Johnson and to Director Hoover, giving them summary information from the technical surveillance.

In a DeLoach conversation with the President, Clark heard mention of discussions concerning the seating of delegates or delegations, of vice presidential candidate possibilities, and the identities of Congressmen and Senators going in and out of King's quarters.

Robert Kennedy's activities were of special interest, including his contacts with King. There was particular interest in learning who was seeking the support of the black leaders and the maneuvering of the black factions with regard to the seating of the Mississippi delegations.

The FBI also relied on paid informants, who infiltrated liberal and Black organizations and reported on their doings to DeLoach as well as FBI supervisor Elmer Todd. One of those paid informants was none other than Julius Hobson, who later became one of Washington's more militant Black spokesmen.* Among Hobson's assignments was reporting regularly on the challenge by the Negro-led Freedom Democratic party of Mississippi, which sent its own delegation to Atlantic City to demand that it be seated instead of the Jim Crow "Regulars."

Johnson was particularly interested in what was taking place inside the primarily Black delegation because he feared it might threaten the tight control he had over the convention. For one thing the President feared that the picketing by civil rights activists in behalf of unseating the mostly white "Regulars" would mar the façade of Democratic unity he was hoping to demonstrate to the country.

And, as Tom Wicker was to observe eleven years later in *The New York Times*, "There is no great difference in wiretapping the Democratic National Committee and the Mississippi Freedom Democratic Party."

"In one sense," Wicker went on, "it might even be to Mr. Nixon's credit that he used his private 'plumbers' in 1972 rather than perverting the FBI as Lyndon Johnson appears to have done in 1964. Nor does it seem likely that Mr. Nixon knew more

---

*An embarrassed Hobson later admitted to being paid $200 by the FBI, but he denied giving the Bureau any vital information. FBI sources, however, termed him "very productive."

of what was being done in his service than Mr. Johnson did, or President Kennedy before that."

At the 1964 Democratic Convention the FBI got false press credentials through NBC and thus was able to insert agents, posing as reporters, within left-wing and civil rights groups. According to an official FBI document, the agents "were furnished with NBC press credentials" through "cooperation with the management of NBC News."* A report on convention activities, written by DeLoach on August 29, 1964, contained these paragraphs:

> Additionally, we utilized a highly successful cover through cooperation of the (deleted) furnished us credentials. I selected several members of the squad to use this cover. As an example, one of our "reporters" was able to gain the confidence (deleted).
>
> Our "reporter" was so successful, in fact, that (deleted) "off the record information" for background purposes, which he requested our "reporter" not to print.
>
> One of our (deleted) successfully established contact with (deleted) Saturday night, August 22nd, and maintained this relationship throughout the course of the entire Convention. By midweek, he had become one of (deleted) confidants. This, of course, proved to be a highly valuable source of intelligence since (deleted) was constantly trying to incite racial groups to violence. . . .
>
> During the period when the Convention was actually in progress, we established a secondary command post at the Convention Hall Rotunda operated by an Agent using his "reporter" cover. As you know, the boardwalk was the center of agitation by dissident elements. Throughout the course of the Convention, pickets were active in the area immediately in front of the Convention Hall entrance. We necessarily kept these people under close observation.**

---

*NBC, in a statement by its chairman Julian Goodman, said that a company investigation had found nothing to corroborate the claim that FBI agents had received press credentials from the network, permitting them to pose as newsmen at the 1964 Democratic Convention. *The New York Times,* which carried the statement on November 23, 1975, quoted "executives at NBC News" as suggesting the possibility that the Democratic National Committee had provided the FBI with false NBC identification. The DNC, which had been playing the martyr's role since Watergate, said nothing. Obviously no one wanted to take responsibility for this "dirty trick."
**The deletions were made in the reproductions of the DeLoach memorandum published in Volume 6 of the hearings conducted by the Senate Intelligence Committee on the activities of the Federal Bureau of Investigation, pp. 496–497.

Counsel for the Freedom Democrats was none other than LBJ's old nemesis, Joe Rauh, and that was enough to trigger one of the President's tirades. When Rauh rejected a compromise proposed by LBJ confidant Fortas, the President himself ordered Walter Reuther to fly to Atlantic City and force Rauh, who was serving as counsel to the United Auto Workers, to accept it.

Not that LBJ gave a damn about the almost lily-white Mississippi delegation. He felt sure that, on returning home, it would wind up supporting Goldwater, which it did. But he believed that the militants were only interested in getting television coverage which would embarrass him. And, in fact, they were succeeding. A reporter later wrote that a top executive of one of the major TV networks was pushed into swift action when his secretary told him the White House was calling. "Get your goddam cameras off the niggers out front and back on the speaker's stand inside, goddam it!" the President shouted on the phone. Within minutes those cameras left the pickets on the outside of Convention Hall and began focusing on the tedium of the speaker's platform!

As it turned out, the conflicts were resolved quietly and commentators on the scene marveled at the perfect control Johnson appeared to be exerting on the proceedings from the White House. "The interesting question is why he had such complete control," wrote Walter Lippmann at the conclusion of the convention. "Quite evidently he is a great politician, but what is the secret of his greatness as a politician?"

It took a decade before the secret was learned. LBJ had known almost everything about what his possible opponents were doing and saying, unbeknownst to them. He had as much mastery over the proceedings as the Kremlin does at one of its "historic" gatherings. Nothing was left to chance. Even the contents of the convention's souvenir book required his approval. A White House aide was backstage to control the duration of the applause whenever LBJ's name was mentioned. Film clips shown to the delegates were to be cropped of all shots of Bobby Kennedy; and a documentary on the late President Kennedy, which was supposed to have been shown the first night, was not projected until the night after the nominations lest a groundswell be touched off for Bobby. Moreover the platform committee could not make a move without LBJ's approval. Among the planks he rejected were those calling for "peaceful demonstrations," legislative reapportionment, and disarmament.

Those who attended the uncontested convention, as did this writer, can only agree that it was probably one of the dullest ever held by either party. Which makes the FBI response to the Washington *Post* disclosure even more shocking. "As a result of a request from the White House," a spokesman said, "the FBI did coordinate the development of intelligence information concerning the plans of subversive, criminal and hoodlum groups attempting to disrupt the Democratic National Convention at Atlantic City in 1964."

There are several things wrong with this explanation. In the first place the targets weren't hoodlums. They were well-known civil rights leaders, including Dr. King. Secondly, if disruption had been the problem, then it didn't make sense for the White House and the FBI to have cut out the Secret Service, the regional FBI office, the local police and, for that matter, Attorney General Kennedy.

The shocking unlawfulness of the entire operation, as outlined by Leo Clark, who has since retired from the FBI after twenty-two years of service, is dramatized by the fact that Kennedy's approval was never requested. Instead, DeLoach indicated, Johnson had given strict orders to bypass the Attorney General.

Even *The New York Times,* which had been leading its constituency to believe that Richard Nixon was guilty of inventing every evil since original sin, became upset by the Clark testimony: "If the strong inferences to be drawn from the former agent's disclosure are correct, the 1964 incident is an even graver offense than the original Watergate break-in, for it represented the turning of a police instrument of Government to illegal activities for political purposes."

And, as Tom Wicker observed in the *Times,* the material in the files of the Watergate Committee "lends credence to Senator Goldwater's belief that, as Mr. Johnson's Republican opponent, he was wiretapped in 1964; and to Mr. Nixon's charge that when he was running against Hubert Humphrey in 1968, Mr. Johnson —still in the White House—eavesdropped on the Republican candidates."

Goldwater not only was wiretapped during the 1964 campaign, but he discovered that his Washington apartment had been "bugged." It had been an amateurish job and the Republican candidate quickly spotted the microphonic device in his living room. As he recalls the episode, he laughed and then yanked the "bug" out from behind a piece of furniture. After discussing the episode with aides, he forgot it during the heat of the campaign.

But in retrospect Goldwater wonders just how the bug had been installed inside his apartment. Obviously a break-in *à la* Watergate was involved. At the time he did not give the episode much thought, believing that was the way LBJ played the game. Nevertheless the candidate did warn Republican Chairman Dean Burch to make sure that LBJ's spies didn't "bug" national headquarters. Burch ordered certain offices soundproofed to prevent such happenings. And the entire headquarters was "swept" frequently to ensure against bugs as well as wiretaps.

At the height of the Watergate furor Goldwater told an Indianapolis press conference that if Democrats had been involved in a Watergate type of break-in, the media would have called it "cute" rather than criminal. "The press never goes after those things when it concerns a Democrat, just a Republican," he added.

"As far as cover ups go," the Arizonan went on, he believed there was more of a cover up involved at Chappaquiddick. "If I had run that girl off that bridge, you wouldn't have heard the end of it," he said.

Recalling 1964, Goldwater said, "I'm convinced that Johnson had my television speeches before I saw them. They seemed to know everything I was going to do, everything I was going to say. But again, if a Democrat does it, that's cute."

That the Democrats had access to Goldwater's speeches was confirmed by John Roche, a speechwriter for the Johnson-Humphrey campaign. "Somehow or other," he wrote, "we used to get advance texts of Senator Goldwater's key speeches. The consequence of this was that before Goldwater had even opened his mouth, we had five speakers primed to reply. Maybe he sent them over as a courtesy, but all I know is that when I innocently inquired how we got them, the reply was 'don't ask.'"

One of the sources of the speeches apparently was none other than E. Howard Hunt, Jr., later convicted as one of the masterminds of the Watergate break-in. In 1964 Hunt was serving as chief of covert action for the CIA's Domestic Operations Division. At that time he was ordered by C. Tracey Barnes to spy on Goldwater's campaign headquarters. He set up a special unit and arranged for a daily pick-up of "any and all information" about Goldwater and his plans. These included advance copies of the candidate's speeches, texts which often had not yet been made available to the press.

According to Hunt, Barnes had received orders to spy on Goldwater directly from the President. Hunt also testified that the materials picked up at Republican headquarters, including press releases and travel schedules, were delivered to White House aide Chester L. Cooper, a former CIA official.

As a Goldwater Republican himself, Hunt said he was opposed to the assignment. In fact he was "shocked by this intrusion into Goldwater's affairs." But he was told that it didn't make any difference, that "Johnson had ordered this activity and that Cooper would be the recipient of the information."

Cooper denied any knowledge of CIA surveillance of Goldwater, or even knowing Hunt. "I knew that we were getting Goldwater's speeches . . . the stuff that was going to the press," he said. "How the hell it got there, I don't know."

Obviously someone's memory appeared to be faulty—and only further probing by appropriate investigatory bodies could have helped ascertain the truth. But Chairman Ervin was not interested in digging into the sins of Democratic administrations.

Part of the story was later confirmed, however. Testifying before the House Select Committee on Intelligence on November 6, 1975, CIA Director William Colby acknowledged that in 1964 a CIA official attached to the National Security Council prepared campaign material for Johnson and, with the help of another CIA employee, got advance texts of Goldwater's speeches and reported regularly on the campaign to the CIA. The official was identified as Chester Cooper, then an assistant deputy director of intelligence. The other employee, a woman secretary, had since retired. No mention was made of Howard Hunt.

But, as Hunt later told *The New York Times,* he most definitely was involved in the CIA procurement of intelligence on LBJ's Republican opposition. And, explaining his involvement in Watergate, he added: "Since I'd done it once before for the CIA, why wouldn't I do it again for the White House?"

Hunt had also told all to Senator Howard Baker in the fall of 1973. Baker, a Republican member of the Watergate Committee, along with Fred Thompson, the minority counsel, had been quizzing the former intelligence agent about the CIA's domestic activities, seeking to determine whether there were any links between the Agency and Watergate.

After news of what Hunt had said during the interview leaked in the press, Goldwater disclosed that he had been informed that Hunt and a team "that could have been as many as thirty people not just working on me, but working on other people, too" had operated out of offices in downtown Washington. That such an office existed, several blocks from the White House, has been established. The office was located in the National Press Building. There Hunt and his staff ran another CIA operation known as Continental Press, which funded "much of the activities of the Frederick D. Praeger Publishing Company in New York," as well as supplying anti-Communist news articles to foreign clients.

During the campaign, Goldwater said, he was aware that he was being kept under surveillance. "I just assumed it was one man or two men assigned at the direction of the President. . . . It never bothered me. I never got upset about it. Oh, I guess (I) should have, but knowing Johnson as I did, I never got upset about it.

"I would naturally be concerned to learn what they did find out," Goldwater added, "not that I did anything wrong."

Goldwater not only believed that LBJ had mounted espionage against him, but he feared that someone within his staff might be playing a double game. The possibility of a double agent in his headquarters was raised by an extraordinary episode: Goldwater had planned a speech announcing the formation of a blue-chip GOP foreign policy advisory committee. Carefully guarded texts were given reporters on the candidate's plane—in the air. When they landed, Goldwater discovered that LBJ had stolen his thunder by announcing his own such committee. And that was just too coincidental.

"Too many funny things were going on," recalls Victor Gold, assistant campaign press secretary.

Talk about dirty tricks. Those used against the Arizonan were enough to make the 1972 campaign look like a Sunday school picnic. Yet, at the time, few in the media appeared to give a damn. If anything the press and television threw its resources into an all-out effort to depict Goldwater as some sort of war-mongering Fascist thug only interested in hurling the world into another war.

A choice example of media defamation of Goldwater was provided by correspondent Daniel Schorr, who reported to CBS from Germany that a post-convention trip to that country, planned by Goldwater, signaled a link between the "right-wing of the United States and that of Bavaria." The smear was plain: Goldwater was somehow involved with neo-Nazis.

"This is the damnedest lie I ever heard," Goldwater said publicly.

In a private conversation with me at the time, the senator said the allegation "made me sick to my stomach. It was a phony story by Schorr. My Jewish forebears were probably turning over in their graves."

A few days later Schorr broadcast this "clarifying statement":

"In speaking the other day of a move by Senator Goldwater to link up with these forces, I did not mean to suggest a conscious effort on his part *of which there is no proof here,* but rather a process of gravitation which is visible here."

Meanwhile the phony story was picked up around the country. The "clarifying statement" never clarified anything. Eventually Schorr returned to Washington, where a decade later he became the CBS expert on the evils of Watergate.

Not to be outdone, *The New York Times* published its own smear. A dispatch out of Germany reported that Goldwater "has been corresponding with the Sudeten-German leader, Hans Christoph Seebohm. . . . Competent informants said today that Mr. Goldwater and Mr. Seebohm, who is Transport Minister in Chancellor Ludwig Erhard's Cabinet, had been in 'frequent and friendly' correspondence for some time. . . . Mr. Seebohm was chastized by Chancellor Erhard last month after . . . he asserted that the Munich Agreement of 1938 remained a legally binding compact."

Several days later the newspaper that prints only the "news that's fit to print" was forced to report that Seebohm had denied that "he had been in friendly correspondence with Senator Goldwater." A Seebohm spokesman made it perfectly clear that the cabinet member had "never seen, never spoken to, and never exchanged letters with Senator Goldwater." The *Times,* caught with a phony story, offered this feeble explanation: ". . . the report was based on information from competent sources known to be informed of Dr. Seebohm's interest in the conservative movement in the United States."

Apparently it never occurred to the good, gray *Times* that the most competent source of information about Goldwater's activities was Goldwater himself.

Murray Kempton had predicted that the 1964 contest promised to be the "vilest" campaign in recent history. He could not have been more accurate. In fact the tactics used by Goldwater's opponents to defeat him were loathsome. He was vilified as a Nazi almost without letup. His sanity was questioned. And Big Media, with few exceptions, cooperated in the Democratic effort to portray the Arizonan as a "trigger-happy" warmonger easily capable of igniting Armegeddon.

Early in the campaign newspaper publisher John S. Knight had this to say: "Barry Goldwater is not my candidate, and I have done nothing to promote his Presidential aspirations. But I do think the Senator is getting shabby treatment from most of the news media." After reading many of the columnists, Knight could find "only a few who are not savagely cutting down Goldwater day after day." As for editorial cartoonists, they portrayed the senator "as belonging to the Neanderthal Age, or as a relic of the 19th Century." The publisher concluded: "Some editors are disturbed because Goldwater is teeing off on the newspapers and other news media for failing to present the news of his candidacy fairly and objectively. I can't say that I blame him. He hasn't had a fair shake."

Ten years later Barry Goldwater was "back in style," as James Naughton phrased it in *The New York Times*. The reason, Naughton wrote, is that "the blunt candor that devastated the Arizona Senator's campaign for the White House in 1964 appears to many to have become something of a national treasure in 1974."

14

IN OCTOBER 1973 BILL MOYERS, FORMER
top aide to President Johnson, devoted an hour-long telecast to
the evils of Watergate over the Public Broadcasting Service. And
he reminisced about the four and a half years he spent in the
White House:

"I . . . can testify as to how tempting it is to put the President's
interests above all others. You begin to confuse the office with the
man. And the man with the country.

"Life inside those iron gates takes on an existential quality. I
think with the President's mind. Therefore I am. To some extent
this happens in every administration. But the men in and around
the White House were measured by their zeal. Pity any grand-
mother who got in the way."

That was of course a reference to Charles Colson, who was
supposed to have said that he would even walk over his grandmo-
ther's grave in order to ensure Nixon's reelection.*

Needless to say, Moyers and his assorted guests, ranging from
the liberal Henry Steele Commager to the conservative George
Will, all disapproved of excessive loyalty to a President—any
President. Moyers, who had been LBJ's press secretary, speechwriter, and confidant, made the customary attack on "efforts to
use the FBI, CIA, IRS and Secret Service for political purposes."

It was quite a program, one which won for Moyers the highly
coveted Emmy Award.

But it should also have won for Moyers a prize for pompous and
hypocritical moralizing.

For we now know that this paragon of righteousness was on the
receiving end of political information garnered by the FBI at the
Democratic Convention in Atlantic City. Another recipient was
White House Chief of Staff Walter Jenkins. And after the convention was over, Moyers sent a note to "Deke" DeLoach thanking

---

*Colson himself denies having said this.

him and his fellow FBI agents for their "fine" work. In return DeLoach wrote Moyers as follows:

Thank you for your very thoughtful and generous note concerning our operation in Atlantic City. Please be assured that it was a pleasure and privilege to be able to be of assistance to the President, and all the boys that were with me felt honored in being selected for the assignment.

I think everything worked out well, and I'm certainly glad that we were able to come through with vital tidbits from time to time which were of assistance to you and Walter. You know you have only to call on us when a similar situation arises. . . .

Another piece of skulduggery in which Moyers was involved occurred two weeks before Election Day. As special assistant to the President he ordered the FBI to run a name check on numerous members of Goldwater's campaign and Senate staffs in an effort to obtain derogatory information about their possible sexual aberrations.

What the President was looking for, Moyers told the FBI, was information about "fags" and other perverts on the Arizonan's staff. Moyers's request came shortly after Jenkins himself had been arrested on a morals charge involving homosexuality. Embarrassed over what had happened to one of his oldest friends, the President insisted that the arrest had resulted from a Republican frame-up. And LBJ wanted to get even. Hence the Moyers request.

The ugly story came out as a result of the February 1975 appearance by Attorney General Edward H. Levi before the House Subcommittee on Constitutional Rights. The subject was the secret file J. Edgar Hoover had amassed over the years, consisting of derogatory information on presidents, members of Congress, federal officials, and others.

After the hearing Deputy Attorney General Laurence H. Silberman disclosed that the misuse of the Bureau's files and manpower had been made by several presidents. And among the examples he disclosed was Moyers's extraordinary request.

The FBI, which had no right to do so, did conduct inquiries into the bedroom proclivities of the Goldwater staffers; but, as the Bureau informed Moyers, it could come up with no derogatory information. That did not stop the President from calling in selected correspondents to the White House and making insinuations about what he knew of leading Republicans and their families, hinting that he would use the material "if they keep after my people."

More recently when asked about the revelations concerning his role in all of this unappetizing skulduggery, Moyers's first reaction was that he had "no recollection" of any of it. Yet within hours he was busy at the typewriter knocking out a column for *Newsweek* telling his side of the story.

In that column Moyers—a former Baptist preacher—came up with a sanitized version of what had occurred at the White House following the Jenkins affair. Johnson had stormed into his office, Moyers claimed, to say that Hoover had informed him that "Goldwater's people" may have "trapped" Walter Jenkins. Whereupon the President had ordered him to make certain that the FBI "find those bastards"—namely, the Republicans who he thought had set up the homosexual rendezvous for Jenkins.

And what did Moyers do?

Considering the criticism aimed at Nixon's staff as being too compliant and spineless—much of it leveled by moralizers like Moyers—what is more pertinent is what he did not do. Johnson's top aide did not arise righteously (and properly) to counsel the President against using a law enforcement agency for personal political ends.

Instead Moyers leaped to the phone, called "Deke" DeLoach, and gave him the President's instructions. Just as his boss had ordered.

So much for what was supposed to be the "unique" paranoia that afflicted the Nixon White House—and for the notion that pre-Nixon presidential aides were pure as Sunday school teachers in their ability to distinguish right from wrong, and to act on their better instincts.

The DeLoach investigation proved as politically brainless as the break-in at Ellsberg's psychiatrist—and as illegal. Walter Jenkins had not been "set up" by "Goldwater's people," as Moyers's boss had hoped to find.

Nevertheless the use of the FBI to conduct such inquiries about political opponents is just as shocking as anything that took place under Nixon. The difference, however, is that those responsible for the Watergate abuses have all suffered at least public opprobrium. But Moyers and other of his former colleagues are doing better than ever. Moyers, in fact, is now moralizing over the CBS Television network.

Like Colson with Nixon, Moyers labored without stint for LBJ.

"That boy has a bleeding ulcer," Johnson once proudly observed. "He works for me like a dog and is just as faithful. He never asks for anything—but for more work. He won't go home with that bleeding ulcer until nine or ten o'clock. I don't know what I'd do without him." And Moyers said the right things about a President "whose full scope of thought, fervor and personality can never be known to one man alive."

When it came to "ass-kissing," as one former LBJ aide told me, Moyers had few peers at the White House. "And there were a hell of a lot of ass-kissers around in those days. LBJ almost demanded it."

The most precious thing in Moyers's life was his relationship with the President; anyone who threatened that relationship could find the young Texan to be nasty indeed. He was constantly looking over his shoulder to see if anyone was gaining on him.

According to Eric Goldman, the in-house intellectual who eventually broke with LBJ, there were those in the White House who called Moyers "Elmer Gantry." Goldman thought the characterization "unfair, but it did suggest the air of completely satisfying rationalization with which he sometimes used stiletto tactics. As one staff man who found himself the victim of a Moyers thrust remarked, 'Whatever he does, he does with every assurance that he is carrying out the will of John the Baptist.' "

During the 1964 campaign itself Moyers achieved a merited reputation as the "hit man" of the Pedernales gang. Prior to Watergate he frequently boasted of the "dirty tricks" he employed against the Goldwater candidacy. For the former preacher shared his boss's determination not simply to beat Goldwater but to roll up the tremendous margin which would give LBJ his "mandate." And one reason LBJ wanted a roaring landslide was to make JFK's 118,000-vote victory of 1960 look, as Eric Goldman put it, "like a pathetic peep." For LBJ had had his bellyful of the so-called Kennedy legend.

These days Moyers doesn't do much boasting about the series of chilling TV commercials which portrayed Goldwater as an H-bomb fanatic. Remember the little girl plucking flower petals and then the world blowing up? Well, those contributions to hysteria were devised by Moyers in collaboration with the advertising agency Doyle Dane Bernbach.

The commercials, which were reviewed by Fortas and Clifford on behalf of the President, included another showing a little girl licking an ice cream cone. A woman's voice told the child how people used to explode atomic weapons in the air, and how the radioactive fallout made children die. She then explained how a man who wanted to be President had voted against a treaty to prevent all but underground nuclear tests. "His name is Barry Goldwater, so if he's elected, they might start testing all over again." The last words were almost drowned out by a crescendo of Geiger-counter clicks. Then came the male announcer's tag-line: "Vote for President Johnson on November Third. The stakes are too high for you to stay home."

Even Johnson supporters were revolted. As a result of various protests the Democrats stopped showing the commercials. But years later, in talking with Nick Thimmesch, Moyers proudly claimed to have "hung the nuclear noose around Goldwater and finished him off."

By this time Moyers had left the White House to become publisher of Long Island's *Newsday*. Then he began pontificating on public television and writing a column for *Newsweek*. It was through these channels that the former "hit man" of the Pedernales let it be known how appalled he was by the "dirty tricks" of the Watergate era.

Another feature of the 1964 campaign was the "Five O'clock Club" meetings at the White House, attended by bright young Democratic lawyers and junior officials. The purpose was to "discuss deviltry" and other tricks (as Theodore White put it) to be inflicted on Goldwater during the campaign. Known to insiders as the Anti-Campaign, it was conceived and watched over by Lyndon Johnson himself. As Evans and Novak later wrote, it was LBJ's "unique contribution to presidential campaigning," conducted with the absolute secrecy befitting a leader to whom "leaks" were anathema. As a result no word of the Anti-Campaign ever got out at the time.

What it was, pure and simple, was a clandestine "black propaganda" operation. Working out of quarters almost directly above the Oval Office itself, the Anti-Campaign had no chairman, kept no minutes, issued no statements, revealed no strategy. Its security-conscious members were well versed in propaganda. Their objective was to keep hitting at Goldwater by any means, fair or foul, in order to keep his campaign off balance.

They were successful. Often there were times when Goldwater did not know what hit him. And Johnson enjoyed every moment of it. As Evans and Novak reported: ". . . [White House Counsel Myer] Feldman was the bridge between Johnson and the propagandists and often rushed downstairs to the Oval Office to get the President's reaction before approving a specific plan."

No stone was left unturned to win for LBJ the greatest landslide in history. A certain winner when he began, early polls had given Johnson 80 percent of the vote. There was absolutely no way he could lose. Yet he unloosed a campaign of defamation against his opponent with few parallels in modern history. And the liberals loved it.

For example, speaking before the Steelworkers, LBJ referred to Goldwater as "a raving, ranting demagogue."

On another occasion he described himself as a man of peace and pictured his opponent as a man of war. At the same time LBJ promised, "We are not going to send American boys nine or ten thousand miles away from home to do what Asian boys ought to be doing for themselves." In still another of his nondemagogic speeches, LBJ bellowed: "Just because we're powerful, we can't mash a button and tell an independent country to go to hell, because they don't want to go to hell, and we don't get very far rattling our rockets or lobbing them into men's rooms. . . . The only real issue in this campaign, the only one that you ought to get concerned about, is who can best keep the peace."

His non-raving runningmate was more explicit. According to Hubert Humphrey, the election of Goldwater would make the United States "a garrison state in a nightmare world, isolated from everything except a nuclear reign of terror." Goldwater was "dead wrong—tragically, dangerously wrong. The solutions he offers are no solutions at all. They are instead a sure path to widening conflict and ultimately to a nuclear holocaust."

There were other voices of reason and moderation (as they billed themselves), some of whom follow.

Martin Luther King: "We see dangerous signs of Hitlerism in the Goldwater campaign. If Goldwater wins, I am absolutely convinced we will see the dark night of social disruption and such intensification of discontent and despair by Negroes that there is certain to be an outbreak of violence."

Postmaster General John Gronouski: "We know what Goldwater is talking about. Extremism is hate and divisiveness. It is spitting on the Ambassador to the United Nations. It is labeling the Chief Justice of the United States Supreme Court a traitor and a Communist. . . . It is justification for turning dogs loose on demonstrators, or bombing churches, or pouring acid in swimming pools."

Senator Fulbright: "Goldwater Republicanism is the closest thing in American politics to an equivalent of Russian Stalinism."

George Meany: "(There is) a parallel between Senator Barry Goldwater and Adolf Hitler."

California Governor "Pat" Brown: "Goldwater's acceptance speech had the stench of fascism. . . . All we needed to hear was 'Heil Hitler.'"

Democratic National Chairman John Bailey: "(Goldwater's platform) looks like a John Birch magazine . . . the platform writers have drawn up an exercise in fantasy, fear, and hate."

Columnist James Reston: "Goldwater must know that most of the extremist tyrants of history, from Caesar and Napoleon to Hitler and Stalin, acted in the name of liberty and justice."

Literary critic Maxwell Geismar: "(Goldwater) is a Doctor Strangelove incarnate; he is possessed, paranoidal, utterly evil, and close to suicidal. . . . I believe he is close to being an out-and-out monster."

Rarely in the history of American politics has so much vulgar rhetoric been loosed against such a good man. No wonder Goldwater said after the election, with his typical good humor, that when he had read all the White House-inspired attacks against him he nearly decided to vote for Johnson. After all, who would want to vote for a man who intended to widen the war in Southeast Asia, for example?

But within a year a bitter joke was circulating. A girl was supposed to have said, "I was told that if I voted for Goldwater we would be at war in six months. I did—and we were."

As it turned out, the man who did widen the war was none other than Johnson. Even while he was blasting Goldwater as a warmonger, LBJ had made up his mind to escalate the conflict by bombing North Vietnam—a fact he later confided to Charles W. Roberts of *Newsweek*. As he did not want to take the Congress into his confidence, he ordered his national security adviser, McGeorge Bundy, to draw up a resolution which would give him a free hand in Vietnam. The idea was to send it to Congress for approval at the proper time. Bundy later confirmed there was such a draft, explaining, "We had always anticipated . . . the possibility that things might take a more drastic turn at any time."

The right moment came after the U.S. destroyer *Maddox* was attacked by North Vietnamese torpedo boats in the Gulf of Tonkin. A second announcement followed quickly: North Vietnamese gunboats had struck again. And on the night of August 4, 1964, Johnson went on television to explain that he had ordered a retaliatory strike against the torpedo boats and their bases in North Vietnam.

Johnson then went to the Congress for a special resolution authorizing him to "take all necessary measures to repel any armed attack against the forces of the United States and to prevent further aggression." This meant that he could use the armed forces just about as he wished in Vietnam. The Congress gave him this blank check by an overwhelming vote.

But had the President deliberately misled the Congress and the American people on the Tonkin episode? Senator Fulbright, who had been LBJ's floor leader on the resolution, thought so after hearing testimony some years later. "I thought Johnson's story was on the level," said Fulbright. "But the story of the attack didn't hold up. It was an arranged incident to get a resolution creating unity behind any action he wanted to take."

In other words LBJ had lied to the American people.

But by rushing the Tonkin Resolution through the Congress, Johnson had also managed to box in Goldwater on Vietnam. Republicans on the attack found it difficult to accuse the President of being "soft on Communism." In fact, by raiding North Vietnam, LBJ looked like a tough hombre indeed.

Everything was coming up roses, Texas-style, for LBJ as the campaign entered its final weeks. Yet still the Democratic candidate was getting awfully annoyed at the hecklers who were crossing his campaign path. His top aide Marvin Watson, who was overseeing the advance work, reported that LBJ was very angry at the demonstrators.

"The President does not want them," Watson notified advance man Jerry Bruno. "See if you can eliminate them."

At the very next stop there was a man with an enormous "Goldwater for President" sign that LBJ could not miss. Watson was fit to be tied.

"I thought I told you we don't want any more signs and hecklers," Watson told Bruno. "Now get that down."

"It's impossible," replied Bruno. "We sent some people over there, but you can't tear down signs. It'll just look really bad."

Bruno thought that was the end of it. But as he was getting ready to leave, Watson called with a great idea.

"What about itching powder?" he asked.

"Itching powder?"

"Sure," said Watson. "Our advance men should carry a can with them. If they saw a heckler shouting or carrying a Goldwater sign, the advance men could throw some powder on the heckler, who'd have to stop what he was doing."

Bruno wrote that he rejected the idea, although he heard that in Houston "somebody did use it on some unfriendly people."

Obviously the "fear of dissent," to use a favorite phrase of *The New York Times*, was not confined to the Nixon era.

Nor were the practical jokes which later landed Donald Segretti and Dwight Chapin in the slammer. The Democratic trickster in 1964 was a Californian named Dick Tuck, who appeared to be spending his life devising schemes to make life miserable for Republicans. And the media loved every minute of it.

There was, for example, the Tuck-inspired caper approved by the Democratic National Committee itself, which involved infiltrating a good-looking brunette aboard the Goldwater campaign train. Her cover was that of a free-lance magazine writer. Her assignment was to slip copies of an anti-Goldwater flyer called *The Whistlestop* under the compartment doors of traveling correspondents.

The girl was twenty-three-year-old Moira O'Conner of Chicago. Shortly after the train left Washington bound for Ohio, Indiana, and Illinois, she got to work. Copies of *Whistlestop* were circulated surreptitiously. It promised to keep everyone informed "and, with considerable assistance from the Senator himself, amused." After listing four Republican newspapers in Ohio that had endorsed LBJ, the newsletter casually reassured the correspondents that fluoride (supposedly the *bête noire* of rightists) had not been added to the train's water supply.

Vic Gold, an assistant Goldwater press secretary, got up before dawn in search of the culprit. Instead he found copies of the second edition already slipped under nearly every compartment door.

"What followed," a dispatch by Charles Mohr to *The New York Times* reported the next day, "had the elements of an episode of an Ian Fleming or Eric Ambler thriller on the Orient Express rushing through the Balkan night.

"There were soft footfalls in the darkened corridors as the gently rocking Goldwater Express went rushing through the West Virginia night. There was a swift and ruthless search of baggage. And then came the pre-dawn discovery and confrontation of Miss O'Connor by . . . Vic Gold.

"She was caught silently slipping under compartment doors a new edition of *Whistlestop* contrasting the crowds Richard M. Nixon drew in Ohio in 1960 with what was expected for Mr. Goldwater today.

"Mr. Gold's words to the pretty Democratic spy were: 'I think you have made your last delivery, my dear.'"

Off she went at Parkersburg, West Virginia—"the spy who was thrown out into the cold," as Mohr reported—but not before admitting she had been assigned to the "mission" by Dick Tuck, who was employed as a "researcher" by the Democratic National Committee. Tuck happily showed up to claim authorship of the caper. And the press couldn't have had a better time reporting every humorous detail.*

For most of his career as a professional "prankster" Tuck concentrated his peculiar talents in efforts to annoy, if not harass, Nixon. And, as he tells it, he was quite successful in his chosen profession.

For a long time, Tuck reaped enormous media coverage with the story of how, when Nixon was in the middle of a whistlestop speech on his 1962 gubernatorial campaign train, it suddenly began pulling out of the station. A switchman had flashed a signal and the train rolled away.

The "switchman," wearing a railman's cap, was none other than Tuck or so the story went.

But what most of those who have written about the episode failed to note was the fact that the prank could easily have resulted in serious injuries to people standing close to the train. Imagine if Segretti had pulled that kind of stunt. He probably would have been imprisoned for life.

But anything went (and still does) when it comes to discomfiting Nixon. As David Halberstam has stated, Tuck's forte over the years was "the haunting of Richard Nixon." And the press loved it. It was only when Segretti began practicing pranks on the Democrats that the media discovered that "sabotage" was involved. The truth is that Segretti was a bumbling amateur compared to Tuck.

---

*The same press failed to see anything funny about the infiltration of another comely creature aboard McGovern's press plane in 1972. Her assignment was to keep the Republicans informed on what the Democratic candidate was saying out in the boondocks, but she did not interfere or play any "dirty tricks" on the Democrats. Yet disclosure of her activities led to cries of horror on the part of the same people who were so amused by Tuck's "spy" of eight years before.

At another Nixon rally in 1962, Tuck claimed credit for switching identification signs on the motorcade buses. One, labeled "Nixon," was ready to rush the candidate to a live television appearance. The other, labeled "VIP's," was standing by to take celebrities to the airport. The result, according to Tuck, was that Nixon found himself at the airport while his guests arrived at the television studio.

In a loving article in *The Village Voice*, Paul Hoffman chronicled several of Tuck's exploits. He noted, "On one of Nixon's California campaign swings, Tuck rode in the press bus, a tape recorder marked 'KRGT' slung over his shoulder—and blithely went his way obtaining advance texts of Nixon's speeches for Governor Brown—until someone on Nixon's staff checked and discovered there was no such station."

Significantly, few of those opposed to "dirty politics" looked askance at Tuck's shenanigans. In fact, Bruce Felknor, then executive director of the Fair Campaign Practices Committee, termed the shenanigans "magnificent nonsense." One wonders how Felknor later would have characterized Segretti's activities.

But even more significant, not once did Nixon or his aides ever complain publicly about Tuck. Annoyed as they were, they took the attitude that all's fair in love and politics.

Tuck next showed up at the 1964 Republican Convention in San Francisco. According to *Newsweek*, he wandered around creating havoc by spreading phony stories about rival candidates and setting one against another—which, the magazine noted, was "a tactic not too far removed from some of Segretti's machinations."

Once Goldwater became his party's nominee, he replaced Nixon as Tuck's chief victim. And one of Tuck's greatest fans was the man in the White House—Lyndon Johnson, who chortled every time he heard of the prankster's capers.

LBJ also chortled at what appeared to be an effort mounted by the Republican National Committee to infiltrate Democratic headquarters with a paid agent. The effort backfired, much to the chagrin of GOP officials.

The prospective spy was Louis Flax, a teletype operator for Reuters, in its Washington bureau. To make a few extra dollars, Flax was moonlighting at Democratic headquarters. His job was to teletype each day's secret schedules and other confidential campaign plans to the Democrats' network around the country.

Late one night Flax received a mysterious call. The caller

made a proposition. "All you would have to do," he whispered, "is get some friends of mine certain information and keep them up to date on any prospective campaign plans that you might come in contact with."

"I'm not interested in anything like that," said Flax.

The caller then delicately referred to "certain things" in Flax's background unknown to his Democratic employers. Quite obviously he was referring to a sixteen-month term Flax had spent in the Maryland House of Correction on a bad check charge.

"Wouldn't you consider this something in the order of blackmail?" the teletypist asked.

"Well," huffed the voice, "let's not use nasty words."

Flax was told to call a certain telephone number, ask for the chief of security, and identify himself as "Mr. Lewis." The telephone number was that of the Republican National Committee and an appointment was made for "Mr. Lewis" to come in.

Flax showed up at the appointed time and met with John Grenier, a top GOP official. A deal was worked out whereby Flax would obtain and deliver materials from Democratic headquarters.

After meeting with Grenier, Flax notified his superiors as to what had occurred. His boss was none other than Wayne Phillips, himself no stranger to political skulduggery. Phillips was absolutely delighted with the story and suggested that Flax play along with the Republicans.

Two days later double agent Flax-Lewis delivered his first shipment—a sheaf of Western Union carbons of secret messages screened by Phillips. Flax-Lewis was paid $1,000 in bills. The teletypist continued his double life for two weeks.

Flax's story was then given to the press. It gave Democratic Chairman Bailey an opportunity to crow over Republican skulduggery in the midst of a Goldwater campaign stressing morality in government.

When Grenier was asked by newsmen about the elaborate plot, he denied he knew anyone named Flax. Goldwater, however, thought the episode was the funniest thing he had heard all day. Besides, he confided, he would never have resorted to bribery since he was sure he'd be able to find a Democratic spy who'd work for nothing.

There was a period during the campaign, however, when things appeared not to be going too well for LBJ's all-out effort to amass the greatest vote in history. The Very Reverend Francis

B. Sayre, Jr.—Woodrow Wilson's grandson and the prestigious dean of the Episcopal Washington Cathedral—unloosed a blast at the Democratic candidate. In fact LBJ and the White House were rocked when Sayre characterized Johnson as "a man whose public house is splendid in its every appearance, but whose private lack of ethic must inevitably introduce termites at the very foundation."

Not that the Very Reverend was endorsing Goldwater. Far from it. He characterized the Republican nominee as "a man of dangerous ignorance." But Sayre, who had suffered through ninety minutes of a bitter name-calling attack directed at him when LBJ was Vice President and both were serving on the President's Committee on Equal Employment Opportunity, concentrated his fire on LBJ. The Washington *Star* commented that Sayre's "harsh pronouncement, we suspect, sums up the real mood of a great part of the electorate."

When Sayre unloosed this blast at his candidacy, LBJ did an uncharacteristic thing. On advice of his associates he bit his tongue and maintained silence. And though there was no official statement, the White House did let it be known that Sayre was an ardent Kennedyite, which, of course, explained everything.

But LBJ suffered an even more telling blow with the sleazy episode involving Walter Jenkins. One of Johnson's closest and most trusted aides, Jenkins had devoted his life to LBJ and had been by his side from the moment he entered the White House.

Ironically it was Jenkins who had sent out a memorandum to all heads of federal departments asking them to be super-careful about not getting caught with any security problems.

As LBJ's chief of staff, Jenkins wrote: "We have been somewhat concerned about our procedures in requesting security name checks . . . for appointees to the federal service. It would be unfortunate if undesirable individuals were put on the Federal payroll simply because sufficient precautions were not taken prior to their appointment."

Jenkins outlined new procedures designed to "prevent considerable embarrassment both to the Government and to the potential employee himself." It was obvious that, with the presidential campaign in full swing, the last thing the administration needed was "embarrassing" appointments.

Of course the man who sent out this warning was himself soon to become LBJ's greatest embarrassment. Just a month before Election Day, Jenkins was arrested in a pay toilet of the men's room of the YMCA, two blocks from the White House. It was not the first time Jenkins had been caught. The police had apprehended him in the same washroom in January 1959 in a similar homosexual episode. But at that time Jenkins chose to forfeit collateral and thus avoid a trial.

Somehow he managed to avoid publicity in the 1959 episode. The big question was whether LBJ had known of his close friend's aberration. Most certainly J. Edgar Hoover knew. Under normal circumstances the director would most certainly have informed LBJ.

Jenkins also tried to keep the news of his newest run-in with the law quiet. But within a week rumors had reached the three Washington dailies. Only one, the *Star*, sent a reporter out to check the arrest book at police headquarters. There he found that a "Jenkins, Walter Wilson (of) 3704 Huntington St., N.W." had been arrested on October 7, 1964, and charged with "disorderly conduct (pervert)."

The reporter then checked with Liz Carpenter, Mrs. Johnson's press secretary, who immediately scoffed at the story. She said she would get back to the reporter. When she did, she said that Jenkins would be in touch with him. But Jenkins never called. Instead he phoned Abe Fortas to say he was in serious trouble.

After listening to the story, Fortas tried to contact the President, who was campaigning in New York. When he was unable to do so, the lawyer acted on his own. He advised Jenkins to check into a hospital in order to be out of reach of reporters. At the same time, accompanied by Clark Clifford, Fortas went to the offices of the *Star* to plead for compassion. He said the unfortunate episode was an isolated incident brought on by hard work and the few drinks he had had at a cocktail party that evening. "Think of Jenkins's wife and six children," he pleaded. Fortas appeared startled when the editors brought up the 1959 episode. Nevertheless they agreed to withhold the story on learning that Jenkins would soon be asked to resign his post.

Fortas and Clifford then raced over to the offices of the *Post* and *Daily News*. After listening to the lawyers, the editors also agreed not to publish the story. As a student of Fortas's career has observed, "The mere fact of his presence at the [newspapers'] offices, along with another of the President's close advisers, amounted to pressure which any editor would have found difficult to resist."

But the rumors could not be contained. Without naming Jenkins, GOP National Chairman Dean Burch issued a one-sentence statement which caused a nationwide sensation: "The White House is desperately trying to suppress a major news story affecting the national security."

Later that day United Press International broke the story over its wires.

Meanwhile, according to Republican Senator Carl Curtis, "the book at the police station containing the Jenkins' arrest record disappeared. But . . . some of the men with whom I was working took a photograph of that particular police blotter before the book disappeared."

By this time Fortas had gotten through to LBJ. The news hit the President like a bombshell. As the guest of honor at the Al Smith dinner at the Waldorf-Astoria LBJ was obviously not himself. He seemed dazed, according to observers, and cut his speech in half, reading the remainder in a distracted monotone.

Fortas had advised the President to announce that he had asked for and received Jenkins's resignation. The announcement was made by Press Secretary George Reedy at an impromptu press conference at the Waldorf.

Fortas had also suggested that LBJ announce he had asked Edgar Hoover to make "an immediate and comprehensive inquiry on the case and report promptly to me and the American people." This too was done. But the credibility of the "inquiry" was immediately placed in jeopardy when it was disclosed that the director had sent a bouquet of flowers to Jenkins at the hospital with a warm personal note, signed "J. Edgar Hoover and Associates."

Nevertheless Jenkins's vulnerability to blackmail did raise the question in some people's minds as to whether he might ever have compromised national security. After all, Jenkins had been privy to every important secret in the White House. There was very little in the way of classified intelligence to which he did not have access. The Republicans, whose campaign had appeared to be floundering, seemed to have gotten a new lease on life. But not for long.

The results of a crash public opinion poll came in the next day. Oliver Quayle, who had taken the poll on LBJ's instructions, reported that the case would have little bearing on the results of the election. Only then did LBJ issue a statement of sympathy for Jenkins, who "has worked with me faithfully for twenty-five years" with "dedication, devotion and tireless labor."

Meanwhile LBJ took such a personal interest in the FBI's investigation ordered by him that he actually told the Bureau what its final report should contain. In substance the President said the report should state that Jenkins was overly tired, that he was a good family man and a hard worker, and that he was not "biologically" a homosexual.

Within the week Hoover sent the results of the Bureau's "extensive investigation" over to Acting Attorney General Nicholas Katzenbach. The FBI investigation, said the director, "disclosed no information that Mr. Jenkins has compromised the security or interests of the United States in any manner." The report, which was issued two weeks before the election, read like a commendation. It claimed that "a favorable appraisal of Mr. Jenkins' loyalty and dedication to the United States was given the FBI by more than three hundred of his associates, both business and social. . . ."

By this time the rush of events abroad completely overshadowed the Jenkins story. For one thing Khrushchev had been deposed in Moscow. Then the Chinese Communists exploded their first nuclear device. At the same time the British elected a Labor government. At home, there was a cliff-hanging World Series between the Yankees and the Cardinals.

But LBJ, now more than ever assured of victory, found it difficult to leave well enough alone. Not only was he harping on his conviction that the Republicans had "framed" Jenkins, but—while campaigning in San Diego—he remarked that Eisenhower had suffered from "the same type of problem" with one of his White House aides. It was a foolish thing to say. If anything, Ike had not hired the young man in the first place. Still, keeping the issue alive was stupid because, by seeking to link Eisenhower with sexual deviates, LBJ was risking political recriminations.

But by then nothing, not even crude mistakes, could prevent an LBJ avalanche. The results were a foregone conclusion.

Meanwhile Clark Clifford, generally known as one of the town's leading "fixers," with clout in the right places, was doing better than ever. Clifford was an expert in back-channel dealing, the sort of thing which was to arouse such horrified concern with the surfacing of what came to be known as the ITT "scandal" during the Nixon years.

Clifford's law firm had been hired in the early sixties by the duPonts of Delaware, when they were ordered to get rid of their General Motors stock because of antitrust implications. This meant that, unless Congress passed extraordinary legislation of forgiveness, the family faced a tax liability of more than $1 billion. According to Bill Greider in the Washington *Post,* Clifford was hired "to guide their argument through the inner branches of the executive branch. . . . Clifford, who was advising President Kennedy on foreign intelligence matters then, arranged some appointments for the folks from Wilmington—private audiences with the Treasury secretary, the Attorney General, the Deputy Attorney General, the Assistant Attorney General for Anti-Trust, and the General Counsel of the Treasury."

The arguments were apparently persuasive because the Justice Department, which had previously opposed special tax consideration for antitrust violators, let it be known that in this case it would make an exception. Before long, with administration approval, Congress passed a law slashing the potential tax liability of the duPonts by approximately $650 million.

Two years later Clifford's closeness to Johnson apparently did him little harm when the duPont tax matter again came up. The lawyer helped negotiate a favorable interpretation of the 1962 settlement—one that saved the duPonts (who probably considered it petty cash) at least $56 million in taxes.

Democratic party ties to Big Business were strengthened under Johnson. The new President took the attitude that people who benefited financially from his administration ought to be able to demonstrate their gratitude. Thus, for the 1964 convention at Atlantic City, the Democratic National Committee prepared a ninety-six-page "program," selling space in it at $15,000 a page. Lo and behold, the pages went like "hot cakes." Everyone—but particularly major defense contractors as well as trucking firms—wanted to advertise their wares in the "program." And why not? It was a good deal. For the Democrats had conveniently obtained an IRS ruling that, far from being considered illegal corporate gifts, the space orders were to be entered on the books as advertising costs which, of course, meant they were tax deductible as legitimate business expenses.

At the same time LBJ invented the President's Club, a device to provide special consideration to those captains of industry who saw the light and contributed accordingly. Among the contributors were August A. Busch and two of his employees at his brewing corporation. In May 1966 they contributed a total of $10,000 to LBJ's President's Club. A month later, in what was then regarded as a surprise decision, the Justice Department announced it was dropping an antitrust suit against the St. Louis company. Shortly after the announcement Vice President Humphrey and Donald Turner, head of Justice's antitrust division, flew out to St. Louis in Busch's private plane to attend the All-Star baseball game in Busch Stadium. This peculiar confluence of events was noticed by two Republican congressmen, Gerald R. Ford and Charles Goodell, who all but called the deal corrupt. But they didn't go that far. What Ford said was this: "The linking of political contributions and dismissal of anti-trust suits was too much of a coincidence to be ignored."

It was ignored. Aside from the Republican sniping, there was little reaction elsewhere. There was no impassioned outcry from the media, for example. That was only to come six years later when the Nixon administration got involved in the ITT case.

15

AMONG THE FRUITS OF THE ELECTRONIC surveillance of Dr. Martin Luther King launched under Attorney General Robert F. Kennedy was a rich lode of tapes on the civil rights leader's private activities in bedrooms across the land.

What those activities had to do with national security—the justification for Kennedy's authorization of the King wiretaps— is difficult to fathom. As the Justice Department itself has lately admitted, the purpose of the surveillance was "investigating the love life of a group leader for dissemination to the press." The "group leader" was later identified as Dr. King.

The electronic surveillance produced a massive number of recordings. Professor Alan Dershowitz of Harvard Law School, writing in *The New Republic,* estimated that 5,000 separate conversations went on tape, violating "the privacy of hundreds, perhaps thousands, of innocent King callers and visitors."

And what is amazing, in retrospect, is that not one of the many persons whose constitutional rights were definitely violated ever sued. Which is interesting in view of the suits later filed by complainants who alleged violation of their rights by the Nixon administration.

One of the secret recordings was of a party held by King and officials of the Southern Christian Leadership Conference, which he headed, at the Willard Hotel in the summer of 1963. This was at the time King was in Washington to deliver his famous "I have a dream" speech before a quarter of a million people in front of the Lincoln Memorial.

It was a mass rally for civil rights which neither President Kennedy nor his brother, the Attorney General, particularly wanted to take place. But they had no choice. Dr. King had informed the President that the demonstration would go on as planned with or without the administration's approval.

A copy of the recording of the Willard festivities was later sent secretly to Dr. King's wife, Coretta, by William C. Sullivan, then in charge of the FBI's counter-intelligence operations, on orders from Hoover.

Mrs. King has confirmed that she received the tape in January 1965. "I received a tape that was rather curious, unlabeled," she said recently. "As a matter of fact, Martin and I listened to the tape and we found much of it unintelligible. We concluded there was nothing in the tape to discredit him." They also concluded, she said, that the tape had been made covertly by the FBI.

But they couldn't prove it at the time. The fact remains that mailing of the tape not only was a violation of Bureau regulations but constituted a potential crime, in that it violated an FCC regulation prohibiting any government agency from disclosing contents of a taped or bugged conversation to a third party.

Wherever Dr. King went, he was the object of electronic surveillance. Room bugs were installed in hotels from coast to coast as the Black leader moved around the country. According to Arthur Murtagh, a retired agent attached to the FBI's Atlanta office, the moves against Dr. King were second in size "only to the way they went after Jimmy Hoffa."

Yet despite this massive surveillance there never was a criminal prosecution of Dr. King for violation of any federal or state law.

But a "monograph" on Dr. King's personal life was circulated among government officials during the Kennedy administration, according to two former FBI officials. *The New York Times* reported that when President Kennedy became aware of what was going on, he ordered Hoover to call back every copy. But the President did not order an end to the surveillance itself.

Nor did Johnson when he assumed the presidency. In fact LBJ eagerly received the tapes and transcripts of King's extracurricular activities. The new President not only read the accounts, which an aide described as being "like an erotic book," but also listened to the tapes, which included the noise of bedsprings. Later on when an aide defended Dr. King's antiwar activities, LBJ angrily retorted, "Goddammit, if only you could hear what that hypocritical preacher does sexually." (This from the same President who sometimes denounced electronic surveillance as "the worst thing in our society.")

According to a staff report of the Senate Intelligence Committee released in 1976, it was none other than Bill Moyers, then an assistant to President Johnson, who "expressly approved" the circulation within the Executive Branch of a secret FBI report on King. One section of the monograph dealt with King's personal life as ascertained from bugs placed in various hotel suites. The purpose of this and other such FBI reports was to destroy and discredit the civil rights leader, according to the Senate study.

Under questioning, Moyers testified that he was generally aware that the FBI reports contained material of a personal nature.

Had he ever asked why the FBI was transmitting this kind of information to the White House?

Moyers said he didn't remember. "I just assumed it was related to a fallout of the investigations concerning the Communist allegations, which is what the President was concerned about."

"Did you ever question the propriety of the FBI's disseminating that type of information?" Moyers was asked.

"I never questioned it, no," Moyers replied. "I thought it was spurious and irrelevant . . ."

"And you found nothing improper about the FBI's sending that information along also?"

"Unnecessary?" Moyers replied. "Improper at that time? No."

"Do you recall anyone in the White House ever questioning the impropriety of the FBI's disseminating this type of material?"

"I think . . . there were comments that tended to ridicule the FBI's doing this, but no."

Moyers said he had not suspected the FBI was covering Dr. King's activities with microphones, although he conceded, "I subsequently realized I should have assumed that. . . . The nature of the general references that were being made I realized later could only have come from that kind of knowledge unless there was an informer in Martin Luther King's presence a good bit of the time."

In his *Newsweek* column of March 10, 1975, Moyers claimed that Johnson's interest in Dr. King began when Attorney General Kennedy told him of the possibility that the civil rights leader might be getting Communist funds. Johnson became quite agitated. "There's not a God-dam thing you and I can do to help this civil rights thing," Moyers quoted LBJ as telling Kennedy, "if we put our arms around King and Jim Eastland [chairman of the Senate Internal Security Subcommittee] suddenly calls a press conference to announce that the good doctor-preacher is a Communist front. And don't think Hoover wouldn't tell him."

According to Moyers, the FBI investigations never established that King was a "Communist front." Instead the investigations turned up "some totally irrelevant information," which Hoover sent over to the White House. Though Moyers did not say it, this apparently was information concerning King's private conduct.

According to Moyers, too, there were times when LBJ "personally feared J. Edgar Hoover." But the President "learned to use Hoover even as Hoover was using him; that he was given to fits of uncontrollable suspicion, once lashing two of his aides for being as 'naive as newborn calves' about the Kennedys, Communists, and *The New York Times;* that he sometimes found gossip about other men's weaknesses a delicious hiatus from work. And that from these grew some of our worst excesses. . . ."

But for more than a decade Moyers did nothing about revealing those excesses, which he only recently indicated led to "constitutional violations." Like Nixon's aides after him, he covered up the transgressions in which he prominently figured. But, unlike Nixon's aides, he has done well and is highly thought of in media circles today.

What is astonishing about all this is that media executives had known for years that Dr. King was the object of illegal surveillance. They knew it when Dr. King was alive. And they knew it because FBI officials had come to them peddling gossip about King's sex life which could only have arisen from surreptitious recordings.

A case in point: In the spring of 1964, an FBI agent called on Eugene Patterson, then editor of the Atlanta *Constitution.* "You people have been giving support to Martin Luther King," the agent told Patterson. "Don't you owe it to your readers to tell them what kind of man he is? Our information is that while he postures as a great moral leader, he is running around with women. Don't you think your readers ought to know this?"

Patterson recalls telling the agent that "we didn't run a keyhole-peeking newspaper" and that "that kind of thing had nothing to do with the civil rights movement."

Nevertheless the agent suggested that the *Constitution* send a reporter and a photographer to a Florida airport that weekend in order to record a meeting between Dr. King and a woman. The agent said the information had come from an "informant," obviously meaning a bug. Patterson refused. As it turned out, the agent later told Patterson, the rendezvous was called off, "so it's a good thing you didn't send anybody down there."

Patterson discussed the episode with his publisher, Ralph McGill. According to Patterson, McGill, who was outraged, spoke of getting in touch with Attorney General Kennedy to advise him of what the FBI was up to. But Patterson never learned whether McGill did so. Patterson says that he himself "personally told this story to John Doar, one of Kennedy's assistants, and was appalled when I got no reaction from him, not even an indication he had heard what I said (and we were speaking face to face). I realized then that Hoover either was beyond Kennedy's control, or else Kennedy knew what Hoover was doing. McGill and I traded disappointed exclamations over this."

Of course Kennedy knew what Hoover was doing. And John Doar, who said nothing about the violations of Dr. King's civil liberties, was to say a great deal ten years later about other such violations as chief counsel of the Nixon impeachment inquiry. Yet, on balance, nothing that was done under Nixon could compare in grossness and inhumanity to what was done to Dr. King under Kennedy and Johnson. And in evaluating the abuses of power under Nixon in the impeachment proceedings, not once did Doar ever seek to place the evidence in the perspective of what he knew at first hand were far greater evils committed by the two presidents whom he so loyally served.

Patterson and McGill were not the only newsmen approached with information about King's alleged philandering. On November 25, 1964, according to the Senate Intelligence Committee, the Washington bureau chief of a "national news publication" told Nicholas B. Katzenbach, then Attorney General, that one of his reporters had been approached by the FBI and offered the opportunity to listen to "interesting" tape recordings involving the civil rights leader. So "shocked" was Katzenbach that he and Burke Marshall, the retiring head of the Civil Rights Division, flew to the LBJ Ranch.

"On that occasion," Katzenbach testified, "he and I informed the President of our conversation with the news editor and expressed in very strong terms our view that this was shocking conduct and politically extremely dangerous to the Presidency. I told the President that it should be stopped immediately and that he should personally contact Mr. Hoover. I received the impression that President Johnson took the matter very seriously and that he would do as I recommended."

The only record of this episode in the FBI files is a memorandum by DeLoach dated December 1, 1964, stating in part:

Bill Moyers, while I was at the White House today, advised that word had gotten to the President this afternoon that (the newsman) was telling all over town . . . that the FBI had told him that Martin Luther King was (excised). (The newsman), according to Moyers, had stated to several people that, "If the FBI will do this to Martin Luther King, they will undoubtedly do it to anyone for personal reasons."

Moyers stated the President wanted to get this word to us so we would know not to trust (the newsman). Moyers also stated that the President felt that (the newsman) lacked integrity and was certainly no lover of the Johnson Administration or the FBI. I told Moyers this was certainly obvious.

Though the name of "the newsman" was excised from the official record, he soon identified himself. It was none other than Ben Bradlee, who confirmed to a questioner that when he was bureau chief of *Newsweek* in 1964 he had informed Katzenbach of the offer made to one of his reporters. While he obviously was outraged at the time, what is significant is that Bradlee never published a word about the sleazy episode.

Also significant was the role of Moyers, who was later to win prizes for expounding on the evils of Watergate. Always the sycophant, the former Baptist preacher had passed on LBJ's warning to beware of the untrustworthy Bradlee who, as everyone in the Johnson administration knew, was an "enemy" because of his close Kennedy associations. But when asked in executive session, Moyers said he had no memory of any aspect of the episode. He recalled nothing about the incident involving Bradlee or about the discussion Katzenbach and Marshall had with the President. Nor did he recall ever hearing anything about the FBI offering to play the King recordings to reporters, or even ever having discussed the matter with DeLoach.

But he conceded under questioning that the DeLoach memo "sounds very plausible. I'm sure the President called me or he told me to tell him whatever" the document reflected.

"Did the President tell you that he understood that Bradlee was saying all over town that the Bureau had been offering tapes?"

"I can't remember the details of that. You know, I can't tell you the number of times the President was sounding off at Bradlee."

Also suffering a loss of memory was Katzenbach, Robert Kennedy's successor as Attorney General. When William Safire suggested that he had condoned the wiretapping and bugging of Dr.

King, for which Hoover had been so much maligned, Katzenbach angrily demanded an apology from the columnist.

Great was Katzenbach's surprise when he was confronted with what appeared to be his initials on documents authorizing the FBI to bug and wiretap Dr. King. He said he had no recollection of ever receiving the several memoranda containing the initials "N. deB. K." and if he had, he would most certainly have recalled them.

"Mr. Katzenbach," he was asked by the minority counsel of the Senate Intelligence Committee, "are you suggesting that what appears to be your initials on these documents in fact represent forgeries?"

"Let me be just as clear about that as I can," Katzenbach replied. "I have no recollection of receiving those documents, and I seriously believe that I would have recollected them had I received them. If they are my initials and if I put them on, then I am clearly mistaken in that recollection."

He insisted that the idea of bugging King's hotel room would have been repugnant to him.

Yet he conceded he had handwritten a note to Hoover on December 10, 1965, cautioning that "these are particularly delicate surveillances" and urging the importance of not involving "non-FBI people" in their installations.

"This document was found in the Bureau's King file," Katzenbach was told. "Do you remember what surveillances you were making references to, what delicate surveillances?"

"I don't recall . . ."

"In your opinion, could this note have referred to the three mentioned electronic surveillances against Dr. King?"

"On the face it says that it did. If I remember any recollection whatsoever of the first three documents, then it would seem to me to be a possibility. I point out that it could refer to almost everything."

Katzenbach's amazing forgetfulness in the face of documents carrying his initials and handwriting aroused none of the dismay which greeted the memory lapses of some Watergate figures. The media said virtually nothing about Katzenbach. More importantly the Special Prosecutor's Office which had, for example, prosecuted Dwight Chapin for not recalling what he had told Segretti, evinced no interest in the Katzenbach case. Chapin, of course, had gone to jail. Katzenbach went on to bigger and better things, one being a directorship of the Washington Post Company. There was a protest, however, at the 1976 corporate meeting. Washington attorney William Moore, holding an "Accuracy in Media" proxy, challenged the nomination on the grounds that, as Attorney General, Katzenbach had approved the FBI's "snoop and smear" tactics against Dr. King. Moore also noted that though at first Katzenbach had denied knowledge of the taps, it developed later that he had authorized them. Questioning whether Katzenbach should be elected to the board of the Washington *Post* if the charges were true, Moore invited the former Attorney General to comment on them. Katzenbach declined to do so. And *Post* publisher Kay Graham didn't think it was necessary either, since, she claimed, he had already done so elsewhere. The *Post*, of course, had achieved a worldwide reputation for its concern about civil liberties and its steadfast opposition to cover ups.

What people did sexually was always of tremendous interest to Lyndon Johnson. Consequently J. Edgar Hoover kept feeding the President startling tidbits about the kinky preferences of the high and mighty. LBJ exploded in laughter when, for example, he was told that a prominent Republican senator had been visiting a high-class Chicago whorehouse where his peculiar tastes were gratified. The informant, LBJ was told, was none other than the madam herself.

The Bureau had also planted bugs in two expensive bordellos in the Washington area. A high-placed source told *Newsweek* that there was a national security rationale for this. "The Bureau hoped to obtain tapes of foreign diplomats in compromising situations, to be used possibly in blackmailing them into working for the U.S."

But on several occasions the bugs picked up congressmen and other prominent Americans. Hoover, said *Newsweek*, would pass such intelligence on to Johnson, who often delighted in placing FBI dossiers on his desk in the Oval Office while subjecting vulnerable congressmen to political armtwisting.

And it was Joe Califano, of all people, who told the story of how his former boss "even had one Senator's mistress contacted to have her persuade her lover to vote to break a filibuster."*

---

*The story is told in Califano's recent book, *A Presidential Nation* (New York: Norton, 1975). The number of times Califano mentions "paranoia" in referring to his White House years is revealing.

Like occupants of the Oval Office before and after him, LBJ had no compunction about "leaking" stories to the press when it benefited him. But he had a "peculiar obsession" with leaks that didn't bear his imprimatur, according to Carl Rowan, who served under LBJ in several capacities. Rowan recalls that in 1961 Vice President Johnson told a startled group of State Department officials: "You're just a bunch of goddamned puppy dogs, running from one fire hydrant to the next."

As President LBJ had no compunction either about calling on the FBI to make "name checks" of media personalities. Years later the Senate Intelligence Committee determined that at least seven prominent journalists were so honored. They included NBC commentator David Brinkley, Associated Press reporter Peter Arnett, columnists Joseph Kraft and Peter Lisagor, and *Life*'s Richard Stolley (now managing editor of *People*).

Like Mrs. Roosevelt LBJ would also make unusual requests of the Bureau. He had heard rumors about the peculiar sexual habits of a boyfriend of one of his daughters. He asked the FBI to check them out discreetly. In this case the President's worst suspicions were confirmed.

According to *The New York Times*, LBJ also received details about Senator Robert Kennedy's personal activities and nightlife in Paris from what were described as "intelligence sources." This apparently was in early 1967 when Bobby charged around Europe talking to diplomats about the Vietnam war—and at night seeking out the company of such beautiful people as Candice Bergen. LBJ wanted all the details.

There had, of course, been rumors about LBJ's own interest in the ladies. Those rumors surfaced recently when Sally Quinn interviewed a young woman, once a confidante of the late President, who claimed that LBJ had even proposed marriage to her. The woman, Doris Kearns, now an associate professor of history at Harvard, was writing a book about LBJ.

Though the Johnson family said nothing about this disclosure, Bill Moyers said it was possible. "While I don't really know whether or not he ever said to Doris what she says he said," said Moyers, "I suspect she heard accurately what he said without understanding what he meant."

"LBJ," Moyers continued, "said many things to many people in the heat of anger, in the wiles of persuasion and in the passion of frustration which every President faces. He was given to stretching the truth to as thin a soup as necessary to feed a lot of people. . . . He never proposed marriage to me, but he made me feel sometimes as if I might be an illegitimate son."

And there were times toward the end of their relationship when LBJ most definitely considered Billie-boy "illegitimate." There was little love, at least on LBJ's part, when the former Baptist minister decided to leave the "plantation," as the White House was being called because of the way LBJ cracked the whip. The reason Moyers quit—LBJ told Walter Trohan—was because he wanted to be Secretary of State and Johnson didn't consider him qualified.

At that time Marvin Watson had become the overseer of the "plantation." He was called in from Dallas, where he had been the assistant to the president of the Lone Star Steel Company as well as chairman of the Texas State Democratic Committee. Joining LBJ's staff as appointments secretary, Watson was introduced to reporters by the President himself. "Marvin," said LBJ, "is as wise as my daddy, gentle as my mama, and loyal to my side as Lady Bird."

Reporters soon discovered that Watson was running a veritable Gestapo in the White House. "To begin with," wrote Joseph Alsop on January 17, 1966,

> a part of the curious espionage system to which members of the White House staff are subjected has been rudely brought into the open. All staff members' telephone calls are noted. All places they visit outside the White House are reported by the government chauffeurs. And these lists of contacts are nightly studied, for symptoms of dangerous associations, by the President's new alter ego, Marvin Watson.

Moyers had come up with an extraordinary explanation for Watson's nightly list perusals. The press secretary said they were solely motivated by a desire to achieve operating economies.

"Yet," Alsop continued,

> it is of course an open secret that the telephone and limousine checks are only parts of a much wider system of surveillance that now covers most of the city of Washington. It is informal, but it works very efficiently.
>
> In brief, a great many sleazy persons are now aware that the quickest way to make brownie points at the White House is to pass the word that X has been seen talking to Y. Thus it is now an odds-on bet that any X-Y meeting in a restaurant or other public

place, will soon be added to the White House's dangerous associations list.

In addition, wrote Alsop, "the President's attempts at news control are much more aggressive, comprehensive, and, one must add, repugnant to the American tradition, than any such attempts by other Presidents." Only sharp protests, for example, prevented a total news control system from being instituted at the State Department.

The explanation by Moyers was most revealing. "It's very important for a President to maintain his options up until the moment of decision. And for someone to speculate, days or weeks in advance, that he is going to do thus and thus, is to deny to the President the latitude he needs in order to make, in the light of the existing circumstances, the best possible decision."

To which Alsop commented:

> Taken literally, this extraordinary statement appears to mean that the President cannot do whatever his duty requires him to do, if someone or other has already suggested in print that this is indeed what his duty will require. . . . Most Presidents have, of course, tried, in one way or another, to manipulate the front and editorial pages of the press. But no previous President has claimed the right to keep from the country the basic facts of the national situation unless he sees fit to divulge them. This is the novelty, and a most alarming novelty it is!

LBJ's interest in other people's private business went back to his days in the Senate, according to Abigail McCarthy. The wife of former Senator Eugene McCarthy, Abigail tells in her book how, in Johnson's years as Majority Leader,

> he frequently boasted in off-the-record sessions that no telephone call went in or out of the Senate wing or the office buildings that he did not know about. News people who visited his ranch and telephoned out their stories told half humorously of incidents when they could hear heavy breathing on the line as they did so. One woman reporter was quoted as having said, "Was that all right, Mr. President?" when she finished. The story was probably apocryphal but was widely believed.

By the summer of 1966, Mrs. McCarthy continued,

> it was taken for granted that most office phones and the phones in officials' houses were tapped. This was probably absurd, considering the number of man-hours that would have been involved in

such wide-scale surveillance. Yet the fact that it was believed and acted upon is evidence of the unhealthy miasma of fear and doubt which hung over the city.

The wife of a high official in the Administration who had been my friend told me quite seriously that we should communicate with each other by note or personal visit in some neutral place.

After Gene McCarthy declared he would contest LBJ for the nomination, the official's wife arranged for Abigail to meet her at New York's Grand Central Station, where it could appear that they had run into each other by accident.

Such was life in LBJ's Washington.

According to the Sullivan memorandum, it was Marvin Watson who asked the FBI to "monitor" the Senate Foreign Relations Committee hearings on the Vietnam war. The President, Watson said, was worried about "his policies losing ground." The President also wanted the Bureau to check out rumors that Chairman Fulbright and perhaps other committee members were receiving information from Communists. But, according to Sullivan, "there was no evidence of this."

A similar White House request, according to an FBI memo prepared for the Senate Intelligence Committee, was channeled through Attorney General Ramsey Clark, who supplied a presidential aide with a summary of information concerning the National Committee for a Sane Nuclear Policy.

LBJ was convinced that the Soviets (if not, the Chicoms) were behind much of the opposition to Vietnam in the Congress and the media. Thanks to the FBI he would boast about how he knew within minutes just what Fulbright had told the Soviet ambassador at lunch at the embassy and what Russian agents had told other members of Congress at cocktail parties.

On another occasion, according to the Sullivan memorandum, LBJ asked the FBI to find out whether top Republicans hadn't encouraged the July 1964 race riots in Manhattan as a means of embarrassing the White House. When the FBI reported it could find no such evidence, the President asked again, "Weren't there at least one or two Republicans involved?" And again the answer was no.

On other occasions Johnson was convinced that the Chinese Communists were bankrolling Black militants in the ghettos as well as the peace marches in the streets. "I damn well know there's Red Chinese money involved," he told aides.

After one big "peace" rally in New York, LBJ told reporters at his ranch that he was carefully reading a lengthy FBI report on who was behind the "anti-war activity." It was after this particular rally, at which Dr. King spoke, that the FBI was given the go-ahead to circulate stories about King's "moral turpitude." Even more significant was the fact that those who wrote to the President protesting his Vietnam policies invariably received replies from the Internal Security Division of the Justice Department.

"Some of President Johnson's requests parallel those of President Roosevelt twenty-five years earlier," commented a staff report of the Senate Intelligence Committee. "The FBI complied with White House requests for name checks on dozens of persons who signed telegrams critical of U.S. Vietnam policy in 1965. The names of other Presidential critics were also sent to the Bureau to be checked and reported on, as were the names of critics of the Warren Commission. The FBI also volunteered reports on Presidential critics."

LBJ also went overboard in sending the FBI into the Dominican Republic when leftists mounted an effort to seize control there. It was a complicated situation, one involving an effort by the ineffectual Juan Bosch to resume the presidency of that tiny Caribbean nation. On sending U.S. Ambassador W. Tapley Bennett back to Santo Domingo, LBJ said sternly that under no condition would he permit "another Cuba in this hemisphere." Above all, the President did not want Bosch back in power. "Giving the Dominican Republic back to Juan Bosch," he said, "would be like turning it over to Arthur Schlesinger, Jr."

Perhaps there was a need for American intervention. But LBJ muddied the waters when he exaggerated the dangers faced by Americans remaining in the Dominican Republic. In fact he made up stories out of the whole cloth to explain the necessity for sending in the Marines.

At one news conference LBJ said: "Some fifteen hundred innocent people were murdered and shot, and their heads cut off, and . . . as we talked to our Ambassador to confirm the horror and tragedy and the unbelievable fact that they were firing on Americans and the American Embassy, he was talking to us from under a desk, while bullets were going through his windows, and he had a thousand American men, women and children assembled in the hotel who were pleading with their President to help preserve their lives."

Testifying later before the Senate Foreign Relations Committee, Bennett termed the whole story a fabrication. No one had been beheaded; no bullets had splattered the embassy; and he had never had to hide under his desk.

The dispatch of FBI agents to a foreign clime was actually unnecessary. They were supposed to look for Communists seeking to seize the Dominican Republic. But, if anything, that was a job for the CIA, not the FBI. As two Bureau officials later told Dan Thomasson of Scripps-Howard News Service, the gesture was "purely political" and "strictly for domestic political consumption." The FBI had no reason to be there.

Also according to Thomasson, LBJ frequently manipulated investigations of his appointees. There was, of course, the President's effort to influence the FBI report on Walter Jenkins. Other examples included a man being considered for an ambassadorial post who had some personal problems. Several former FBI officials claimed that Johnson asked them to "interview twenty-five persons, and when we turned up derogatory information he asked for thirty-five and then forty-five to balance off the bad data." At last LBJ ordered Clyde Tolson, Hoover's top assistant, to conduct a "final interview," and LBJ made the appointment on the basis of that interview.

Rarely had any other Chief Executive taken such a direct interest in the FBI and its functions. This went for other federal agencies as well. Thus LBJ kept personally informed on major tax cases. And the President, who had no right to such information, would enjoy talking about confidential IRS findings with his cronies. Of course this was nothing new.

Biographer Alfred Steinberg tells the story of how LBJ reacted when a TV news commentator on the 11:00 P.M. news made a mildly critical comment about the President. "I was expecting a tax refund from Internal Revenue at the time," the commentator said, "but a few days later I was notified that court action would soon be instituted against me for failure to pay my taxes. I was certain the IRS had made a mistake, but my lawyer told me that I was in for real trouble: Johnson had heard me make the offending remark. So I took the only course available to me. I called Sheldon Cohen, the director of IRS, and told him I wanted to run a special half-hour show directly with him and also work up a series of a half-dozen shows on the wonders of the Internal Revenue Service. The tax action was dropped."

LBJ was particularly sensitive, and justifiably so, about false rumors concerning his own possible complicity in the Kennedy assassination. From the moment the evil deed occurred, irresponsible rumormongers began noting that it had taken place in LBJ's own state on a political mission that had been urgently requested by Johnson.

The new President immediately set up a blue-ribbon commission headed by Chief Justice Warren to make a painstaking investigation of the tragic events of November 22 and issue a report on its findings to the nation. The Warren Commission issued a document of nearly 900 pages which, claiming there was no plot, pointed the finger directly at Lee Harvey Oswald as the sole slayer.

From the beginning, however, there were critics of the Warren Report. Some of them, for example, did not believe that Oswald—if he were indeed involved—was the sole killer. Others could not believe that a single bullet could have passed through the bodies of both Kennedy and Governor John Connally.

The "assassination critics," as they were called, began to receive a great amount of attention. One of them, in fact, wrote a best-selling book called *Rush to Judgment.* All of which renewed doubts about Dallas, as well as promoting conspiracy theories.

In 1965 Marvin Watson asked the FBI to provide the White House with background information on seven of the critics. Members of the commission also received copies of the FBI data. In January 1975 Hale Boggs, Jr., disclosed that his father, the late Representative Hale Boggs, who had been a member of the commission, received a file from the FBI with derogatory information about the critics of the commission's work.* But the report that went to the White House apparently was much more detailed than that received by the Louisiana Democrat. Portions of the FBI document were leaked to friendly newsmen. And Lyndon Johnson was pleased that the leftwing backgrounds of several of the critics were well publicized. For he felt that many of the critics had been aiming their shafts at him.

Like other presidents LBJ could brook no criticism. But he responded in a particularly ill-tempered manner when Eartha Kitt attacked the Vietnam war at a White House luncheon given by Lady Bird. It was a boorish thing for the Black songstress to

---

*Hoover would frequently refer to Boggs as "the old drunk from Louisiana." Boggs, in later years, would insist that he and other members of Congress had been wiretapped by the FBI, but he was never able to produce any proof to support his charge.

do; but it hardly called for a CIA investigation—which is exactly what occurred.

A file on Miss Kitt's background was hastily compiled and transmitted to the White House. It contained numerous allegations concerning her romantic attachments. What they had to do with national security is difficult to understand. The reason the CIA was brought in, it was said, was because of Miss Kitt's long residence in foreign countries. But the FBI was active, too, as it turned out. In her book *Alone with Me,* Miss Kitt contends that LBJ personally ordered a "subversive name check" on her just hours after her clash with Mrs. Johnson. And she reproduced sections of an FBI dossier compiled on her activities by several government agencies, including the CIA and the National Security Agency.

At a Washington *Post* Book and Author Luncheon in February 1976 Miss Kitt challenged former LBJ aide Jack Valenti's syrupy appraisal of the late President. "You said that he had a good side to him," Miss Kitt said in her sultry voice. But, she went on, "there was one thing that struck me so strongly, that personally I have knowledge of, that he was mean." She claimed that after the White House episode her career as an entertainer was severely damaged in the United States.

The CIA became involved with domestic dissidents in a big way after numerous requests by Johnson for information linking the "peaceniks" with Communist governments. On August 15, 1967, Richard Helms, then CIA director, set up a unit within the Agency's Counterintelligence Office to check into the possibility of such foreign links.

Johnson, meanwhile, had appointed a commission headed by Governor Otto Kerner of Illinois to study racial outbreaks and find a way to prevent more of them. One of the first requests of the Kerner Commission was to the CIA for any information the Agency might have developed about foreign stimulation of the ghetto riots. Helms wrote back, saying that while the Agency had no involvement in domestic security, the CIA did have some limited material from abroad which might be of interest.

In all, files on about 10,000 American citizens were eventually established in the Counterintelligence Office. About two-thirds of them were originated because of requests by the FBI for information on the activities of Americans abroad, or by the filing of reports received from the FBI. These were the files made famous by Seymour M. Hersh in *The New York Times.* According to Hersh, the CIA had "conducted a massive illegal domestic intelligence operation during the Nixon Administration against the anti-war movement and other dissident groups in the United States." The trouble with his story was not only that it exaggerated what had taken place but that it pinned the blame largely on the Nixon administration. The truth is that much of what were alleged to have been direct violations of the CIA charter originated and were carried out under Johnson.

A number of former Johnson administration officials claimed there was no presidential directive ordering the CIA to set up a special office to handle domestic intelligence about radical and antiwar groups. Helms had testified under oath that he had initiated the special office "in response to the express concern of the President."

One of those officials, however, Dean Rusk, did recall that the administration had developed some "hard evidence" that foreign governments were indeed involved in supporting the antiwar efforts. The administration decided against making its information available, Rusk said, because "we didn't want to smear all the others who were legitimately against the war."

Joe Califano, who had been a special assistant to LBJ and later general counsel to the Democratic National Committee, said he was "stunned, really stunned" when he read the story about Dick Helms's testimony. The former aide said he had no knowledge of any presidential directive authorizing the CIA to monitor radical activities. Califano, who had been directly involved in the White House response to the civil rights riots and other disturbances in the 1960s, said, "I had to ask myself after reading it— were there two White Houses in 1967?"

There also appeared to be two Ramsey Clarks. One was the more widely known liberal Clark, so liberal, in fact, that in one of his more private moments Johnson said of his Attorney General: "If Stokely Carmichael was knocking at the White House door with a Bowie knife in one hand and a pistol in the other, Ramsey Clark wouldn't arrest him."

The other, perhaps the more real Clark, was Attorney General when domestic spying was escalated to an enormous operation, aimed at Black community leaders, antiwar activists, New Left radicals—anyone the administration regarded as a threat to national security. And all of this was done on Clark's express directions.

Ever since 1968 when he left Washington, however, Clark has

been in the forefront of movements to defend dissenters, violent or otherwise. Not only did he emerge as a leader of the American Civil Liberties Union, but he has devoted considerable time as an attorney to representing extremists in trouble with the law. Needless to say, he is now opposed to the very kind of secret government activities which he himself assiduously promoted as Attorney General.

Except that Clark has never leveled with his public on what kind of shady activities he engaged in as the nation's chief legal officer—that is, "shady" in light of the post-Watergate morality.

The story was told in part by the President's Commission on CIA Activities Within the United States, which was headed by Vice President Rockefeller. Generally overlooked in the coverage of the report to President Ford was the startling finding that it was "the Justice Department under Attorney General Ramsey Clark (which) established the first in a series of secret units designed to collate and evaluate information concerning the growing domestic disorder and violence."

The finding was especially startling because of Clark's image as one who has been excessively liberal in his approach to dissenters. And it was because of that image that Nixon, during his 1968 campaign, argued the necessity of ridding Washington of the overly permissive Clark for a tougher Attorney General.

Just as startling was the Rockefeller Commission's disclosure of the identity of the man who assisted Clark in getting the "goods" on dissenters. Why, it was none other than that paragon of virtue, the Honorable John Doar, who later was to make a name for himself as the "fearless" counsel to the House Judiciary Committee in its Nixon impeachment proceedings. (Among the charges leveled against Nixon by Doar was that the President had trampled on the civil liberties of antiwar people and other nonconformists.)

To quote the Rockefeller Report:

> In early fall, 1967, Attorney General Clark asked John Doar, Assistant Attorney General for Civil Rights, to report on the Department's facilities for organizing information on individuals involved in civil disorders. On September 27, 1967, Doar recommended establishment of a "single intelligence unit to analyze the FBI information we receive about certain persons and groups who make the urban ghetto their base of operation."
>
> The FBI was to constitute only one source of information for the proposed unit. As additional sources, Doar suggested federal pov-

erty programs, Labor Department programs, and neighborhood legal services. Doar recognized the "sensitivity" of using such additional sources, but he nevertheless thought these sources would have access to relevant facts. Other sources of dissident information suggested by Doar included the intelligence unit of the Internal Revenue Service and perhaps the Post Office Department. The CIA was not among the proposed sources.

In a memorandum dated November 9, 1967, Attorney General Clark gave full approval to Doar's recommendation. Clark found it "imperative" that the Justice Department obtain "the most comprehensive intelligence possible regarding organized or other purposeful stimulation of domestic dissension, civil disorders and riots." He appointed a committee of four assistant attorneys general to make recommendations concerning the organization and functioning of the proposed unit.

"Planning and creation of the unit must be kept in strictest confidence," Clark's memorandum stated.

On December 6, 1967, the committee suggested that the new unit, in addition to analyzing FBI information, should develop contacts with other intelligence agencies, including the CIA, as sources of possible information. Following this recommendation, Clark directed the organization of the Interdivision Information Unit.

Objectives of the IDIU were: ". . . reviewing and reducing to quickly retrievable form all information that may come to this Department relating to organizations and individuals throughout the country who may play a role, whether purposefully or not, either in instigating or spreading civil disorders or in preventing or checking them."

After its organization, the IDIU also began collecting, collating, and computerizing information on antiwar activists and other dissidents. Daily reports went directly to Ramsey Clark's office. Regular reports went to the White House.

Doar's memo to Clark, written September 27, 1967, after he had returned to Washington following the Detroit riots, noted that a "special problem" existed with the Community Relations Service, an agency formed by the 1964 Civil Rights Act to help solve disputes in that area. "Generally," said Doar, "the service feels that if it passes on information it learns in the course of its business about activities in the urban areas that [sic] it will lose its credibility with people in the ghetto. My personal view is that the service is in the Department of Justice and should bring to the Department's attention any information which you request it to furnish."

Roger Wilkins, then head of the Community Relations Service, thought otherwise. He claimed his people were already too busy trying to break down the suspicion in Black areas that they were spies. Now a member of the editorial board of *The New York Times,* Wilkins says he "made it clear to Ramsey Clark" that he would not seek to turn over such information.

Nevertheless Doar's memo did lead to the creation of a computerized intelligence file that eventually grew to contain some 18,000 names of all kinds of dissidents and troublemakers.

So now we know, thanks particularly to the Rockefeller Report, that not all the Watergate-type activity started with the Nixon administration. Much of it was begun by those who bellowed the loudest about Watergate—namely, liberals like Clark and Doar.

And while we do not yet know the entire story of this turbulent period, it is clear from the fragmentary record that, as William Greider reported in the Washington *Post,* "thousands of informers were recruited in black neighborhoods, phones were tapped, mail and bank accounts were inspected, community organizations infiltrated, campus groups watched." There were also illegal break-ins.

Many of these activities were exposed when thieves broke into the FBI offices in Media, Pennsylvania, and "liberated" 1,200 confidential Bureau documents. The thieves, calling themselves the Citizen's Commission to Investigate the FBI, sent Xerox copies of the documents to newspapermen and other interested parties. Among other things the documents demonstrated that the FBI was following Clark's orders to enlist undercover agents in the ghettos in order to obtain advance warning of riots and other outbursts.

And as a former FBI official explained, "We used the same kind of program against the dissidents and the revolutionaries as we used against the Klan." But some of the informers, according to court testimony, became *agents provocateurs,* encouraging or even leading the targets of their spying into acts of violence.

According to Greider, "neither Republicans nor Democrats were eager to investigate the implications" of the "Media papers"—"not even Senator Ervin, whose Judiciary Subcommittee on Constitutional Rights was alarmed by Army spying but not by FBI spying."

Military spying on civilians was another operation unleashed by the Johnson administration. Originating under Secretary of Defense McNamara, the covert actions were deemed necessary because of "national security" considerations. Much of the army surveillance was directed against antiwar militants, some of whom were plotting to sabotage military installations. The army brass, for the most part, objected to this unwanted activity. As did the FBI, whose director felt it constituted competition by not-too-well-trained sleuths. Eventually, under the glare of embarrassing publicity, the program was abolished.

During the Johnson years espionage, wiretapping, and other "dirty tricks" were not only used against radical dissenters but against LBJ's political adversaries. Thus, during the 1968 campaign, Nixon found himself the object of FBI surveillance. As he later told James J. Kilpatrick, "There was not only surveillance by the FBI, but bugging by the FBI, and Hoover told me that my plane in the last two weeks was bugged." Hoover told Nixon this when he visited the President-elect at the Hotel Pierre in New York during the 1968 interregnum.

There can be little doubt that Johnson was anxious to learn everything he could about the Republican candidate and runningmate Spiro Agnew. In fact a file of "sensitive" information about the relatively unknown former governor of Maryland was assembled by the FBI for transmittal to the White House. What LBJ was looking for, as usual, was personal dirt to be used to promote Humphrey's campaign for the presidency.

In addition LBJ ordered the FBI through "Deke" DeLoach to make a check of phone calls made by Agnew from his campaign plane. Also requested were the telephone toll records of members of the Agnew staff. Again the rationale was "national security."

One of the FBI's major assignments was to find out whether Agnew or anyone on his staff was in touch with South Vietnamese officials in Washington in an effort to sabotage the Paris peace talks launched by Johnson. The National Security Agency reportedly had intercepted a cable to Saigon transmitted from its Washington Embassy advising the Thieu régime that it would get a better deal from Washington if the Nixon-Agnew ticket were elected.

When a copy of that cable reached LBJ, an irate President demanded an immediate FBI investigation. The ensuing developments were described in testimony before the Senate Intelligence Committee by "Deke" DeLoach:

"I received a call from Mr. James Jones, who was the top assistant to the President . . . late one evening, and he indicated the President wanted information concerning either Mr. Nixon or Mr. Agnew insofar as toll calls being made from Albuquerque, New Mexico, were concerned. I told Mr. Jones I felt this was not a correct thing to do, particularly at this time of night, and while we would try to comply with the President's specific request, we would not do it that night.

"The President then called me personally in my office late that night and indicated that did he understand my refusal to Mr. Jones correctly; and I said, yes, he did. I said I thought that it would be wrong for us to try to obtain such information that late at night. The President then proceeded to tell me that he was the Commander in Chief and that when he needed information of that nature, he should get it. However, (after) I reiterated my objections . . . the President indicated all right, try to get it the following day."

Which is what DeLoach did. The next morning he received Hoover's permission to proceed with the investigation. The first move was to have the FBI field office in Albuquerque check the record of toll calls made from the Agnew plane when it was in New Mexico some days previously. And, according to former Governor David F. Cargo of New Mexico, the phones in the governor's mansion in Santa Fe were tapped during a visit by the vice presidential candidate.

Also initiated with LBJ's approval was the wiretapping and physical surveillance of Anna Chennault, widow of famed World War II Flying Tiger General Claire Chennault and an avid money raiser for the 1968 Nixon campaign. It was LBJ's belief that Mrs. Chennault was seeking to mobilize the opposition of the Taiwan, South Korean, and South Vietnamese governments to the Paris peace talks seeking an end to U.S. involvement in Southeast Asia. And how did LBJ get any such idea? According to Theodore White, Mrs. Chennault had "neglected to take the most elementary precautions of an intriguer, and her communications with Asia had been tapped by the American Government and brought directly to the perusal of President Johnson."

LBJ, though not a candidate for reelection in 1968, wanted to do everything possible to get Humphrey to replace him in the Oval Office. So he notified Humphrey of what White described as "the sabotage of the negotiations and the recalcitrance of the Saigon Government."

In other words, what had been obtained in the name of "national security" was being used for domestic political purposes.

DeLoach was also in charge of this operation. As he testified, it was his recollection that "the Executive Secretary of the National Security Council, Mr. J. Bromley Smith, called me on one occasion and indicated the President of the United States wanted this done. I told Mr. Smith that I thought what he should do is call the Attorney General concerning this matter, and I believe either Mr. Hoover or I later received a call from the Attorney General indicating that this should be done."

"Was it done?" asked Senator John Tower of Texas.

"There was a physical surveillance on Mrs. Chennault, yes, sir."

"What did it include?"

"The usual physical surveillance, as I recall, Senator, following her to places where she went in the city of Washington, and . . . also a trip that she made to New York."

"Did it involve the constant monitoring of any and all of her incoming and outgoing telephone calls?"

"I believe the instructions of the President and the specific instruction and approval of the Attorney General, that a wiretap was placed on her telephone, sir."

"So during the period of time between October 30 and November 7, all her telephonic communications were monitored by the Bureau?"

"I don't recall the specific dates, Senator, but I do know that such surveillance was established."

"Who was the Attorney General at the time?"

"I believe that would have been Mr. Clark."*

Whether Humphrey was aware that the Chennault material had been obtained through illegal wiretapping and physical surveillance is not known. But the Democratic candidate conceded that he sent his own campaign aide, James Rowe, to the South Vietnamese ambassador with a warning that the Thieu régime had better cooperate in Paris lest, should Humphrey be elected,

---

*Clark's position on wiretapping as Attorney General was erratic. Though he approved the Chennault operation, he had turned down previous FBI requests to install "a technical surveillance" at offices of New Left organizations planning demonstrations at the 1968 Democratic National Convention.

Marshal Thieu "would rue the day." Humphrey later denied that he knew anything of wiretapping and physical surveillance of the Chinese-born socialite.

And Mrs. Chennault denied she had anything to do with any conspiracy to thwart the peace talks, claiming she was being made a "scapegoat." Even if she had, she still was within her constitutional rights to urge foreign governments to do whatever she wanted them to do. In her denial, however, she castigated "inaccurate political calculations in high places by those who presumably had all instrumentalities of intelligence at their disposal."

Humphrey was aware of what the FBI had done during the 1964 Democratic Convention. He knew, for example, that Johnson had used a special FBI team equipped with wiretaps and bugs to spy on troublemakers in Atlantic City. According to a memo from Hoover to his top associates including DeLoach, the director told of a conversation he had with William Connell, executive assistant to Humphrey. Dated August 15, 1968, the memo stated: "William Connell . . . had talked to the Vice President about the team I sent into the Convention area in 1964 that was so helpful. He stated he was hoping perhaps I might be able to do the same thing for the Vice President out in Chicago and have my men directly in contact with him [Connell]."

Though Humphrey did obtain limited FBI assistance, the Vice President did not get "the same thing" that LBJ had gotten four years previously. The reason was that Attorney General Clark, who had been willing to approve the Doar plan to spy on dissidents, not being a Humphrey man, refused to authorize the "telephone surveillance" requested by the FBI. "There has not been an adequate demonstration of a direct threat to the national security," Clark informed Hoover.

A week after Connell had talked to Hoover, "Deke" DeLoach received a call from John Criswell, treasurer of the Democratic National Committee. And in a memo dated August 22, 1968, DeLoach reported that Criswell had had dinner the previous night with Marvin Watson. Then Postmaster General, Watson "had informed him of the great service performed by the FBI during the last Democratic Convention in Atlantic City . . . Criswell wanted to know if the same services could be performed this time in Chicago. He also asked if I could personally go out and take charge, as was the case in Atlantic City."

DeLoach informed Criswell that Connell had already talked to

Director Hoover about the matter. "I stated the Director had made complete arrangements to have a topflight group of experienced agents, under the supervision of the Special Agent in Charge of the Chicago Office, handle this assignment. I told Criswell I felt certain these men would do an excellent job and the Vice President's office would be kept fully advised at all times of need-to-know information."

The significance of the memo is that a functionary of the Democratic National Committee could feel free to call on a top FBI official for assistance in gathering political intelligence.

The CIA had also gotten into the act. One of its agents, posing as a private detective, investigated the personal life of one of Nixon's aides during the 1968 campaign. The target of the inquiry was Richard V. Allen, the Republican candidate's pre-Kissinger foreign policy adviser.

The CIA operative was identified as Franklin R. Geraty. On June 25, 1968, two weeks after Allen joined the Nixon staff, Geraty appeared in the offices of a banker in Palo Alto, California, where Allen had been living. Displaying credentials indicating his connection with the Fidelity Reporting Service of New York City, Geraty asked for any personal information the banker might have on Allen. He explained he was doing background checks on Nixon aides for the Republicans.

Suspicious, the banker divulged nothing to his visitor. Later he telephoned Nixon's personal secretary, Rose Mary Woods, to find out what was going on. Miss Woods phoned back to report that no one had been authorized to conduct an investigation of Allen.

John J. Caulfield, who was then chief of staff security for Nixon, checked into the matter. He discovered that the Fidelity Reporting Service, which Geraty said he represented, was a "CIA outfit."

If anything, as Allen himself later noted, the CIA's covert efforts to obtain information about him, whether for legitimate or political motives, was "a clear violation of the charter of the CIA." But the Nixon high command decided not to expose the improper use of the CIA, as it was later explained, because any attack on the Johnson administration could move President Johnson to more enthusiastic support of Humphrey.

"We went out of our way not to provoke Lyndon," a top Nixon aide said, "even though we knew he had authorized some shady ventures against us."

The fact remains that improper investigations, wiretapping,

bugging, and physical surveillance of Republicans did take place on orders of President Johnson. All of which constituted a flagrant disregard of individual civil liberties, as well as a definite misuse of federal police agencies for partisan political advantage.

Yet years later when the facts began to emerge, there was a profound disinterest on the part of the same media that went bananas over Watergate. As Professor Noam Chomsky, the authority on linguistics who was involved in most antiwar protests of the sixties, put it: "Illegal FBI operations [under Kennedy and Johnson] . . . while incomparably more serious than anything charged in the Congressional Articles of Impeachment or other denunciations of Nixon, aroused scant interest and little concern, specifically, in the organs of American liberalism that were so agitated over the latest tax trickery or tape erasure.

"Ergo," concluded Professor Chomsky, "Nixon's defenders do have a case."

And Nicholas von Hoffman, who was not often accused of being a Nixon apologist, wrote: "In the months since his departure, his defense looks better. Half a dozen Congressional committees have brought forth volumes of information all adducing that the break-ins, the tapping, snooping and harassment have been routine government activities for a generation at least."

Much of this had long been known in the halls of Congress. During the hearings of the Ervin Committee, for example, there was a determined effort to prevent information on Democratic precedents to Watergate from leaking out. And those investigative reporters, later to be immortalized by Robert Redford and Dustin Hoffman, made no effort to dig out the material.

For good reason, too, from their point of view. "Because," as William Safire noted, "the public, if possessed of the whole truth, might not have acted as the public opinion manipulators wanted them to. If the whole truth were let out, Mr. Nixon might have escaped. . . ."

In his book *At That Point in Time** Fred Thompson, the minority counsel of the Senate Watergate Committee, explained why even the Republicans on the committee did not call former FBI Deputy Directors Sullivan and DeLoach to testify about their first-hand knowledge of abuses of power under Democratic Presidents. "[Senator Lowell] Weicker was adamantly opposed," wrote Thompson.

---

*(New York: Quadrangle, 1975), pp. 143-144.

"He said it would look like an attempt to justify some of the actions of the Nixon Administration. [Senator Edward] Gurney reluctantly agreed. He didn't want to further tarnish the image of the FBI. He also felt, as I think we all did, that the press would downplay the story and treat it as a Republican attempt to take the heat off of Nixon. The fact that FDR and LBJ had used the FBI for political purposes might be a significant story at another time, but not while Nixon was on the ropes.

And so the greatest cover up of all took place. All evidence concerning the incredible abuses of power under the Democrats was officially suppressed, lest there be any amelioration of the tremendous hatred being focused on Richard Nixon.

Only later, long after Nixon was gone from center stage, did the unpalatable facts about Democratic presidents begin to emerge. Not all of them, by any means, but enough to cause dismay among those who had been so tumultuously aggrieved by Watergate. The sound and fury which had marked the Nixon years had died down to a whimper.

16

By THE TIME LYNDON JOHNSON LEFT OF-
fice, his administration was under bitter attack by the media and
its subsidiary organizations. Thus in 1968 the journalism society
Sigma Delta Chi had this to say: "The Credibility Gap, which has
reached awesome proportions under the Johnson Administration, continued to be a grave handicap. Secrecy, lies, half-truths,
deception—this was the daily fare."

In turn there were those who felt that the press had its own
credibility problems. Douglas Cater, special assistant to President Johnson, suggested that too often newsmen presumed an
expertise they quite obviously didn't have.

"I'm concerned about the little demigods of TV who make an
instant analysis of complicated events," said Cater. "There
should be bounds on what TV men do, so much of which is
delivered with flippant abandon."

Cater, of course, was and is of the liberal persuasion. His remarks concerning "instant analysis" were generally overlooked
at the time. A year or so later Vice President Spiro Agnew used
the same phrase in condemning television coverage of presidential speeches—and all hell broke loose. The reaction ran true to
form. The liberals claimed the remarks augured—in the words of
the International Press Institute in Zürich—"the most serious
threat to the freedom of information in the Western world." And
commentators like Walter Cronkite agreed.

But down in Texas the former President wondered out loud
whether "Ted" Agnew had been politic in saying what he did.
It wasn't that Citizen Johnson disagreed with what was said.
Shortly after the 1968 election he had sought to warn the Vice
President-elect about the antagonistic nature of the media.

"Young man," he had told Agnew, "we have in this country
two big television networks, NBC and CBS. We have two news
magazines, *Newsweek* and *Time.* We have two wire services, AP
and UPI. We have two pollsters, Gallup and Harris. We have two

big newspapers—the *Washington Post* and *The New York Times.* They're all so damned big they think they own the country. But, young man, don't get any ideas about fighting. . . ."

Well, Agnew got precisely that idea and came out swinging. Lyndon, of course, had also battled with the media and been bloodied in the process. He had even lost control of the Democratic Convention held that terrible year of 1968. So fearful was he of angry outbursts from many of the delegates, particularly on Vietnam, that the President did not even put in an appearance at the Chicago Stockyards.

Another reason was the furies in the streets. Chicago just was not safe for the President. Thousands of antiwar youths rampaged through the Loop district, shouting obscene slogans and battling with the cops. The resultant scenes on national television were devastating.

And no one was more aware of that than Hubert Humphrey as he was being nominated for the presidency of the United States. The exemplar of the "politics of joy" had been watching the nominating speeches in his hotel room on television. Just as Carl Stokes, the Black mayor of Cleveland, took the rostrum to make a seconding speech, the screen switched to filmed coverage of the violence in the streets. Blood showed up in living color. And Hubert was beside himself.

As the ubiquitous Teddy White made notes, Humphrey denounced the television coverage as injurious to his chances. "I'm going to be President someday," he said angrily. "I'm going to appoint the FCC—we're going to look into all this!"

The implication was, of course, that as President, Humphrey intended to wreak vengeance on the broadcast media. But the threat did not appear to arouse much concern on the part of people like White, who later was to write in detail about the hubris of the Nixon administration.

Needless to say, Humphrey never got the chance to meddle with the FCC. But his hurt remained. For a long time he felt the media had done him in. And, like Nixon, he felt that some reporters had deliberately sought to "get" him.

There could be little doubt that certain sections of the media had overplayed the violence in the streets. Leading Democrats felt it was all deliberate. The final irony was that the convention coverage undoubtedly helped tilt the closely contested election to Nixon.

Moreover, in covering the big stories, media people were not above taking the law into their hands. On September 6, 1968, for example, the National Broadcasting Company acknowledged that some of its personnel had conducted illegal electronic surveillance on the Democrats at their recently concluded convention.

According to an NBC statement, "overzealous and overeager employes, acting without authority" (sound familiar?), had planted a microphone in a closed meeting of the Democratic platform committee at the Sheraton-Blackstone Hotel.

Representative Hale Boggs, the committee chairman, disclosed that the microphone had been discovered under a cushion behind a curtain. He said that it "was attached to a cable leading directly to the recording facilities of the National Broadcasting Company in the same hotel."

A member of the committee told *The New York Times* that the supposedly confidential proceedings had been interrupted for about fifteen or twenty minutes when the bug was discovered. "There was also some belief that an earlier meeting a day or two before had been bugged," he added, "because the Chicago papers had such complete details of the closed meeting."

Boggs, meanwhile, announced he had requested an investigation of the incident, noting that the laws must apply equally to all men and that wiretapping, bugging, and eavesdropping, except in matters of national security or organized crime, constituted direct violations of federal and state statutes.

"The matter now is for determination by the appropriate Federal and state law enforcement agencies," he added.

In a telegram to Boggs NBC News President Reuven Frank said that NBC intended "to take stern disciplinary action against any personnel who acted improperly." In a separate statement NBC claimed that no material obtained by the bugging was used in any way, that the network deeply regretted the episode which, it added, was not "condoned or encouraged by NBC News."

Several weeks later Drew Pearson and Jack Anderson reported in their column that NBC was about to be indicted and that one of its producers, Enid Roth, who had allegedly planted the bug, had been selected as the "scapegoat."

"This action," the columnists added, "marks the first time in history that the Government has cracked down on the high-handed operations of the networks, which in the past have helped instigate riots, played a part in encouraging trouble during the Little Rock school crisis, and slanted the news brazenly at the Chicago convention."

Pearson and Anderson also reported that Chairman Harley Staggers of the House Interstate Commerce Committee had ordered an investigation of news slanting by the networks. Investigators had reported, among other things, that while Humphrey was delivering his acceptance speech, an NBC director made sure that only unflattering shots of the Vice President were used.

And Senator Gale McGee had supplied the committee with information regarding an episode he personally witnessed on a Chicago street. The Wyoming Democrat said he saw a TV producer lining up several female protesters before his cameras. Not one of them had been hurt, menaced, or threatened. Yet when the producer gave the cue, they began to scream: "Don't hit me! Don't hit me!"

According to Pearson and Anderson, the networks also went out of their way to present Mayor Daley in the worst possible light. And, they reported, TV film clips of the Chicago riots, "some of them partially whipped up by TV producers," were transmitted "all over the Communist and non-Communist world."

But the Staggers probe never got off the ground.

Nor, as it turned out, was NBC indicted for breaking the law. What ultimately happened was that on March 20, 1969, "scapegoat" Enid Roth was indicted and charged with two counts of "wilfully endeavoring to use an electronic device to intercept oral communications." In February 1970 Miss Roth pleaded no defense to one count of the indictment, was fined $1,000 as well as costs, and given a suspended sentence. More recently Miss Roth, still with NBC, turned up at both 1976 conventions as the television network's on-the-air director.

Needless to say, the lawbreakers in Watergate did not fare as well.

But what is significant about all of this is that it went virtually ignored by the rest of the media. The press only became aroused about such lawbreaking during Watergate. Then no network spent as much time, day in and day out, in exposing "the crime of the century" as did NBC. Hypocrisy obviously is not confined to politicians.

Of course such "escapades"—as *The New York Times* described them—were nothing new. As an example the newspaper noted how at the Republican Convention in Miami Beach some weeks previously a delegate from Florida concealed a tape recorder at a closed meeting at which Richard Nixon addressed Southern delegates. The tape was turned over to the Miami *Herald* and the St. Petersburg *Times,* both of which published stories based on Nixon's secretly recorded remarks. As it turned out, it was an enterprising *Herald* reporter who provided the delegate with the recording equipment.

Jack Anderson himself was no stranger to electronic surveillance. In July 1958 he was caught in a hotel room with a congressional investigator spying on Bernard Goldfine, the wealthy industrialist whose gift of a vicuna coat to Sherman Adams, a presidential assistant, became a major scandal of the Eisenhower administration.

Anderson was mortified about being caught red-handed participating in the invasion of someone's privacy. But his boss, Drew Pearson, shrugged off proposals from close friends that he fire Jack. Instead Pearson issued a statement which paraphrased Eisenhower's defense of Adams. "Anderson might have been imprudent," said Pearson, "but I need him."

Not as fortunate was Baron I. Shacklette, the chief investigator of the House Special Subcommittee on Legislative Oversight which had been looking into Goldfine's peculiar links to the Eisenhower administration. As a result of the Goldfine "bugging" Shacklette was forced to resign. Years later this background was ignored by Representative Wright Patman when the Texas Democrat hired Shacklette as his administrative assistant. Patman, incidentally, was among the first in Congress to become alarmed about the ramifications of Watergate.

Perhaps because his improper activities had been directed against the likes of Goldfine, the media laid off Shacklette. At most the investigator suffered little more than momentary embarrassment. His caper was quickly forgotten. However Howard Hunt and Gordon Liddy paid a far greater price for conspiring to do exactly what Shacklette did.

"Bugging" had long been considered a major tool of investigative reporters. What Anderson did, therefore, was nothing new. And it didn't hurt him a bit. In fact it helped in his extraordinary career. As he told Susan Sheehan of *The New Yorker* in 1972, "getting caught like that was the most embarrassing thing that ever happened to me . . . but I later found out it didn't hurt me at all. Everyone thought it proved we were getting just the kind of keyhole evidence they suspected we were getting."

In his book *The Truman Presidency* Cabell Phillips tells how reporters bugged a caucus of the Illinois delegation at the 1952 Democratic Convention in Chicago. The episode took place on the afternoon of Sunday, July 20, when the delegation met in a private dining room of the Morrison Hotel.

As Phillips relates the story,

> The press had been excluded from the meeting. But the room had been "bugged" by an enterprising radio correspondent, and a group of other reporters, clustered behind a plastic room divider behind the speaker's table, overheard the entire proceedings. Even before the caucus broke up, news wires across the country were cracking with speculations "on the highest and most unimpeachable authority" that Adlai Stevenson's name would be put in nomination and that he would not block it.

Some of the nation's better known political reporters of the time were in on the caper. They included Edward T. Folliard of the Washington *Post*, nationally syndicated columnist Doris Fleeson, and Charlie Cleveland of the Chicago *Daily News*. Their stories quoted Governor Stevenson as saying he was not being coy or indecisive; he just didn't want to run for President. "I have no fitness—temperamentally, mentally or physically for the job," Stevenson said. Without knowing that their words were being overheard, one delegate after another rose to say the governor had no choice but to run. And it soon became obvious that, regardless of his wishes, Stevenson's name would go before the convention.

Significantly, in describing the episode, Phillips used the adjective "enterprising." There was no condemnation of media people for employing such tactics. If anything there was tacit approval. The same adjective was used by three British journalists in their book on the 1968 campaign in describing the Miami *Herald* reporter who persuaded a Florida delegate covertly to tape a Nixon speech.

The point of all this is that the media has long relied on Watergate-type tactics to obtain stories, and has rarely criticized itself for doing so. In fact spying has long been considered a virtue in the ranks of journalists.

In the October 1973 issue of that sprightly, iconoclastic journal *The Alternative,* Richard Wheeler gave some personal insights into the realities of so-called investigative reporting. "A couple of years ago," wrote Wheeler, when I was a journalist in Montana, I attended a meeting under news management auspices in which our speaker was a Helena bureau chief freshly returned from a seminar at the American Press Institute on investigative reporting.

"Our speaker

discussed what he had learned in New York about investigative reporting, which is often a euphemism for such deep digging tactics as espionage, bullying information out of people, buying information—and electronic spying. Among the participants at the API seminar . . . were a couple of *Life* reporters who instructed the group on the uses of electronic spying, and discussed pridefully their successful use of bugs to supply the material for several exposé type stories in the magazine.

Our speaker named several such stories, and noted that at the API seminar there had been little malaise about such illegal activity, because it helped newsmen fulfill their watchdog function. In fact, he reported, some had felt that bugs were a positive good, and a vital investigating tool. Now of course, all this is hearsay, but I have no reason to doubt the truth of it, especially when the speaker was waving an issue of *Life* containing, he said, a story acquired by illegal bugging. The response among my colleagues was equally enthused; indeed, I was nearly the only one there who felt that the end did not justify such nefarious means. . . .

So we are entitled to ask whether the press' opposition to electronic spying is principled. If it is true that *Life* reporters bugged sources illegally, would the gentlemen of the press agree that such reporters should get the same twenty to thirty-five year sentences meted out to the Watergate conspirators? One suspects, after all, that such sentences are draconian, and that one does not normally spend a quarter or a third of a lifetime in prison for a first offense of breaking and entering.

But has the press respectfully pleaded with Judge Sirica for a more temperate sentence? The judge is a reasonable man, and would surely listen if a respectful request for a better justice were directed to him by the press. But the press is in a vengeful mood, and is inclined to approve the Watergate justice. One wishes that each reporter who had similarly used bugs illegally might spend an equal time behind bars.

Of course, Richard Wheeler really doesn't expect that ever to happen. The fact is, as we shall see, that despite all the so-called lessons of Watergate, there continue to be invasions of privacy by the media. And one of the worst offenders continues to be the Washington *Post*, which has long had an undistinguished record of such sleazy behavior. A recent example was the assignment by Ben Bradlee of two reporters to snoop into the private life of Congressman Wayne Hays. Does the "right to know" include the right to listen in on boudoir conversations? Granted that Hays was an old scoundrel, but even scoundrels have rights. And where will it all end? The next thing might well be some enterprising reporter demanding to know more about Kay Graham's private life, which the *Post* publisher insists is no one's business but her own.

It was the Washington *Post*, utilizing the services of a self-described political spy in the 1950s, which nearly came a cropper when it developed that the individual in question was nothing more than a semiliterate confidence man wily enough to rip off some of the nation's leading liberals. Based on information provided by this confidence man, the *Post* had prepared twelve articles exposing the supposedly evil doings of Senator Joseph McCarthy of Wisconsin. Fortunately for the *Post* someone had the presence of mind to decide almost at the last minute to check out the material. All of it proved to be phony.*

But it wasn't only the *Post* that willingly became involved in one of the sleaziest episodes in American political history, one now conveniently forgotten by those who like to look back with horror. Some of the most powerful members of the liberal fraternity willingly condoned the very use of confidential informants, dossiers, and political spies which they condemned in others. They felt that their purpose was above reproach. Any means, in their view, justified the end of destroying Joe McCarthy.

Consider the names of some of the "biggies" involved in the plot to "get" McCarthy. They included Joseph L. Rauh, Jr., chairman of Americans for Democratic Action; Telford Taylor, Chairman of the National Committee for an Effective Congress; James Wechsler, editor of the *New York Post;* Clayton Fritchey, more recently a columnist for the Washington *Post;* and the three top officials of the Washington *Post* at the time, Philip Graham, James Russell Wiggins, and Alfred Friendly.

Also involved were Robert Eichholtz, a Washington lawyer and Rome representative of the Marshall Plan during the Tru-

---

*The full and amazing story of how the con man got himself financed by the cream of American liberalism can be found in William F. Buckley's article, "The Case of Paul A. Hughes, The Liberal Light that Failed," *National Review*, Feb. 13, 1960, pp. 101–105.

man administration; Paul Porter, partner in one of Washington's most prestigious law firms, and a former high official of the Roosevelt and Truman administrations; and Clark Clifford, another prestigious lawyer who had been special counsel and leading adviser to Democratic presidents.

The story began in late 1953 when a recently discharged airman named Paul Hughes approached the staff director of Senator McCarthy's Subcommittee on Investigations with an eye-popping story of high treason at an American air force base in Saudi Arabia where he had been stationed. Staff director Francis Carr took notes, checked the story, found it to be a fabrication, and told Hughes to get lost. Hughes then took his wild yarn to the FBI, where his story was also checked, and he was shown the door.

Switching stories, Hughes then approached General Cornelius Mara, who had been a White House aide and intimate of President Truman. So overwhelmed was Mara with what Hughes told him that the general turned him over to Clayton Fritchey, then editor of the Democratic party's official magazine *Democratic Digest*. According to the story Hughes now told, he was a covert agent of the McCarthy Committee. As such, he had come across information that shocked him. And he was offering to report on the secret doings of the committee. An agreement was reached. Mara and Fritchey agreed to pay Hughes his "expenses." And they also agreed to the aliases "Yale" and "Ewing" respectively. Aha, they must have felt, what a great way of getting the goods on Joe McCarthy!

Hughes then sought out another mark, Joe Rauh, who was most receptive. Particularly after he heard Hughes's shocking tale of the secret horrors perpetrated by McCarthy. In fact Rauh's appetite for anti-McCarthyana was insatiable. He demanded more. And Hughes obliged, bringing in a ninety-four-page document full of "goodies." Satisfied, Rauh placed Hughes on his private payroll.

The document, as it was later disclosed in a courtroom, was a masterpiece. Reading it, Bill Buckley said it could easily have been "the work of a master psychiatrist seeking, simultaneously, to assuage and to aggravate a patient of unbalanced political outlook. The salve was there—for here was confirmation in abundance of the worst one could imagine about McCarthy; and also the galvanizer—here was a call to glory, a call for extraordinary exertions to destroy the monster McCarthy."

Consider the "revelations" which Hughes unfolded for Rauh's "eyes only." They concerned the secret and dark alliance between Eisenhower and McCarthy (their open hostility was, in effect, play-acting); marital problems developing between Senator and Mrs. McCarthy; a clandestine White House meeting at which a smear campaign against the Democratic party was programmed; secret McCarthy informers scattered about the White House, the CIA, the State Department, and elsewhere in the federal bureaucracy; McCarthy's personal views on a host of miscellaneous subjects ranging from ethics to Drew Pearson. The package included "documentation" consisting of notes, official communications, inter-office memoranda, and secret transcripts. Like the good con man he was, Hughes had worked hard to convince the mark. He could well have provided inspiration for the characters played by Paul Newman and Robert Redford in *The Sting*.

The Hughes memorandum made these recommendations:

. . . as McCarthy is presently violating some very serious military and civil laws, we should obtain photographs and written evidence and witnesses to that effect. The result of evidence of this nature is not only elimination but also prosecution by the Federal Government as well. You must make a decision relative to whether you want McCarthy removed permanently or not. If you do, it is relatively a simple legal matter. . . .

There are many important military and civil officials in the Washington area alone willing to go to any extremes to remove McCarthyism from the political scene. Any coordination desired in this matter is relatively simple to obtain. Surely no obstacle exists in coordinated observation of me during my unauthorized procurement of classified material and my subsequent handling and disposition of same. Under coordinated but secure surveillance, observation will disclose that I surreptitiously procured [according to instructions from McCarthy] various amounts of classified data; photographic evidence, controlled, will pinpoint McCarthy personnel receiving unauthorized classified material from me.

Phone taps can be utilized, initially, to tie in all illegal incidents performed by me to specific McCarthy staff personnel. Phone taps can be further utilized for admissions by staff personnel of security violations and compromises of classified military projects. . . .

. . . Being nice, too ethical, or squeamish, will accomplish less than nothing where McCarthy is concerned. . . .

Joe Rauh bought all these Watergate-type recommendations to the tune of 8,500 of his own dollars. He made an arrangement whereby Hughes was to report to him directly and regularly on the activities of McCarthy and his Investigations Committee. In so doing, Rauh placed no limits on what Hughes was to do in obtaining his secret information—including illegal phone taps.

Of course Rauh had long been bitterly opposed to such anti-civil libertarian tactics when they were used against liberals or even confirmed subversives. In fact in the May 1950 issue of *The Progressive* he had insisted, "Let us do away with confidential informants, dossiers, political spies. . . . No one can guess where this process of informing will end."

In Rauh's case the process of informing ended up in a federal courtroom in Manhattan. Two years after he had hired Paul Hughes, Rauh's use of confidential informants, dossiers, and political spies led a jury of his peers to refuse to take his word over that of a self-confessed liar and confidence man.

The case involved allegations of perjury on Hughes's part. One count, for example, contended that Hughes had lied when he told a grand jury that Rauh had known all along that he was a phony. In other words Hughes had contended that Rauh was a knave.

Thus when he took the witness stand, Rauh in effect was forced to argue that, no, he was not a knave, but a fool. Despite all the sophistication he had picked up in many years of political involvement, he had not known he was being taken, he insisted. The jury chose not to believe him.

At any rate it was Rauh's contention that the reason he had hired Hughes was to seek to develop a legal case against McCarthy, not to look for prurient details of the senator's personal affairs. But as it turned out under questioning, Rauh never did advise Hughes to limit his reports only to evidence of legal wrongdoing. And Alfred Friendly, managing editor of the Washington *Post*, likewise found it difficult to explain why he had written down numerous notes about McCarthy which had absolutely nothing to do with illegal activities. Some of them were prurient indeed.

Also taking the line that his interest in McCarthy was limited was that paragon of anti-McCarthyism, Clayton Fritchey. Then why, asked the judge, was he so interested in Hughes's claim that a McCarthy sympathizer worked on the Louisville *Courier-Journal?* "What did *that,*" the judge went on, "have to do with illegal activities?" Fritchey's response: "It happened—a friend of mine happened to be a publisher of the *Courier-Journal....*"

Under questioning by the defense counsel, Rauh testified that Hughes had informed him that McCarthy's spy on the *New York Post* was—would you believe?—the *Post*'s cooking editor.

COUNSEL: Did you call Mr. Wechsler, editor of the *Post*, and tell him?

RAUH: Yes, sir.

COUNSEL: You didn't feel that the cooking editor was going to slant any recipes in McCarthy's favor, did you?

RAUH: That wasn't the purpose. That wouldn't have been the purpose to have somebody there.

COUNSEL: What *was* the purpose of McCarthy having a spy as the cooking editor?

RAUH: Because a cooking editor like anybody else has access to all the records, files and clips and other matters on the paper and to all the discussion. It doesn't matter who the person is. I didn't feel he should have *anybody* on the paper.

THE COURT *(interrupting):* You don't believe in having spies?

RAUH: No, sir.

COUNSEL: Unless they are your own?

RAUH: Unless you are trying to uncover illegal activity which I was trying to do.

COUNSEL: You didn't think McCarthy was trying to uncover illegal activity?

RAUH: No, I didn't.

COUNSEL: You thought you were the only one trying to do that?

RAUH: I thought the Washington *Post* and I were the only ones trying to do that.

Of course when it came to loyalty risks holding jobs in the U.S. government, Joe Rauh had other views.

The court was also interested in why, if Hughes's employers were so concerned about McCarthy's illegalities, they did not turn to the Justice Department and, particularly, Attorney General Herbert Brownell. For example the judge asked General Mara, "Did you explain to Mr. Hughes why you called in Mr. Fritchey and, let's say, not Mr. Brownell?" The general seemed a bit shaken. "I don't quite—well," he mumbled, "the only reason I called in Mr. Fritchey was, I felt he had newspaper background, that he could analyze this thing. . . ."

Under questioning Fritchey was asked if he recalled "whether Hughes at any time expressed any opinions which caused you seriously to doubt his ethics or morality?"

– 234 –

"No," he replied, "not one single thing, no."

Whereupon there was inserted into the record a memorandum which Hughes had submitted to Fritchey and later Rauh. Excerpts from the document, dated December 1953, are as follows:

> Phone taps can be utilized [against McCarthy]. . . . Don't discount the tremendous value in just bargaining power of recorded phone discussions. . . . A program of this type, although not nice, can result in harm to no one except [McCarthy]. . . . As mentioned earlier, being nice, too ethical or squeamish, will accomplish less than nothing, where McCarthy is concerned. McCarthy has stated many times, "Ethics went out the window with buttoned shoes." So therefore I don't see the necessity for us to send a boy to do a man's work. If both federal and civil law enforcement agencies use the same unethical procedures to bring to justice criminals, are we not justified in using similar methods to expose [McCarthy] . . . ? It is most easy to prove and document [McCarthy's guilt] . . . by relaxing somewhat on ethics. This perhaps is probably what I'm best suited for. . . .

Thus twenty years before Watergate several of America's leading liberals agreed to a plan in which wiretapping was proposed as a means of dealing with a hated political enemy. Not only that, they shelled out cold cash to the author of a memorandum advocating numerous outright illegalities. These were the same liberals who would so vociferously castigate the Nixon administration.

At any rate Paul Hughes began to submit numerous reports about the evil doings of McCarthy and his gang. But the report which really had everyone shook up was the claim by Hughes that Joe and his staff had amassed a cache of pistols, Lugers, and submachine guns in the basement of the Senate Office Building. The implication was obvious. The McCarthyites were planning a putsch aimed at seizing the government!

By this time the Washington *Post* was preparing a series of articles based on the exclusive revelations provided by the paid informer. When twelve pieces were completed under tight security, someone in the *Post*'s hierarchy thought it would be wise to check out some of the sensational material. After checking some of the sources of the anti-McCarthyiana, reporter Murray Marder quickly determined that the stories, already in type, were phonies. Whereupon the series was killed.

And then silence!

Not one word of how it had been "taken in" by an adventurer was published in the *Post,* even though it had exclusive access to all the details. And Joe Rauh failed to take the matter to the authorities, even though he had been ripped off for a considerable sum by a phony who went around flashing false credentials as a Senate investigator, in itself an illegal act. That present-day moralist, Clayton Fritchey, said nary a word to the police about a man who subsequently sought to blackmail him. Also saying nothing to anyone in authority was General Mara, to whom Hughes had given a bad check.

What these liberal worthies wanted above all else was to forget their embarrassing, if not illegal, transgressions. But it was not to be. When Hughes once again tried to con the FBI, he was hauled before a grand jury. Whereupon he was indicted on six counts of alleged perjury. Two counts concerned Hughes's contention that Rauh was aware that his claim to being a McCarthy investigator was false, and that his reports on McCarthy's doings were doctored.

On February 3, 1956, following a jury trial, Hughes was acquitted. Two years later the government recommended that Hughes not be retried. Its reason: "During the trial the credibility of the major Government witnesses was severely attacked by its defense. . . . There is no reason to believe that a second jury would be any less receptive to the contentions made by the defense." In other words, according to the government, the credibility of such witnesses as Joe Rauh, Clay Fritchey, and Al Friendly left much to be desired.

When the *National Review,* shortly after the conclusion of the Hughes trial, chided liberal publicists for not commenting on the case, Richard Rovere wrote editor Buckley, saying, "I agree with you that the Hughes case is full of import. . . . I know that I shall deal with the Hughes case in (my forthcoming book.)" The book turned out to be a study of Senator McCarthy; but it did not contain a single reference to Hughes.

Eventually the Washington *Post* did publish a brief, self-serving editorial. And that was all. Forgetting its own deep involvement with a secret informer, the *Post* continued to condemn such practices when used by anti-Communist "witch-hunters." When Watergate broke, however, the *Post* again sought out secret informers which it described as "reliable sources." One or a combination of those sources will forever be known as "Deep Throat."

Of course the *Post* has long believed in the right to privacy for everyone but Richard Nixon. Thus it was the first American newspaper to publish a story involving Henry Kissinger's private remarks concerning his former employer and other prominent figures.

All this took place at a state dinner held in Kissinger's honor in Ottawa in October of 1975. Talking animatedly, the Secretary of State came up with some startling (for Canadians) views concerning his former leader. According to Henry, Nixon was an "odd, artificial and unpleasant man." At the same time he conceded that Nixon was "one of our better Presidents. . . . He was very decisive in his own way. He went to the heart of the problem."

On and on he prattled, little knowing that his seemingly private comments were being transmitted by a microphone to newsmen gathered elsewhere. Two days later the Secretary's babblings were published on the front page of the Washington *Post*.

Most everyone in the media enjoyed the story. Only one journalist worried aloud about its import. In a radio commentary Hugh Sidey of *Time* observed, "It seems that everybody but we journalists apologized. . . . As one of the trade, I am disturbed that there was not someone somewhere who said, wait, this is not only ungentlemanly but decidedly unfair. Kissinger should have been told what was happening. . . . The pursuit of the facts needs to be relentless, but if all the rules of decent conduct are ignored along the way, we may find we have defeated ourselves."

A flabbergasted Kissinger meanwhile tried to make amends by telephoning his "profuse apologies" to Nixon. The Secretary claimed he had been quoted out of context—the usual excuse for such *faux pas*. But both he and Nixon knew better. For Henry had been saying pretty much the same things elsewhere, but without benefit of a prying media. And reports of these indiscretions had reached San Clemente.

None of which has endeared Kissinger to the man who made the Secretary what he is today. And it must have given Gerald Ford some cause for alarm. What, the President must have thought, will Henry be saying about me when he no longer needs me?

During the Nixon years Kissinger went out of his way to butter up the President. His praise of Nixon was unstinted. In private conversations he described the President as "a genius whose understanding of foreign policy is unparalleled." At the same time (at least to this writer) he went out of his way to attack John F. Kennedy as a "dilettante," whose "opening to the left" had led the nation into deep trouble "from which we have yet to recover."

Of course in his *sotto voce* comments on Nixon, Kissinger was seeking to placate his liberal friends, whose hatred of the former President knew no bounds. But, in so doing, the Secretary made a serious mistake. For the word soon was out that no longer would Nixon's friends seek to protect him from allegations that it was he who helped initiate the wiretapping of numerous persons, including former aides, one of whom, Morton Halperin, was suing him.

Indeed as the facts began to be assembled, it became increasingly obvious that it was largely because of Kissinger's almost hysterical preoccupation with plugging "leaks" of national security information that the secret "plumbers" unit was established at the White House.

And out of the plumbers' activities came Watergate.

17

P R O B A B L Y   T H E   M O S T   E X T R A O R D I N A R Y   A S -
pect of Watergate was the fact that so many outsiders—including
officials of the Democratic National Committee—were among
those who had knowledge of the break-in many weeks before it
occurred. Yet some of these individuals later conceded that they
did nothing to prevent the episode. Indeed it would appear that
some of them welcomed it.

Evidence that the victims of the break-in had been warned of
what was being planned was developed by the minority staff of
the Senate Watergate Committee. Sworn testimony was taken in
executive sessions from three officials of the Democratic National
Committee, columnist Jack Anderson, and the two individuals
who had given the warning: A. J. Woolston-Smith, a New York
private investigator, and William F. Haddad, a former official of
the Kennedy and Johnson administrations.

From the beginning these investigators, headed by minority
counsel Fred Thompson, found themselves being hampered by
witnesses who contradicted themselves and each other, had incredible lapses of memory, and who misplaced or lost important
documents. As Thompson was later to put it, "An obvious effort
had been made to conceal the facts." But, he added, he had no
doubt that "several people, including some at the Democratic
headquarters, had advance knowledge of the Watergate break-in
on June 17, 1972."

Because they were unable to find a "smoking gun" in anyone's
hands, as Thompson put it, and because of the press of Watergate
business, "we knew that we could not justify the expenditure of
any more time, effort and money on a matter that, even if our
hunches turned out to be true, might add up to a finding of
historical interest only. We realized that we had played out the
string, and we let the matter drop, reluctantly, with a gnawing
feeling in our stomachs."

Nevertheless since nearly all the information came from testimony given under oath, a thoroughly documented summary was prepared and a major effort was made to include it in the committee's final report. But, as expected, Senator Ervin agreed with the majority staff's opinion that the Republican effort was "too speculative," and it was never published.

According to the transcripts of the once-secret testimony, among the first to be warned of the forthcoming break-in was none other than Lawrence F. O'Brien, the Democratic national chairman who was the major target of the caper. One of O'Brien's old friends from the days of Camelot, William Haddad, had written him a letter, saying he had been hearing "some very disturbing stories about GOP sophisticated surveillance techniques now being used for campaign purposes and of an interesting group here in New York where some of this 'intelligence' activity is centered."

Haddad said that the stories had come to him "from a counter-wiretapper who helped me once in a very difficult situation in Michigan." Haddad thought the information he had available was so important that it might be wise for O'Brien to "have someone call me so you can get the info first hand and take whatever actions you deem necessary."

O'Brien immediately instructed the DNC's director of communications, John Stewart, to follow up on the matter. Stewart flew to New York for an April 26, 1972, meeting at Haddad's office. The meeting was attended by Stewart, Haddad, Woolston-Smith, and Ben Winter, the vice president of a New York bank. Haddad later testified that Winter, a friend, happened to be in his office and that he invited the banker to sit in on the meeting "to hear something fascinating."

It was at this meeting that Haddad suggested that "little Cuba in Miami" was involved in the planned bugging of the office of the Democratic National Committee and that what the Republicans were after was evidence that the Democrats were being subsidized by Castro's Cuba. According to Haddad's testimony, the discussion centered on ways in which the funding of the espionage operation might be traced. Also discussed was a Republican organization in New York called the November Group that had some connection with someone named G. Gordon Liddy. The name of Attorney General Mitchell was mentioned.

Woolston-Smith's sworn testimony also indicated that these were among the matters discussed in Haddad's office. And he added that James McCord, who participated in the Watergate burglary, had been mentioned at the meeting. According to Woolston-Smith, John Stewart was "very interested" in the Cuban money angle.

For Thompson's investigators, Mike Madigan and Howard Liebengood, all this testimony was a "bombshell." For it meant that six weeks before the Watergate burglars were apprehended, Haddad knew that Cuban-Americans would be involved and that they would be looking for evidence that Castro was helping subsidize the DNC.

And who was Woolston-Smith? A short, roundfaced, balding man, he described himself as a "security consultant" to a firm calling itself the Science Security Associates, Inc., with offices at 441 Lexington Avenue in New York City. A one-time British intelligence agent—he said he carried a New Zealand passport—Woolston-Smith's immigration status was that of a permanent resident of the United States. Following the Bay of Pigs, he testified, his offices in New York were used by the CIA as a clearinghouse for those returning from the aborted invasion. Woolston-Smith said his contacts with what he described as the "intelligence community" were excellent. Which, he indicated, was how he first heard rumors about what later became known as Watergate.

Haddad's banker friend, Ben Winter, testified that Woolston-Smith had displayed a "sophisticated bug" at the April 26 meeting and had handed it to both Stewart and Haddad. Winter thought that the investigator's information was based on hard evidence obtained through surveillance, rather than theory. During his interview Woolston-Smith insisted that he did only "defensive wiretapping," i.e., detection of bugging. The bug he exhibited at the meeting, he said, was only a fake model intended to show the type of equipment available in the market. But he did confirm that he had visited the building in which the November Group was located, but insisted that he had remained in the hallway and never entered the suite.

Two days after the April 26 meeting Haddad wrote a letter to Stewart, saying that Woolston-Smith had "good information" and that, as a former investigative reporter, it was his judgment "that the story is true and explosive." Seeming to respond to a question from Stewart about whether the private detective wanted to be paid for continuing his investigation, Haddad wrote that Woolston-Smith "did want to cover expenses." Haddad added: "Instead of pursuing this with money, I decided to see what a good investigative reporting operation could do with it now. So I went ahead along these lines. If they draw a blank, I'll be back to you on how to proceed, and I'll keep you informed."

At the same time, Haddad told the Senate investigators, he transmitted all the material in his file to Jack Anderson with a covering letter. But, he said, he did not keep any copies of either the material or the letter.

As Thompson later said, "We wondered what there was that was 'true and explosive,' as Haddad had put it in his letter. Whatever it was, it was in the files sent to Anderson, and they did not want us to know its contents."

Having been warned that there were plans afoot to bug their offices, did the Democrats notify the police, have their premises "swept" for bugs, hire guards, or even ask the staff to take precautions? Not on your life. Stanley L. Griegg, then deputy chairman of the DNC, said that even though John Stewart had told him that Woolston-Smith had warned there might be electronic surveillance and possibly breaking and entering, he felt that the information was too fragmentary. Besides, he told Stewart, the DNC "didn't have the finances for an elaborate security program."

Woolston-Smith however was astonished that, despite his repeated warnings, the Democrats had done nothing to secure their headquarters. "I don't think I could have spelled it out more," he said. "It's no use asking me why they did nothing. It's all beyond me."

"In retrospect," said Larry O'Brien, whose private office and telephone had been the targets of the break-ins, "we should have paid more attention to it, but my recollection was that there were no specifics or clear lines. I don't recall I got any recommendation about what to do about it, and if there was one, the question was how did we pay for it?"

Thus great pains were taken to create the impression that the Democrats had not taken the warnings seriously. And no one appears to have asked why they did not at least tip off the authorities of what they had been told. The fact is they already knew their offices had been broken into. During the first week of May, according to Griegg's testimony, unknown burglars had removed various documents and checks. And on another occasion there had been an unsuccessful effort to force the locks. Under these circumstances the Democrats' total inaction over the bugging warning appears strange indeed. Though no one admitted it, the minority investigators did think it conceivable that a search had been made for bugs and that one had been found in O'Brien's office. The June 17 break-in, which resulted in the apprehension of the Watergate burglars, was made largely because that bug was not functioning properly. The feeling was that the O'Brien bug may not have died a natural death.

In his testimony Woolston-Smith said that the DNC's interest in his information continued right up to the time of the June 17 break-in. He said that he and Stewart talked on the phone several times a week, denying that Stewart's interest had waned at any time. "It was hot right up until the end and after the end." Their last pre-Watergate discussion was, as Woolston-Smith later recalled, "along the lines of 'something is about to happen.'"

And happen it did on a muggy Saturday in mid-June when five men wearing business suits and surgical gloves, carrying $100 bills and a walkie-talkie, were arrested in the middle of the night. Later that day Stewart tried to reach Woolston-Smith, but the investigator was away for the weekend. Stewart finally reached him on Monday, June 19. According to Woolston-Smith, Stewart was "elated." Asked what he was elated about, the private detective said, "Elated that we had more or less called it the way it happened."

Asked to elaborate further, Woolston-Smith said, "This enthusiasm seemed to have been, well, we may not have this election, but boy, we have got them in real great position." He said this was because Stewart thought there was definite involvement in the break-in of the Committee to Re-elect the President (CRP). Woolston-Smith said that the DNC people were "expecting the newspapers to develop it."

Stewart painted a very different picture. According to his testimony, his contact with Woolston-Smith was extremely limited and the investigator's information was "so unsubstantiated that it certainly was not the basis for action on our part." He indicated that he had only one telephone conversation with him before Watergate. At first he could not recall any meeting with him prior to June 17. Only when he was told that others had testified he had met with Haddad, Woolston-Smith, and Winter would Stewart admit that it was possible. Stewart also had difficulty recalling the letter Haddad had sent him dated April 28, two days after the New York meeting. Though the letter had described Woolston-Smith's story as "true and explosive," Stewart said he had no recollection of having seen it, though that too was possible. But he did say that following the Watergate arrests, he had recalled Woolston-Smith's warning and gave him a call to ask whether he had any additional information. But, according to Stewart, Woolston-Smith said he knew nothing more.

It was obvious to Thompson and his investigators that someone wasn't telling the truth. While Haddad and Woolston-Smith often gave the impression of being fuzzy and less than candid in their testimony, Stewart seemed to go to unusual lengths to play down his meetings and conversations with Haddad and Woolston-Smith. So lacking in credibility was Stewart's testimony that his inquisitors wondered what he was afraid of. Would the admission that the Democratic high command had taken Woolston-Smith's warning seriously have been so damaging?

Apparently it would. For if the DNC had taken the warning seriously, it would have been difficult to explain why no obvious defensive measures had been taken. Woolston-Smith did not accept the idea that there was no money available for security. He noted that field force meters to detect bugs could have been purchased at little cost. And he pointed out that while the DNC was crying poverty, Larry O'Brien was hitting the committee for numerous "perks," including a round-the-clock chauffeured limousine.

Woolston-Smith's conclusion, as he told Senate investigators, was that the DNC had a plan to let the break-in and bugging take place and then capitalize on it.

Whether that was indeed the plan has never been fully established. What is intriguing, though, is the speed with which the DNC proceeded to file a $1 million lawsuit against the Committee to Re-elect the President. On the Tuesday following the weekend arrests, Larry O'Brien announced the suit which, he said, was an attempt to force the issue into examination in U.S. District Court.

Thompson and his staff finally were forced to terminate their investigation of the prior-knowledge angle before they could obtain answers to some perplexing questions. Just how did Haddad and Woolston-Smith manage to amass such accurate information on the Watergate break-in in advance? Did they have access to information obtained by electronic surveillance? Or was there a double agent within the ranks of the Watergate burglars?

Suspicions had fallen on James McCord, who had bungled the break-in, kept in touch with the CIA, confessed to federal Judge

John Sirica, and ended up serving very little time in jail. McCord's name had come up at the April 26 meeting in Haddad's office. While looking into the November Group, Woolston-Smith had learned that McCord had come up from Washington to check whether, as suspected, the group's phones were being tapped. The lines most definitely had been tampered with. On one occasion an office conversation on the WATS line was interrupted by an unknown party who began cursing out Nixon as a "murderer" of women and children in Vietnam.

It wasn't too long before Woolston-Smith learned that McCord, a former FBI agent as well as a CIA employee, considered himself to be "a bit of a wireman"—in other words, something of an expert in electronic surveillance. And the investigator also learned that McCord was buying all sorts of electronic equipment, paying for it with $100 bills and, in one case, leaving his CRP calling card. The word soon got out in the inbred world of intelligence operatives that the security chief for the Nixon campaign effort was up to something.

But why did Woolston-Smith become interested in the November Group in the first place? According to his testimony, the private eye first began probing into its affairs in December 1971. As it turned out, the November Group was a legitimate enterprise set up by the Nixon reelection campaign to handle its newspaper advertising and television commercials. Yet Woolston-Smith became so suspicious of what he thought it was doing that he personally cased its premises. He testified, however, that he did this from the hallway, never going inside. But why? And why, as it later developed, did the CIA keep a dossier on Woolston-Smith?

Jack Anderson, who later informed investigators he had misplaced the letter containing the Haddad file on the bugging plans, reported that he was not able to develop any further information on the basis of what Haddad had provided. The columnist recalled receiving a rather "sloppy" one-page letter ("kind of dashed off hurriedly") from Haddad some time in April 1972, advising that the November Group was going to wiretap the Democratic National Committee. He said he had run into a stone wall and just dropped the matter. For one thing he looked into the November Group and found it to be perfectly above board. However, as he disclosed in his column, he subsequently learned that McCord, while in New York checking out the group's phones, had "made the mistake of confiding his plans to bug the

Democrats to old FBI friends. The word spread through the investigative community, reaching us in Washington two months before the celebrated Watergate break-in."

By coincidence Anderson was a friend of one of the Miamians apprehended at the Watergate—Frank Sturgis, a non-Cuban soldier of fortune who had connections with the CIA and had participated in anti-Castro activities. It was through Sturgis that Anderson became knowledgeable about Cuban underground affairs. For example he had once met Bernard Barker, later the team leader of the break-in, through Sturgis. They had spoken of a mysterious "Eduardo," their CIA superior during the Bay of Pigs, and only after Watergate did Anderson realize they were speaking of E. Howard Hunt.

In an article in the July 22, 1973, issue of *Parade* magazine, thirteen months after the Watergate break-in, Anderson made what appeared to Thompson's investigators to be an amazing revelation. The columnist reported that on June 16, 1972, less than twenty-four hours before the break-in, he had "run into" Sturgis at Washington's National Airport. Anderson wrote that he was surprised to see his old friend because usually the Miamian would call him before he came to Washington. Though he was in a hurry to catch a plane for Cleveland, Anderson stopped to chat. He asked Sturgis what he was doing in Washington. "Private business," replied Sturgis, who then introduced him to Virgilio Gonzalez, the Cuban locksmith who was to pick the Watergate locks the next day.

Two days later Anderson learned the nature of Sturgis's "private business." The front pages carried the story of the Watergate arrests. Anderson then paid a visit to the District of Columbia jail to see Sturgis. In fact he got there before the jailers even had Sturgis's correct name. Sturgis had been booked under an alias, Anderson testified, and he had a hard time finding him. The columnist said he found his old friend "tight lipped," saying only that the Watergate project had been part of the struggle against Castro. In return for their services, Sturgis said he and his fellow burglars had been promised, among other things, that some Cuban refugees living in Europe would be permitted to resettle in Miami. After this visit Anderson sought to have Sturgis released to his custody, but the Justice Department was adamantly opposed.

"My court appearance in Sturgis' behalf also disturbed the Democrats," wrote Anderson. "After I printed details of Larry

O'Brien's expense accounts, the Democrats issued a statement suggesting I had received information stolen from their offices by the Waterbuggers. I had managed, as usual, to gain the enmity of both political parties."

According to Thompson, there were other unanswered questions concerning who else may have had prior knowledge of the Watergate break-in. But under the press of a deadline and handicapped by representing a minority party at the mercy of an antagonistic majority, Thompson's small staff didn't have the time or the resources to pursue every lead or to force the reconciliation of every contradiction. And contradictions there were aplenty.

Probably the most intriguing area of investigation conducted by Thompson under the aegis of Senator Howard Baker, vice chairman of the Watergate Committee, had to do with exactly what the CIA knew—and when. The investigation came up with no hard answers, only more questions, the main reason being the obvious unwillingness of the CIA to come clean on what it knew. And apparently the Agency knew plenty.

That the White House wasn't always pleased with the CIA was established in testimony. Indeed one witness, David Young, told how his boss Kissinger would sometimes write, "This is a piece of crap," across CIA estimates and return them to Langley. When Young and Egil Krogh were assigned to establish the "plumbers" —the White House task force formed to plug national security leaks—the CIA realized it had a competitor, and subsequently there were a number of connections between the CIA and the plumbers. Which raised the question whether the CIA had sabotaged the Watergate break-in in order to weaken the White House and strengthen the Agency. After all the CIA had done jobs like that before.

Consider what happened at the home of James McCord shortly after he and the other Watergate burglars had been apprehended. His wife began burning his papers. Present at the time was a CIA operative named Lee R. Pennington, Jr. Though Pennington later testified that his presence had been strictly coincidental, Baker flatly charged that Pennington had "destroyed documents which might show a link between McCord and the CIA." But McCord's connection with the Agency was not exactly a secret. So why the burning of the documents? The only conceivable answer was that they might have established a CIA relationship with McCord at the time of the break-in.

– 247 –

But even more startling was the frenzied effort by the CIA to mislead the FBI about the incident; when the Bureau inquired about a "Pennington" in August 1972, the CIA furnished information about a former employee with a similar name who—as Baker later noted—"was obviously not the man the FBI was interested in." If ever there was an effort to obstruct justice, this was it. Information about the "real" Pennington was provided to Watergate probers in February 1974, a year and a half later, only after a low-echelon CIA employee protested an order to remove the material from the Agency's Watergate files to prevent its disclosure. The unnamed "personnel security officer #1" informed his superiors, according to closed-door testimony, that he would not be party to the destruction of the Pennington documents.

Another murky episode was the destruction of tape recordings of certain room and telephone conversations on orders of Richard Helms just before he departed as CIA director to become ambassador to Iran. This was approximately a week after Helms had received a letter from Senate Majority Leader Mike Mansfield requesting that the Agency safeguard all evidence pertaining to Watergate. Some of the lost tapes were phone conversations with President Nixon, H. R. Haldeman, and John Ehrlichman. Helms later insisted that none of the conversations had anything to do with Watergate. Moreover he said that the tape wipeout was customary whenever a new director took over. But according to Baker's final report, two facts seem clear: "First, the only other destruction for which the CIA has any record was on January 21, 1972, when tapes for 1964 and 1965 were destroyed (there are no records of periodic destructions); and secondly, never before had there been a destruction of all existing tapes." Which, in effect, raised questions concerning Helms's precipitate behavior which, according to Baker, were never resolved.

A third area of focus in the Baker report was the relationship of E. Howard Hunt with the CIA. There can be little doubt that the relationship was extensive. A longtime employee who retired from the Agency in 1970, Hunt—at White House request—was given full CIA cooperation in the Daniel Ellsberg incident. Thus, among other things, the Agency assigned its psychiatrists to assemble a "profile" of the intense young intellectual who had purloined the Pentagon Papers and then released them to the press.

The Baker report noted that CIA assistance to Hunt—which

included the furnishing of false driver's licenses and identification papers, pocket litter, a voice changer, wig, fake glasses, a
Uher recorder disguised in a typewriter case, a camera hidden
in a tobacco pouch, and the like—was not terminated until August 27, 1971, one week before the break-in at the offices of Ellsberg's psychiatrist, Dr. Lewis Fielding. CIA laboratories also developed photos taken by Hunt and Liddy when they "cased" Dr.
Fielding's office in Beverly Hills. One CIA official who reviewed
the film testified that he found the photos "intriguing" and recognized they were taken in southern California. He then ordered
one of the photos enlarged. The blow-up revealed Dr. Fielding's
name in the parking lot next to his office, which information was
immediately taken to higher-ups at the CIA.

And although the CIA publicly claimed it had no contact
"whatsoever" with Hunt after August 1971, the Senate investigation disclosed at least a half-dozen later contacts continuing into
the spring of 1972. In fact the CIA psychiatric study of Ellsberg
was not completed until November 1971. All of which led Senator
Baker to contend that "documents and conflicting testimony of
CIA personnel" had raised questions about "whether the CIA
had advance knowledge of the Fielding break-in."

Hunt maintained still another CIA connection. After leaving
the Agency in 1970, he joined the Robert R. Mullen & Co. on a
parttime basis. The Mullen organization was a Washington public relations firm which had long provided a "cover" for CIA
operatives in Europe and Asia. President of Mullen was Robert
F. Bennett, the son of Senator Wallace Bennett, a Utah Republican. Shortly after he joined the Mullen firm in 1971, Bennett was
introduced to the firm's CIA case officer. In joining Mullen, Bennett brought over a prestigious public relations account—that of
the Hughes Tool Company, Howard Hughes's major corporation. According to CIA records, the Agency had given consideration to utilizing the Mullen-Hughes Tool relationship to provide
a "cover" arrangement in South America, as well as to gather
information on Robert Maheu, the CIA's former go-between
with the Mafia in the unsuccessful Castro assassination plots. Why
the Agency wanted information on Maheu was never made
clear. But Maheu had been fired by Hughes, an act which had
resulted in a bitter court fight.

Bennett's accessibility to the CIA raised questions in Baker's
mind concerning possible Agency involvement in, or knowledge
of, his relations with Hunt's activities in the White House plum-

bers. Bennett, for example, helped arrange a Hunt interview with someone who had claimed to know something about Ted Kennedy and Chappaquiddick. It turned out he knew nothing. Bennett also coordinated the release of a statement by lobbyist Dita Beard intended to clear the Nixon administration of any impropriety in its dealings with ITT. Hunt had flown to her hospital bedside in Denver after Bennett learned of her whereabouts from a Hughes executive. And it was Bennett who reported that a safe in Las Vegas contained material which could be of extreme interest to both Hughes and the CRP. The safe was that of Hank Greenspun, a newspaper publisher who had aroused the ire of Howard Hughes. And among the items in the safe reportedly were memoranda from the billionaire recluse himself. Plans for a break-in were aborted however, largely because Hughes's attorneys said their employer could live without recovery of the documents. It was Bennett, too, who asked for and received from Hunt an estimate on what it would cost to wiretap Clifford Irving, then writing the spurious Hughes "autobiography." The Hughes people decided the venture wasn't worth the risk.

Bennett was also in on Hunt's recruitment of a young student, Tom Gregory, to act as a spy in both the Muskie and McGovern campaigns. In fact when Gregory had second thoughts about plans to wiretap the phones at McGovern's headquarters, he went to Bennett and told him he was quitting. This was on June 16, 1972, the day before the Watergate break-in. Two days after the Watergate episode, which was before Hunt's name surfaced in the press, Bennett talked with Hunt and apparently all but confirmed his strong suspicion that his parttime employee was deeply involved with the burglary. Bennett, according to Baker, provided "detailed knowledge of the Watergate incident to his CIA case officer" on July 10, 1972, less than a month after the break-in. The case officer's report, which was handwritten, was hand delivered to Director Helms on or before July 14, 1972; but the information was never relayed to the FBI which, after all, was investigating the case.

Immediately after the break-in Bennett began to serve as liaison between Hunt and Liddy, all the while presumably reporting to his CIA case officer. Yet none of this was relayed to the FBI. In fact Bennett later conceded he had not been fully responsive while appearing before the grand jury—a fact that took on added importance when it was disclosed that the CIA had paid half of his attorney's fees when he testified.

Some of the information which Bennett withheld from the grand jury he transmitted to Edward Bennett Williams, counsel to the Democratic National Committee which had filed suit against CRP. Bennett had reported to his case officer that he had established this "back door entry" to Williams in order to "kill off" revelations of the CIA's relationship with the Mullen organization. At the same time Bennett reported that he was planting phony stories with the media, specifically *Newsweek* magazine, which would lead investigators away from any CIA involvement. He seemed to take particular relish in fingering Charles Colson as being implicated in Hunt's activities. Bennett also claimed to have been feeding stories to the Washington *Post*'s Bob Woodward, who was "suitably grateful" and was "protecting" Bennett and the Mullen Company.

Obviously the CIA had known plenty of the operations of the "plumbers" unit at the White House. But what did the Agency know in advance about the break-in at the Watergate? In the period between March and May of 1972, according to the Baker report, Hunt contacted the CIA's External Employment Assistance Branch for former Agency personnel who might be willing to become involved in espionage operations. Hunt was particularly seeking to hire a "retired lock-picker," an "entry man," and other similarly gifted operatives.

At the same time the Agency was aware that Hunt had been in contact with one of its Cuban informants, Eugenio Martinez. A former fulltime employee then on retainer to the Agency, Martinez had participated in the Hunt-directed break-in of the office of Ellsberg's former psychiatrist in early September of 1971.

That Martinez discussed his relationship with Hunt with both his CIA case officer and the Miami chief of station has been established by Senator Baker's investigation. In March 1972 when Hunt began recruiting Cuban exiles for the Watergate caper, he again made contact with Martinez in Miami. At that time Martinez somewhat cryptically advised the CIA station chief that Hunt was employed by the White House and "asked the Chief of Station if he was sure that he had been apprised of all Agency activities in the Miami area." So concerned was the station chief, he later testified, that he wrote a letter to CIA headquarters asking about Hunt's status. The response from headquarters was that Hunt was on "domestic White House business of an un-known nature," and that the station chief should "cool it." Why the CIA didn't show more interest in Hunt's doings was later to perplex Baker and his investigators. The station chief himself was to testify about his astonishment.

Actually, as Baker's probers discovered, Martinez had two case officers during 1971 and 1972. The first one, according to the CIA, was on "African safari" at the time of the Watergate break-in, an assertion which raised the eyebrows of the investigators. But this was contradicted by the second case officer, who said that his predecessor was still in Miami on June 19, 1972, two days after the break-in. And when Baker asked that the first case officer be brought back for interrogation, the Agency said it couldn't be done since he had been reassigned to Indochina. At the same time the CIA denied the investigators access to the Martinez case officer reports. In other words the Agency did everything conceivably possible to prevent a thorough investigation. Why? That is the question that continues to haunt Baker, Thompson, and their tiny team of investigators.

And why did the CIA unloose all its media weapons in a desperate effort to discredit the Baker investigation? When the senator first began digging into the CIA's mysteries, the question was raised in the press whether Baker was looking for facts or for an alibi for Nixon. And in their syndicated columns, Tom Braden, an old CIA agent himself, as well as Evans and Novak, both friends of Helms, assailed Baker for seeking to advance his own political aims even though his investigation could harm the CIA. When Baker, under the press of a deadline, finally came up with an admittedly incomplete report of the CIA's possible involvement with Watergate, the Washington *Post* predictably concluded that the senator had "done a difficult job unsatisfactorily."

With former CIA operatives on the Watergate burglar squad; with a CIA man suddenly turning up at James McCord's home and destroying documents that might link McCord and the CIA; with Director Helms admitting that CIA tapes of conversations involving Nixon, Haldeman, Ehrlichman, and other White House officials were destroyed; with powerful Washington figures including Senator Stuart Symington protecting CIA—was it any wonder that Senator Baker, in exasperation, declared there were "animals crashing around in the forest"? Again Chairman Ervin refused the minority request to include their CIA findings in the final report of the Watergate Committee. And he had the support of most of the other senators on the committee, including Republican Lowell Weicker. After reading the Baker report, Ervin said he had learned nothing new about the CIA role. "I think it made some foolish mistakes," he said; he was not interested in checking out the extraordinary array of contradictions in testimony elicited by Baker's men.

Thus the Chairman made sure that the focus remained resolutely on the main task—"getting" Richard Nixon.

18

AS IT TURNED OUT, THE ONE PERSON WHO
had absolutely no advance knowledge of the Watergate break-in
was Richard M. Nixon.

A careful examination of the various tapes that Nixon was
forced to turn over to the Special Watergate Prosecutor demonstrated beyond question that the President didn't have the slight-
est inkling that a group of "jackasses"—as he was later to describe
them in what he believed to be the privacy of the Oval Office—
was planning the caper whose unraveling was eventually to lead
to his resignation.

Nixon's lack of knowledge was made clear, even before the
existence of the White House tapes became known, by Jeb Stuart
Magruder. In his testimony before the Senate Watergate Committee on June 14, 1973, the former deputy director of CRP
stated: "As far as I know, at no point during this entire period,
from the time of planning the Watergate to the time of trying to
keep it from public view, did the President have any knowledge
of our errors in this matter. He had confidence in his aides, and
I must confess that some of us failed him."

This finding was confirmed by an even more credible authority. Following the Watergate cover-up trial the chief U.S. prosecutor, James Neal, was asked by *Time* correspondent Hays
Gorey: "Did Nixon authorize the Watergate bugging?"

"No," replied Neal. "The tapes show some surprise on Nixon's
part when he was told of the break-in." And he gave as an example what he heard on the crucial so-called smoking gun tape of
June 23, 1972. A week after the break-in at Democratic headquarters, Nixon asked his chief of staff H. R. (Bob) Haldeman, "Who
was the asshole that did it? Was it Liddy?"

On February 28, 1973, in a conversation with White House
Counsel John Dean III, the President stated: "Of course, I am not
dumb and I will never forget when I heard about this (adjective
deleted) forced entry and bugging. I thought, what in the hell is

this? What is the matter with these people? Are they crazy? I thought they were nuts! A prank! But it wasn't! It wasn't very funny. I think that our Democratic friends know that, too. They know what the hell it was. They don't think we'd be involved in such."

"I think they do too," Dean said.

"Maybe they don't. They don't think I would be involved in such stuff. They think I have people capable of it. And they are correct, in that Colson would do anything."

As it turned out, Colson was never officially accused of having had anything to do with the break-in. He eventually served time after pleading guilty to a totally unrelated charge, that he had interfered with justice by conspiring to "defame" Daniel Ellsberg—as hoked up a charge as ever came down the pike.

Dean himself strongly disclaimed to the President that anyone at the White House had any prior knowledge of the break-in. On the morning of March 21, 1973, the lawyer observed, "I honestly believe that no one over here knew that. I know that as God is my maker I had no knowledge that they were going to do this."

Still the break-in did occur. But to many Watergate buffs the big mystery—as yet unexplained—is why the burglary-cum-bugging was ordered in the first place. The feeling persists, many years after the event, that no logical motive for the senseless deed has yet been provided. Perversely enough Ron Ziegler's characterization of Watergate as a "third-rate burglary" remains the only rational explanation.

Actually Watergate isn't that much of a mystery. The basic story can be found in the transcripts of the presidential tapes.

On the morning of March 21, 1973, John Dean III entered the Oval Office for a long talk with President Nixon. An ambitious young protégé of Attorney General Mitchell at the Justice Department, Dean had been named White House counsel after John Ehrlichman had been named assistant to the President for domestic affairs.

After some chit chat Dean got to the point. "The reason that I thought we ought to talk this morning is because in our conversations, I have the impression that you don't know everything I know. . . . We have a cancer—within—close to the presidency, that's growing. It is growing daily. It's compounded, growing geometrically now, because it compounds itself. . . .

"How did it all start," Dean went on, "where did it all start? It started with an instruction to me from Bob Haldeman to see if we couldn't set up a perfectly legitimate campaign intelligence operation over at the Re-Election Committee. Not being in this business, I turned to somebody who had been in this business, Jack Caulfield. I don't remember whether you remember Jack or not. He was your original bodyguard before they had the candidate protection, an old city policeman."

The President remembered Caulfield. A former New York City police officer, Caulfield's official job at the White House was to act as liaison with various law enforcement agencies. His immediate superior, at the beginning, was Ehrlichman. He was then transferred over to Dean.

At Dean's suggestion Caulfield came up with a plan to gather intelligence about the political opposition. Dean told the President that he had taken the plan to both Ehrlichman and Mitchell, "and the consensus was that Caulfield was not the man to do this. In retrospect, that might have been a bad call because he is an incredibly cautious person and wouldn't have put the situation where it is today."

In retrospect too, dumping the "incredibly cautious" Caulfield may well have been the first major blunder of the Watergate affair. For, under pressure to find someone else to take over the intelligence assignment, Dean came up with G. Gordon Liddy. First off, as Dean told the President, Liddy was a lawyer. Then, because of his FBI background, he "had an intelligence background." Moreover Dean was aware that "he had done some extremely sensitive things for the White House . . . and he had apparently done them well."

Among other things Liddy had "worked with leaks," tracking them down, said Dean. Egil Krogh, who had headed the plumbers, had reported that "he was a hell of a good man . . . and could set up a proper operation," according to Dean.

After he was hired by the CRP, Liddy was asked to put together a plan to gather intelligence about the political opposition. In January 1972 Magruder called Dean to attend a meeting at Mitchell's office in order to listen to Liddy explain his plan.

At first, Dean told the President, he was reticent about going. "I said I don't really know if I am the man, but if you want me there I will be happy to. So I came over and Liddy laid out a million dollar plan that was the most incredible thing I have ever laid my eyes on: all in codes, and involved black bag operations, kidnapping, providing prostitutes to weaken the opposition, bugging, mugging teams. It was an incredible thing."

"Tell me this," the President interrupted, "did Mitchell go along—?"

"No, no, not at all. Mitchell just sat there puffing and laughing. I could tell from—after Liddy left the office I said that is the most incredible thing I have ever seen. He said, 'I agree.' And so Liddy was told to go back to the drawing board and come up with something realistic. So there was a second meeting. They asked me to come over to that. I came into the tail end of the meeting. I wasn't there for the first part."

When he arrived, Dean discovered that they were discussing bugging, kidnapping, and the like. Dean was alarmed. He broke in and said, "These are not the sort of things that are ever to be discussed in the office of the Attorney General of the United States . . . and I am personally incensed."

Dean told the President he had been "trying to get Mitchell off the hook. He is a nice person and doesn't like to have to say no when he is talking with people he is going to have to work with."

"That's right," the President said.

"So I let it be known. I said, 'You all pack that stuff up and get it the hell out of here. You just can't talk this way in this office and you should re-examine your whole thinking.' "

"Who all was present?" the President asked.

"It was Magruder, Mitchell, Liddy and myself. I came back right after the meeting and told Bob [Haldeman], 'Bob, we have a growing disaster on our hands if they are thinking this way,' and I said, 'The White House has got to stay out of this and I, frankly, am not going to be involved in it." Bob said, 'I agree John.' "

At this point, Dean told the President, he thought the plan had been "turned off because it was an absurd proposal." And while he had some other dealings with Liddy, they never discussed the matter again. "Now that would be hard to believe for some people, but we never did. That is the fact of the matter."

At any rate, Dean continued, from what he was later able to learn by putting the pieces together, Liddy returned to his CRP office "and tried to come up with another plan that he could sell. They were telling him that he was putting too much money in it. I don't think they were discounting the illegal points. Jeb is not a lawyer. He did not know whether this is the way the game was played and what it was all about. They came up, apparently, with another plan, but they couldn't get it approved by anybody over there. So Liddy and Hunt apparently came to see Chuck Colson, and Colson picked up the telephone and called Magruder and said, 'You all either fish or cut bait. This is absurd to have these guys over there and not using them. If you are not going to use them, I may use them.' Things of this nature."

"When was this?" the President asked.

"This was apparently in February of seventy-two."

"Did Colson know what they were talking about?"

"I can only assume, because of his close relationship with Hunt, that he had a damn good idea what they were talking about, a damn good idea. He would probably deny it today. . . ."*

Did Dean think that Colson was "the person who pushed," the President asked.

"I think he helped to get the thing off the dime. Now something else occurred though—"

Had Colson talked to anyone at the White House?

"No, I think this was—"

"Did he talk with Haldeman?"

"No, I don't think so. But there is the next thing that comes in the chain. I think Bob was assuming that they had something that was proper over there, some intelligence gathering operation that Liddy was operating. And [Gordon] Strachan, who was [Haldeman's] tickler, started pushing them to get some information and they—Magruder—took that as a signal to probably go to Mitchell and to say, 'They are pushing us like crazy for this from the White House.' "

"And so," Dean continued, almost without catching his breath, "Mitchell probably puffed on his pipe and said, 'Go ahead,' and never really reflected on what it was all about. So they had some plan that obviously had, I gather, some different targets. . . . They were going to infiltrate, and bug, and do all this sort of thing to a lot of these targets. This is knowledge I have after the fact. Apparently after they had initially broken in and bugged the DNC, they were getting information. The information was coming over here to Strachan and some of it was given to Haldeman, there is no doubt about it."

"Did (Haldeman) know where it was coming from?" the President interjected.

"I don't really know if he would," Dean replied.

"Not necessarily?"

---

*Colson did deny it. Though he did make the phone call in question, he later said he did not believe that the Hunt-Liddy scheme involved illegalities.

"Not necessarily. Strachan knew it. There is no doubt about it, and whether Strachan—I have never come to press these people on these points because it hurts them to give up that next inch, so I had to piece things together. Strachan was aware of receiving information, reporting to Bob. At one point Bob even gave instructions to change their capabilities from Muskie to McGovern, and passed this back through Strachan to Magruder and apparently to Liddy. And Liddy was starting to make arrangements to go in and bug the McGovern operation."

"They had never bugged Muskie, though, did they?"

"No, they hadn't, but they had infiltrated it by a secretary."

"By a secretary?"

"By a secretary and a chauffeur. There is nothing illegal about that. So the information was coming over here and then I, finally, after—. The next point in time that I became aware of anything was on June seventeenth when I got the word that there had been this break-in at the DNC and somebody from our Committee had been caught in the DNC. And I said, 'Oh (expletive deleted).' You know, eventually putting the pieces together—"

"You knew what it was."

"I knew who it was. So I called Liddy on Monday morning and said, 'First, Gordon, I want to know whether anybody in the White House was involved in this.' And he said, 'No, they weren't.' I said, 'Well I want to know how in (adjective deleted) name this happened.' He said, 'Well, I was pushed without mercy by Magruder to get in there and to get more information. That the information was not satisfactory. That Magruder said, 'The White House is not happy with what we are getting.' "

"The White House?"

"The White House. Yeah!"

"Who," the President asked, "do you think was pushing him?"

"Well, I think it was probably Strachan thinking that Bob wanted things, because I have seen that happen on other occasions where things have been said to have been of very prime importance when they really weren't."

"Why at that point in time I wonder?" the President asked. "I am just trying to think. We had just finished the Moscow trip. The Democrats had just nominated McGovern.* I mean, (expletive deleted), what in the hell were these people doing? I can see

---

*Nixon's time sequence was confused; actually George McGovern was nominated as the Democratic candidate for President a month later in Miami Beach.

their doing it earlier. I can see the pressures, but I don't see why all the pressure was on then."

"I don't know, other than the fact that they might have been looking for information about the conventions."

"That's right."

"Because, I understand that after the fact that there was a plan to bug Larry O'Brien's suite down in Florida. So Liddy told me that this is what had happened and this is why it had happened."

"Where did he learn that there were plans to bug Larry O'Brien's suite?"

"From Magruder, long after the fact."

"Magruder is (unintelligible)."

"Yeah. Magruder is totally knowledgeable on the whole thing. . . . I know that Magruder has perjured himself in the Grand Jury. I know that [Herbert] Porter has perjured himself in the Grand Jury."

"Who is Porter?"

"He is one of Magruder's deputies. They set up this scenario which they ran by me. They said, 'How about this?' I said, 'I don't know. If this is what you are going to hang on, fine.'"

"What did they say in the Grand Jury?"

"They said . . . that Liddy had come over as Counsel and we knew he had these capacities to do legitimate intelligence. We had no idea what he was doing. He was given an authorization of $250,000 to collect information, because our surrogates were out on the road. They had no protection, and we had information that there were going to be demonstrations against them, and that we had to have a plan as to what they were going to be confronted with and Liddy was charged with doing this. We had no knowledge that he was going to bug the DNC."

"The point is, that is not true?"

"That's right."

"Magruder did know it was going to take place."

"Magruder gave the instructions to be back in the DNC."

"He did?"

"Yes."

"You know that?"

"Yes."

"I see. O.K."

"I honestly believe that no one over here knew that," said Dean. "I know that as God is my maker, I had no knowledge that they were going to do this."

From Dean's account to the President it becomes obvious that the break-in, at the very least, was not carefully conceived. If anything, it was largely the brainchild of G. Gordon Liddy. A flamboyant character, Liddy had been an FBI agent in the early 1960s, then an assistant district attorney in New York's Dutchess County. In 1968 Liddy had run unsuccessfully for the Republican nomination in what was then New York's 28th Congressional District. Congressman Hamilton Fish, Jr., the man who beat him, recommended Liddy for a job with the Nixon administration.

His first job was at the Treasury Department, where he aroused the ire of his superiors for his unabashed opposition—publicly—to gun-control legislation. From there he kept getting tossed around like a hot potato. For a time he worked with Bud Krogh at the White House on drug-related projects, then with the plumbers. Then he was sent over to CRP as general counsel. Within four months he moved over to the finance committee as counsel. Stories of his eccentricities abounded, but no one had quite the guts to fire him.

Magruder, for example, couldn't whip up enough courage to get rid of him. In his Senate testimony he told of meeting Liddy in a hallway.

"I simply put my hand on Mr. Liddy's shoulder and he asked me to remove it and indicated that if I did not serious consequences would occur," Magruder testified.

"Was he more specific than serious consequences?"

"Well, he indicated he would kill me."

Fear of Liddy and his seeming penchant for violence, in the final analysis, may well have been the reason why his colleagues gave him leeway in carrying out some of his crackpot schemes. And to assist him in gathering intelligence, Liddy hired a former CIA agent named E. Howard Hunt on a parttime basis. They had worked together on several plumbers assignments, including the effort to obtain defamatory material on Ellsberg. And they got along quite well.

By this time Hunt was also working for the Mullen Company, the public relations firm with CIA ties. In fact Hunt had made the connection as a result of an intervention by Richard Helms. Bob Mullen, the founder of the firm, later said that the CIA director had "twisted my arm" to give Hunt a job. Hunt had retired from the CIA a day before.

When Robert Bennett later joined the Mullen firm, he brought with him a choice public relations account. He had been named

Howard Hughes's Washington representative, succeeding Larry O'Brien, who had been on the Hughes payroll for a fee of $15,000 a month. In all O'Brien served the multimillionaire recluse for sixteen months. For eleven of those months O'Brien also served as chairman of the Democratic National Committee. As Ron Rosenbaum noted in *The Village Voice:*

> It might be unfair to call O'Brien a high-level fixer for Hughes, but with Democratic majorities in both Houses of Congress and on most of the federal regulatory agencies it probably didn't do Hughes any harm to have the Democratic National Chairman on the payroll. O'Brien never denied or attempted to cover up the fact that he was working for Howard Hughes, but he certainly didn't publicize the relationship very strenuously and he never revealed how much he was getting paid. In eleven months of serving two masters, O'Brien received $165,000 from Howard Hughes. While there may be no violation of the law in such conduct, consider the outcry if, for instance, it were revealed that Republican National Chairman George Bush was receiving a $500 per day salary from Exxon.

While O'Brien never denied his Hughes connection, very few people in his own party knew about it. And exactly what he did for all that bread was never officially disclosed. There were reports that he had tried to help arrange an out-of-court settlement of the Hughes-TWA lawsuit. And there was some talk of his publicizing the "humanitarian efforts" of the Hughes Medical Foundation. But his efforts did not appear to be overly successful.

At any rate it was at Hughes's personal instructions that O'Brien had been hired. The recruiting was done by the multimillionaire's chief lieutenant Robert Maheu. Hughes had gotten interested in O'Brien following Robert F. Kennedy's assassination. O'Brien had served as campaign manager in Bobby's tragically aborted run for the presidential nomination. Hughes wrote this memo to Maheu, "What is O'Brien going to do? Why don't we get hold of him?"

Eventually they got hold of him.

The point is that Hughes didn't give a damn about a man's politics—whether he be Democrat or Republican, liberal or conservative. All that mattered was how much good that individual could do for Hughes. Thus he frequently financed Democrats and Republicans seeking the same office, but always tailoring his contribution to a candidate's chances of winning, giving more heavily to the front runner. In 1968, for example, Hughes transmitted $25,000 to Robert Kennedy for his presidential primary battles. Later he contributed to both Humphrey and Nixon, who were contesting each other for the presidency.

After the 1968 election when Congress was considering legislation affecting tax-exempt organizations such as the Howard Hughes Medical Institute, Hughes hired the Washington law firm of Clifford, Warnke, Glass, McIlwain & Finney, whose senior partners included longtime advisers to Democratic presidents—former Defense Secretary Clark Clifford among them. And eight years before, at the start of the Kennedy administration, when Hughes was contesting TWA's directors for control of the airline, he sent Bob Maheu to meet with Lyndon Johnson about the problem. The Vice President suggested the hiring of the firm of Arnold, Fortas & Porter, of which LBJ's longtime friend and associate Abe Fortas was then a senior partner. This Hughes did.

O'Brien's profitable arrangement with Hughes was terminated in early 1971 when the multimillionaire had a falling out with Maheu, sparking a bitter court fight. That's when Bennett entered the picture. And that's when Bennett began using Hunt in connection with the all-important Hughes account. Thus, according to Hunt, he was informed by Bennett of being approached by "the Hughes people" about the possibility of bugging Clifford Irving's home. And it was Bennett who suggested that there were documents in the safe of Las Vegas publisher Hank Greenspun which could be of decided interest to both "the Hughes people" and the CRP.

Already in place was the burglary team which had previously broken into the offices of the Ellsberg psychiatrist. And Hunt, who had directed that bungled caper, was not adverse to using the team in behalf of what he perceived to be the interests of Howard Hughes. In fact Hunt conceived of a combined operation, involving the entry team and the Hughes people, aimed at cracking into the Greenspun safe. What Hunt wanted from the Hughes organization was a getaway plane to fly the team to a Central American country.

"Gee," a Hughes man recalled asking Hunt, "suppose you get caught?"

"We're professionals," replied Hunt. "Don't worry about that."

The Hughes people rejected the proposal. But they were most decidedly interested in what Maheu was up to, particularly his relations with Larry O'Brien.

Which may well provide the answer to the still-recurring question as to why the Watergate burglars sought to wiretap O'Brien. Hunt thus had hit upon the seemingly brilliant idea of combining public and private service. By supposedly obtaining political ammunition aimed at the Democrats, he would also be serving the interests of "the Hughes people."

O'Brien at the time headed a party that was $9 million in debt and whose membership was so divided that he could not lure all its representatives to the same dinner table. As he later observed, "The Democrats didn't seem to think much of me; but to the Republicans, I was a giant."

An equally tantalizing question is why the phone of R. Spencer Oliver, Jr., was selected for tapping. Comparatively unknown in the political world, Oliver was the youthful executive director of the Association of Democratic State Chairmen, a post which did not involve much crucial decisionmaking. But by coincidence Oliver's father, Robert Oliver, was an account executive at the Mullen company. In fact Bennett had placed him in day-to-day charge of the firm's most important account—that of the Hughes Tool Company. There had even been discussions at one point about young Oliver buying into the Mullen firm. And it was known that Hunt was not too happy about the idea of having a liberal Democrat around the premises.

As it turned out, the Oliver tap was the only one that functioned following the first Watergate break-in. The O'Brien tap had failed to work. But the material garnered from the Oliver tap was considered "garbage" by those who, like Jeb Magruder, perused it. As John Ehrlichman was later to testify, "They learned a great deal more about Mr. Oliver than anybody really wanted to know."

From the very beginning Watergate had more the elements of high farce than great tragedy. A group of bunglers had been turned loose to gather political intelligence and, needless to say, they did everything wrong. Probably contributing the most to the botched-up caper was James W. McCord, Jr., who had taken over as the CRP's fulltime security chief on January 1, 1972. He had been recommended for the job by Jack Caulfield and Al Wong, an old friend who was then deputy assistant director of the Secret Service. (One of Wong's assignments was the installation of the taping system at the White House.)

McCord's credentials seemed impressive. He had spent twenty-five years in government service, seventeen of them with the CIA. When he retired from the Agency in August 1970, he was presented with a distinguished service award for outstanding performance of duty by none other than Director Helms himself. McCord then organized his own security consulting business, McCord Associates, Inc., in Rockville, Maryland. But business wasn't too good. Offered the CRP job, McCord grabbed it. In fact McCord's business "would have been hopelessly in debt," said Earl Silbert, the head of the original Watergate prosecution team, if he had not received three $10,000 checks in the spring of 1972, "presumably money for the Watergate operation."

Before long McCord had become acquainted with Liddy. They had something in common. Both had been FBI agents, and Liddy enjoyed telling "war stories" about his days in the Bureau. Before long, too, Liddy and McCord began discussing the problem of political violence. Liddy told McCord that the White House was concerned that the radicals might seek to duplicate the bloody events of the 1968 Democratic Convention in Chicago at the forthcoming Republican Convention. Several violence-oriented groups had already publicized their plans to disrupt the convention, then scheduled for San Diego. (The convention site eventually was transferred to Miami Beach, where security could be more effectively implemented.)

Of more immediate concern were the threats of violence being directed at Republican headquarters around the country. One weekend in February 1972, for example, there were demonstrations in Manchester, New Hampshire, against the opening of CRP offices. A few days later McCord learned that four "pipe bombs" had been found near Manchester's police and fire departments. One of the bombs had exploded, mangling the arm of a young man involved in planting them. A young woman, apprehended as she was fleeing the scene, was found to be carrying letters addressed to New Hampshire newspapers stating that "we have bombed the offices of the Committee to Re-Elect the President." A search of her apartment revealed still more parts of pipe bombs.

Other bomb incidents were reported to McCord, including one explosion on the ground floor of the Alameda County Republican Headquarters in Oakland, California. At the same time plans were announced for a massive antiwar demonstration in Washington. According to McCord, the most militant of the groups, at least in its rhetoric, appeared to be the Vietnam Veterans Against the War (VVAW). "I had no issue to take with them on their plans to demonstrate; it was the matter of violence they propounded against the Republican efforts, especially at the convention site, which held my interest. My job was that of protecting lives and property against violence. Property could be restored. Lives could not."

"Liddy's job," McCord went on, "was intelligence-gathering regarding such groups' plans. Mine was the security of our own personnel. . . . Early in his campaign, McGovern's political base appeared to include an element of the groups talking disruption or violence. We were to receive some reports in May 1972 that the VVAW and McGovern's headquarters had linked forces in a west coast college barn-storming tour, in a station wagon leased by the staff of McGovern headquarters. The party on the barn-storming tour reportedly included three VVAW personnel and one of McGovern's staffers as a driver. Did collusion exist between McGovern headquarters, Democratic National Committee headquarters and such anti-war groups? This was one of the questions uppermost in my mind."

At any rate the decision was made to break into DNC headquarters. On or about April 1, 1972, Liddy called McCord and announced, "The operation has been approved." He said he was going across the street to meet with Hunt at the Mullen offices. Hunt was being brought into the picture because he had a "team" of men with whom he had worked before; and McCord had the feeling that Liddy knew the men. On April 12, Liddy handed McCord a manila envelope containing $65,000 in $100 bills and said, "Get the equipment as quickly as you can." Which McCord proceeded to do, arousing suspicions wherever he went.

Meanwhile the team was being assembled. McCord had hired a former FBI agent named Alfred Baldwin to act as a bodyguard for Martha Mitchell. He had found Baldwin's name in the register of the Society of Former Special Agents of the FBI. But Mrs. Mitchell didn't like him. And McCord told Baldwin he had other work in mind for him. That work, of course, involved monitoring the tapped phones at the DNC.

The rest of the team was brought in by Hunt. Except for Frank Sturgis, they consisted of Cuban-Americans with a passionate hatred of Castro. All of them had been veterans of the Bay of Pigs, several had participated in the Ellsberg venture, and some still maintained CIA ties. Their mission was to find evidence proving that the Democrats were receiving covert funds from Castro or from leftist, violence-prone organizations.

There were, of course, two break-ins at the DNC. The first took several nights to complete. From the beginning it was obvious—in the words of Eugenio Martinez—that "there wasn't adequate operational preparation. There was no floor plan of the building; no one knew the disposition of the elevators, how many guards there were, or even what time the guards checked the building. Gonzales did not know what kind of door he was supposed to open. There weren't even any contingency plans."

One immediate result of this lack of preparation was the inability of Virgilio Gonzalez, the locksmith, to open the DNC door on the sixth floor of the Watergate Office Building. And all the time he was working on the door, McCord—who had led the group into the building—would be going to the eighth floor. "It is still a mystery to me what he was doing there," Martinez later wrote in *Harper's*. "At 2:00 A.M. I went up to tell him about our problems, and there I saw him talking to two guards. What happened? I thought. Have we been caught? No, he knew the guards. So I did not ask questions, but I thought McCord was working there. It was the only thing that made sense. He was the one who led us to the place and it would not have made sense for us to have rooms at the Watergate and go on this operation if there was not someone there on the inside. Anyway, I joined the group, and pretty soon we picked up our briefcases and walked out the front door."

Hunt was furious. He insisted that Gonzalez return to Miami in order to obtain the proper tools. So, with practically no sleep, the locksmith flew South. He came back on Sunday afternoon, May 27, 1972. And early the next morning a successful entry was made. While McCord installed the phone taps, the others were busy photographing what they believed to be records of contributions. As Martinez wrote, "I had hopes that we might have done something valuable. We all had heard rumors in Miami that McGovern was receiving money from Castro. That was nothing new. We believe that today."

As it turned out, the fruits of the break-in which were turned over to Magruder were worthless. The photographed documents included unpaid bills owed by the Democrats. And the transcripts of the wiretapped conversations told a great deal about the social lives of the members of the DNC staff, but little of political consequence. Liddy was told the stuff wasn't worth the paper it was printed on. The problem was, Liddy lamely explained, that "one of the bugs isn't working. And they put one of them on O'Brien's secretary's phone instead of O'Brien's phone. But I'll get everything straightened out right away."

McCord had fouled up on his assignment. Despite this, he insisted he could repair the damage. A new entry was planned.

The rest is well-told history. The Watergate burglars were discovered when a night watchman, Frank Wills, while making his rounds, found tape over the lock on the garage door. Thinking the tape had been left by the maintenance crew, Wills removed it and then went across the street to Howard Johnson's for a cup of coffee. Back on his rounds, the guard discovered that the door had been retaped. He then called the police.

A year later four of the Miamians who were apprehended the night of June 17, 1972, were interviewed at the federal penitentiary in Danbury, Connecticut, by Senator Weicker. Two of the four, according to the notes taken by the senator, expressed considerable suspicion of their convicted fellow conspirator James McCord, suggesting at least by implication that he may have been a double agent who had deliberately led them into a trap.

According to the notes, which were not verbatim, Eugenio Martinez told the senator "that when they made their entry, they were in all right, but because McCord was late, they had to put tape on the door the second time. And when he finally joined them, they asked him whether he had removed the tapes when he came up and he said he had. But the fact of the matter is, he hadn't, and that's what led to their getting caught."

Another of the convicted conspirators, Sturgis, "presented a series of facts concerning McCord's involvement which he implied certainly cast some question on whether or not McCord had a different role than the one they thought he did," the notes said.

"For example," said Sturgis, "McCord got us equipment that didn't work, Baldwin was stationed across the street but when the police were searching the building, the men inside had not been warned and tipped off. McCord came late to the rendezvous and not only came late but told them he had taken the tape off the door when it turned out he had not."

McCord also instructed Barker to turn off his walkie-talkie, thus cutting off communications with Baldwin, who was stationed at Howard Johnson's across the street. As a result Baldwin was unable to warn his cohorts when the police arrived.

And as Sturgis noted, "It's also strange that three policemen were cruising in that very area, three policemen in plain clothes. McCord was the first one after [the arrests] to open up and spill the beans. And yet . . . McCord was the one who had ordered (us) not to talk."

All four prisoners (the others were Bernard Barker and Virgilio Gonzalez) agreed that from the very beginning the break-ins were marked by incredible bungling. According to the notes, Martinez told Weicker that, "had they not been caught he had already made up his mind that he would not do any more missions for this group (of) highly unprofessional bunglers."

Martinez, the notes added, "said he was totally disgusted with all of this and very puzzled. He couldn't understand the amateurism and the sloppiness and was very concerned about it. But he said he kept being reassured that they knew what they were doing, that they were the experts, that they were the leaders and that they knew what they were doing."

There is one other puzzling piece of information about McCord. That had to do with his relationship with Louis Russell, a former congressional investigator down on his luck. For a time Russell had been employed by the General Security Services, which provided the guards for the Watergate Office Building. And despite his outspoken dislike of Nixon, Russell had been placed on the payroll by McCord as a night watchman for the President's reelection committee, a job terminated following McCord's arrest. But most interesting was the fact that on the night of the second break-in, Russell had had dinner at the Howard Johnson's just across the street from Watergate. Later he told investigators that he had dined there for "sentimental reasons"; he once had a girlfriend who worked nearby.

McCord's conduct following his arrest was even more bizarre. Not only did he vehemently deny CIA responsibility for Watergate, but he threatened to expose White House involvement if any effort were made to blame "the company." Yet it was McCord who, immediately upon his apprehension, told one of the arresting officers that all the men being picked up were former CIA employees. Later McCord charged that his lawyer Gerald Alch had suggested that in his defense he should claim Watergate was a CIA operation. He said that Alch claimed he could arrange to have McCord's records appropriately doctored to show that McCord was still in the CIA's employ at the time of the break-in. Alch, he claimed, had stated he could get the incoming CIA director James Schlesinger to handle the matter. But

Alch, an outstanding Boston lawyer of unblemished reputation, flatly and vigorously denied the allegations under oath while testifying before the Ervin Committee. In other words he called McCord a liar. And to prove the point he suggested that both he and McCord be given polygraph tests.

But this did not meet with the approval of Sam Ervin, who launched into a discourse on the inadmissibility of lie-detector tests as evidence. It was just as likely, however, that the senator wanted to dispose of Alch as quickly as possible. An effective witness, the Bostonian had completely shredded McCord's highly publicized testimony. Alch meanwhile went ahead on his own and took a polygraph examination. He sent the results, which, he felt, proved his point, to Ervin. But the solon from North Carolina never recalled McCord for further testimony.

Previously McCord had obtained additional counsel, Bernard Fensterwald, who had been introduced to McCord by Lou Russell. Almost immediately he offered to help raise the money for McCord's bail. And, according to Alch, Fensterwald did indeed raise $40,000 of the required $100,000. Mrs. McCord got the rest. Though it seemed strange that Fensterwald would be doing this for someone he hardly knew, Alch said, "I was not about to look a gift horse in the mouth."

Alch did work with Fensterwald in McCord's behalf for a short period. And Alch testified that Fensterwald had once told him in a telephone conversation, "We're going after the President of the United States."

When Alch retorted that he was not interested "in any vendettas against the President, but only in the best interest of my client," Fensterwald was quoted as saying, "Well, you'll see; that's who we're going after—the President."

Demonstrating his extreme partisanship, Ervin refused to get to the bottom of the argument between Alch and McCord. It may well have been that the Tarheel senator was of the opinion that his committee should begin to concentrate on the main issues. Nevertheless Ervin permitted the record to be cluttered with all kinds of other statements which would never have been permitted in any court of law.

Of considerable interest, however, was the role played by Fensterwald. Senator Baker, the ranking Republican, agreed that all parties to the dispute—Alch, McCord, and Fensterwald—be given lie-detector tests. Baker observed that the results would be at least as informative as the extraordinary amount of hearsay evidence cluttering the record. But Ervin said he was not interested in any such "twentieth century witchcraft."

Still there were other questions which were never resolved. Just exactly when did Fensterwald become involved with McCord? Why did he help raise the princely sum of $40,000 in bail funds to get McCord out of jail? Where did he get the funds?

And who exactly was Fensterwald? Around Washington he was known as an eccentric lawyer, whose main hobby had been to promote further investigations into the assassinations of John F. Kennedy and Martin Luther King. In fact he set up a special committee aimed at discovering the "truth" about the two tragedies. And while he had denied the statements attributed to him by Alch, he has since publicly conceded that as a longtime Democrat he had an interest in going after President Nixon.

But that would have been a question that could well have been asked of him by the Ervin Committee—if it had been truly interested in looking into all the ramifications of Watergate. And the committee could also have checked into a *New York Times* story which impeached Fensterwald's credibility in another area. According to investigative reporter Denny Walsh, Fensterwald "made false statements and false implications during his questioning of a key witness while serving as counsel to a Senate subcommittee investigating electronic snooping in the mid-nineteen sixties. . . ." Sources close to that investigation quoted Fensterwald as having asked government agents for "sexy and sensational" material for use in public hearings. He also told the agents he was seeking evidence "with some publicity value."

Except for the *Times,* no other newspaper—not even the Washington *Post* always searching for new Watergate angles—unloosed investigatory resources on Fensterwald's controversial background. Likewise the networks kept hands off.

But that shouldn't have prevented the Ervin Committee from spending some time on the matter. After all what was at stake was the people's right to know all the facts—even those which may have cast discredit on anti-Nixon witnesses.

19

A S   W A T E R G A T E   B E G A N   T O   U N R A V E L   I N   T H E
spring of 1973, commencement speakers had a field day deplor-
ing the scandal. And W. Allen Wallis, chancellor of the University
of Rochester, was no exception. Addressing the graduating class
at Roberts Wesleyan College, Wallis said that he agreed with
other speakers across the nation that "Watergate is deplorable,
disgraceful, immoral, shocking, inexcusable, alarming, reprehensible, and quite a few other things besides, none of them nice."

"But," he went on, "the saddest thing about Watergate is that
in important respects it is far from unique, or even unusual. It is
another of those many instances in which the end is regarded as
justifying the means. One thing different about Watergate, however, is that the end is not acceptable to the academic-journalistic
complex, as were the ends pursued by Daniel Ellsberg, the Berrigan brothers, the anti-war rioters, the Black Panthers, and innu-
merable others stretching back to the sit-in strikers of the 1930's."

According to Wallis, "the perpetrators of Watergate appear to
be men of good character by their own lights, who put conscience and patriotism above civil law. In that regard, they are
exactly like Daniel Ellsberg. Yet the press, the ministers, and the
politicians who condemn the Watergate convicts praise Ellsberg,
the Berrigans, and others who have used comparable means for
different ends. . . .

"This is why I said earlier that the reaction by journalists and
politicians to the Watergate break-in has been morally even
more corrupt than the Watergate activities themselves."

In the final analysis Watergate was largely a media event—the
most spectacular in the history of American journalism. The
break-in itself was chiefly the result of a combination of poor
judgment and innocuous stupidity on the part of the perpetrators. Yet the episode was blown up through incessant publicity,
and an inane caper was transformed into "the crime of the century." And though not to be condoned, the so-called cover up

and obstruction of justice constituted a natural human reaction rather than the heinous crime trumpeted by a largely liberal media.

Similar, if not far worse, crimes had been committed in previous administrations, but the lack of interest in them on the part of the media was notorious. Had the Watergate break-in taken place during the Kennedy administration, for example, it is safe to say that the matter, while perhaps duly noted, would have been forgotten quickly. As so many other Kennedy abuses of power were.

The main reason for the double standard was JFK's popularity with the press corps. Kennedy had spent an inordinate amount of time catering to influential columnists, correspondents, and broadcast personalities. Many of them, like Ben Bradlee, were close personal friends. In their eyes, "Jack" could do no wrong. And if he did wrong, they rarely got emotional about it.

Nixon, on the other hand, was much more wary of the press. He did not go out of his way to cultivate correspondents and columnists. Generally he felt uneasy around them. All through his long, controversial career in politics, he felt that the major news media was out to "get" him.

Not that he was entirely wrong. As the late Stewart Alsop once pointed out, "The notion that Mr. Nixon is a sort of monster has been almost an article of faith" among liberal journalists. The surprise in their ranks generated by Nixon's approach to the People's Republic of China was due to a preconceived and mistaken notion that he was a doctrinaire whose administration would be devoid of new approaches.

Nixon himself has long believed that the hostility of the liberal media toward him began early in his political career when he took the lead in exposing Alger Hiss. A former State Department official, Hiss had been accused by Whittaker Chambers of having been a member of an underground Communist group in the nation's capital. Nixon, then thirty-five years of age and a member of the House Committee on Un-American Activities, pressed hard to determine the truth. Eventually Hiss was prosecuted by the Justice Department under President Truman and was convicted on a perjury charge when he denied having slipped confidential U.S. government material to an admitted spy courier. And, though the Hiss case made Nixon a household word, he also became a marked man among liberals, many of whom swore they would never forgive his "witch-hunting."

Nixon discussed the climate of opinion generated by the Hiss case in his book *Six Crises,* which was published in 1962. "Hiss," he wrote,

> was clearly the symbol of a considerable number of perfectly loyal citizens whose theaters of operation are the nation's mass media and universities, its scholarly foundations, and its government bureaucracies . . . They are not Communists (but) they are of a mind-set as doctrinaire as those on the extreme right. . . . As soon as the Hiss case broke and well before a full bill of particulars was even available, much less open to close critical analysis, they leaped to the defense of Alger Hiss—and to a counter attack of unparalleled venom and irrational fury on his accusers.

Nixon next faced what he termed "the overwhelmingly hostile reaction of the press" when he ran for Vice President in 1952. The issue was a so-called secret fund which had been raised by his supporters to help him pay the costs of political activities— postage, travel expenses, and the like—during his term as a senator. In all $18,000 was involved. The *New York Post* was first to break the story. Its front page on September 18 was dominated with the big, black words: SECRET NIXON FUND! The story itself was given on page two, under the headline: SECRET RICH MEN'S TRUST FUND KEEPS NIXON IN STYLE BEYOND HIS SALARY. As it turned out, the story was an exaggerated version of the facts. There was nothing "secret" about the fund. Other politicians, including the *Post*'s candidate for President, Adlai Stevenson, had made similar arrangements.

Years later such funds were specifically approved in the code of rules and ethics adopted by the U.S. Senate. And when the post-Watergate Federal Election Commission sought to regulate these privately funded "office accounts," the Senate by a close vote on October 8, 1975, said no. Such accounts are funded by leftover campaign donations as well as contributions from outside donors. They are in no way different from Nixon's so-called slush fund of a quarter century ago.

But back in 1952 most of the liberal furies were directed at Nixon. There were demands, even among leading Republicans, that he quit the ticket headed by Eisenhower. However Nixon managed to turn the issue around with a broadcast appearance which became known as the "Checkers" speech.

Some influential press organs refused to let up. Typical was the front-page story published in the St. Louis *Post-Dispatch* on October 30, 1952, five days before the election. The story alleged that Nixon had been seen in a gambling casino in Havana the previous April, presumably living it up with "secret" funds. The story was quickly picked up and widely used throughout the country. It turned out that Nixon had been making speeches in Hawaii at the time the *Post-Dispatch* placed him in Cuba. But by the time the truth was made known, the phony story had done its damage.

The hostility of much of the press continued throughout Nixon's eight years as Vice President. During his 1960 run for the presidency most of the correspondents covering the campaign made no secret of their support of Kennedy.

"In 1960," wrote Timothy Crouse in *The Boys on the Bus,** "many reporters had become shills for Kennedy.... The reporters on Kennedy's plane referred to the candidate as 'Jack,' talked constantly about his 'style' and 'grace,' cheered his speeches, and sang anti-Nixon songs with Kennedy staffers around hotel bars. The Kennedy people encouraged this claque atmosphere...."

Nixon's own bitterness at such press treatment was exacerbated during his 1962 run for governor of California. The morning after he lost his race, Nixon told reporters, "You won't have Nixon to kick around any more, because, gentlemen, this is my last press conference..." Pat Brown, who had been watching his defeated opponent on television, said: "Nixon is going to regret all his life that he made that speech. The press will never let him forget it."

Covering Nixon's 1968 campaign for the presidency, Gloria Steinem wrote in *New York* Magazine: "In fact, the reporters *don't* like Richard Nixon. As far as I've been able to find out, only two members of the ninety-odd press corps are likely to vote for him: the *U.S. News & World Report* man, who was also for Nixon in '60, and the Voice of America correspondent, who is thought to be Republican because he doesn't join in anti-Nixon bull sessions and smokes an unlit pipe."

In *The Making of the President 1968,* Ted White commented that what he called the new culture "dominates the heights of national communications, subtly but profoundly influences those who sit astride the daily news flow in New York and Washington, and thus stains, increasingly, the prisms of reporting through which the nation as a whole must see itself."

---

*(New York: Random House, 1973), p. 182.

And, of all people, Mrs. Katherine Graham, president of the Washington Post Company, had this to say to Sigma Delta Chi, the journalism fraternity, in November 1970: "There is some validity in the allegation that we tend to draw our reporters from a common, narrow base. One of our staff members put it this way in a memo: 'Inevitably, the *Post* reflects the background biases of the people who put it out. We are for the most part a collection of Easterners . . . generally liberal.' "

A similar situation applies in television, according to ABC commentator Howard K. Smith. In a pre-Watergate commentary Smith described the staffs of the network news departments as generally liberal, with a "strong leftward bias." Smith, who considers himself "left of center," deplored what he termed the pervasiveness of a "party line" in reporting the news. "Our liberal friends have become dogmatic," he said. "They have a set of automatic reactions. They react the way political cartoonists do—with over-simplification. They're pleasing the Washington *Post*, they're pleasing the editors of *The New York Times*, they're pleasing one another."

It's not that there is a conspiracy among the press, but there most definitely is conformity. That the overwhelming majority of Washington newsmen have a similar "liberal" political viewpoint is a fact of life accepted by most politicians. As a consequence objectivity in reporting has largely gone by the boards and there is an increasing tendency toward advocacy in the news columns. Noting this, the late Arthur Krock, one of the giants of Washington journalism, wrote in 1971 of the "highly subjective nature," "the name-calling and emotionalism," and the "liberty that verges so readily into license" in the treatment of Washington news.

On no subject was the Washington press corps more united than in a general dislike, if not hatred, of Richard Nixon. And Nixon reacted in kind. To him, as he would say privately, "the press is the enemy." To him, news people constituted—with some exceptions—an unelected, unrepresentative, and unbelievably arrogant élite.

There were a few newsmen who did not permit their presumed liberalism to affect their reporting. One of them was David Broder, of the Washington *Post*, whose reputation as a political analyst is respected in all camps. In the fall of 1969, after Nixon had served for nine months, Broder riled many liberals with a column accusing the antiwar movement of trying "to break the President." He put it this way:

> . . . The men and the movement that broke Lyndon Johnson's authority in 1968 are out to break Richard M. Nixon in 1969. The likelihood is great that they will succeed again, for breaking a President is, like most feats, easier to accomplish the second time around. . . . First, the breakers arrogate to themselves a position of moral superiority. For that reason, a war that is unpopular, expensive and very probably unwise is labeled as immoral, indecent and intolerable.

Broder concluded:

> The orators who remind us that Mr. Nixon has been in office for nine months should remind themselves that he will remain there for thirty-nine more months—unless, of course, they are willing to put their convictions to the test by moving to impeach him. Is that not, really, the proper course, rather than destroying his capacity to lead while leaving him in office, rather than leaving the nation with a broken President at its head for three years?

One columnist who was to make no secret of his desire to "break" the President was Tom Wicker of *The New York Times.* He compared the first Nixon Inaugural unfavorably with that of President Kennedy eight years previously which, he wrote, had brought to Americans the feeling that "they were taking the first steps into a bold new era." (Forgotten, of course, was the fact they were also taking the first steps to the Bay of Pigs and Vietnam.) In contrast, Wicker wrote, the Nixon inauguration "brought no sense of excitement, of ground-breaking of new worlds," with the new President offering only "the old values and the old assumptions and even the old rhetoric." He also complained about the Marine band "playing such square music as *This Is My Country* and *God Bless America.*"

With the passage of time Wicker got more vehement. On February 22, 1971, at an antiwar teach-in at Harvard, the columnist urged 2,000 students to "engage in civil disobedience of all kinds" as a means of demonstrating opposition to the Nixon administration's policy in Vietnam. "We got one President out and perhaps we can do that again," he said, referring to LBJ's 1968 decision not to seek reelection.

Getting American forces out of Vietnam without handing the country over to the Communists was Nixon's major objective during his first term. What Nixon was seeking, as he said repeatedly, was "peace with honor." Eventually he came up with a program which he labeled "Vietnamization." At the same time he sought to negotiate secretly with the enemy.

Before long *The New York Times* claimed that the United States was moving toward unilateral withdrawal. The story came at a particularly unpropitious time for the new administration since the President was seeking to assure the South Vietnamese that no "sellout" was in the works. The *Times* published other exclusive stories on foreign policy obviously based on "leaks"—that is, the surreptitious release of sensitive information. As Kissinger was to tell a Senate committee, the spring of 1969 was a "particularly sensitive time with regard to the formulation of this country's foreign policies and the establishment of our future relations with other nations. During this period, policies were being considered which would establish the fundamental approach to major foreign policy issues such as the United States' strategic posture, Strategic Arms Limitation Talks (SALT), Vietnam and many other national security issues. Because of the sensitive nature of these matters, the secrecy of each was of vital importance, and the success or failure of each program turned in many instances upon the maintenance of necessary security. However, notwithstanding the critical need for such security during this period, we were confronted with leaks to the press of information of the greatest importance to the national security."

Kissinger, as the President's chief security adviser, was almost paranoid about leaks. And this was not necessarily a bad trait. For, at Nixon's instructions, the former Harvard professor was engaged in complicated dealings with foreign adversaries. And Kissinger agreed with the President that the only serious negotiations were those that were kept secret. True, critics were to label this attitude a Nixonian obsession. But how else could sensitive foreign relations be carried on? For example, without secrecy it would have been most difficult to have opened the door to the People's Republic of China.

It wasn't that Kissinger was adverse to dealing with the press. He spent an inordinate amount of time worrying about what the papers were going to say about him. He was probably the most image-conscious member of the Nixon administration. Nor was he adverse to "leaking," as long as he controlled the process. At his very first staff meeting in January 1969 he announced firmly, "If anybody leaks anything, I will do the leaking."

Thus when national security leaks were involved, it was Kissinger who played a major role in arranging for wiretaps of his own staff as well as newsmen. In this he had the President's full approval. The object, of course, was to determine who was doing the leaking. Nixon was later to say that he regarded the operation as completely legal under the law. Moreover, he said, J. Edgar Hoover had assured him that such procedures had been used by previous administrations to find leaks—a fact which has been established during recent congressional probes.

On September 7, 1973, at hearings of the Senate Foreign Relations Committee on his confirmation as Secretary of State, Kissinger explained why the FBI wiretaps were ordered.

"When this Administration came into office," he testified, "for a period of many months it was confronted with leaks to the press of documents of the greatest importance to the national security. These included discussions of National Security Council deliberations, of procedures in case of emergency contingency planning, and of specific military operations.

"The last conversation I had with President Eisenhower was when he called me from Walter Reed Hospital to protest that information that had been given to him by the President only two days before as extremely confidential had found its way into a newspaper on the day that he called."

Barry Goldwater had a similar experience. He tells of attending "a meeting of top officials in the White House," and the next day he "read all about it in the morning paper . . . I am not talking about just any meeting. I am talking about a meeting that I felt was so confidential that I did not even discuss it with my staff. Yet, the next day I found a completely accurate account in the newspaper. It was so accurate that even the words I spoke were correctly attributed. You almost have to have it happen to you to understand the feeling such an experience gives you. I called the President and suggested that something would have to be done to seal off the leaks of information from the executive branch."

Goldwater, of course, was not then aware that the President was indeed trying to do something. How successful he was is debatable. Concerning the wiretaps, Nixon told John Dean on February 28, 1973: "They never helped us. Just gobs and gobs of material; gossip and bullshitting—the tapping was very, very unproductive. . . ."

Kissinger, who probably had better knowledge of the productivity, said at his confirmation hearing, "There were some cases in which the sources of some leaks were discovered and in which appropriate action was taken."

The wiretapping program was ended in February 1971. In July Assistant Attorney General Robert Mardian discussed the disposal of the tapes with President Nixon at the Western White House in San Clemente. In later testimony Mardian said that Nixon explained the taping was related to national security leaks which had to be stopped. The President was concerned that information from the National Security Council relating to the American position on the current SALT talks had been in the possession of the Russians before one of the meetings. "In that context," Mardian went on, "he expressed great concern not only about SALT, but also his ability to govern if he could not maintain the confidentiality of the White House."

By this time there had occurred the most massive security leak in our diplomatic history. This was the publication of numerous documents which became known as the Pentagon Papers. Carefully edited portions of the papers—a history of the Vietnam war and U.S. involvement as prepared by Defense Department experts—began to appear in *The New York Times*. The first article, which was published on June 13, 1971, curiously enough did not appear to arouse too much concern in the Oval Office. If anything the material included revelations that could be embarrassing only to Lyndon Johnson and his top advisers. Since the study ended in early 1968, the material was hardly likely to embarrass the Nixon administration.

But Kissinger felt different. As National Security Council director he was then negotiating secretly with North Vietnamese officials in Paris seeking an end to the war in Vietnam. At the same time there were negotiations with the People's Republic of China for a confidential visit to Peking by Kissinger—with the hope of paving the way for a rapprochement with the Communist régime. The fear was that the Chinese might back out because the United States was incapable of keeping confidences with other nations.

When it became known that Daniel J. Ellsberg was the former government official who had purloined the Pentagon documents and then given them to the *Times*, Kissinger was even more upset. Kissinger had known Ellsberg. They had worked together on a paper dealing with U.S. options in Vietnam at the Nixon transition headquarters in New York. Ellsberg was then on the payroll of the Rand Corporation, a West Coast think tank with close government connections. What Kissinger did not know at the time was that Ellsberg, who had been a fanatical "hawk" on Vietnam, by now had become an even more fanatical "dove."

According to Colson, Kissinger was "even more alarmed" by the publication of the Pentagon Papers than Nixon, and he communicated his alarm to the President. In an affidavit made public by a federal judge on April 29, 1974, the former presidential counsel asserted that Kissinger "believed that the leaks must be stopped at all costs, that Ellsberg must be stopped from making further disclosures of classified information and that those acting in concert with him must be stopped."

Colson told of one high-level White House meeting at which "Dr. Kissinger also reported on Ellsberg's private habits and certain of his activities in Vietnam." This of course was a reference to what a CIA psychiatrist was to refer to as Ellsberg's "blatant" and variegated sexual habits.

Ehrlichman, who also met with the President and Kissinger, later quoted Kissinger as describing Ellsberg as "a fanatic," as well as a "known drug abuser," who had "knowledge of very critical defense secrets of current validity, such as nuclear deterrent targeting." The latter referred to Ellsberg's having worked on nuclear targeting plans for Defense Secretary Robert Strange McNamara in the mid-sixties. These closely held nuclear secrets were contained in a highly classified document—the Single Integrated Operations Plan (SIOP). Kissinger informed Nixon that a leak of SIOP would be devastating to national security. SIOP spelled out the timing and attack patterns of American nuclear bombs in case of war; it contained specific targeting information for every military objective behind the Iron and Bamboo curtains, including the number and power of nuclear warheads programmed for each target.

Contributing to the fears was a report from an FBI counterspy that the Soviet Embassy in Washington had received a full set of the Pentagon Papers prior to their publication. The immediate suspicion was that it was Ellsberg who had passed on the secret documents. According to a *New York Times* story, one former

Nixon official recalled Kissinger's "literally pounding the President's table" over all of this.

By this time Nixon had come to see in Ellsberg another Hiss. Pressured by Kissinger to do something about the "madman's" activities, the President called in Colson and Haldeman and said: "I don't give a damn how it is done, do whatever has to be done to stop these leaks and prevent further unauthorized disclosures; I don't want to be told why it can't be done. This Government cannot survive, it cannot function if anyone can run out and leak whatever documents he wants to."

Colson said the President had demanded to learn "how and why the 'counter-government' is at work. I don't want excuses. I want results. I want it done, whatever the costs."

There was another reason for presidential anger. The feeling was that Ellsberg's release of the Pentagon Papers had thwarted a peace offer made by the United States to North Vietnam. The offer was delivered in Paris by Kissinger in May 1971. He, Nixon, and other U.S. officials believed it would be accepted. But, according to Colson, when Hanoi rejected the offer "without giving any reasons" thirteen days after the *Times* began publishing the papers on June 13, 1971, "the White House felt their publication weakened support given to the United States by other countries and led North Vietnam to expect further weakening of our position." Later Colson estimated that this probably delayed the end of the war by eighteen months.

That "the Nixon Administration's concern with Ellsberg was not unreasonable" was a point made by the *Wall Street Journal* in an editorial on July 16, 1974, following the conviction of Ehrlichman and others for the break-in at Ellsberg's psychiatrist's office. "He had access to a great deal of classified information far more important than the Pentagon Papers, and his motivations and psychological make-up were highly pertinent in trying to guess what else he might release. And as we now after all know, sporadic and sensitive negotiations were under way to extricate the U.S. from the Vietnam war."

It is of course easy at this point in time—to use a Watergate phrase—to forget what the political climate was like back in the Nixon years. But it was a most painful period in American life: one of great tension and polarization, of angry rhetoric and demonstrations, of conspiracies real and imagined, of casual talk about overthrowing everything. Often it was more than talk.

Scanlan's, a now-defunct anti-Establishment monthly, claimed in January 1971 that there was a dramatic increase in "guerrilla acts and terrorism." As evidence it listed over 1,200 acts of violence perpetrated during the period of 1965 to June 1970. They included sniping, bombing, dynamiting, arson, the use of Molotov cocktails, and terrorism. The violence of the New Left appeared to be sanctioned in the seemingly lofty pages of *The New York Review of Books.* Andrew Kopkind, for example, enunciated his memorable observation: "Morality, like politics, starts at the barrel of a gun." Kopkind seemed to be championing rioting, and the young responded on the campuses. This was the time when the *Review* published an illustration on its cover on how to manufacture a Molotov Cocktail, a provocative act which was to haunt the weekly's editors despite Murray Kempton's funny remark that people in Newark found the cocktail formula didn't work.

Leaders of both political parties were alarmed. Following the 1967 antiwar demonstration at the Pentagon, at which Vietcong flags were unfurled, Democratic floor leader Carl Albert charged that the huge demonstration was "basically organized by international Communism." And Republican floor leader Gerald Ford revealed that President Johnson, at a White House meeting, had read to him and other GOP leaders a secret report contending that the demonstration had been organized by the international Communist movement. Ford claimed to have asked that the report be made public. But, he said, Attorney General Clark and Secretary of State Rusk both claimed that doing so would compromise sources of information and create a "new wave of McCarthyism."

Later Senator Henry Jackson met with President Nixon in the Oval Office to complain bitterly about the easy access Soviet agents were having up on the Hill to argue against such major defense proposals as the anti-ballistic missile. The way "Scoop" had it, KGB agents were actually being welcomed into the offices of a number of senators and congressmen; moreover there wasn't a blessed thing the FBI could do about it. For under restrictions agreed to by Director Hoover, none of his agents were permitted —except under rare circumstances—to conduct surveillance on Capitol grounds.

And following the publication of the Pentagon Papers, Governor Jimmy Carter of Georgia called on a senator to urge, in his words, "the enactment of Federal legislation that would make news organizations criminally liable."

It was in this environment that the Special Investigations Unit —later to become more familiar as the "plumbers"—was born. The White House felt—rightly or wrongly—that the FBI had been dragging its feet in the Ellsberg case. For one thing there was Hoover's friendship with Ellsberg's father-in-law Louis Marx. A wealthy toy manufacturer, Marx was far from sympathetic with his son-in-law's exotic politics. Nevertheless Hoover did not want his friend interviewed by any of his agents. Somehow the director's wishes were ignored. Through a mixup Marx was interrogated. After which the FBI official in charge was reassigned to a less desirable post.

Moreover Hoover believed—again rightly or wrongly—that an intensive investigation into how the Pentagon Papers came to be published would only create public relations problems for his Bureau. At this stage of his long life Hoover was too weary to do battle with his old foes in the media. The director felt that the Ellsberg case constituted a no-win situation.

All of which helped to create still more dissatisfaction with the FBI at the White House. For some time Nixon and his aides had been annoyed at the Bureau's inability to cope with the New Left, and particularly with the rash of bombings that were taking place across the country. The feeling was that while Hoover had done a good job infiltrating organizations like the Communist party and the Ku Klux Klan, the director's old-fashioned methods were not appropriate for combating the new extremists. At the same time the White House disliked dealing with the FBI because, as Ehrlichman told me at the time, "the Bureau leaks like a sieve." For a while Nixon was urged by some aides to put Hoover out to pasture. But they quickly learned there was no way they could get the director to agree to a well-earned retirement.

Thus with Ehrlichman as the head honcho, the plumbers came into being. But Ehrlichman, then presidential assistant in charge of domestic affairs, was too busy to involve himself very deeply in investigative matters. He turned over the principal chores to two young lawyers on the White House staff. They were David R. Young, Jr., thirty-two, and Egil M. ("Bud") Krogh, Jr., thirty-one, neither of whom had any investigative experience to speak of.

Krogh had gone to work at the White House in May 1969 as an aide to Ehrlichman, for whom he had worked briefly in a Seattle law firm. Like Ehrlichman he was a Christian Scientist. After graduating from Principia College in Illinois, Krogh served for two years in the navy. In 1968 he was graduated from the University of Washington law school. At the White House his work was outstanding. Among other things he acted as liaison with the District of Columbia.

District problems had concerned Nixon from the moment he entered the White House. The erupting crime rate in the nation's capital had been forcefully brought to his attention by an ad hoc committee composed of some of the town's leading citizens who, as it happened, were mostly of the liberal persuasion. Those who met with Attorney General Mitchell to call for action on the part of the new administration included Katherine Graham, publisher of the Washington *Post;* attorney Edward Bennett Williams, a noted civil libertarian; and Joe Califano, former aide to President Johnson and later counsel to the Democratic National Committee. As Mitchell recalled their conversation, they described the situation in Washington as being so bad that they feared for their lives. Among other things they suggested the stationing of federal troops throughout the capital for the emergency.

The irony of the leading lights of the liberal Establishment calling for such extremist measures was not lost on Nixon. Though elected on a "law and order" platform, the President did not want to launch his administration by virtually declaring martial law. That, of course, had been the case not too many months earlier during the racial rioting that greeted the assassination of Dr. King. Instead Nixon felt that beefing up the local police forces would be a better response. And Krogh, as liaison with the District of Columbia, was right in the thick of things, helping push through Congress various measures sought by the local government. He also traveled to Europe, Asia, the Middle East, and Latin America, coordinating administration efforts to check the world heroin trade.

And so Krogh became co-chief of the plumbers, his partner being Dave Young, a trusted aide to Kissinger. Young had known Henry for some time before coming to Washington. They had met at the Rockefeller brothers' office in midtown Manhattan. An Oxford graduate, Young had been a member of the law firm of Milbank-Tweed when he was assigned to work at the Rockefeller office. He became chief researcher for Nancy Maginnes (now Mrs. Kissinger), who directed foreign policy analyses for the Rockefellers. When Kissinger went to work for Nixon, he invited the young lawyer to become his appointments secretary. With his new bride, the former Susie Kelley, who had also worked for the Rockefellers, Young moved to Washington and settled on Foxhall Road.

Working for Kissinger didn't prove overly exciting for Young, who found himself doing all kinds of odd chores, such as handling Henry's social schedule and personal business. "Dave's wife even did Henry's laundry," one former official said. So Young wasn't overly distressed when he was assigned to investigate leaks.

Testifying at his confirmation hearings to be Secretary of State, Kissinger said under oath that he had no knowledge "of any such [illegal] activites that David Young may have engaged in. I did not know of the existence of the Plumbers group, by that or any other name. Nor did I know that David Young was concerned with internal security matters."

Kissinger did concede that, though Young had been trans-ferred to Ehrlichman's staff in June 1971, his former aide re-mained on Kissinger's payroll until forced out of the government in May 1973. Kissinger testified he had understood that Young was working on a declassification project. Which, of course, was the "cover" for Young's role with the plumbers. "I had no contact with David Young either by telephone or in my office or in any other way after he left my staff, although I continued to have a high regard for him."

Two weeks after he was approved as Secretary, the Watergate Committee released an affidavit which in effect called into ques-tion Kissinger's knowledge of the plumbers. The affidavit dis-closed that on August 12, 1971, David Young met with a CIA psychiatrist named Dr. Bernard Malloy to arrange for a psychiat-ric profile of Ellsberg. This was at a time when Kissinger had testified he was unaware of his former aide's doings. According to the affidavit, however, "Mr. Young stated that the Ellsberg study had the highest priority, and had been requested by Mr. Ehrlichman and Dr. Kissinger."

Malloy's study of Ellsberg, based as it was on newspaper clip-pings, magazine articles, and a few State Department documents and FBI reports, proved unsatisfactory. Also unsatisfactory was an FBI visit to the Beverly Hills offices of Ellsberg's former psy-chiatrist. On advice of counsel Dr. Lewis J. Fielding refused to cooperate with the Bureau by discussing his former patient's mental problems.

The plumbers, augmented by G. Gordon Liddy and Howard Hunt, discussed the possibility of a "bag job"—or an illegal entry of the Fielding premises—by the FBI. But J. Edgar Hoover had previously ordered the end of such operations. As for using the Secret Service, the feeling was—as reported by Liddy—that its agents could not be trusted on such sensitive assignments.

Meanwhile, Ehrlichman kept the President informed about what the plumbers were up to. Nixon's only beef was that "their effort . . . was not vigorous enough." At one point the President told Ehrlichman that "Krogh should, of course, do whatever he considered necessary to get to the bottom of the matter—to learn what Ellsberg's motives and potential further harmful action might be." Which was what Krogh sought to do. With what he believed to be Ehrlichman's approval, Krogh authorized "a covert operation . . . to examine all the medical files still held by Ellsberg's psychoanalyst covering the two-year period in which he was undergoing analysis." Among other things, said Krogh, he was seeking information possibly leading to other conspirators. But as Krogh himself later made clear, after he received a six-month jail term on charges growing out of the burglary of Dr. Fielding's offices, "I received no specific instruction or authority whatsoever regarding the break-in from the President, directly or indirectly."

The burglary itself was a botched job. The Cuban-Americans who had broken into the psychiatrist's offices could find nothing of interest. They took some photos showing that they had, indeed, been on the job; and then they went back to the Beverly Hilton where, for some unaccountable reason, Hunt broke out the champagne as if to celebrate. But celebrate what? To this day the Cubans have been perplexed by "Eduardo's" behavior.

On their return to Washington Hunt and Liddy reported their mission was unaccomplished. They showed Krogh the pictures of the damage that was done to Fielding's office. The reason for the damage, they said, was to make it appear that a burglar was searching for money and/or drugs. Then Hunt and Liddy sought permission to break into Dr. Fielding's apartment since they felt that, after the FBI visit, the psychiatrist might have taken the Ellsberg file home. But Ehrlichman told Krogh, "The thing should be terminated, discontinued, finalized, stopped."

It was almost two years later when Nixon first learned of the episode. This came during a conversation with Dean on March 17, 1973:

DEAN: . . . The other potential problem is Ehrlichman's and this is—

PRESIDENT: In connection with Hunt?

DEAN: In connection with Hunt and Liddy both.

PRESIDENT: They worked for him?

DEAN: They—these fellows had to be some idiots as we've learned after the fact. They went out and went into Dr. Ellsberg's doctor's office and they had, they were geared up with all this CIA equipment—cameras and the like. . . .

PRESIDENT: What in the world—what in the name of God was Ehrlichman having something (unintelligible) in the Ellsberg (unintelligible)?

DEAN: They were trying to—this was a part of an operation that —in connection with the Pentagon Papers. They were—the whole thing—they wanted to get Ellsberg's psychiatric records for some reason. I don't know.

PRESIDENT: This is the first I ever heard of this. I, I (unintelligible) care about Ellsberg was not our problem.

All through the summer of 1971 the leaks continued. On July 24 the President met with Ehrlichman and Krogh to complain bitterly about a *New York Times* dispatch which disclosed the U.S. back-up position in its arms limitation talks with the Soviet Union. When Krogh reported that the "prime suspect" was a Pentagon official who had talked to the *Times* reporter that week, Nixon exploded: "If the son-of-a-bitch leaked, he's not for the Government . . . little people do not leak . . . this crap to the effect: well, a stenographer did it, or the waste paper basket did it. It's never that case. I've studied these cases long enough, and it's always a son-of-a-bitch that leaks."

How to get the "sons-of-bitches" out of government was a subject much on White House minds. One published story was particularly sensitive since it could only have come from a CIA informant within the government of India. The story, published in the *Times*, reported that Moscow had urged India not to recognize East Pakistan as an independent nation. The informant incidentally was not heard from after that, but Krogh was led to believe he may well have lost his life.

Then came a series of columns by Jack Anderson disclosing that the Nixon administration, while publicly professing neutrality, had privately "tilted" toward Pakistan in its dispute with

– 289 –

India. The columns were particularly sensitive since they contained material obviously taken from the minutes of the Washington Special Action Group, a super-secret outfit set up by the White House to deal with major crises. In one of his columns, for example, Anderson quoted Kissinger as saying, "I'm getting hell every half-hour from the President that we're not being tough enough on India. He has just called me again. He doesn't believe we're carrying out his wishes. He wants us to tilt in favor of Pakistan."*

By this time the plumbers had already been disbanded. But both Krogh and Young were called back to duty and ordered to look for Anderson's source. They not only quickly discovered who they believed to be the source but, in so doing, learned of the existence of a "ring" of military officers who were spying on the activities of the National Security Council. The discovery sent alarm bells ringing throughout the White House.

Most of the investigatory work was done by Young. And Young had determined that a Yeoman First Class Charles E. Radford had rifled files, briefcases, and "burn bags" for documents to be clandestinely transmitted to the joint chiefs at the Pentagon. Whether this could be considered espionage in the traditional sense is debatable. Obviously the joint chiefs wanted to know what the hell was going on inside "Henry's shop." Like the President Kissinger preferred to play his cards close to his vest, telling as few people as possible what they were up to. And what they were up to—particularly in regard to détente with the Soviets and the Chinese, as well as in limitation of strategic arms—was what the joint chiefs apparently felt they had a right to know.

Nevertheless Kissinger was outraged at the discovery of what was to become known as "Pentagon spying." Not only did he order the liaison office shut down, but he arranged for the transfers of Rear Admiral Robert O. Welander and his assistant Yeoman Radford. Welander was sent out to command a cruiser flotilla; Radford (who was also suspected of being Anderson's source) was transferred to a reserve recruiting station in the Far

---

*Actually Nixon had sought to dissuade India's prime minister Indira Gandhi from waging war with neighboring Pakistan. The President felt Pakistan should be given time to work out problems with her eastern wing, now known as Bangladesh. Nixon argued that no one would benefit from that war. Considering the problems of Bangladesh and now of India, under Gandhi's authoritarian rule, Nixon was not too far off the mark.

West. Apparently on orders from President Nixon a major effort was made to keep the messy affair under wraps.

Several years later after the story was broken by the Chicago *Tribune*, Kissinger continued to deny that he had had any knowledge of the plumbers. At a press conference in January 1974 the Secretary of State conceded that he had been aware that his former assistant had interrogated Admiral Welander, "but from this one could not suppose that David Young was conducting an investigation."

The more Kissinger attempted to explain, the more he perplexed seasoned correspondents. Even his best friends in the press corps were displeased by his double talk. The Washington *Post*, for example, observed editorially that Kissinger's sworn assurances that he had known nothing of David Young and/or the plumbers "look very strange now." And Nick Thimmesch summed it all up by saying that, while he could understand Dr. Kissinger's valid worry about leaks,

> what I can't understand is why Kissinger, in the Year of Watergate, hasn't owned up to his role in the wiretapping of a number of his own staff and other government figures, his deep involvement with David Young and his knowledge of the plumber's activities. His denial of the latter, as found in his testimony before the Senate Foreign Relations Committee, could get Dr. Kissinger into serious trouble, possibly into a charge of perjury.

In other words Kissinger could well have defended actions he was obviously involved with. After all, whatever wrong came out of wiretapping and the plumbers' activities could hardly be laid to him, for he certainly did not order criminality.

But, unlike more hapless individuals in the Nixon administration including eventually the President himself, Kissinger had many good friends in such critical places as the Congress and the media. And they came to his rescue in June 1974 when, still riding high on a number of foreign policy successes, Kissinger threatened to resign unless he was cleared of allegations that he had participated in "illegal or shady activity" in government wiretapping of individuals. The Secretary had expected a hero's welcome when he returned to Washington following exhausting and successful negotiations in the Middle East. Instead he was jolted by blunt news conference questions as to whether he was retaining counsel for a possible perjury trial.

How deeply wounded Kissinger felt at the questioning of his veracity was demonstrated a few days later when he angrily voiced his threat to resign at an unscheduled press conference in Salzburg, Austria, where he and Nixon had paused before their trip through Israel and the Arab nations. Scarcely had his anguished words echoed through the halls of Congress when fifty-two senators of both parties, without waiting for all the evidence, raced to sign a resolution stating that Kissinger's "integrity and veracity are beyond reproach."

With some major exceptions (*The New York Times,* for example, accused the Secretary of "dissembling"), editorialists and columnists in Washington and across the country also rushed to Kissinger's defense. In general they argued that the search for Watergate culprits had gone too far. Joseph Alsop wondered

> why it was so shocking for a servant of the Nixon Administration to worry about national security to the extent of knowingly approving under a score of wiretaps. After all, national security wiretaps were very much more numerous in the Truman Administration, and they were vastly more numerous in the administration of President Kennedy. This reporter, with a known three wiretaps to his credit, all pre-Nixon, has long held the doctrine that if you have not been tapped, you have been slacking on your job. . . . In short, the servants of the Nixon Administration are plainly being judged by different tests than those that prevailed in happier times.

Nevertheless there was a pronounced lack of desire to go after Kissinger with the same prosecutorial zeal demonstrated against other figures in the Nixon entourage. Even for those who thought Henry had not been telling the whole story, as *Newsweek* reported at the time, "there seems little enthusiasm for pursuing the matter." Kissinger was the only political hero left in the dying days of the Nixon administration. Even perjury should be forgiven when it came to Henry, said his old friend Joseph Kraft, who had been zestfully punching away at Nixon and his aides. "While he may have lied," Kraft informed his readers, "the untruths are matters of little consequence when weighed against his service to the state."

It was obvious, as then noted by one of Kissinger's wiretapping victims, that different standards were being applied in judging the conduct of Nixon and his much-admired Secretary of State.

Apparently, wrote Daniel I. Davidson, who had been a member of Kissinger's staff, "the normal rules of conduct are not applicable to Henry Kissinger superstar. If those rules are not applicable to him, should they be applicable to Richard Nixon, who also deserves credit for foreign policy achievements?"

20

IRONICALLY, DESPITE REPEATED CONTEN-
tions to the contrary, the 1972 presidential campaign proved to
be one of the cleanest in American history. All of the "dirty
tricks" performed by the Nixonites had "the weight of a feather"
in determining the final outcome, as Theodore H. White phrased
it in *The Making of the President 1972*. If anything Nixon's 61–38
percent margin might have been larger if 3 or 4 million Americans had not been turned off by Watergate.

Actually the biggest "dirty trick" of the campaign was one the
Democrats played on themselves—the nomination of George
McGovern as their standardbearer. For in presidential terms the
senator from South Dakota was a goner by the night he was
nominated. Rarely had the American electorate seen as bizarre
a gathering as the delegates who came together at Miami Beach
for the quadrennial Democratic Convention. And it was all there
on the tube several days running. To many stay-at-home Democrats the spectacle was far from edifying. At the White House
where he occasionally glanced at his set, the incumbent knew he
had it made. The election was over before it actually began.

A year later, toward the tail end of the Watergate hearings,
Hubert Humphrey—who had himself sought the 1972 nomination—appeared on *Meet the Press*. In response to a question the
senator from Minnesota observed that "the dirtiest trick that was
played was the Democrats playing it on themselves, their crazy
system of quotas and sub-quotas and partial voting, all kinds of
gymnastics, political gymnastics that we went through to divide
our party. No Republican could have conceived of a program
that did as much to tear the Democratic party apart as we ourselves."

Of course Humphrey did his bit to assure McGovern's defeat.
After Ed Muskie had been eliminated as a front-runner, the
Minnesotan delivered upon McGovern as devastating an attack
as anyone in the White House could have dreamed of. Hum-

phrey made the case against McGovern better than any of his subsequent Republican attackers. Writing in *Life* magazine, Pierre Salinger, who had been one of McGovern's top aides, contended that Humphrey and the high command of the AFL-CIO had "succeeded beyond their wildest expectations" in painting McGovern as a "dangerous radical." Literature aimed at defense workers claimed that a McGovern presidency would cost them their jobs. Jews were handed pamphlets saying that McGovern would sell out Israel. In televised debates Humphrey pronounced McGovern's economic program as irresponsible and his tax program as confiscatory. "McGovern's positions were shamelessly distorted beyond recognition and the damage was done," wrote Salinger. "I am not saying that the Nixon campaign would not have done the same thing, but Hubert Humphrey had credibility with Democrats which Nixon never possessed."

There were issues in the 1972 campaign and McGovern lost on them. In the March 1974 issue of *The Atlantic,* David Broder wrote: "Every serious analysis of the 1972 election shows that issues had a larger importance than ever before—and worked badly to the Democrats' detriment. What few Democrats in Congress, but many outside, see is that, despite Watergate chicanery, Richard Nixon won on the issues in 1972—as he was able to define them."

And while McGovern himself refused to agree that he had lost on the issues, the ill-fated candidate did finally concede that the electorate had overwhelmingly rejected what "they perceived to be a confusion and uncertainty of leadership"—that is, McGovern's leadership. "To a large degree the failure of that campaign was its own fault, and I bear the largest share of responsibility," McGovern said in October 1975—three years after his defeat. It was the first time he had publicly taken upon himself the blame for his party's débâcle. The senator listed among his "mistakes": "the inadequate preparation" of his proposal for a $1,000 guaranteed annual income, which he never properly explained; "staff disorganization and disputes"; delivering his acceptance speech at 3:00 A.M. when the television audience was asleep; and the "vice presidential problem"—namely, the selection and subsequent removal of Senator Thomas F. Eagleton as his running-mate without thorough checking. The Eagleton episode, said McGovern, "was the most serious error of the campaign."

McGovern could also have listed among his "mistakes" his intemperate rhetoric. As he was battling to stay alive politically, he could hardly contain himself. "It is McGovern, not Nixon, who has been driven to the harsh and shrill extremes," noted John Osborne in *The New Republic*. Among other things McGovern likened Nixon to Hitler, repeatedly saying, "The main issue in this whole campaign is Richard M. Nixon." And at a Midwest airport in the final week of the campaign the Democratic candidate greeted a heckler with the historic words, "Kiss my ass." By this time McGovern had also had it with conservative newspaper columnists. "I find them pretty despicable characters," he observed. "They're really propagandists for a narrow and outmoded cause." So bitter were the McGovernites toward some of the gentlemen of the press that Frank Mankiewicz personally ordered Robert Novak, of Evans & Novak, barred from the candidate's plane and relegated to the "Zoo plane," usually filled with television technicians and the like. When he heard of the shift, a livid Novak encountered Mankiewicz and shouted, "Okay, Frank. No more Mr. Nice Guy!"

Not one of McGovern's "mistakes" could in any way have been attributed to Nixon's "dirty tricksters," the most notorious of whom was Donald H. Segretti. In fact when news of the break-in hit the newspapers, all such activity was called off. Segretti himself scurried into hiding. And from mid-June McGovern was able to head up a campaign in which, as a disillusioned Dick Tuck has suggested, the only "dirty tricks" were "the ones the McGovern campaigners played on each other."

Tuck, of course, was the Democrats' "dirty trickster," who had long made a career out of harassing Republicans, particularly Nixon. Except that his many media friends would lovingly refer to his dubious activities as "pranks." Frank Mankiewicz however, for whom Tuck had worked during the McGovern campaign, did describe Tuck as what he really was—"the grand old man of dirty tricks." (It was a title which "the grand old man" did not appreciate, particularly after Watergate when some of his past capers came back to haunt him.)

Mankiewicz, incidentally, was not opposed to "dirty tricks" when they were practiced against McGovern's enemies during the 1972 primaries. And he made that perfectly clear in a book entitled *Perfectly Clear*, a rousing attack on Nixon. In reviewing the book for the Washington *Post*, Lou Cannon, an expert on California politics, noted that Mankiewicz's effort presents Nixon "not as man but as monster. Even more, the book reveals a persistent double standard that does Mankiewicz no credit.

McGovern's 'pranks' against John Lindsay are great fun. Dick Tuck is glorified (with no mention of his paste-and-scissors campaign against a decent Democratic state senator). . . ."

The McGovernite pranks against Lindsay constituted a textbook case of overkill. They occurred during the primary in Florida where the New York mayor sought to establish himself as a Democratic contender. McGovern's main objective was to stop Lindsay, whom he considered the prime obstacle in his battle for the championship of the left. To this end McGovern had a strange ally in Matthew Troy, Jr., the Queens Democratic leader who hated Lindsay's guts. Among other things Troy had gained renown when he climbed the roof at City Hall to raise the flag after Lindsay had ordered it flown at half-mast following the tragic events at Kent State. For, if anything, Troy represented the earthy patriotism of New York's hard-hat voters, a fact which, according to Mankiewicz, "made him a special hero to us." Politics do indeed make strange bedfellows.

Working closely with Mankiewicz, Troy headed up efforts to "destabilize" the Lindsay effort. Aides were flown to Florida, where they concentrated on reminding transplanted New Yorkers about the horrors that Lindsay had wreaked on the Big Apple. For example they hired a small plane to cruise up and down Miami Beach, towing a banner with the message: "Lindsay means Tsouris." For the Gentiles who may not have understood, another plane towed a second banner: "And Tsouris means Trouble." At the same time Tuck had a band of volunteers whose job it was to wave embarrassing signs at Lindsay rallies and to heckle the mayor. Tuck's minions even infiltrated legitimate press conferences to ask Lindsay about New York's problems.

Mankiewicz was particularly proud of one such conference. It was in fact the big one called by Lindsay to announce his official entry into Florida's primary. The McGovernites tried to think of a question that would surely fluster the mayor. "We came up with it, and we got lucky," wrote Mankiewicz. The McGovern infiltrator was the first one recognized by Lindsay. And as three network and five local cameras zeroed in, the planted tormentor asked, "Mayor Lindsay, if you are elected President, how would you change U.S. policy toward Mexico?"

His Honor was noticeably rattled. As Mankiewicz later wrote, "The puzzled look on Lindsay's face made it all worthwhile."

Under Tuck's guidance the McGovern forces also played tricks on Senator Muskie, who was contesting in the primary. Muskie had once told questioners that he would not take a Black man as his runningmate since that would guarantee his defeat. So Tuck arranged for Muskie to be constantly needled about why he didn't think a Black man was qualified for high office.

Muskie, then considered the front-runner, was a major target of the McGovernites. And Mankiewicz still chortles over the practical joke they had planned for the Maine Democrat. Muskie had been scheduled to address an AFL-CIO picnic in Alameda County, California. It happened that Democratic County Chairman William Lockyer was also the McGovern coordinator for northern California. As chairman, Lockyer was asked to arrange to get Muskie from the airport to the picnic grounds. According to Mankiewicz, Lockyer rented a long black limousine and arranged for a Black chauffeur, in full livery, who was prepared to bow when he opened the door for Muskie. "I added the suggestion that he be prevailed upon to tug once or twice at his forelock as the news cameras zeroed in," wrote Mankiewicz. But when the candidate came off the plane, he quickly sized up the situation and arranged to be taken away in a more modest automobile. If the McGovernites had pulled it off, says Mankiewicz, it "would have been the great political stunt of the campaign."

Why all this harassment? Explained McGovern's research director Ted Van Dyk: "Our tactics were simple: challenge Muskie to debate; crowd his famous temper; have McGovern supporters and signs present at all his rallies; question his late-blooming conversion to the peace movement; encourage him to spread himself too thin among the many primary states; outorganize him in states where we had a chance. It was, in [Pat] Buchanan's phrase, sometimes 'political hardball.'"

Of course Muskie's "famous temper" finally got the better of him. Who could ever forget the extraordinary scene when the Maine senator lost control of his emotions while standing in front of the offices of the Manchester *Union-Leader* in New Hampshire? There was Muskie bare-headed in the snow, tears streaming down his face, as he denounced publisher William Loeb as a "liar" and a "gutless coward" for having attacked his wife. Actually what the *Union-Leader* had done was to reprint an interview with Mrs. Muskie by a reporter from *Women's Wear Daily*, which in turn had been reproduced by *Newsweek*, a magazine published by the Washington Post Company.

The *Union-Leader* had also published what appeared to be a spurious letter which claimed that Muskie, while in Florida, had laughed at a description of French-Canadians—of whom there are many in New Hampshire—as "Cannocks." The word actually is "Canucks" and it is considered offensive. At any rate Muskie couldn't contain himself. "I was just goddamned mad and choked up over my anger," he said later. But the episode did dramatize certain disabling personal weaknesses. And that meant the end of Muskie's front-running candidacy.*

Who was responsible for the "Canuck" letter? Conventional wisdom suggests that the Nixon "dirty tricks" operation may have done the job. But *no concrete evidence* to that effect was ever produced, despite exhaustive investigative effort by both the Ervin Committee and the media. And no one ever asked who benefited most directly from the episode. It was, of course, George McGovern.

Nevertheless as John Roche has observed, "the Muskie development was sheer political luck; it could never have been predicted."

Meanwhile Segretti was also dreaming up "political stunts," most of them not much different from what the McGovernites had been doing. The Republican worker, however, concentrated on manufacturing and distributing phony leaflets. Hundreds of copies of one of them, reading: "If you like Hitler, you'll love Wallace," were slipped under the windshield wipers of cars parked at a rally for the Alabama governor in St. Petersburg, Florida. Other leaflets signed "Mothers for Muskie" advocated "more busing" for schoolchildren at a time when the issue was most controversial. Segretti eventually came a cropper with a letter duplicated on "Citizens for Muskie" stationery which purportedly gave the "facts" concerning bizarre sexual conduct and excessive drinking on the part of Senators Humphrey and Jackson. "I came back from two, three glasses of wine at the local pub and wrote it off the top of my head," Segretti later said. "It wasn't done for anybody to believe in the damned thing. It was intended to be outrageous. I didn't expect anyone to believe it." Nevertheless, ludicrous as it was, the letter resulted in Segretti

---

*Ironically during the 1968 campaign Muskie had frequently alluded to Nixon's emotional state. Before one campaign audience Muskie declared, "You remember that press conference when he broke down completely under pressure" (referring to the famous 1962 meeting with newsmen). "If he can't take that kind of pressure, how's he going to take the pressure of being President?" Muskie asked.

being charged with distributing illegal campaign literature.*

In New Hampshire when news of these pranks spread through McGovern's primary headquarters, "there was mixed reaction— laughter, of course, but also nervousness," wrote Kristi Witker, Mankiewicz's deputy press secretary.** "Who was doing these things? Was it Humphrey, Jackson, Wallace, or us?" Kristi was not too happy about the idea of McGovernites putting out such material:

> There were others at our campaign office, though, who thought a little political sabotage a good thing and who were quick to take credit for the work itself or at least some prior knowledge of it. Several campaign workers admitted in amplified tones, that although they couldn't go into it, they knew our campaign had a spy "very high up" in the Muskie campaign who had been helpful in "liberating" some key documents as well as coordinating some "unfortunate events." It all pointed to Dick Tuck. . . .

But Witker didn't believe Tuck had been working inside the Muskie operation. For one thing he was too well known, "and he was also prominently in evidence at the McGovern press suite bar. Perhaps he was coordinator of the unfortunate events. But that didn't seem likely either, because only one of these events had the Dick Tuck touch"—that was when guests at the opening of Muskie's New Hampshire headquarters looked down at the bottom of their coffee cups to read: "McGovern for President."

That the McGovernites were interested in obtaining confidential intelligence from inside the camps of their political adversaries was also made perfectly clear by Mankiewicz. Thus Mankiewicz tells how one of his subordinates, Yancey Martin, began collecting stories about how much money the Lindsay campaign was paying local Black politicians in Florida, ostensibly for "organization work." The implication was that the payments were actually bribes. When Martin "had a few of the stories nailed

---

*The use of sexual innuendo against Nixon became standard practice in *The Village Voice*. Absolutely phony stories were published regarding the President and his friends. One reader, Mary Gallagher, protested in a letter published in the November 1, 1973 issue: "Sexual guesswork about Nixon and his coterie . . . is a smear tactic at least as shoddy as the Segretti letters used against Muskie in the Florida primary. . . ."

**Miss Witker's recollections of the McGovern campaign are contained in a very amusing book entitled *How to Lose Everything in Politics (Except Massachusetts)* (New York: Mason & Lipscomb, 1974).

down," writes Mankiewicz, "we made the story public. It annoyed the black leaders who had not been paid—or who had not been paid enough—and couldn't have helped very much with those Floridians who weren't yet sure that blacks should even vote, let alone be organized." In other words the McGovernites —despite their oft-expressed liberalism—did not mind catering to the racism of some Floridians.

There was apparently even one Liddy-type operation indulged in by the McGovernites. From a favorable April 25, 1972, article in the *Wall Street Journal:* "It's sometimes hard for McGovern workers to get hold of [Democratic] party lists. In Wichita, a local party leader refused to allow the lists to be photocopied; but McGovern workers managed to smuggle out the lists at night and copy them." Was a break-in in the dark of night involved?

The McGovernites did receive "one piece of political intelligence from within the Humphrey camp" which, according to Mankiewicz, turned out to be worthless. "A few weeks before the primary election, someone purporting to be a Humphrey 'insider' told us that a private plane at the Burbank airport was at the disposal of the candidate and that he would fly in it to Las Vegas to pick up a substantial cash contribution to his campaign. The informant even gave us the plane's registration number. There *was* a plane at Burbank with this number, and there it stayed throughout the campaign. . . ." The point is that the McGovernites did check the story out, obviously hoping somehow to embarrass Hubert Humphrey by linking him to shady characters in Las Vegas.

Somehow the story managed to leak out. And one of those who heard it was none other than Dr. Hunter S. Thompson of *Rolling Stone,* the affluent organ of the Counter-Culture. Since the story was second-hand by the time it got to him, he decided to check it out. Finally, as he explained in his book,* Dr. Thompson decided, "for reasons better left unexplained, at this point—that the only two people even half-likely to know anything about such a bizarre story were Mankiewicz and Dick Tuck." Unable to raise Tuck on the horn, Thompson managed to trap Mankiewicz outside the McGovern press room in Beverly Hills. He told Man-

---

*Fear and Loathing: On the Campaign Trail '72. (San Francisco: Straight Arrow Books, 1973).

kiewicz what he had learned. "What can you tell me about it?" he asked.

"Nothing," said Mankiewicz. Then, as an afterthought, "When's your next issue coming out?"

"Thursday."

"Before the election?"

"Yeah, and so far I don't have anything worth a shit to write about—but this thing sounds interesting."

Mankiewicz nodded, then shook his head. "Listen," he said. "You could cause a lot of trouble for us by printing a thing like that. They'd know where it came from, and they'd jerk our man right out."

"What man?"

Mankiewicz did not say. But the implication is obvious. The McGovernites had a man planted inside the Humphrey organization—the "insider," as Mankiewicz described him—who was feeding them juicy tidbits about a feared political opponent.*

Later on the McGovernites sought to obtain intelligence on Nixon. According to Mankiewicz, he was told by "guarded telephone callers" at least four or five times that the shah of Iran had made a secret one million dollar contribution to the Nixon campaign on the occasion of the presidential visit to Teheran in May of 1972. But Mankiewicz said his people did not raise the charge because "we were never able to produce even a trace of supporting evidence." Not for lack of trying, however. The point is that the McGovernites were not adverse to digging up dirt about opponents. Which was one reason why Walter Sheridan, who had headed up Robert F. Kennedy's "Get Hoffa" investigative squad, was hired. Among other things, according to Mankiewicz, Sheridan was assigned to perform background checks on members of the Democrats for Nixon group headed by John B. Connally. The idea was to determine whether any of them had legal problems with the Justice Department.

There was even a plan to plant spies aboard the Republican campaign planes. During the Ervin hearings GOP investigators produced a sworn affidavit by Richard M. Cohen, an associate producer for ABC-TV, who said a McGovern campaign official

*The Humphrey story can be found in *Fear and Loathing*. It is an extraordinary book. Where else could you read about Thompson's encounter with McGovern at a urinal in a New Hampshire men's room. "How's it going, Senator?"

had made the proposal. "The primary purpose of the project was to convey information from public statements rapidly to the McGovern headquarters and a secondary function would be to relate embarrassing incidents which might occur" on the campaign planes of President Nixon and Vice President Agnew. In his affidavit Cohen said it was Ted Van Dyk who suggested the project and had tentatively agreed to pay him a salary of $150 a week. Van Dyk confirmed the story. The McGovern research director said that he had hoped "we might catch the Vice President in another 'fat Jap'-type remark." But Van Dyk and Mankiewicz decided to scrap the plan after finance director Henry Kimelman objected to it on financial grounds.

The McGovernites did not hesitate to use rough tactics against Nixon, according to sworn testimony taken in the final hours of the Ervin hearings. For example Fred Taugher, who had been the Southern California campaign coordinator for the Democratic candidate, acknowledged that he had permitted persons planning an antiwar demonstration against the President to use McGovern phones for two days to round up support for their protest. According to Taugher, the use of the phones was also approved by Richard Stearns, the McGovern coordinator for the Western states. Leaflets advertising the anti-Nixon rally were also permitted to be placed in about 100 McGovern storefront offices around Los Angeles. The rally, a noisy one, resulted in the arrest of three people.

The Watergate Committee, in proceedings barely reported by the media, also heard testimony about the disruption of a Nixon rally in Fresno, California, by members of the United Farm Workers, a union whose vote-registration drive had been subsidized to the tune of $52,000 by the McGovern campaign. And there were witnesses who told of scurrilous anti-Nixon literature distributed throughout the country. A Los Angeles student, Michael Heller, testified about a pamphlet passed out in Jewish neighborhoods in Los Angeles which stated, "Nixon is *Treyf*," that is, unclean. One line asserted: "Nixon brings the ovens to the people rather than the people to the ovens," an apparent effort to link the President's Vietnam policies with the slaughter of 6 million Jews by the Nazis. According to Heller, the pamphlet was passed out by McGovern workers. The final witness was Jeremiah Sullivan, a Boston police superintendent, who described a demonstration that occurred outside a fund-raising dinner in Boston attended by Mrs. Nixon. Sullivan said the demonstration resulted in about twenty arrests and injuries to nine policemen, as well as considerable damage to property.

But the majority Democrats on the Ervin Committee, like the media, were totally disinterested in any of these revelations. So in order to save the committee the time it would take to present first person testimony, Senator Baker submitted about forty affidavits for the record, most of which concerned violence, property destruction, heckling, and disruption committed against Republicans and Nixon reelection offices during the 1972 campaign.

One affidavit was from Dr. John Lungren, Nixon's personal physician, who described a break-in at his Long Beach, California, office discovered on September 21, 1972. Lungren said that Nixon's medical records "were strewn about the floor" and had apparently been examined and perhaps photographed by intruders, who disturbed nothing else. No arrests were ever made in the break-in, he said. No interest was shown in what occurred in the Lungren office by either Senator Ervin or Senator Weicker, both of whom, of course, had been up in arms about the break-in at the Ellsberg psychiatrist's office. The Lungren episode was quickly forgotten.

Of course none of these dirty tricks did much to prevent Nixon's overwhelming victory at the polls. And likewise the Nixonite dirty tricks did little more than annoy and harass the Democrats. Some of the pranks were indeed gamey; but others were as remarkably inventive and funny as any dreamed up by the irrepressible Dick Tuck. For sheer whimsy there was the disruption of a Muskie fund-raising dinner at the Washington Hilton on April 17, 1972. Segretti and two assistants ordered a $300 supply of liquor; a $50 floral arrangement; goodies from the Watergate pastry shop; and 200 pizzas. Two magicians arrived, one having flown in from the Virgin Islands, to perform—as they said—"for the children." Also invited were a dozen or so African diplomats who arrived, appropriately dressed in national costume, in chauffeur-driven limousines, the bills for which were submitted to the Muskie people. But it could have been worse. As Segretti later testified, "We also made inquiries about renting an elephant, but wereunabletomakethenecessaryarrangements."

Testifying before the Ervin Committee, H. R. Haldeman told how the Segretti operation came about. He said that presidential aides Dwight Chapin and Gordon Strachan had come up with the idea of hiring a "Dick Tuck for our side," that is, setting up someone to function independently of the campaign organization in order to generate the same kind of activities carried out by the Democratic prankster whose "basic stock in trade was embarrassing Republican candidates." Haldeman added: "The repertoire of the political prankster includes such activities as printing up embarrassing signs for the opponent, posing in trainman's clothes and waving the campaign train out of the station, placing an agent on the opponent's campaign train to produce witty newsletters mocking the candidates, distributing opposition signs at rallies for use by members of the crowd, encouraging band leaders to play rival songs at rallies and so forth." In short the kind of activities for which Dick Tuck had received enormous—and friendly—press attention.

Chapin and Strachan informed Haldeman that they had someone in mind, Donald Segretti, an old chum from USC who was about to leave army service.

Nixon had not been informed of the Segretti operation. Meeting with Dean on February 28, 1973, the President referred to the prankster as "such a dumb figure, I don't see how our boys could have gone for him."

"But nevertheless," he went on, "they did. It was really juvenile! But, what the hell did he do? What in the (characterization deleted) did he do? Shouldn't we be trying to get intelligence? Weren't they trying to get intelligence from us?"

"Absolutely!" replied Dean.

The President observed that his rallies had been punctuated by violence. "They threw rocks, ran demonstrations, shouted, cut the sound system, and let the tear gas in at night. What the hell is that all about? Did we do that?"

Dean noted that "McGovern had Dick Tuck on his payroll, and Dick Tuck was down in Texas when you were down at the Connally ranch and set up to do a prank down there. But it never came off."*

"What did Segretti do that came off?" the President said.

"He did some humorous things. For example, there would be a fund-raising dinner, and he hired Wayne the Wizard to fly in from the Virgin Islands to perform a magic show. He sent invita-

_____
*Tuck claimed he had suggested that "when Nixon visited John Connally at his ranch in Texas, we should have a Brinks armored truck roll in saying they had come to collect the money, and have it followed by a laundry truck with Mexican license plates." The pointed reminder of Mexican "laundering" of Nixon campaign funds was not approved, according to Tuck.

– 306 –

tions to all the black diplomats and sent limousines out to have them picked up, and they all showed up and they hadn't been invited. He had four hundred pizzas sent to another—"

"What the hell!" the President broke in. "Pranks! Tuck did all those things in 1960, and all the rest."

"I think we can keep the Segretti stuff in perspective because it is not that bad. Chapin's involvement is not that deep. He was the catalyst, and that is about the extent of it."

"Sure," said the President, "he knew him and recommended him."

"That's right."

"But he didn't run him," the President noted. "He was too busy with us."

Segretti's appearance before the Ervin Committee came after senior staff members had spent most of the summer of 1973 touting the committee's forthcoming exploration of dirty tricks. That phase of the investigation would be even more explosive than the probe of the actual break-in, it was said. As David E. Rosenbaum reported in *The New York Times,* the committee's lawyers claimed privately that the testimony would show that the Republicans had systematically sabotaged the campaigns of the various candidates for the nomination and had thus engineered the nomination of McGovern, supposedly the weakest possible opponent for Nixon.

Finally, after the big buildup, Segretti took the witness chair on October 3, 1973. A tiny man, he stood 5 feet 4, had a moon face and a teenager's voice. Nevertheless appearances could have been deceiving. After all this was the man whom Woodward and Bernstein had exposed a year before in the Washington *Post* as the alleged Guy Fawkes of the 1972 campaign, the man who had conducted "a massive campaign of political spying and sabotage." The next day Segretti's partners-in-pranks, Martin Kelly and Robert Benz, testified. Kelly told the committee how he released two white mice and a finch in a room where Muskie was holding a press conference. He also hired a girl for $20 to run naked, shouting: "I love Ed Muskie!" in front of the senator's hotel room in Gainesville, Florida. About the most serious thing Segretti confessed to was sending out that phony letter on Muskie stationery accusing Humphrey and Jackson of totally fictitious sexual misconduct.

"When they had finished their testimony," reported Rosenbaum, "it was apparent that what they had done was tasteless, at times vicious, for the most part humorless and probably unprecedented in American Presidential campaigns. But it was equally clear that their efforts had made no difference in the outcome of the Democrats' nominating procedure. . . ."

In other words the "massive campaign of political spying and sabotage," as Woodward and Bernstein had described Segretti's activities, turned out to be journalistic hype. All the Ervin Committee could turn up in its "dirty tricks" phase were largely pranks of a collegiate variety; and while no doubt they were all annoying to the candidates and their staffs, they hardly imperiled —as James Reston once lugubriously put it—the "fragile process" of democracy.

Still the myth persists that the Nixon people helped nominate McGovern, which McGovern himself described as "nonsense." The truth is that the South Dakotan won the nomination fair and square, by doing better than most party pols had expected in the primaries, and by attracting a tremendous number of young people to his banner because of his position on Vietnam and other social issues.

As for the impact of dirty tricks, McGovern told Elizabeth Drew in a television interview that "added all together," they "probably didn't influence the primaries very much. They might have cost a few hundred votes at some point."

Of course neither Ms. Drew nor any other interviewer ever asked McGovern about the dirty tricks performed in his campaign.

Tuck's presence was felt at the 1972 Republican Convention in Miami Beach. There he published a daily four-page newspaper called *Reliable Source.* His penchant was printing confidential memoranda written by White House personnel holed up at the Doral Hotel under tight security. How Tuck got these documents he has never explained. But he did obtain what he called a "security" memo, which had been sent to White House staffers, telling them how to use the shredders and burn bags. And he did publish the private phone numbers of all Nixon campaign officials. And it was Tuck, as Pat Buchanan recalled with a chuckle before the Ervin Committee, who sent a group of pregnant Black women to parade outside Nixon headquarters in Miami Beach with signs reading "Nixon's the One."

But Tuck never did get the opportunity to reveal the tricks of his trade. Though interviewed by committee investigators in

September 1973, it was decided by the Democratic majority that Tuck should not be called as a witness because most of his mischief was perpetrated prior to the 1972 campaign—the focus of the committee's mandate. One staff member who participated in the interrogation was quoted as describing Tuck as "scared silly." And Tuck did not quarrel with that description, saying, "I won't kid you—I'm not dying to appear." He never did.

Once McGovern was nominated, the dirty tricks were few and far between. However Frank Mankiewicz did tell of a few in his appearance before the Ervin Committee. He claimed that just before a major McGovern rally in Los Angeles, "every radio station in the city was called by someone purporting to be from the McGovern campaign, saying the rally had been cancelled. That cost us a full house." And he also recalled that "an insulting telephone call was placed to AFL-CIO President George Meany in June 1972 by someone masquerading as the McGovern campaign manager, Gary Hart. How much of Mr. Meany's hostility to Senator McGovern's campaign can be attributed to this or other such incidents is difficult to measure."

Then in September 1972 Walter Cronkite called "to ask if I had telephoned him the day before," Mankiewicz continued. "I said no, I had not. He said that he'd had a very curious call from someone claiming to be me who said, 'You know, Walter, we have this arrangement where McGovern gets eighty percent of the coverage and Nixon only twenty percent and I just want you to know I think it's working very well.' Cronkite speculated the caller might have hoped he would confirm the existence of some such arrangement. Cronkite thought perhaps he was being set up," said Mankiewicz.

Exactly who was responsible for these pranks was never learned, but every effort was made to place the blame on the Nixonites. There were even allegations that the efforts of pro-McGovern homosexuals were generated to bedevil the Democratic campaign. One such allegation was published in the Washington *Star* in an article by John Fialka, entitled "Odd Events Dogged McGovern," which stated that "people presenting themselves as spokesmen for homosexual groups handed out flyers saying 'Gays for McGovern' "—the implication being that the organization might have been set up to embarrass the Democratic candidate.

But as Robert W. Corbett pointed out in a letter to the *Star*,

Gays for McGovern was a "perfectly legitimate campaign group, as was Dentists for McGovern or Black Americans for McGovern." Corbett, who had been a salaried district coordinator for McGovern, and prior to that an organizer of "gay" groups throughout New York City, said that Gays for McGovern was organized to do what the name implied—namely, to campaign for McGovern in the gay community. "Many noted gay leaders lent their names to this group. It operated with campaign funds from New York, San Francisco and Los Angeles. In New York State, the Walt Whitman Democratic Club paid the bill for the 'Gays for McGovern' leaflet."

It is true the Nixonites kept close tabs on what McGovern and his people were doing during the campaign. They set up an "attack group," composed of White House and CRP aides, to keep on top of what the Democratic candidate was saying with the idea of spotting and making the most of his mistakes and weaknesses. Though the "attack group" was not highly visible, it was no secret. In fact John Osborne wrote about it at length toward the end of the campaign, in the October 21, 1972, issue of *The New Republic.*

"The original assignment of the attack group was to get George McGovern down," said Osborne.

> Now it is to keep him down. Its visible way of doing this is to track his every word and action, partly from press reports and partly from the personal and more or less covert observation that occurs in all national political campaigns. . . . Nixon observers are present at every McGovern appearance just as—or so the Nixonites assume—McGovern observers are at every Nixon and Nixon surrogate performance. The Nixon tacticians have arranged, as they assume their McGovern counterparts have, to have friendly watchers and informants in newspaper offices, television and radio studios and, where and as they can manage it, among the opponent's workers and supporters at campaign centers from the national headquarters down to precincts.
>
> This is standard campaign procedure, within accepted political norms.

Despite the intensive exposure of dirty tricks by the Senate and the media, such practices were continued in, of all places, the Congress. The victims this time were conservatives of both parties, who were embarrassed by bogus remarks inserted in their names in the *Congressional Record.* True, an investigation was launched by the FBI to determine who was responsible for the pranks, but what was surprising was that the media which was so loud about hunting down Donald Segretti now had so little to say.

The victims were Congressmen Earl R. Landgrebe of Indiana, John M. Ashbrook of Ohio, and Otto E. Passman of Louisiana. The false statement inserted in the *Record* in Landgrebe's name dealt with Nixon's resignation. In an irreverent takeoff on Nixon's farewell address to his White House staff, the insertion said: "Mr. Speaker, former President Nixon's mother was a saint, by his own admission . . . but he omitted mention of his own saintly qualities in that wonderful and touching address." Landgrebe, who had been a stout defender of Nixon, was also quoted as saying: "As you know, I was a faithful supporter of our embattled President to the bitter, sour end, stating even that I would be shot with him if necessary. Many wonderful people wrote me recommending this course." The forged speech had this to say about the Watergate break-in: "Who, after all, he was [sic] bugging at the DNC? Leftist fellow-travelers, Mr. Speaker. By God, I should hope he listened closely." The material, entitled "Rectifying the Untimely Removal of President Nixon," concluded by suggesting that President Ford name Nixon as his new Vice President, then resign himself to allow the former President to again take up the reins of power.

Two pages later, in the section reserved for "extensions of remarks," Ashbrook was quoted as praising the new military régime governing Chile. "Mr. Speaker," the Ohioan was quoted, "I have been disgusted and dismayed by the ranting of the pink fellow-travelers and libral [sic] dupes in our great Nation against the government of our military allies in the beleaguered land of Chile."

Both Landgrebe and Ashbrook protested the forgeries and Speaker Albert said he viewed the matter "with extreme concern." The FBI investigated and came up with nothing, Albert later informed Ashbrook. Meanwhile Congressman Michael J. Harrington acknowledged that a separate incident involving another bogus statement attributed to Congressman Passman, the pro-Nixon Democrat from Louisiana, had been perpetrated by a few college students working as summer interns in the Harrington office. Aides of Harrington, one of the leading House liberals, called Passman to apologize for what were described as "profane" remarks. Passman took a philosophic attitude toward the episode. He told Harrington's aides, "Don't be too hard on the young men who did it."

Segretti, who apologized personally to Senators Jackson and Humphrey for the dirty trick he played on them, was not as lucky. Sentenced to six months in the slammer, he served four and a half months of that term.

Another story of political shenanigans which broke after the 1972 election concerned an illegitimate child born in Fort Wayne, Indiana. The 1941 birth certificate listed the father as "George S. McGovern of Mitchell, South Dakota." The story surfaced in the summer of 1973, after someone leaked a memo purportedly from H. R. Haldeman proposing that the illegitimate child story be given to the press. Apparently someone else had better sense, for the story never came out during the campaign.

The Washington *Post*, however, rectified that. On August 2, 1973, the Watergate-obsessed daily let the world know of the Haldeman memo and that the senator's name was on the birth record. The mother, though conceding she had known McGovern briefly, denied the senator was the father. After that the story was generally forgotten.

The Fort Wayne *News-Sentinel* kept after it however, and not for reasons of prurience. As editor Davis told Ron Rosenbaum of *The Village Voice*, he didn't give a damn whether McGovern had an illegitimate child or not, "although I was convinced he did. What I wanted to know was who had expunged the public record on the copy of the birth certificate at the Board of Health" during the 1972 campaign.

In other words a cover up.

According to Davis, the father's name was "clumsily eradicated" from the document. And that infuriated Davis. "I'm concerned about preserving the purity of the public record," he said. "If you don't have that then where the hell are you?"

Davis had to get a court order to examine the birth certificate. When he discovered the mutilation, he sought to examine the original copy maintained in Indianapolis. Refused permission, he took the matter to the State Supreme Court. There he lost.

"The Nixon contention," commented Rosenbaum, "that the press has one standard for him and another one for the conduct of his opponents is much ridiculed in the press. But imagine if it was rumored that 'Richard M. Nixon of Whittier, California' was the name clumsily eradicated from the Fort Wayne copy of the birth certificate. People would be knocking down the doors of the Indiana State Board of Health to document the 'coverup scheme.' All in the interest of preserving the public record, of course."

21

THROUGHOUT THE 1972 CAMPAIGN THERE
was anguish in the McGovern camp over what appeared to be
massive indifference on the part of the electorate toward what
was then being described as the Watergate bugging case. This
despite numerous—and frantic—efforts on the part of McGovern
and runningmate R. Sargent Shriver to make the case the major
issue of the election. Again and again Senator McGovern made
the most stinging attacks on the President personally, calling him
a "bungling, bugging burglar," and likening him to Hitler.

Still the opinion polls indicated that most of the public couldn't
have cared less. And it wasn't because the American people
weren't informed. Two weeks before the election Crosby S.
Noyes, writing in the Washington *Star,* suggested that

> it may be that many people see no great difference between the
> bugging of Democratic National Committee headquarters and the
> systematic pilfering of secret documents from a whole series of
> federal agencies that has become so fashionable in recent years.
> . . . Far more real political damage has been done to this and
> previous Administrations by these breaches of security than by
> anything that happened at the Democratic headquarters.

There was of course Daniel Ellsberg, then under indictment
on a number of counts involving the theft of government property in the case of the Pentagon Papers. Ellsberg conceded he
was aware of the possibility of going to jail for his actions. But for
him, breaking the law was a matter of political conscience. In the
upside-down world of Watergate, Ellsberg became an heroic
figure to a large number of people and what he did was widely
regarded as a public service.*

---

*"Poor Liddy & Hunt," wrote Pat Buchanan on the Op-Ed page of *The New York Times,* August 3, 1973, "if only, like Ellsberg, they had dropped their stolen papers off at the national desk of *The New York Times,* instead of the campaign desk of Jeb Magruder, they might be sharing the Pulitzer Prize."

"But where does one draw the line between theft in the public service and plain theft?" asked Noyes. "What is the real difference between agents and informants who turn over reams of secret Government documents to sympathetic newspapers and columnists and a crew that tries to tap the phones and read the mail of the political opposition?"

Then, too, there was the feeling among many that trying to find out what the opposition was doing had long been part of the American political scene. "Which," wrote Noyes, "may be why the Watergate affair has had so little impact in spite of the publicity it has received and why it seems unlikely to affect the result of the election in the long run." And as it turned out, despite Watergate, the American people went to the polls and voted overwhelmingly for Nixon.*

The Watergate affair probably would have run its course had it not been for the violations of the rights of the seven defendants at the break-in trial by a federal jurist whose prior judicial conduct had long aroused the ire of all true civil libertarians. And a few did protest Judge John Sirica's handling—or mishandling—of the case. "It seems ironic," wrote Joseph Rauh, Jr., former national chairman of Americans for Democratic Action, "that those most opposed to Mr. Nixon's lifetime espousal of ends justifying means should now make a hero of a judge who practiced this formula to the detriment of a fair trial for the Watergate Seven."

The *Washingtonian,* a monthly of liberal leanings, had a similar analysis. Listing judges who should be removed from the bench, the magazine prominently included Judge Sirica, citing his "careless legal errors, his short temper, his inattentiveness to court proceedings, his misguided view of the purpose of judicial power, his lack of compassion for his fellow human beings, and strange as it now seems, his lack of interest in the truth." In the Watergate case Sirica "badgered, accused, and castigated witnesses, prosecutors and defense lawyers. He read transcripts of confidential bench conferences to the jury. He used the threat of lengthy sentences to force defendants into abandoning their constitutional rights. He turned the trial into an inquisition, and justice into a charade."

---

*Asked about Watergate after the election, Senator Tom Eagleton—McGovern's original runningmate—replied, "All political parties spy on one another; the Republicans got caught at it."

Five of the original defendants had pleaded guilty to burglary. The other two had stood trial and were convicted. Telling them that they knew more about the case than they had told, Sirica provisionally meted out sentences of thirty-five to forty years. If they cooperated and confessed all, he said he would reconsider the sentences. Not for nothing was Sirica known as "Maximum John."

Since then Sirica has basked in the adulation of much of the media. The fact that "Maximum John" had once been a close friend of Joseph R. McCarthy—and an ardent espouser of the late senator's views—did not deter Mary McGrory from gushing over "the immigrant's son who . . . pried up the rock to show the maggots and worms underneath." In fact Ms. McGrory urged in her column that the J. Edgar Hoover Building be leveled "with our bare hands, if necessary" and the ground made into a park named after "Judge John J. Sirica, the man to whom we owe our liberty, if we still have any."

A few civil libertarians were appalled. Nat Hentoff of *The Village Voice* for example observed: "When most of those who are otherwise concerned with judicial fairness laud a judge for putting on the screws—or are silent—a dangerous precedent has been set."

Another surprising entry in the liberal pantheon was none other than Senator Ervin, who had previously led Southern filibusters against civil rights laws. But all that anti-Nigruh stuff was forgotten when the North Carolinian took over as chairman of the Watergate Committee. The liberals even forgave him his staunch opposition to the Equal Rights Amendment, which would grant legal parity to women, when he let it be known he would show Nixon no quarter.

The Ervin Committee had its origins in the spadework done by staff members of Ted Kennedy's Subcommittee on Administrative Practices and Procedures. This was back in October 1972 when James Flug, the subcommittee's chief counsel, and Carmine Bellino, its chief investigator, looked into Donald Segretti's contacts with the White House. Apparently deciding it would be best to remain behind the scenes, rather than be accused of a political vendetta, Kennedy played a key role in convincing Ervin to take over the investigation.

But it was Majority Leader Mike Mansfield who made the final decision. He chose Ervin, Mansfield said, because he "was the only man . . . on either side of the aisle who'd have the respect of the Senate as a whole. We could've got the fist-pounding, free-wheeling boys out there. I don't know what that would have accomplished. We're not looking for a TV melodrama. We're looking for a good, fair, impartial investigation."

Which is exactly what Ervin did not provide. If ever there was a partisan investigation, this was it. From the start it was obvious that Ervin's main purpose was to get the goods on Richard Nixon and his associates, and there were goods to get. When it came to investigating Democrats, however, there was small enthusiasm.

It was a Democratic-controlled show from the very beginning. The Republicans had tried desperately to enlarge the committee's scope of investigation from the 1972 campaign to those conducted in 1964 and 1968. They also tried to get an even break on committee representation, contending that otherwise the hearings would become a partisan witch-hunt. The majority Democrats in the Senate rebuffed them on both counts.

Mansfield may not have been looking for a "TV melodrama," but the hearings were soon converted into a television extravaganza providing more entertainment than enlightenment. But that was not Ervin's purpose, according to his statement authorizing the televising of the hearings. Though conceding that the coverage could be prejudicial to the rights of the accused persons, Ervin stated: "It is more important for the American people to know the truth . . . than sending one or two people to jail." Especially, the great constitutionalist added, because "justice has a habit of treading on leaden feet." In other words lynch them —at least figuratively—since the courts are too slow in meting out the punishment they deserve.

Likewise much of the press couldn't have cared less about due process when it came to those accused in Watergate. The Nixon-haters had a field day at the hearings. Almost maniacal to "get" the administration, some of them passed questions to senators interrogating witnesses, thus participating in, rather than reporting, the drama. Dan Schorr of CBS, for example, got so annoyed with the questioning of Haldeman that he cornered Majority Counsel Samuel Dash to tick off a number of questions he said had been unanswered. The reason for such unprecedented behavior was explained by Mary McGrory: "Reporters have been covering the story for so long they are more familiar with it than the Senators, and there are such gaps of information. The reporters can't get at it, and they hope the Senators can get it for them." And few in the press corps were more exercised over the proceedings than Ms. McGrory who, Fred Thompson has noted, never smiled in all those months, for "hers was an all-consuming mission of vengeance, with every committee member graded by the number of verbal lashes he administered across the backs of White House witnesses." Finally it occurred to the Republican counsel that McGrory's attitude may well have been colored by the fact that, alone among the major columnists, she had predicted victory for George McGovern in 1972.

Thomas Collins, writing in *Newsday,* compared the Watergate press corps to "an army holding a strategically vital position. It holds the high ground, so to speak, in the Battle of Watergate, and its presence symbolizes the fact that the press has a proprietary interest in this story as it seldom has had before."

By and large, according to Collins, the reporters covering Watergate were "an anti-Nixon crowd" which, generally regarding the proceedings in the Caucus Room as show business or "good theater," developed a cynical tolerance for the "star" value of Ervin and company.

In all of this the media had the active cooperation of a majority staff largely composed of young zealots who made no secret of their passionate hatred of the administration. Heavily funded, feeling no compunction about the ethics of leaking material, and not reined in by Ervin, they made a mockery of fair inquiry. As Thompson put it, "Here was a way for a young man on the staff to make his mark in history, possibly even to bring down a President."

Directing the staff was Samuel Dash, the chief counsel. Dash's liberal credentials appeared to be in order. A Democrat who had supported George McGovern, he had also been a member of Americans for Democratic Action. A law professor, he had served for a time as a district attorney in Philadelphia. But that was back in the mid-fifties when Dash was a more enthusiastic supporter of wiretapping—much more, in fact, than either E. Howard Hunt or James W. McCord. "We would be powerless to protect the country if we couldn't wiretap," Dash said at the time. "To outlaw wiretapping is similar to chopping off your head to take care of the pimple on your nose." After leaving the DA's office, Dash signed on with the Ford Foundation to study wiretapping. He came away convinced that wiretapping, at least in the volume he himself had once encouraged, was not necessarily beneficial. Now he felt that the practice "leads to corruption . . . it affects the quality of life."

As chief counsel Dash was quickly labeled a *nebbish* by certain members of the press who felt that, because of his bumbling efforts, the hearings would go nowhere. For example, as chief investigator of illegal electronic surveillance Dash hired a San Francisco private eye who it turned out had himself been convicted in a New York bugging case in 1966. The private eye was quickly let go.

Then there was Terry Lenzner who made no secret of his hatred of the Nixon administration. Lenzner had served briefly as head of the Office of Legal Services in the anti-poverty program. Following an internal dispute he was dismissed by Donald Rumsfeld, the director of the Office of Economic Opportunity, for channeling federal anti-poverty dollars to such groups as the Black Panthers and Students for a Democratic Society (SDS) in violation of OEO regulations. Previously Lenzner had been a defense counsel for the Berrigan brothers, the two antiwar priests who had been indicted for destroying federal draft records.

Another of Dash's investigators, Scott Armstrong, was a close friend of Bob Woodward of the Washington *Post*, then running exclusive stories on Watergate based on "informed sources" within the committee. Woodward had recommended Armstrong to Dash, after Dash had offered Woodward a job with the committee.*

And, of course, there was Carmine Bellino, the aging investigator who had long served the Kennedys. He came over from Senator Kennedy's Subcommittee on Administrative Practices and Procedures, where he had concentrated on Segretti's contacts at the White House.

It was with this band of zealots that the probe into Nixon misdeeds was launched. And from the beginning the Ervin Committee itself was guilty of numerous misdeeds, including the very kind of dirty tricks it supposedly was investigating. Eventually Richard Wilson enumerated ten general categories in investigative procedure which, he said, gave great concern to strict constructionists of constitutional rights:

---

*Armstrong, who had known Woodward from their days at Yale, was best man at Woodward's wedding. Later he went to work for Woodward and his collaborator, Carl Bernstein, as a researcher for their second book, *The Final Days*. After that he was hired by the Washington *Post* as a reporter.

1. Hearsay evidence was unlimited.

2. Opinion and conclusion of witnesses involving the guilt, innocence and motives of second and third parties.

3. Moralistic lectures based on political ideology.

4. Invasion of privacy by demands for repentance.

5. Preclusion of fair trial by notoriety via television.

6. Accusation without corroboration.

7. Bullying and ridicule of witnesses.

8. Immunity to tell all to the TV jury but not to the grand jury.

9. Repetition ad infinitum for censorious effect.

10. Bible quoting for discrediting effect.

"Some of the foregoing practices in the Ervin committee bear upon Constitutional rights of accused persons and others relate merely to common decency," wrote Wilson. "In both areas the sky has been the limit under the Ervin doctrine that it is better to expose and destroy than to convict by due process."

On the other side of the ideological fence Nat Hentoff made the point that the Ervin hearings ought to be regarded by his fellow liberals critically and skeptically. "Yet in the current celebratory anti-Nixon atmosphere, nearly all the criticism of what's happening to due process comes from the right. The left will have its hangover when the cycle turns."

And somewhere in the middle of the ideological spectrum Professor Theodore J. Lowi of Cornell University raised the question, "Are liberals only concerned about legality and justice when the cause of action affects the Left?" Lowi, author of *The End of Liberalism,* added, "Liberals ought to have joined in the defense of the Watergate witnesses. They should have been clamoring for the rebuke of the Ervin Committee and its staff." As for Ervin himself, Lowi said that the senator "sounds like Congress's keeper of the Constitution only because so few others are ready to stand up and call his Bible-bearing bluff. . . . The Ervin Committee seems to recognize no limits at all."

Rarely did the committee demonstrate its extreme partisanship more clearly than in its treatment of Richard Moore, special counsel to the President and a man universally respected in and out of the White House. Moore was called at the suggestion of White House Counsel Fred Buzhardt. The purpose was for Moore, a former television executive of unblemished reputation, to refute John Dean. Dean had testified that while he had told the President all he knew about the break-in and cover up on March 21, 1973, he believed that the President was aware of the cover up as early as September 15, 1972.

Prior to his appearance Moore met privately with Lenzner and Thompson to go over his testimony. What he planned to put on the record, Moore said, was the meeting he had had with Dean in which the White House counsel had flatly told him that the President was not aware of the cover up before March 21, 1973, six months after the date Dean had cited in his testimony. Moore also said that following the March 21 meeting, Dean had said the President was genuinely surprised at Dean's information.

But the subject was not brought up the next afternoon when Lenzner began questioning Moore in public session. The first question he asked was, "Do you have a recollection of a meeting on March 14, 1973, at 8:30 in the morning also attended by Mr. Kleindienst and Mr. Mitchell?" Moore was visibly taken aback. He had no such recollection. Lenzner kept boring in. He asked a series of questions totally unrelated to the main issues. As Thompson later recalled, "It was an effective trial lawyer's tactic: challenge the witness's memory on collateral matters; if he does not remember those, perhaps his memory can be challenged on the matters at issue."

The next morning Thompson took over the questioning. By this time Moore had regained his composure, and responded forthrightly to questions about his meeting with Dean. His testimony was not only clear, it was significant. He repeated what he had told Thompson and Lenzner at their original interview— namely, that Dean had told him that he was convinced the President was in the dark about the cover-up activities prior to March 21, 1973.

Confirming Moore's impression of Dean's state of mind during this period was Egil Krogh, chief of the White House "plumbers." Krogh, interviewed by Mike Wallace of CBS, said he was convinced from conversations with Dean that President Nixon did not know about the cover up as early as Dean claimed he did. Krogh told of a two-hour meeting he had with the then White House counsel on March 20, 1973, and he quoted Dean as saying, "Bud, the President is being badly served. He just doesn't know what's going on." Significantly Krogh's testimony on this point had not been sought by the Ervin Committee.

By now the Ervin Committee was routinely engaged in character assassination of White House witnesses. Most times the witnesses were too terrified to protest. One White House aide, speechwriter Patrick J. Buchanan, appeared at the hearings unafraid. Accused beforehand, through the usual leaks to the press, of being a "dirty tricks" strategist, Buchanan sprang from his corner at the opening bell and punched his inquisitors silly—with justification. In a prepared statement he noted that the committee had not granted him the elementary courtesy of notifying him that he would be called as a witness before the news was flashed over television. "Of greater concern to me, however, has been an apparent campaign orchestrated from within the committee staff, to malign my reputation in the public press prior to my appearance. In the hours immediately following my well-publicized invitation, there appeared in the *Washington Post, The New York Times,* the *Baltimore Sun,* the *Chicago Tribune* and on the national networks, separate stories all attributed to committee sources alleging that I was the architect of a campaign of political espionage or dirty tricks."

"Mr. Chairman," Buchanan went on, "this covert campaign of vilification, carried on by staff members of your committee, is in direct violation of Rule 40 of the rules of procedure for the select committee. . . . Repeatedly I have asked of Mr. Dash and Mr. Lenzner information that they might have to justify such allegations. Repeatedly, they have denied to me that they have such documents. When I asked Mr. Lenzner who on the committee staff was responsible, he responded, 'Mr. Buchanan, you ought to know that you can't believe everything you read in the newspapers.' It was his joke and my reputation. So it seems fair to me to ask, how can this select committee set itself up as the ultimate arbiter of American political ethics if it cannot even control the character assassins within its own ranks?"

When Buchanan finished, Ervin "deplored" the use of leaks to smear innocent people, as did Dash, but both professed an inability to check them. "I know of no staff member who has done it," said Dash. "I have searched to find such staff members if there were any. We have had a problem like this before and I think we all know that the problem of leaks is one that isn't always to be solved."

Buchanan proceeded to demolish the committee, standing up to Dash and even one-upping Ervin. When the senator invoked Andrew Jackson, the witness noted that President Jackson had been the "father of the spoils system." Declaring that the Watergate break-in had been "a crime" and that electronic surveillance had no place in politics, Buchanan insisted that none of the strategems, overt or covert, which did have a White House imprimatur had exceeded the limits of time-honored political tradition. His only regret was that the "exaggerated metaphors" in his private memos ("We ought to go down to the kennels and turn all the dogs loose" on Senator Muskie) had become public property.*

And as Buchanan pointedly reminded the committee, campaigns do cause some extreme rhetoric, such as McGovern's comparison of U.S. war policy in Indochina with the extermination of the Jews, and Nixon with Hitler. But, of course, the committee had no intention of looking into that. Asked what kind of political activity he advocated, Buchanan responded, "Anything that was not considered immoral, unethical, illegal—or unprecedented in previous Democratic campaigns."

With one exception the Republicans on the committee appeared to enjoy Buchanan's performance. The exception was Senator Weicker, the Connecticut statesman who expressed unhappiness that Buchanan seemed to be lumping pranks and hardball tactics in with the break-in as if there were no differences. Buchanan quickly assured the senator that "I did not consider Watergate a prank; it was a crime." The wind out of his inquisitorial sails, Weicker meekly thanked Buchanan for saying so in public.

When Buchanan left the witness table, the White House celebrated what one worker there called "the only day of the hearings I've really enjoyed." And Senator Edward J. Gurney of Florida, the lone Nixon stalwart among the panel's Republicans, proclaimed it "one of the most amusing days" of his life. The Democrats, however, were not that amused. Senator Herman Talmadge of Georgia, characterizing the day's proceedings an "unmitigated disaster," wondered how long the committee planned to continue its hearings.

---

*Only William Safire in his column in *The New York Times* noted the "dangerously illiberal turn" the committee had taken in questioning Buchanan about memos dealing with political strategy. "The search is no longer for unethical acts that require legislative remedies, or for ways to 'get to the truth' about Watergate. . . . What right does any arm of Government have to demand to know the political strategy, past or present, of any party or individual? Would it be a good idea to send the FBI over to Senator Kennedy's office to ask for the file on his political strategy? . . ."

Following Buchanan's appearance, Senator James Buckley of New York sent a letter to Ervin asking him to put members of his staff under oath to discover who was leaking damaging material about prospective witnesses. Ervin declined to do this for a number of reasons, among which were his concerns that a search for leakers would "divert" the committee from important tasks and that it would hurt staff morale. Imagine Buckley's surprise, therefore, when he read in *The New York Times* of November 20, 1973, a dispatch reporting that an investigator had been suspended because Sam Dash believed he was the source of an article that was highly critical of the committee staff.

The article, by Timothy Crouse, entitled "Senators, Sandbaggers and Soap Operas," was published in *Rolling Stone*. Quoting anonymous sources, it presented a far from flattering picture of the behind-the-scenes work of the committee.

When Dash read the piece and saw "that bit about his being an egomaniac, he went bananas," a staff member told *The New York Times*. "There was no stopping him. Nobody else who mattered gave a damn but Dash." With Ervin's permission Dash dropped everything to launch a full plumbers-type search for the culprit who had leaked to *Rolling Stone*. After a week Dash discovered that the leaker was none other than Scott Armstrong, the investigator whom he had hired at the suggestion of Bob Woodward. What to do about it caused a split within the committee. Some investigators demanded his dismissal; after all, he had cast discredit on their work. Terry Lenzner, however, urged Armstrong's retention. Finally in a Solomon-like decision Dash ordered him suspended from the staff without pay for a month.

Almost immediately Weicker—whom *Rolling Stone* had referred to as one senator who "does his homework"—praised Armstrong and offered him a job on his own separate investigative team.

Despite Armstrong's temporary suspension the problem of leaks continued to bedevil the Ervin Committee. So much so that when Dash sent out a rough draft of the final report to the member-senators, he appended a memo warning the staff to protect security on the document. Dash noted that CBS correspondent Dan Schorr "has told us that he has been promised a copy of the draft by a member of the Committee as soon as it is received. I am sure this is merely a boast, but I would urge very careful security of the draft. . . . Each draft has a control number. At the staff level, we have 'shredded' working papers and are keeping a few copies of the draft (for editing purposes) tightly secured. . . ."

The irony of the situation apparently was lost on Dash. The plumbers whom the committee had been investigating for so many months had been organized to plug leaks, and much had been made of the way in which, shortly after the Watergate arrests, G. Gordon Liddy had been seen headed for the shredder with various documents. Now, it turned out, Dash himself had employed a shredder.

But the greater irony was that while Dash was busy plugging the possible leak to Schorr, another CBS correspondent, Lesley Stahl, somehow obtained a copy of the report and promptly put it on the air.

Another irony was that as chief counsel of a committee probing dirty tricks, Sam Dash himself was not adverse to playing one on Republican staffers. With Ervin's approval, Dash told them to take a holiday during the Memorial Day recess. He did not tell them he and other Ervin people intended to write the committee's final report during that period and present it to them as a *fait accompli.*

"When Fred Thompson and the committee returned from the Memorial Day recess, we had a draft of the final report ready for them. Fred seemed resentful and insisted on his staff going over each section . . ."*

Probably the biggest leaker was Weicker. For a Republican, the senator was an oddity. He had actually fought for his job on the committee while most Republicans were running the other way. From the very beginning Weicker operated on his own with a team of five investigators who became known as the Third Front. Also from the very beginning Weicker made no secret of his intention of "getting" Richard Nixon.

Ironically Weicker had been elected to the Senate with Nixon's support. At the behest of the President's chief political adviser, Murray Chotiner, money from a secret White House fund collected for the 1970 congressional campaign was siphoned off to aid a duly appreciative Weicker. As a result Weicker held Chotiner in high esteem. When Chotiner died in 1974, one of those prominent in attendance at the Washington Hebrew Congregation services was Weicker. (Also there was President Nixon, bidding farewell to an old comrade; such are the vagaries of politics.)

Chief Counsel: Inside the Ervin Committee (New York: Random House, 1976).

Weicker had made his way into the Senate through a fluke. He ran against two opponents. The endorsed Democrat was a free-lance clergyman and ADA Poohbah named Joseph Duffey; but a great many unreconstructed Democrats preferred the incumbent Tom Dodd, who had been censured by his peers on charges most people by now have forgotten. "It was a delightful campaign," wrote C. H. Simonds in *The Alternative.* "While Weicker went about portraying him as a one-man Weatherman bomb-and-orgy squad, poor Duffey devoted his scanty energies to refereeing staff disputes over whether or not to bill himself as *The Reverend;* Dodd, meanwhile, bumbled along with chin up and smile bright and every hair in place.... And so Weicker went to Washington, giving the last laugh to Dodd, who must be laughing still as he beholds the pompous clowns who censured him, yawning and squirming through his successor's weepy tirades."

In one programmed outburst during the Watergate hearings, Weicker—making sure the cameras were focused on him—had cried out, "Republicans do not cover up, Republicans do not go ahead and commit illegal acts, and God knows Republicans don't view their fellow Americans as enemies to be harassed; but rather I can assure you that Republicans . . . look upon every American as a human being to be loved and won." At the same time he denounced the White House for allegedly seeking to smear him, claiming that Charles Colson had been leaking nasty things about him to the press. Naturally Weicker was opposed to leaking. Except of course when he did the leaking. For, as it turned out, Weicker and his staff were feeding out confidential materials to press people on an almost daily basis. Weicker's arrogant disregard of the rules shocked most of his colleagues. As columnist Nick Thimmesch observed, the senator "acted every bit as high-handed as anyone in Nixon's White House ever did and could have well been a Watergate himself if he had the opportunity."

Consider, for example, the dirty trick he played on Colson. Having heard the senator's emotional outburst on television, Colson immediately called Weicker's office. But the senator would not take the call, insisting through his secretary that Colson appear at his office the next morning. That meeting became almost as celebrated as the TV hearings. When Colson and lawyer David Shapiro arrived, they were surprised to discover five men seated around the senator's desk. And Weicker looked even angrier than he did on television.

"Sit down, Mr. Colson," Weicker growled, barely rising to shake Colson's outstretched hand.

Seeking to soothe the Senator's ire, Colson began to speak. "Senator, I appreciate your seeing me. I think there has been some mistake. I'm not the fellow who tried to stir up stories about you in the press."

Weicker ignored the statement and began denouncing Colson for other White House actions. Both men raised their voices in anger. Finally, leaning across his desk, Weicker shouted, "You guys in the White House make me sick. I don't know you—but I do know what you stand for, Mr. Colson, and we live in two different worlds. I deal in hard-nosed politics; you deal in crap. You make me so mad, I'd like to break your Goddamn nose."

Rising to his full 6 feet 4 inches, the senator came around the desk and pointed to the door. "You make me sick," he roared. "Get your ass out of my office."

Within hours a transcript of the supposedly private encounter was circulated among reporters, and aides to the millionaire senator told newsmen that Weicker had thrown Colson out of the office after the twelve-minute meeting. The story was played prominently in newspapers across the country. As Colson later wrote,

> In the whole sordid Watergate struggle, the Weicker episode for me was the most unpleasant; being falsely accused before millions on national TV, then coming almost to blows with a United States Senator. I was used to playing as rough as the next guy, but Watergate was creating a madness I had never witnessed in twenty years in Washington, reducing political morality to the level of bayonet warfare.

A previous example of the Washington madness had been provided by Weicker in using confidential IRS records for his political purposes—this, after denouncing the Nixon administration for purportedly doing the same thing. The IRS, the senator stated, had been "behaving like a lending library," passing out the tax reports of celebrities to anyone in government overcome by curiosity about these people's financial affairs. "Clearly this is not material that should be in the hands of anyone but the taxpayer and the IRS," he said, addressing himself to the tax deficiency claims against these notables.

Whereupon the self-proclaimed "idealist" made available to newsmen confidential tax information on audits of John Wayne,

Sammy Davis, Jr., Frank Sinatra, Jerry Lewis, Richard Boone, Lucille Ball, and Ronald Reagan, all of whom, it seems, had troubles with the tax collector. The Weicker material included specific amounts assessed against each for back taxes. But what was perhaps not coincidental was that the senator saw fit to disclose confidential information only of persons who were known to have supported Nixon. Weicker's implication was that the White House had been using the tax intelligence to protect Nixon's friends. All of which aroused Vermont Royster to note in the *Wall Street Journal:*

> Since we would have known none of this except for the gossiping of Senator Weicker, I can't help wondering how this fits in with his splendid sentiment that a person's tax information ought not to be bandied about to the curious. And that set me to wondering too about the Senator's views on the tax returns of Richard Nixon, which have hardly been kept as a private matter between the taxpayer and the IRS.

John Wayne had the last word. In a telegram fired off to the publicity-hungry senator, the nation's number one box office star at the time said: "Senator Weicker, for your information, I have never asked for, nor have I received IRS favors, nor have I needed them. What I need is protection from cheap politicians like you. The IRS has reviewed my taxes annually and I deeply resent your using your senatorial privilege in throwing my name around."

From the very beginning of the Watergate probe Nixon's critics insisted that the President could demonstrate his willingness to cooperate in the search for truth by permitting his top aides to testify before the Ervin Committee. So Nixon permitted his aides to go before the senators, and only one—John Dean—sought to implicate him. All the others either insisted that the President had not been involved in the scandals or swore that they had no knowledge that he had been involved.

"Looking back over the testimony," commented the *Wall Street Journal,* "its outstanding feature is the total lack of corroboration for Mr. Dean's account."

In later years when he had more time to think, H. R. Haldeman often wondered how he, a perfectionist, permitted a man like Dean to get on the White House staff. "If I had seen Dean's FBI dossier it would have barred him from the White House. Allegations about a conflict-of-interest charge, however slight, involving his prior affiliation with a law firm would have been enough to concern me about the smoke, whether or not there was any fire."

Haldeman was referring to the fact that Dean had been fired from his first job as a lawyer for "unethical conduct." But when Dean was hired at the White House, his once angry boss softened the recollection to "a basic disagreement" within the law firm.

Later on Dean admitted that he had removed $4,000 from the White House safe without permission, ostensibly to pay for his honeymoon. And as Barry Goldwater once told Nick Thimmesch, he couldn't understand why "that little bastard" had to do that "because he always has had plenty of money." The senator knew Dean through Barry Jr., who was his classmate at Staunton Military Academy, a neighbor in Alexandria, Virginia, and best man at Dean's second wedding.

As Nixon increasingly found himself enmeshed in the web of Watergate, Dean purred his way into the President's favor, in addition to committing crimes. But when the going got tough, Dean got going. In order to "save my ass," as he later put it, he turned informer, going first to the U.S. Attorney's Office and then to the Senate committee. And with him he took various White House documents which he had secreted away in his safe deposit box.

One of those documents came to be known as the Huston Plan. The plan, so named because it was developed by an interagency committee chaired by White House aide Tom Charles Huston, recommended mail covers, electronic surveillance, and even clandestine entries—as preventive law enforcement measures against violence-prone political extremists. Bearing the signatures of the top officials of CIA, FBI, Defense Intelligence Agency, National Security Agency, and each of the military intelligence services, this plan was signed by the President on July 23, 1970. Five days later, on July 28, 1970, it was withdrawn at J. Edgar Hoover's insistence.

Contrary to opinion voiced during the Ervin hearings, however, the measure was not aimed at domestic dissenters or political demonstrators. It was aimed mainly at the extreme left, which by 1970 was growing in prominence, numbers, and degree of violence at an alarming rate. It was aimed at the kind of individuals who were murdering judges in their courtrooms and policemen on their beats. It was aimed, too, at the kind of minds responsible for thousands of bombings of buildings, including the

United States Capitol, resulting in millions of dollars of property damage and several deaths. And it was aimed at organizations whose members hijacked American planes to Cuba and Algeria, and murdered an Israeli diplomat outside his home in suburban Chevy Chase.

But there was another motivation behind the Huston Plan. As Huston himself later explained, "a handful of people can't frontally overthrow the Government. But if they can engender enough fear, they can generate an atmosphere that will bring out of the woodwork every repressive demagogue in the country. Unless this stuff was stopped, the country was going to fall into the wrong hands."

Thus the plan was not at all the product of wild-eyed reactionaries. Rather it was conceived as an effort to spare the nation from the threat of a violent clash between the New Left and repressive demagogues seeking to fill the vacuum left by a government powerless in the face of mounting violence.

In any event the Huston Plan was quickly vetoed by the President. But Nixon's short-lived approval, in the face of Huston's caveat that some of the proposals could be considered illegal, was later to form the basis for one of the three articles of impeachment voted against him by the House Judiciary Committee.

"In fairness," as William V. Shannon observed in *The New York Times,* "one also has to say that each of Mr. Nixon's several predecessors at least as far back as Franklin D. Roosevelt might also be subject to impeachment on the same grounds. . . . There was nothing really new or unprecedented in the methods proposed in the 1970 plan. They had at various times in the past been used against native Communists, gangsters and foreign agents."

As it turned out, the intelligence agencies had already been doing what the plan proposed—and neither Nixon nor Huston had any knowledge that these activities were being pursued independently. Surreptitious entries for example, which had begun in 1942, continued right through 1976. One of them involved an illegal break-in at the headquarters of an Arab organization in Dallas, Texas, and, according to former Associate FBI Director Mark Felt, may well have helped save the lives of several Jewish targets.

But none of this came through during the hearings conducted by Ervin. Rather the Huston Plan was made to appear to be part and parcel of the Watergate syndrome. Ervin and his colleagues had apparently decided that the fact that Huston had once worked for Nixon's White House was *prima facie* evidence of his complicity in some plot to turn the United States into another Chile. Despite his professed concern for due process Ervin did not permit Huston a chance to present his case before the public.

Then came the revelation that Nixon had taped his White House conversations. The critics roared that only by releasing the tapes and submitting to interrogation himself could the President prove his innocence. Suddenly the sworn testimony of all the witnesses seemed to become meaningless. All, that is, except Dean's; his testimony the critics liked.

And what they particularly liked was testimony which had absolutely nothing to do with Watergate or the cover up. Ears perked up when Dean began talking about so-called enemy lists. There were several of these. One was compiled by a member of Colson's staff and, according to Colson, was intended primarily for the use of the social and personnel offices in considering White House invitations and appointments. But the major list, as it turned out, was put together by none other than Dean himself. Under the heading, "Dealing with Our Political Enemies," he wrote these immortal words:

"This memorandum addresses the matter of how we can maximize the fact of our incumbency in dealing with persons known to be active in their opposition to our Administration. Stated a bit more bluntly—how we can use the available Federal machinery to screw our political enemies."

Disclosure of the "enemy lists" was enough to set presumably serious people to talking about how close the United States had come to being a "police state."

Among the names on the "enemy lists" were those of members of the Senate, the House, and the news media. But some of the senators listed by Dean as "enemies" took the trouble to deny they ever had been blacklisted by the White House, among them Clifford Case and Jacob Javits, both of whom had at times voted against Nixon programs. In fact Case issued a statement on the subject: "I am unaware of any discriminatory treatment by either the President or the White House staff. The President has always been most cordial to me personally. The White House went out of its way to make clear it had no interest in a primary contest for the seat I held. And in the important area of judicial and U.S. attorney appointments my suggestions, almost without exception, have been accepted."

Later on it developed that Dean had prepared another list, this one of McGovern supporters, which he had transmitted to the IRS with a request for special audits of their returns. But IRS Commissioner Johnnie Walters took the matter up with Treasury Secretary George P. Shultz, who told him to "do nothing." According to Shultz, Walters's notes showed that Dean had informed him that the President had no knowledge of the list.

In this case Dean's only avenue for getting a tax audit on one of the President's "enemies" was to write an anonymous letter to the IRS.

Still the lists proved exceedingly embarrassing to the President. For, as Nixon later observed, "they must have been prepared by idiots." Some of the names included were those of Nixon supporters; for example, much to his amazement, Dr. Michael DeBakey, the Houston heart specialist, discovered his name on one of them. Purely by coincidence DeBakey was scheduled to visit with the President shortly after his name was publicized. "I don't regard myself as an enemy," DeBakey said at San Clemente. "I was surprised to learn of it. I didn't know what it meant." Neither did the President.

Subsequently a congressional committee—headed by two Democrats, Representative Wilbur Mills of Arkansas and Senator Russell Long of Louisiana—took a long, hard look at how the IRS had treated the White House "enemies." The conclusion by the staff of the Joint Committee on Taxation was that a number of " 'enemies' either were not audited or were audited too leniently." Even more startling was the finding that a number of those on the lists had not even bothered to file income tax returns. And, according to the report, there was no evidence that audits of so-called enemies were on the average conducted more harshly than normal. "Indeed, if anything, the opposite is true. Several individuals on the lists appear to pose collection problems for the IRS. The service has been quite lenient in granting extensions to file in many cases, and has not yet attempted to collect taxes from several political opponents who have failed to file returns or even to ascertain the reason for failure to file."

In other words those lucky enough to have been included in the White House lists seem to have had a good chance of getting away with nonpayment of income taxes. Some police state.

As the Ervin hearings drew to a recess in August 1973, it was becoming apparent that the committee was floundering. Both Ehrlichman and Haldeman had plainly stymied the senators. As Haldeman suggested, the hearings may have created a climate so deficient in perspective that the eye of a fly becomes a terrifying object. And, as the Washington *Star* noted,

> once again, the committee and its staff displayed their frustration. Senator Weicker especially rose to new heights of outrage. Majority Counsel Dash got himself in trouble. . . . Put alot of this down to just plain weariness. But not all of it. We venture to say that the Ervin Committee had become a little too full of itself, a little too eager to take on, and bring down, the two men who already are fixed in legend as the big, bad guys of the Nixon White House. Why, it might be asked, wasn't the Committee equally eager to put John Dean through such a wringer?

With the growing air of frustration and conflict within the committee the feeling developed that public opinion was beginning to swing toward the embattled President. Committee members themselves began to sense a significant backlash. The folks back home were openly wondering whether they weren't hounding the President. And perhaps even more fatal for the committee, general boredom—now that the principal witnesses had testified—was beginning to set in.

The *Wall Street Journal* commented:

> The President's critics are starting to worry that they may not be able to pin the cover-up on him after all. So they point to the spending on his homes. If that starts to slip away, they point to the ITT anti-trust case. If that falters, on to the Cambodian bombing and on and on. So impeach Nixon, they suggest, regardless of his specific culpability in Watergate—impeach him, indeed, regardless of his specific culpability in any of the successive charges.

The longer these charges are analyzed, the *Journal* went on, "the less black-and-white they become. They involve various insensitivities and misjudgments, but none of them looks much like a gross breach of American law or democratic tradition, if it is placed in its true context. But as attention flits from one allegation to the next, none of them is placed in any context at all."

As an example the spending on presidential security at San Clemente and elsewhere

> is discussed as if the assassination of John F. Kennedy had never taken place. In the wake of that tragedy Congress passed laws calling for open-ended spending on presidential security. The great bulk of the questioned spending was clearly pursuant to the hang-the-cost intent of those laws or simply to provide the necessarily elaborate communications. Yet, by now it seems the public

is persuaded the entire $10 million somehow went to line Mr. Nixon's pocket, though in fact efforts to specify an improper expenditure seems to have foundered.

Similarly, the most minute attention is focused on who knew what about the ITT case, but no one steps back to look at the whole picture: Here was an antitrust case based on legal theories previous Democratic administrations would not touch, and which had been uniformly unsuccessful in the lower-court jousting with ITT. The Government settled the case on the basis of the largest divestiture in history, and a ten-year ban on future major acquisitions by ITT. It will take a great deal of minutiae to persuade us this was a sell-out.

With regard to the Cambodian bombing, also, there was a war going on. If Presidential power as Commander-in-Chief means anything at all it must mean he can bomb troop concentrations of an enemy with whom we are in active combat. International law, also, clearly considers it irrelevant that such hostile concentrations are on the territory of a third nation. . . .

Now, it is far from our intention to absolve the Administration of all blame in any of these incidents. . . . But nothing here strikes us as . . . an impeachable offense. Except for Watergate itself, indeed, the incidents strike us as the normal mistakes, coincidences and embarrassments that would turn up if opponents guided by turncoats were turned loose on the record of any Administration that has ruled for four years, especially four years as difficult as the last four have been.

The inconclusiveness of the hearings proved disconcerting to much of the media which had sought to establish direct presidential culpability in Watergate. And while the public appeared to be turning against the inquiry with a huge yawn, the media had no alternative but to keep the story alive. As Richard Wilson wrote:

What will happen, if the trail is lost before it reaches the Oval Office, is that the press will be held guilty of as great and dangerous an excess of zeal as has been charged against the Nixon Administration. Nixon's statement that a systematic effort has been made to destroy the President of the United States will be engraved on the mastheads of powerful newspapers along with their record of Pulitzer prizes.

So the battle lines were fully drawn. At stake was not only the fate of the President but the power of the press. One or the other would have to emerge triumphant. There was no turning back. The die was cast.

By then, however, Nixon was facing a new challenge—this one from the Watergate Special Prosecution Force headed by Archibald Cox. Despite pronounced misgivings the President had gone along with Cox's appointment. That was the price he had to pay to get Elliot Richardson approved as his new Attorney General.

Nixon was not unaware of Cox's ideological proclivities. A long-time Kennedy partisan, Cox had been described as the "informal dean of the Kennedy brain trust" during the 1960 campaign. And following that election, JFK had rewarded him with the post of Solicitor General—the third-ranking job in the Justice Department. Cox's liberal credentials were demonstrated anew in 1968 when he headed a commission to investigate disorders at Columbia University. The Cox group decided that while the students ought not to have been violent, their irascibility resulted from their grievances and, therefore, the university administration was to blame. Four years later Cox was an avid McGovern supporter. Shortly before he was designated special prosecutor, Cox made remarks critical of the administration's policies on civil rights and civil liberties at a news conference in California. Moreover he acknowledged such "philosophical and ideological" differences with the Justice Department that he felt he could never consider taking a job there.

On May 25, 1973, Cox was sworn in as special prosecutor, armed with full powers to investigate an administration which he had previously conceded he personally detested. Among those attending the ceremony were Ethel Kennedy, Senator Edward M. Kennedy, and his aide James Flug.

But what disturbed the White House even more was the news that Cox was loading his staff with former aides to both John and Robert Kennedy. An ancient vendetta was taking a new form. In charge of the Watergate task force for example was James Neal, a Nashville attorney who had been special assistant to Attorney General Kennedy from 1961 to 1964. As such he helped prosecute Jimmy Hoffa, a prosecution which led some civil libertarians to question whether it wasn't persecution. His assistant, Richard Ben-Veniste, had been an assistant U.S. attorney in New York. In one case, according to the *Washingtonian*, Ben-Veniste and others had concocted a scheme to entrap certain individuals into committing bribery. In reversing the convictions that resulted, Judge Henry Friendly of the U.S. Court of Appeals accused Ben-Veniste and his cohorts of holding "an arrogant disregard for the sanctity of the state judicial and police process." The judge ruled that they had employed a "pattern of deception," and described their overall conduct as "offensive."

Another member of "Cox's Army" was William H. Merrill, a chief assistant U.S. attorney during both the Kennedy and Johnson administrations, who was chairman of the Michigan Citizens for Robert Kennedy for President in 1968, and was placed by Cox in charge of the "plumbers" task force. Merrill, who twice ran for office as a Democrat, told an interviewer, "We'll set standards of conduct or show what they could be." Which, needless to say, is not the role of a prosecutor. This extraordinary attitude was carried a step further by Thomas F. McBride, another former member of the Kennedy Justice Department. While heading up the task force examining "campaign contributions," McBride told the same interviewer that he saw in his new job the opportunity "to use law enforcement as an instrument of social reform" possibly equal to the Progressive movement at the turn of the century. Which isn't exactly the purpose of law enforcement.

Eventually Cox's staff numbered eighty or so. Armed with a superbroad mandate, the Kennedyite lawyers were assigned to probe an enormous range of potential trouble areas in the weakened Nixon presidency—most of them far afield from the Watergate break-in. No rumor or false implication was too wild for the investigators to dig into.

With avid Kennedyites fully expecting to be gnawing away at the administration for three and a half years, a confrontation was unavoidable. No government could endure a continual inquisition constantly refueled by leaks of information. The noose was out for Nixon and he knew it. At the same time he was facing a crisis in the Middle East—one that could conceivably lead to World War III. On the eve of Yom Kippur the Egyptians staged a surprise attack on Israeli positions across the Suez. The Israelis, after setbacks, began to hit back. But they were running short on materiel. At this juncture, given the risks involved, Nixon made a courageous decision. He ordered a massive military airlift to Israel. Also courageous was his decision to face down the Soviet threat to send troops to the Middle East unilaterally. He ordered a worldwide alert of U.S. forces. And though that helped cool the crisis, the President got precious little credit. For his enemies were now suggesting that the U.S.-Soviet face-down was just a Nixon effort to divert attention from his troubles. As we now know, the suspicion was totally without foundation.

It was during the Mideast crisis that the President also decided to get rid of Cox. The President had agreed to a compromise on the White House tapes which he believed conformed to a memorandum the Court of Appeals had made public "asking Mr. Cox and the President's lawyers to agree on some compromise which would avoid a sharp constitutional encounter." Seeking a quick resolution to the Watergate affair, the President accepted a plan whereby the respected Senator John Stennis of Mississippi would prepare a verified version of the subpoenaed tapes. The plan won the approval of Chairman Ervin and Howard Baker. And, just as important, it was a compromise dear to the heart of Attorney General Richardson. But Richardson wasn't able to sell it to his old Harvard teacher Archie Cox. All of which led to what the White House chief of staff Al Haig was to call "the day of the firestorm."

Saturday, October 20, 1973, had been a beautiful, crisp autumn day. It began with Cox going before the cameras to announce he was not buying the Stennis compromise. The White House considered this defiance and the President felt he had no choice but to order Cox's dismissal. Richardson and his deputy, William Ruckelshaus, then resigned, even though both of them had approved of the compromise. Richardson in fact made clear in a letter to the President that his resignation was not a *protest* against Nixon's action, the reasons for which he fully "respects." Rather, he said, he was resigning for the formal and honorable reason that he had assured the Senate that Cox would have certain rights which the President had felt it necessary to revoke.

All that Saturday evening the news bulletins repeatedly interrupting the prime time television shows made the nation's capital seem like downtown Santiago. From the frenzied, breathless, on-the-spot reporting on the tube, one would have thought that the storm troopers had seized control. The fact that the President was well within his rights in dismissing Cox—a fact noted by Yale Law Professor Alexander Bickel, among others—was completely overshadowed by hysterical comments such as that of Edmund Muskie: "It smacks of dictatorship." Senator Kennedy called Cox's firing "a reckless act of desperation by a President who is afraid of the Supreme Court, who has no respect for law and no regard for men of conscience." Generated by the hysteria of the media, an avalanche of telegrams calling for the President's impeachment or resignation descended on Washington. Editorials, even in hitherto friendly newspapers, condemned the President across the land. The Chicago *Tribune*, while warning against the reaction becoming "hysterical, inflammatory and divisive," called the President's action "the worst blunder in the history of the presidency."

Yet, as the Washington *Star* pointed out,

Mr. Nixon has broken no law, defied no court, padlocked no legislature, muzzled no member of the press. The jackboots that some observers seem to hear echoing in the streets of Washington are largely in their own minds. . . . In short, we could use a little more *gravitas* in the treatment of the President of the United States. There has been too much slander, innuendo and loose rhetoric about Mr. Nixon's possible deeds and presumed motives. He has yet to be found guilty of anything other than having underlings and associates accused and some guilty of misdeeds. Nor is he, insofar as we know, mentally unbalanced, an insinuation which some have made. . . . Thinking men used to hold that the blood of kings can be shed, but never lightly. Richard Nixon is not our monarch but he is our president, and the only one we happen to have. To destroy him out of pique, at the cost of destroying the nation, would be a shallow victory for some and a defeat for all.

Barely seventy-two hours after firing Cox, Nixon reversed his position and agreed to provide Judge Sirica with subpoenaed tapes. On hearing the news, Cox went straight to the offices of Senator Kennedy because, as he explained, "I don't have any office any more." A week later, appearing before the Senate Judiciary Committee, Cox conceded he was guilty of an "inexcusable" breach of confidence in having passed confidential information concerning the ITT case to Kennedy, among others. The information, acquired when Cox was special prosecutor, had come from former Attorney General Richard Kleindienst. Yes, Cox told the Senate committee, he had broken his word to Kleindienst by letting the secret information drop in relaxed conversation with Senators Kennedy and Hart, and two of their aides. "Of course," he said, "I shouldn't have done it. It was carelessness, not malice." Somehow the information had found its way onto the front page of *The New York Times.* Cox denied he had leaked the story. As did the two senators.

In effect Cox had weakened his image of impartiality and had given the administration an issue to use in trying to justify his dismissal. Deputy Press Secretary Gerald Warren said that the leak "makes clear to us at the White House his partisan attitude that has characterized his activities in recent months." And he pointed out that of the ten top lawyers on the Cox staff, all but one had strong Democratic connections. Republican Senator Hugh Scott, who had condemned the Cox dismissal, also denounced the leak as part of a continuing pattern, adding that the Cox staff is "a hostile adversary staff."

There had been talk that some members of the staff would resign in protest. But that was not to be. Instead most of them remained, voicing suspicions however about Cox's successor Leon Jaworski. An LBJ Democrat from Houston, Jaworski quickly reassured the staff Cox left behind. They were to continue their investigations; and there would be no "cover ups."

Except, of course, those involving Democratic misdeeds. And that became more than apparent when the new Attorney General, William B. Saxbe, telephoned Jaworski to inform him of a file found in his office which revealed widespread wiretapping during the Kennedy and Johnson years. After describing the contents of the file, Saxbe asked Jaworski whether he could use it in his investigations. According to Saxbe, Jaworski called back later and said no.

At the same time Jaworski made a major decision in the case of John Dean, choosing not to proceed with perjury charges, despite a record indicating that Dean had not always been a paragon of truthfulness.

As an example there was the case of the shredded documents. On November 5, 1973, Assistant Special Prosecutor Ben-Veniste informed Judge Sirica in open court that "members of our staff interviewed Mr. Dean and questioned him with respect to the contents of Mr. Hunt's safe. Mr. Dean related that at some time in late January 1973, he discovered a file folder in his office containing the President's estate plan, two clothbound notebooks with cardboard covers and lined pages containing some handwriting. Dean at that time recalled that these had come from Howard Hunt's safe."

Dean had said that he never even looked at the contents of the notebooks, which he had casually "discovered" while going through a file. And what did he do with these notebooks, the existence of which was never disclosed to the FBI? Why, according to Ben-Veniste, "he shredded both notebooks in his shredder. At the same time he also discovered a pop-up address book containing some names with each page X-ed out in ink. Dean threw this pop-up notebook into the wastebasket at this time."

Dean's disclosure that he had deliberately destroyed evidence caused only a minor sensation. Unlike other "horrors" attributed to men more loyal to Nixon, the story was quickly forgotten. The reason was simple. The story could cast doubt on the veracity of the President's chief accuser.

For when he had previously testified under oath before Ervin, Dean had told a different tale. At that time he told of how troubled he was when John Ehrlichman had suggested that he "deep six" (or throw into the Potomac) some of the evidence found in Hunt's safe. "After leaving Mr. Ehrlichman's office," Dean swore, "I thought about what he had told me to do and was very troubled. I raised it with [Fred] Fielding and he shared my feelings that this would be an incredible action to destroy potential evidence."

What he did not say, of course, was that he had shredded the two Hunt notebooks. Instead he told how "everything found in the safe had been turned over to the FBI"—in the person of Director Pat Gray. But he had not turned over "everything found in the safe" to Gray. And that could well have proved to be Dean's undoing, as well as a severe blow to whatever prosecutions depended on his testimony.

As William Safire pointed out at the time, there was still another way for Jaworski to determine whether Dean's credibility was—in legal parlance—"subject to question." He could have called Justice Department prosecutors whom Howard Hunt had told about the notebooks shortly after his arrest. Late in 1972 they had described the purloined notebooks to Dean, whose immediate reaction was to deny any knowledge of them. The denial, of course, was one reason why Dean felt he had to destroy them.

Despite all this Jaworski went on television to insist, "We have found no basis for a perjury charge" against Dean. Nor was he charged with having lied to federal investigators, a violation of paragraph 1001 of Title 18 of the U.S. Code, the statute under which a minor Watergate figure, Bart Porter, had only recently been sent to jail.

Despite Cox's ouster, however, things did not get better for Nixon and his embattled subordinates. The power was now more strongly in the hands of zealous prosecutors, who believed they could do no wrong because right was on their side. And what Safire described as a "reign of terror" ensued. The functionings of the White House were crippled as dozens of aides were called in repeatedly for questioning at the fearsome offices of the special prosecutor on K Street. Civil rights, let alone the amenities, were ignored as the investigators smelled blood.

To his credit William Greider of the Washington *Post* took note of what he described as

> a reversal of roles which seems to mock both sides. The White House men, feared and hated because they trampled on the Bill of Rights, are now espousing . . . human conceptions of law and individual liberty, notions of crime and punishment and decent limits of political power, ideas which some would call liberal. The reaction is ho-hum.
>
> A lot of liberals, meanwhile, have become law-and-order zealots, imitating unconsciously the hard-nosed ethos which they once thought so frightening in Mr. Nixon's Department of Justice. People who once argued that conspiracy indictments are dangerous to civil rights now spin webs for the Watergate conspiracy case. Reformers who wanted to empty the prisons now grumble about short sentences for the Watergate gang.

One could almost feel the blood lust. And the White House responded in kind. Much of the mutual hatred could be felt at the daily news briefings at the White House. Illustrative is this exchange, which occurred in December 1973 between some correspondents and press spokesman Gerald Warren. Warren had been asked by Adam Clymer of the Baltimore *Sun* whether the White House was involved in any way in the burglary of the home of Jill Wine Volner, the Watergate assistant prosecutor who at the time was cross-examining Rose Mary Woods in U.S. District Court.

"How in the world would I know?" replied Warren.

"But Jerry," said another reporter, "with all deference, in following up Adam's question, I know it does seem rather silly to be asking the White House about a burglary that occurred in Washington, but we have heard about certain burglaries before. Has the White House taken any steps or contacted the police or contacted the Justice Department or anyone to gather information or make an inquiry concerning the burglary . . . ?"

Warren responded, "I would think that the police department would be the agency which would be qualified to investigate this matter. If that fine department requests assistance of the Justice Department or the FBI or anyone else, I am sure that assistance would be forthcoming. But I thoroughly reject the implication of the questions."

Then Norman Kempster, of the Washington *Star,* asked, "Can you state categorically that no one employed by the White House now or previously was involved in this burglary; not in investigating it but in doing it?"

"As soon as the burglary is solved, I will be able to answer that question for you, Norm," Warren said. "Now can you state categorically that no one presently or formerly employed by the *Evening Star* was involved in that burglary?"

"Yes," Kempster replied.

"How?" Warren demanded. "How can you do that? I think this is ridiculous. May we move ahead?"

The briefing moved on, but not ahead.

At a public meeting Walter Cronkite was asked whether he would "walk the streets of San Clemente" conducting interviews with President Nixon the way he conducted those with the late President Johnson at LBJ ranch.

"San Clemente or San Quentin?" replied Cronkite.

The crowd roared and Cronkite quickly added, "That's wrong. I am an objective newsman."

All kinds of speculation began to appear in print concerning Nixon's mental stability, not because of any evidence that there was anything to be concerned about, but because it was assumed that any man should have cracked under such pressures. Which explains the play given to the allegation that Nixon had slapped a man while he was greeting bystanders at an airport in Orlando. It turned out that the "slap" amounted to a pat on the cheek, which the man described as "the greatest honor I've ever had . . . I won't wash my face." But the damage was done. Many readers were left with the impression that the President was losing his senses.

"Nixon's right," wrote Nicholas von Hoffman in *New Times.* "The media has gone rabid, and pathologically arrogant. You can't hardly crack open a newspaper or turn on a TV without getting unsubstantiated garbage leaked out of a grand jury room, a barroom or some other place where rumors are trapped and collected."

As the obsessive assault on the President continued with even greater intensity, more and more Americans were becoming increasingly dismayed and fed up. They began to call for a resolution of the crisis, one way or the other. Impeachment no longer was a dirty word.

So foul had the atmosphere become toward the President of

the United States by this time that it was difficult to remember that only a year before Richard Nixon had been inaugurated for a second term after achieving one of the greatest landslides in American history. "What they used to call McCarthyism is now a virtue, because Nixon is the goat," wrote the late Senator McCarthy's counsel, Roy Cohn, in a commentary for *Newsday*.

> Let's try to control our killer instincts enough to give to Nixon the same constitutional and moral presumptions we would give to anyone else in so hapless a predicament. If we do, perhaps everything will end up happily ever after. John Dean can marry Martha Mitchell, and the Democrats may ride into office in 1976 on a ticket pledged to restore that credibility and integrity that will certainly be a major plank in the platform they adopt at their nominating convention in Chappaquiddick.

On the other side of the ideological spectrum Eugene McCarthy also appealed for calm in the growing crisis. In a speech in New York the former senator said, "little good would be served by the impeachment of President Nixon—except to satisfy public outrage over Watergate," adding that "impeachment proceedings might interrupt the conduct of foreign policy which, with Henry Kissinger as Secretary of State, has been as good or better than what might have been supported by recent Democratic Presidents and candidates." But McCarthy found scant support for his heretical views among his former followers, one of whom said angrily, "That is just too much to take."

Indicative of the ugly mood was the playing of a subpoenaed White House tape as a big laugh at a Georgetown party. Attorney William Dobrovir, on retainer from Ralph Nader and several consumer groups, had sued Secretary of Agriculture Earl Butz and others on charges that the Nixon administration had illegally raised milk subsidies in return for campaign contributions. The suit had been filed in January 1972. In December 1973, almost two years later, Dobrovir succeeded in obtaining a recording of a meeting that the President and other administration officials had with dairy industry representatives in March 1971. The White House had not claimed executive privilege for the tape.

Dobrovir borrowed a tape recorder from Fred Graham, a CBS correspondent, in order to make two copies of the tape. At the same time he permitted Graham to listen to the tape on what was described as an "off the record" basis. Feeling somewhat elated, Dobrovir telephoned a friend who invited him over to a small party she was having. When he arrived, he told the guests, "I've got in my pocket the hottest news item in town."

While the guests were "sitting around the fireplace, eating salami and chopped liver, having a drink," (as Dobrovir later explained) he played the tape. Well, it wasn't as good as Dobrovir had advertised. None of the guests could come up with any presidential directive to raise the milk price for the benefit of the Grand Old Party. What they did hear, it turned out, was several attempts at humor on the part of the President, which as yet had not been suggested as grounds for impeachment.

One of the guests was Kevin Delany, an assistant bureau chief in Washington for ABC News. Delany tipped off correspondent David Schoumacher, who called Dobrovir and asked if he could listen to the tape. When Dobrovir refused, Schoumacher asked, "Well, didn't you play it at this cocktail party?"

"Well," Dobrovir replied, "that was just for fun."

Fun or not, Schoumacher broke the story on the evening news. Two days later U.S. District Judge William B. Jones summoned Dobrovir for an explanation. The abashed lawyer told the judge, "I made a very foolish mistake." He said he was "extremely sorry." Jones termed the matter "very serious," and suggested that if the Justice Department felt that Dobrovir committed a serious breach of legal ethics, the case should be referred to the District of Columbia Bar Association. But eventually the matter was dropped. Dobrovir had gotten away with playing the subpoenaed tape, an act which even the Washington *Post* had found to be incredible. The Washington *Star* noted that "the playing of the tape at a cocktail party lends weight to Mr. Nixon's argument that executive confidentiality is being breached by requiring him to turn over Watergate tapes to courts and investigators."

Then the story died. There were no follow ups. Dobrovir went on to lobby among the members of Congress for the impeachment of President Nixon for high crimes and misdemeanors.

Also overlooked was a speech delivered on November 5, 1973, by Daniel Schorr in Rochester, New York, in which the CBS correspondent declared: "This past year, a new kind of journalism developed, and I found myself doing on a daily routine some things I would never have done before. There was a vacuum in investigation, and the press began to try men in the most effective court in the country. The men involved in Watergate were convicted by the media, perhaps in a more meaningful way than any jail sentence they will eventually get. We've gotten good at uncovering those stories we shouldn't be covering at all. Luckily, most of what we reported turned out to be true. I'm proud. Yes, I'm happy. No. We ought to withdraw from it as soon as possible."

It was a speech so incoherent that, at times, it sounded like some of the White House tapes which eventually were released.

About that time a new leader emerged in the national spotlight. He was Peter Rodino, who as chairman of the House Judiciary Committee had begun the process of considering impeachment of the President. Rodino, an obscure congressman from Newark, New Jersey, had previously conducted hearings into the fitness of Gerald Ford to be Vice President. When Ford's name was finally placed in nomination, Rodino remarked that never before had any man undergone such investigation and emerged so well. So what did Rodino then do? He voted *against* confirming Ford.

Later Rodino was to explain that his vote on the floor in no way reflected on Ford's integrity or qualifications. Rodino, who represents a largely Black constituency, said he voted "no" because he had a fundamental difference in perception with Ford on the government's role "in serving the needs of all our citizens."

"But," Rodino added, "Jerry wrote me a beautiful letter afterward."

22

O C C U P Y I N G   A   P R O M I N E N T   S P O T   O N   T H E
coffee table in the office of Chairman Rodino was a thick book
with a red, white, and blue jacket. Its title was *The Imperial
Presidency* and it was autographed by its author, Arthur Schlesinger, Jr., as follows:

"To Chairman Peter Rodino, A belated valentine. This book
doesn't provide answers, but it does lay out some of our history
and it raises some important questions about the Presidency."

In the book Schlesinger traced the growth of an autocratic
presidency, discussed the Watergate scandal and its potential
impact on the White House, and concluded that "neither impeachment nor repentance would make much difference if the
people themselves had come to an unconscious acceptance of the
imperial Presidency."

Schlesinger failed to discuss his own role in selling the American people on the Imperial presidency. In previous works he had
glorified such strong Presidents as Andrew Jackson and Franklin
Roosevelt and such would-be strong ones as JFK, arguing for
executive prerogative, and contending that Congress was excessively powerful while the President was hampered by congressional interference. As the Dallas *Morning News* observed of
Schlesinger's attacking the growth of presidential powers, "that
is roughly similar to a book by the Boston Strangler attacking the
decline of chivalry."

Schlesinger recognized his problem. So he sought to draw a
line between "a strong presidency within the Constitution" as
practiced by his former heroes and the "imperial Presidency" of
Nixon. The point seemed to be that FDR and JFK were capital
fellows, to be commended despite occasional transgressions.
Nixon, however, was a rogue and should be dealt with accordingly. Of course in his partisan approach to history Schlesinger
deliberately failed to recognize that when it came to abuses of
power, his presidential heroes far outstripped the despised

Nixon. More germane was the fact that, faced with a bitterly hostile Congress, press, and intellectual Establishment, Nixon ultimately became appreciably less powerful than his predecessors, who generally had these auxiliaries working for them. The "imperial Presidency," by now, was turning to ashes.

In Congress many years before coming to public notice, Rodino had never expected to be courted by the likes of Schlesinger, one of the nation's more publicized intellectuals. And in all probability Schlesinger had never expected to be courting the likes of Rodino, a product of the Essex County Democratic organization. But the stakes were high. What Schlesinger wanted more than anything was the consummation of a long-held dream —the destruction of Richard Nixon, whose very existence affronted the in-house historian of the Kennedy administration. "Impeachment may have grievous consequences," Schlesinger had written in *Harper's*. "Refusal to impeach the President will have consequences even more grievous and far more enduring."

Schlesinger needn't have worried. One of his pals from Camelot days was now actually running the impeachment inquiry. He was none other than John Doar, formerly head of the Civil Rights Division in Robert Kennedy's Justice Department. This of course was the same Doar who, when informed of the FBI's campaign to denigrate Martin Luther King, had done nothing to stop it. And it was the same Doar who had urged Attorney General Clark in 1967 to seek intelligence information from government workers in the nation's Black communities. Doar's memorandum, written September 27, 1967, following the Detroit riots, led to the creation of a computerized intelligence file that eventually grew to contain some 18,000 names, mainly of Black militants. This was the kind of activity which Doar and others on the impeachment panel soon sought to characterize as "abuses of power" under Nixon.

As president of the New York City Board of Education in 1969, Doar did a switch. He catered to the Black militants, refusing for example to dismiss extremist teachers who made anti-Semitic remarks in class. Arnold Forster and Benjámin R. Epstein of the Anti-Defamation League pointed out that "when William O. Marley, chairman of the Brownsville Model Cities Committee, in a long anti-Semitic diatribe, repeatedly attacked Jews as dominant in the school system . . . there was no challenge from President Doar. . . ."

Doar had not been Rodino's first choice as special counsel.

Initially Rodino had approached liberal Republican Albert E. Jenner, Jr., of Chicago. But Jenner turned the job down, citing a backlog in his private practice; instead he recommended Doar. Eventually Jenner took the minority counsel post, only after the "Illinois boys"—meaning Congressmen Robert McClory and Tom Railsback—"worked hard on me." Following his appointment with unanimous Republican approval, it became known that Jenner had concealed the fact that the previous fall he had been co-host at a business breakfast in Chicago for Senator Adlai E. Stevenson 3rd, an Illinois Democrat. Jenner, an old friend of the Stevenson family, attended a fund-raising dinner for the senator and contributed $1,000 to his reelection campaign. Stevenson then had publicly predicted that Nixon would not "survive three more months in office."

Hardly had Jenner been ensconced in his new post when he made an astonishing appearance on Chicago television, asserting that the President should be held responsible for some of the actions of his aides even if he had not known about them in advance. He went on to cite the activities of the "plumbers" as the sort of actions for which a President should be held accountable. The remark, coming just as the inquiry was getting under way, astonished the Republicans. If nothing else, Congressman Charles E. Wiggins of California told Jenner in a letter, no member of the staff should be making pronouncements of that kind. Instead they should be maintaining a judicious silence. But Jenner did not take the hint. He kept on voicing anti-Nixon opinions.

From all this it was obvious from the very beginning of the impeachment inquiry that the cards were stacked against Nixon. As William Safire put it on January 17, 1974, "By its choice of counsel, the House Judiciary Committee has made it plain that it intends to look busy for a few months and then recommend the impeachment of the President."

Rodino promised that the committee would work "expeditiously," saying it would proceed only as fast as "the principles of fairness and completeness" would allow. "Whatever we learn or conclude," he added with a Churchillian flourish, "let us now proceed—with such care and decency and thoroughness and honor—that the vast majority of the American people, and their children after them, will say: 'That was the right course. There was no other way.'"

The composition of the committee, however, guaranteed against fairness. Ignored for the most part by a media always seeking conflicts of interest was the fact that Rodino had accepted a whopping $31,000 campaign contribution from the AFL-CIO, whose leadership was fiercely pro-impeachment. In all, according to Representative John Erlenborn, an Illinois Republican, the nineteen Democrats on Judiciary received $189,000 in contributions from labor unions in 1972—about 14 percent of their financing. Rodino incidentally had also received enormous funds from the milk lobby—though there hasn't been a cow in Newark for fifty years.

Revealing too was the fact that of the thirty-five votes cast in the House against Gerald Ford's nomination as Vice President, nine came from the committee's liberal Democrats, including Rodino—despite the fact that the investigation into Ford's qualifications showed him to be whistle clean. No wonder then that the White House had been complaining that these Democrats were as prejudiced against Nixon as a lynch mob that has already tossed its rope over the lamppost. Indeed Massachusetts's Robert Drinan, a Jesuit priest of liberal credentials, had been the first congressman to introduce a resolution calling for impeachment. And California's Waldie had backed several impeachment resolutions. As the hearings got under way, other members of the committee indicated rather clearly that they had already made up their minds before hearing any of the evidence.

"Unquestionably," wrote Arthur Schlesinger, Jr., "one element in the Democratic drive for impeachment is a desire to humiliate Mr. Nixon, a politician Democrats have despised for more than a quarter of a century." Schlesinger himself had long held a well-publicized hatred for Richard Nixon, a hatred which often led to such irrationalities as his predicting in the midsummer of 1972 that George McGovern would win by a landslide.

The clamor for the end of Richard Nixon could be heard everywhere. "In a very real sense," wrote Nick Thimmesch, "we are in a time comparable to the worst hours of the Joe McCarthy era, for reason is diminished, and passion flows freely. . . . The difference between that hysterical period and now is that then one man, Joe McCarthy, flailed against the world, and now, a world of opponents flails against one man, Richard Nixon. Where have all the civil libertarians gone?"

Well, the American Civil Liberties Union was still around. It had mounted a huge campaign aimed at ousting Nixon. As far as the ACLU was concerned, Nixon was not entitled to the civil liberties of, say, an Angela Davis. He was guilty even before he was charged.

Charles Morgan, Jr., who was leading the ACLU's campaign, told how the impeachment cause was reuniting a lot of old friends from left of center: "There's no civil rights movement. There's no war. There's no social-action movement. I hate to use the word, but it's liberal chic. Impeachment is there. It's not ecology, but then whatever happened to ecology?"

That outstanding liberal Murray Kempton, while sharing the impulse to impeach, deplored the character of the ACLU campaign and its stampede-the-Congress strategy. "We seem to have entered one of those periods when virtuous men feel driven toward quite vicious devices," he observed in a CBS-Spectrum commentary. He noted that "polluting is a very dubious remedy for pollution."

Likewise Milton Viorst, no Nixon fan, was shocked at the antics of organized liberals. He wrote that the impeachment crisis was

> also exposing some of the worst characteristics of some of his persistent enemies. . . . I wish the ACLU would go back to worrying about civil liberties. I wish the National Committee for an Effective Congress would refocus its attention to the effectiveness of Congress. I'd be happy if the Americans for Democratic Action thought a little more about democracy. As for Common Cause, I have the feeling that its cause—the impeachment of Richard M. Nixon—has become so common that it's humdrum. I admired the organization more when it was more selective in its goals.

Impeachment is "an act of religious devotion" for these liberal organizations, Viorst concluded.

Ironically the John Birch Society was also calling for Nixon's scalp. As founding Bircher Robert Welch pointed out, he had had Nixon's number as far back as 1958 when he called the then Vice President one of "the most disingenuous and slipperiest politicians that ever showed up on the American scene." Now Welch, who had also called Dwight Eisenhower a "willing tool" of the Communist conspiracy, contended that Nixon was out to conquer the world. "That's been Richard Nixon's aim for twenty years," said the sage of Belmont, Massachusetts, relishing all the impeachment talk.*

---

*The Birch Society was no stranger to impeachment. Its members had long called for the impeachment of Earl Warren as Chief Justice of the Supreme Court.

If that wasn't enough, there began to flow from the Judiciary Committee a torrent of leaks of material damaging to the President. And this from a committee whose chairman had pledged that the inquiry would be handled in a fair and even-handed manner, without violations of the confidentiality of evidence in its possession. It was to be expected that the White House would seize on the leaks as coming from, in Pat Buchanan's words, "nameless, faceless character assassins." But even *The New York Times,* which incidentally was publishing the leaked material, conceded there was a large element of truth in what Buchanan was saying. "The leakers," wrote the *Times,* "apparently impatient with the rules of secrecy adopted by the Committee and presumably anxious to 'get the President,' are subjecting him to trial by the court of public opinion based upon fragmentary and unrebutted evidence and analysis."

One senator did praise those who leaked information from the Judiciary Committee. Lowell Weicker proudly announced that he himself had leaked information which he had obtained from such as Acting FBI Director L. Patrick Gray III. And if he could do it, why not his colleagues on the other side of the Hill? The only leaks he didn't like were those coming from the White House.

Arousing particular controversy was the unauthorized release of a series of memoranda prepared by a staff member for four of the more vociferous anti-Nixon members of the Judiciary Committee—Conyers, Brooks, Drinan, and Kastenmeier. The memos, all of which were particularly harmful to Nixon, were prepared by William P. Dixon, who had been a coordinator in the 1972 campaign of George McGovern. Ironically Dixon was also one of those named in a General Accounting Office report alleging campaign funding violations in McGovern's Wisconsin effort.

Most of the Dixon material was based on his own extremely prejudicial interpretation of the White House tapes, which had finally been handed over to the Judiciary Committee by an unwilling President. The fact was that opposite conclusions were reached by different committee members on the same evidence. A good example of the confusion engendered over meaning was provided on June 6, 1974, when *The New York Times* carried this headline on its front page: NIXON TAPE IS SAID TO LINK MILK PRICE TO POLITICAL GIFT. That very morning the Washington *Post* front-page headline read: TAPE PROVIDES NO NIXON LINK

TO MILK FUNDS. Which led a somewhat "startled" Senator Buckley to say on the floor of the Senate that day, "This experience has shattered my faith in the infallibility of the undisclosed sources of one or the other of these papers. The question that now bedevils me is, which am I to believe?"

Still the leaks continued, invariably in the President's disfavor. There was the report for example that the President, in dictating his recollections of March 21, 1973, described the day as "uneventful." March 21, 1973, was a crucial date; it represented the foundation stone of the Nixon defense. For that was the day in which, the President said, John Dean finally leveled with him about the cover up. Thus if the President, in recording his impressions, summarized the day as "uneventful," the conclusion would be inescapable and staggering: Dean's disclosures were not news to the President; he had already known! Such a conclusion was the one obviously hoped for by the leaker. Yet the leak, like so many others, was born of calculated malice. What the President had actually dictated into his Dictabelt machine were these words: "As far as the day was concerned, it was uneventful except for the talk with Dean."

Actually the published transcripts show that in the weeks after March 21 the President appeared to be truly amazed by the revelations coming his way. Talking to a friend after he released the documents, Nixon emphasized how much Dean had withheld from him on March 21. "What he didn't tell me was more important than what he did," he said, according to William Safire. And what Dean hadn't told the President that day was how he had coached Jeb Magruder to perjure himself; how he had handled payoff money himself; how he had offered clemency to Magruder and McCord; and how he had shredded evidence, including notebooks taken from Hunt's safe.

The foul temper of the times was caught by columnist Charles Bartlett, who wrote:

> Already the raspings of a lynch spirit can be heard among those Democratic members of the Judiciary Committee who race out each evening to tell the TV audiences what they have learned in the committee rooms. The shallow spirit of contemporary politics is epitomized by those who seek maximum visibility to leak to the public what they have been told in confidence. Nixon is going to be quickly absolved by the public if he is indicted every night on television by these opportunists.

In short the impeachment proceedings were turning into a three-ringed circus. "Rodino's failure to plug these leaks," wrote James J. Kilpatrick, "is one more reflection upon his lack of capacity for his job. . . . By serving as a willing ally to the Committee's hatchetmen, the conniving newspapers inevitably create the impression that their purpose is not to pursue the news, but to pursue a vendetta instead. It is an ugly image, harming the press as a whole."

John F. Bridge, writing in the *National Observer,* observed that the press had played a very active part in the Watergate drama, "including the rising clamor for impeachment." And "whether it was too much an active part and not enough that of a reasonably objective onlooker will be part of the General Accountability for the media."

"In my view," Bridge noted,

> there is a widespread attitude that public officials must be more moral than the rest of us. I have been bemused, for example, by a situation in one Washington suburb dominated by a wealthy left-leaning moral elite that has been apoplectic over Watergate; high-level bureaucrats, well-known members of the media, and concerned professional people. Yet the local luxury grocer has had to put his stock of caviar under lock and key because of shoplifting; closed-circuit television cameras scan the aisles at all times.

And Clare Boothe Luce, widow of *Time* co-founder Henry R. Luce, in a letter to the editor irately lambasted *Time* for its "overinvestment in the destruction of the President" and for its "phobic Watergate reporting." She added:

> No President of the U.S. except Lincoln (in retrospect, now to be considered another impeachable character) has ever been more savaged by the press than Nixon. . . . And he has shown that he can take it and take it and take it, with cool and courage. But few journalists—none on *Time*—have had even the sportsmanship, no less the journalistic objectivity, to report that whatever Nixon is or is not, he is one helluva gutsy fighter. To be sure, the capacity to take punishment as well as dish it out is not widely associated with journalists, which is no doubt why they do not recognize it as a virtue in Nixon.

Also noteworthy and surprising was the statement of Archibald Cox, who had been such a hero to the Nixon critics. "The media," said Cox, "certainly (are) turning gradually to a more active role in shaping the course of events. . . . I think it's true of the *Wash-*

ington Post, The New York Times, Newsweek . . . and I rather think it seems to be true of some of the network presentations. It does seem to me that the selection of items emphasized often reflects the sort of notion that the press is the fourth branch of Government and it should play a major role in Government. I'm not sure that I want it that way when there are only three networks—to me that's an awful lot of power to give to whoever runs the three networks." Cox concluded by noting that he had no grounds for complaint about the way in which the media had treated him. "Indeed, they've treated me much better than I deserve."

Ignored by much of the media was a startling remark uttered by Sam Ervin in a moment of candor. On March 10, 1974, this was the night lead of a UPI story filed out of Cleveland: "No evidence was produced in the Senate Watergate hearings to support impeachment of President Nixon, Watergate Committee Chairman Sam Ervin, D.-N.C., said Sunday. 'I think this is one section of the Constitution on which Dick Nixon and I agree,' he said."

No evidence to support impeachment, according to Ervin? Even in paraphrase that was a major assessment on the part of a senator whose investigations had lasted many months at a cost of millions of dollars. The UPI story was written by Pete Spudich. His account was confirmed by another reporter present, Bud Weidenthal, of the Cleveland *Press,* who wrote that Ervin "also said that he learned nothing during the long Senate investigation that indicated to him that Nixon had committed an impeachable offense."

After Nixon's defenders seized on Ervin's statement, the sage from North Carolina panicked. He did what most politicians do when they commit a blunder: he denied he ever said it. But the Cleveland reporters stuck by their guns.

Finally Nixon's lawyer in the impeachment proceedings, James St. Clair, demanded that the Judiciary Committee open its secret sessions to the public. The committee had suffered still another leak and St. Clair argued that since piecemeal revelations were coming out anyway, it might as well all hang out.

What had specifically aroused St. Clair's ire was the leak of a taped conversation of September 15, 1972, in which the President had expressed sour feelings about the Washington *Post* and lawyer Edward Bennett Williams. Though the *Post* was to claim that the remarks constituted a threat to its valuable television licenses, it was more plausible to conclude that Nixon was venting his anger. For at that time Williams was serving as counsel to the *Post* and to the Democratic National Committee, and that—to Nixon—hardly looked kosher. "I wouldn't want to be in Edward Bennett Williams' position after this election," the President had said. "We are going to fix the son of a bitch, believe me . . ." As for the *Post*, the President predicted that the newspaper would have "damnable, damnable problems out of this one—they have a television station and they are going to have to get it renewed."

St. Clair called this tidbit "irrelevant" to the impeachment inquiry and claimed that the leak had violated committee rules and was prejudicial to the President's case. He also could well have argued that there was nothing in the record to indicate that the President had ever done anything about his alleged threat.

All that the leaked story proved therefore was that Nixon had a temper and was far from being the plastic man his critics sometimes made him out to be. At times he could get very emotional; and most times he thought he could indulge himself in letting off steam. As Haldeman put it in his celebrated interview with Mike Wallace of CBS, he and "all the rest of the senior assistants" had felt that "one of our principal duties had been not to carry out some of the President's orders." He explained, "It was not a matter of disloyalty. It was a matter of loyalty in not carrying them out. One of the means by which the President let off steam was to issue orders that were clearly orders not intended to be carried out."

Haldeman offered this example: "The President called me into his room between meetings—he was in a rush—and he said, 'I want lie-detector tests given to . . .' and he listed categories of people. He said 'I want them done today. I don't want any arguments back' and he put in some of his blunter expletive-type language, I guess.

"I said, 'Yes, sir,' and left because he was mad. I went out and did not do what he told me to do. And so he blew up. He said, 'I told you to get it done and I expect you to get it done.' "

Haldeman then told the President he did not intend to follow the order because he believed it to be "a bad idea."

"I bought the time," Haldeman told Wallace. "The next day, he said, 'What have you done on that?' and he kind of laughed and I said, 'I haven't done anything.' And he said, 'I knew you wouldn't.' And I said, 'Well, I knew you knew I wouldn't . . . ' "

Secretary of State William Rogers was another who knew how to resist an intemperate presidential order. As Safire tells the story in his book on the Nixon years, the President had received reports about some U.S. diplomats in Laos who had failed to carry out some White House directive or other. Miffed, the President sent Rogers a note telling him to "fire everybody in Laos." Rogers, who had known Nixon for a long time, let it pass. But some weeks later the Secretary told the President that he had not carried out his order. Nixon gave Rogers a funny look and asked what he was talking about. "You said to 'fire everybody in Laos,' remember?" Rogers said. "Oh, hell, Bill," the President laughed, "you know me better than that."*

Much of this kind of material appeared in the transcripts of the Watergate tapes reluctantly submitted by the White House to the House Judiciary Committee on April 30, 1974. The tapes, of course, were never intended for public dissemination without the editing out of what Nixon himself was later to describe as "blemishes."

On hearing of the Nixon taping system, Arthur Schlesinger, Jr., predictably announced he was dismayed. It was "absolutely inconceivable" that anyone in the Kennedy administration would get involved in secret recording, he said. "It was not the sort of thing Kennedy would have done. The kind of people in the White House then would not have thought of doing something like that."

Imagine then Artie's horror on learning that there were at least seventy tapes in the Kennedy Library of confidential conversations made by John Kennedy. "And," wrote Bill Buckley, "when they are made public, I am going to line up and listen to what Arthur said to Jack during the Bay of Pigs."

Ironically Nixon originally did not want any tapes at all. Shortly after he assumed office, he ordered the removal of the taping system which Lyndon Johnson had left behind. But two years later he installed a new—and more extensive—recording system, largely at the urging of his predecessor. "President Johnson said that the recordings he had made of his conversations while President had proved to be exceedingly valuable in preparing his memoirs and he urged that I reinstall the recording devices," Nixon said.

Of course the transcripts which Nixon was forced to make

---

*Other episodes of this kind are described in detail in the Safire book, *Before the Fall* (New York: Doubleday, 1975), probably the most authoritative written thus far on the Nixon presidency.

public constituted only a minuscule part of his five-and-a-half-year presidency. And they showed him and his staff presumably at their worst. Because the transcripts dealt mainly with Watergate discussions, they necessarily were out of context. No discussions on domestic or foreign policy or the operations of the government, in which the President could take pride, were released in an effort to balance the record.

As Haldeman explained, "The conversations we were having (were) based on a long working relationship, an ability to talk in shorthand at some times, and other times to let your hair down and grind through a whole series of things without really thinking about the enormity of what you were saying."

To the disappointment of his bitterest critics the transcripts effectively ruled out the possibility that Nixon knew of the Watergate burglary in advance. And despite some ambiguities they generally supported his contention that he wasn't aware of the cover up until Dean enlightened him on March 21, 1973. (The June 23, 1972, "smoking gun" tape, which many observers feel constituted *prima facie* evidence of the President's complicity in the cover up, had not yet been made public.) In the March 21 transcript, the question of the million-dollar hush money payment to and possible clemency for the Watergate defendants arises. Here the text appears to support the President's claim that he vetoed both. The conversation, in which various options are considered, is long and repetitive. But the conclusion was that clemency was impossible, as was blackmail:

PRESIDENT: . . . But in the end, we are going to be bled to death. And, in the end, it is all going to come out anyway. Then you get the worst of both worlds. We are going to lose, and people are going to—

HALDEMAN: And look like dopes!

PRESIDENT: And, in effect, look like a cover up. So that we can't do.

Many passages became the subject of dispute. As early as September 15, 1972, for example, the President congratulated Dean on his handling of the Watergate matter.

PRESIDENT: Oh well, this is a can of worms, as you know, a lot of this stuff that went on. . . . But the way you have handled all this seems to me has been very skillful, putting your fingers in the leaks that have sprung up here and spring there. . . .

Some commentators immediately interpreted the passage as indicating that Nixon knew of or at least suspected high-level involvement. But such an interpretation is inconsistent with the March 13, 17, and 21 conversations, the last being the one in which Dean told the President that "I have the impression that you don't know everything I know." Nixon's position on his "fingers in the leaks" statement, however, was that it referred to Dean's success in putting off various pending civil suits that could have been embarrassing as the election approached.

If anything, the 200,000 words that made up the 1,293 pages of transcript showed that the participants in the discussions were human beings—not cartoon caricatures, figments of press agentry, or actors before the television cameras. All their doubts, confusions, fears, and evasions are displayed—embarrassingly so —with the bark off. Probably the most realistic, even poignant, statement was made by Haldeman, whose public image was that of the toughest of them all: "We are so (adjective deleted) square that we get caught at everything."

Nixon himself comes off as a somewhat beleaguered and bewildered prisoner of circumstances rather than, as portrayed in liberal mythology, the malicious ringleader of a gigantic conspiracy to subvert the Constitution. What the transcripts do show is a President loath to move against longtime associates who somehow had blundered into an untenable position. The President found himself in a no-win situation. Had he acted quickly at the very beginning, he undoubtedly would have been accused of a lack of loyalty to those who had served him. Now with the release of the transcripts the moralists were scornful because he had not flayed about in righteous wrath.

The inability of much of the media to treat the admittedly ambiguous transcripts in a fair and reasonable manner could only be attributed to an anti-Nixon psychosis which, by that time, was out of control. Thus *The New York Times* would have had its readers believe that Nixon never discussed right or wrong with his subordinates. Therefore the President must have been "immoral." Here too the truth is otherwise. For the transcripts demonstrate the very "moral" concern the President felt about how to handle allegations that Haldeman and Ehrlichman were implicated. The issue facing the President was whether he should dismiss his two most trusted aides—a difficult decision indeed, since it would also seem to prejudge their guilt. At one point he says plaintively, "I want to know what is the right thing to do." It is difficult to observe this agonizing without feeling some sympathy. And then the President told Attorney General Kleindienst, "The Justice Department and the presidency are going to come out clean because I don't tolerate this kind of stuff. But the point is, Dick, I can't let an innocent man down. That's my point."

About the only judicious appraisal of the situation in which Nixon found himself at this "point in time" was provided by the *National Review,* the conservative magazine which had not always cottoned to the President's more "liberal" policies:

> A generation hence, looking back on Watergate, historians are likely to marvel at how much was made of it, and how White House bumbling made of so trivial an event the lever by which Mr. Nixon may be overturned. The original Watergate break-in was trivial and ridiculous. The original burglars deserved thirty-day suspended sentences. By the time Nixon got all the threads, or most of them, in his hand—March 21—the situation had become a lot messier. The air is now filled with all manner of resonant phrases: subornation of perjury, obstruction of justice, high crimes and misdemeanors, and all the rest of it. The media have treated Watergate like the biggest thing since the wooden horse was insinuated into Troy. But even the crimes which were committed, and those which may have been committed, were trivial in comparison with the political consequences they have been made to yield.

John Doar however was not satisfied with the transcripts. He announced that, while he was not charging deliberate distortion, some of the "unintelligible" passages were indeed intelligible to his own experts. For one thing, he contended, the committee had high-quality playback equipment far superior to that at the White House.

Eventually the committee released its own transcripts. One of them quoted the President as voicing concern about someone named "Earl Nash." This was in a conversation on March 22, 1973, with John Mitchell. On that occasion the former Attorney General had asked about the general political state of affairs. And according to the Judiciary version of the tape:

PRESIDENT: Yeah, we're all doing fine. I think, though that as long as, uh, everyone and so forth, is a, uh—(unintelligible) still (unintelligible).

MITCHELL: All of Washington—the public interest in this thing, you know.

PRESIDENT: Isn't Nash, (unintelligible) Earl Nash worries the shit out of us here in regard, regarding (unintelligible).

MITCHELL: Just in time.

PRESIDENT: But the point is that, uh, I don't—There's no need for him to testify. I have nothing but intuition, but hell, I don't know. I, but—Again you really have to protect the Presidency, too. That's the point.

MITCHELL: Well this does no violence to the Presidency at all, this concept—

PRESIDENT: The whole scenario.

MITCHELL: Yeah.

The reference to "Earl Nash" sent newsmen frantically scurrying around in an effort to determine who the mysterious gentleman was and why he was worrying the shit out of the President. Finally a librarian at the Los Angeles *Times*, after rifling through numerous reference books, found, "Nash, Harold Earl" in *Who's Who in Government*. Nash was identified as an underwater sound expert working for a navy laboratory in New London, Connecticut. Watergate reporters began to salivate with interest; an acoustical sound expert, no less.

A reporter called the laboratory. He was told that Nash was away on assignment with the Sixth Fleet in the Mediterranean. Nash was then traced to an apartment in Naples, Italy. When his phone rang in Naples, there was no answer. A Military Intelligence officer kept the story alive, however, by telling the reporter that "the name sounds familiar."

But the story of the mysterious "Earl Nash" was finally killed when Doar's experts listened again to the tape. "Earl Nash," it turned out, was "National Security." And that's what had been worrying the President. What the episode proved, therefore, was that Nixon was truly concerned that the Watergate disclosures were doing damage to national security. It was not something that he had conjured up in a desperate effort to conceal the truth. But none of the commentators followed this up. The "Earl Nash" fiasco was quickly forgotten.

There were, of course, deliberate distortions of what was on the tapes. Probably the most significant was the quote which had the President saying, "I want you all to stonewall it . . ." Headlines featured the quote. Cartoonists, who specialize in wrenching things out of context, had a field day with it. *Newsweek* featured it on its cover.

But the full quote, as it appeared in the Judiciary transcripts, was something else again. It came up in the context of Nixon saying that Eisenhower had been too tough in firing his aide Sherman Adams. He added:

> And, uh, for that reason, I am perfectly willing to—I don't give a shit what happens. I want you all to stonewall it, let them plead the Fifth Amendment, cover-up or anything else, if it'll save it—save the plan. That's the whole point. On the other hand, uh, uh, I would prefer, as I said to you, that you do it the other way. And I would particularly prefer to do it that other way if it's going to come out that way anyway. And that my view, that, uh, with the number of jackass people that they've got that they can call, they're going to—the story they get out through leaks, charges, and so forth, and innuendos, will be a hell of a lot worse than the story they're going to get out by just letting it out there.

Watergate had more than its share of inaccurate reporting. As an illustration *Newsweek*, in what appeared to have been based on an interview with Dean, had disclosed that he would reveal in his public testimony that some "low-level" White House officials had planned to assassinate the military ruler of Panama, but that the plan had been aborted at the last minute. This "exclusive" story constituted still one more indictment of an "immoral" administration. The problem was that it just wasn't true; in fact it turned out that Dean did not so testify. Significantly *Newsweek* neither corrected nor explained the discrepancy.

Still another inaccurate story was bannered across page one of the Washington *Post*—HUNT TOLD ASSOCIATES OF ORDERS TO KILL JACK ANDERSON. And it reported that "according to reliable sources," E. Howard Hunt, Jr., "told associates after the Watergate break-in that he was ordered in December, 1971 or January, 1972, to assassinate" the columnist. According to the article, Hunt had said that the order, which came from a "senior official in the Nixon White House," was "cancelled at the last minute but only after a plan had been devised to make Anderson's death appear accidental."

But an investigation of the story by the Senate Intelligence Committee produced "no evidence of a plan to assassinate Jack Anderson." The committee did ascertain that an effort had been made by Hunt to determine the possibility of drugging Anderson so as to render him incoherent before a public appearance. When Hunt learned of the impracticality of the venture, the matter was dropped. The question was whether Hunt had acted on the order of Colson. This Colson flatly denied. However he recalled Hunt "on a couple of occasions coming to me with some hare-brained schemes, something to do with drugging involving Jack Anderson." But he said he never authorized any such project. And there is no independent evidence he did.

The Washington *Post* "exclusive"—and it really was exclusive —was written by Bob Woodward. And Woodward, along with Carl Bernstein, was the great hero of Watergate. The popular perception of the two young reporters (buttressed by *All the President's Men,* as well as the film based on the best-selling book) is that, in the words of the dust jacket, their "brilliant investigative journalism smashed the Watergate scandal wide open." But that isn't exactly the truth. As Lester Markel, former Sunday editor of *The New York Times,* put it: "The *Washington Post's* coverage was not investigative reporting in the real sense because the original facts were dug up by others." Or as Nicholas von Hoffman wrote in the Washington *Post,* of all places, about the "brilliant investigative journalism:" "If you believe that, you also probably can be convinced that if you kiss a toad, it'll turn into a prince."

Woodward and Bernstein did "break" the Mexican connection through which money from the CRP was transmitted to the Watergate burglars. But they did not find this out through their own investigations; rather they obtained the information from federal and local investigators. At best they often were able to publish information a few days in advance of its normal public disclosure. As Edward Jay Epstein argued in *Commentary,* "It was not the press which exposed Watergate; it was the agencies of Government itself." Epstein in effect dismissed the efforts of Woodward and Bernstein; they did, "of course, add fuel to the fire. But . . . they were not the only ones publicizing the case."

Their one original discovery actually had nothing to do with Watergate. It involved Donald Segretti, whose dirty tricks had nothing to do with the break-in. Yet from the start of their investigation Woodward and Bernstein believed there was a direct connection between dirty tricks and Watergate. Which, in a far-fetched way, was like linking Dick Tuck's "pranks" with the harassment of Martin Luther King. There just was no connection. In retrospect it was the enormous play given the Segretti story by the Washington *Post* which resulted in indictments. The authorities felt they had no choice but to go after Segretti and Dwight Chapin. Thus they would be able to avoid the cry of "cover up." And in the end Segretti served time, after pleading guilty to three counts of distributing illegal campaign literature. Chapin was convicted on two counts of perjury for not telling the truth about his knowledge of a misdemeanor. He too served time.

Finally therefore it wasn't Woodward and Bernstein (or Redford and Hoffman) who smashed Watergate wide open. The cover up began to unravel when James McCord, fearful of going to jail, wrote a letter to Judge Sirica charging that other persons besides those convicted of the break-in had been involved. In the final analysis it was Richard Nixon who ironically helped break the case when he ordered his staff, including Dean, to testify before the grand jury without taking any claims of executive privilege. And he gave the same order with regard to the Senate Watergate Committee.

Little of this can be found in the book *All the President's Men,* in which Woodward and Bernstein exaggerated their role as, in effect, the saviours of our freedoms. For a time they were invested with magical powers by members of the journalistic fraternity who were looking for their own heroes.

The very title of their book is misleading. Not "all the President's men" were involved in Watergate—that's guilt by association with a vengeance. Only a relative handful of top officials were even accused of wrongdoing. The book is replete with more specific implications that are demonstrably false. Dita Beard, for example, is described as "the author of the famous memo which showed that there was a connection between ITT's promise of several hundred thousand dollars to help the Republican convention and a favorable antitrust settlement." The record shows that Mrs. Beard swore under oath that she did not write the memo, which she charged was an outright forgery. Moreover the memo itself did not "show" anything, except perhaps a certain tenuous connection. And contrary to popular impression the ITT pledge of money was not to the Republicans but to the San Diego Convention Bureau. Moreover the antitrust settlement was far from favorable to ITT. If anything it was the most stringent antitrust settlement in history, a fact conceded even by Archibald Cox. But more importantly Special Prosecutor Jaworski found no wrongdoing in the transaction. So the impression Woodward and Bernstein leave here is decidedly misleading.

Then there were the "revelations" provided by "a source in the Executive Branch" dubbed "Deep Throat," a nickname suggestive of fellatio. According to Woodward, the source was so secret that he did not even reveal it to Bernstein. But whether he ever existed or was a figment of Woodward's vivid imagination is a subject still in contention. Consider the James Bondish melodramatics in the book; Woodward rushing out at 2:00 A.M. to meet Deep Throat in deserted garages. Then there were Deep Throat's warnings that "everyone's life is in danger," and that the CIA was conducting "electronic surveillance" on the intrepid *Post* reporters. Great stuff for the film, but hardly in keeping with the record. About the only danger Woodward faced was the possibility of getting mugged while rendezvousing in the middle of the night with Deep Throat. As for electronic surveillance by the CIA, no such evidence was ever produced by anyone. But it all played well on film.

Exactly how much did Deep Throat—if he, she, or it, existed —really know? At one point the secret source purportedly told Woodward that there were "more than fifty" dirty tricksters, operating under White House and CRP control, for the purpose of destroying the opposition, "no holds barred." And Woodstein published a page-one story, quoting "sources," about a massive campaign of sabotage and espionage aimed at the Democrats. As it turned out, the story was vastly exaggerated. All Woodward and Bernstein had to go on were the juvenile antics of Segretti and a handful of pranksters.

On another occasion Deep Throat claimed that the Nixon administration had been bugging throughout its tenure and, therefore, the bugging of the DNC was "only natural," the mysterious source adding that "the arrests in the Watergate sent everybody off the edge because the break-in could uncover the whole program." Woodstein also quoted other sources as saying that Watergate and Segretti were just "the tip of the iceberg." All of which, on the basis of facts later uncovered by numerous investigations, was highly exaggerated. There just was no iceberg under the tip. There was no massive wiretapping operation, no emerging police state. There was Segretti and his few dirty tricks. And there were the break-in and the cover up. But if one were to believe Woodward and Bernstein, had it not been for their ceaseless labors, Nixon would have been inaugurated in January 1977 to the singing of the Horst Wessel Song.

Woodward and Bernstein did concede making several errors. One of them was particularly damaging to the parties involved. Relying on confidential sources, they had reported that material obtained from the first Watergate break-in had been delivered to Bill Timmons of the White House, and Rob Odle and J. Glenn Sedam of the CRP. This, of course, tied the three men to criminality. "But," Woodstein wrote, "the report was incorrect, and the decision to rush it into print was a mistake. . . . Three men had been wronged. They had been unfairly accused on the front page of the *Washington Post,* the hometown newspaper of their families, neighbors and friends." For some reason the Washington *Post* never apologized to the men it had wronged so dreadfully.

Woodward and Bernstein do tell how they sought to question members of the grand jury about what witnesses had been saying under oath. The fact that this was in absolute violation of the law seemed to be lost on the intrepid reporters. Grand juries are supposed to act in secret; and grand jurors are sworn to secrecy. One of the jurors had told the prosecutors he had been visited by a *Post* reporter. The prosecutors immediately notified Judge Sirica. Informed of this, Edward Bennett Williams, counsel to the Washington *Post,* instructed Ben Bradlee to direct his two reporters to "sit tight." Things looked bad; old "Maximum John" could well decide to throw the book at Woodward and Bernstein. But as Bradlee later informed his frightened reporters, "Williams talked to Sirica and to the prosecutors; he thinks he can keep you out of the slam."

Then came an irony normally to be found only in fiction. The young reporters were called to open court, where Sirica chided them for their misconduct but never mentioned them by name. Despite Sirica's harsh reputation they had gotten off scot-free. "In Britain," commented John Roche, "they would probably be breaking rocks for a couple of years, and Ben Bradlee . . . would be on his knees at the bar of the House of Commons for publishing their material, apologizing and asking for clemency."

Thankful that they had not been treated like other lawbreakers, Woodward and Bernstein left Sirica's courtroom somewhat confused, amid a barrage of questions from other reporters as to whether they were the "news media representative" the judge had excoriated. When Dan Schorr suggested that the judge was referring to them, Bernstein cried "hearsay, innuendo and character assassination." Previously Woodward and Bernstein "had reluctantly agreed during a rush to the halls that only as a last resort would they deny the allegation outright; maybe they would get by with indignation and artful footwork." When asked directly whether they were the culprits, they bobbed and weaved, refusing to tell the truth. As Woodward and Bernstein report of themselves in the book, "They had chosen expediency over principle and, caught in the act, their role had been covered up. They had dodged, misrepresented, suggested and intimidated, even if they had not lied outright." In short, a mini-Watergate.

More than journalism was involved in the Washington *Post's* pursuance of Watergate. Bradlee and publisher Katherine Graham were pictured as having an almost psychopathic hatred for President Nixon. There is Bradlee, for example, when he learns of the resignations of Haldeman and Ehrlichman:

> For a split second, Ben Bradlee's mouth dropped open with an expression of sheer delight. Then he put one cheek on the desk, eyes closed and banged the desk repeatedly with his right fist. In a moment, he recovered. "How do you like them apples?" he said. . . . Bradlee couldn't restrain himself. He . . . shouted across rows of desks to Woodward. . . ."Not bad, Bob. Not half bad!" Howard Simons interjected a note of caution. "Don't gloat," he murmured, as *Post* staff members began to gather around. "We can't afford to gloat."

An unhappier time for Bradlee had been when he considered the possibility of Mrs. Graham and others being subpoenaed for notes taken during the paper's investigations. Benjy was beside himself. "Of course we're going to fight this one all the way up, and if the Judge wants to send anyone to jail, he's going to have to send Mrs. Graham. And, my God, the lady says she'll go! Then the Judge can have that on his conscience. Can't you see the pictures of her limousine pulling up to the Women's Detention Center and out gets our gal, going to jail to uphold the First Amendment? . . . There might be a revolution." So removed from reality was Benjamin Crowninshield Bradlee that he could actually conceive of a revolution over a multimillionairess going to the slammer. Imagine the "wretched of the earth" storming the barricades to salvage Graham's limousine!

It took an English press lord to blow the whistle on press efforts to "crucify" President Nixon. Addressing himself to such newspapers as the Washington *Post,* Lord Thomson, publisher of *The Times* of London, declared that Nixon "was found guilty by newspapers before he was proven guilty." And he went on: "This kind of character assassination is much more difficult in England because British laws provide more safeguards for a man's reputation."

By that time Nixon's reputation was being torn to shreds in other ways. No President since FDR was as reviled, scorned, and mocked. It had gotten to the point where there was serious discussion of whether Nixon could take his dogs on Air Force One without reimbursing the government. Roosevelt, who had actually arranged special trips for Fala, was able to turn it around, getting the best of such critics as Westbrook Pegler. Nixon however was in no position to fight back. And in *The New York Times* Eileen Shanahan reported breathlessly that Nixon's tax accountant had deducted a total of $224 from Nixon's gross income in the four-year period 1969–1972 for California gasoline taxes, thereby saving the President nearly $19.63 a year in federal income taxes. Since Nixon was riding around in official cars most of the time during those years, Ms. Shanahan thought the deduction was "seriously inflated"—a dazzling insight which, according to William Rusher, won her the 1974 Prize for Creative Microeconomics: "one slightly bent safety-pin."

Meanwhile Nixon was being called every dirty name in the book: ridiculed at the Kennedy Center for the Performing Arts by a comedian making obscene remarks about the President's sexual prowess; served as subject of endless cartoons and graffiti everywhere; reviled on talk shows, including Johnny Carson's; and denounced in printed expression, ranging from scholarly knife to four-letter words. A young man in Saginaw, Michigan, was shown on the tube declaring, "I hate him." And Nixon-watchers in the media made no secret of their fear and loathing. They began scrutinizing the President as the officers of the U.S.S. *Caine* scrutinized Captain Queeg, ready to elevate a moment of irritation into possible mental breakdown. Rumors spread that Nixon was on drugs; some reporters predicted suicide; there was even a diligent attempt to find a psychiatrist Nixon was rumored to be seeing currently. Eventually Woodward and Bernstein would begin asking close associates whether it was true that Nixon had been talking to portraits on the wall of the family quarters. The answers were not wholly satisfactory—for there were only landscapes, not portraits, in the upper floors of the White House. But that didn't stop the intrepid *Post* reporters from finally quoting Ed Cox (who never talked to them) as saying that his father-in-law had been roaming around talking to portraits of former presidents in his last days.*

Respected newspapers which used to glory in relaying only news fit to print now published falsehoods in their campaign to topple the President. Thus *The New York Times*, in a front-page story by Seymour M. Hersh, reported that the President had been heard to utter anti-Semitic and other ethnic remarks on taped conversations he had had with Dean on February 28 and March 20, 1973. Hersh had gone ahead with the story despite denials by the White House and, perhaps more importantly, by James Doyle, press officer for the special prosecutor. Doyle had listened to the two tapes in question and had not heard the President indulging in slurs. But Hersh went ahead anyway, reporting that Nixon had referred to "Jew boys" and had called Sirica a "goddam wop." Actually, as it later developed, it was Dean who used the phrase "Jewish boys" in talking to the President. As for "goddam wop," the President's words on the scratchy recording in fact were "That's the kind I want," a reference to Sirica's reputation as a tough jurist. There was an unfortunate Nixon reference to Jews in the arts—"they're left wing"— in the so-called smoking gun tape of June 23, 1972. Talking to Haldeman, the President had recounted some upsetting experience endured by his daughters while visiting art galleries and the like. Nixon didn't want them scheduled for such locales in the future. "In other words, stay away," he said.**

The Hersh story sent quivers of excitement down the spines of Nixon-haters. Writing in the *New York Post*, Pete Hamill called on New York's "wops" and "Jew boys" to prepare a counterattack against Nixon. He wrote that the President's "disregard for the Constitution" was such that tomorrow, if not today, the President could direct "a military coup d'etat" from Washington; Governor Wilson and Mayor Beame should immediately

> begin planning a program of self-defense. . . . (They) should order all New York police and National Guard units to draw up a plan of resistance. . . . In addition, there should be a system that would

---

*Of *The Final Days* John Osborne, one of the more respected correspondents on the Washington scene, wrote in *The New Republic:* "It is on the whole the worst job of nationally noted reporting that I've observed during forty-nine years in the business."

**Though Nixon derided left-wing Jews in the arts, he appointed a widely respected right-wing Jew, Dr. Ronald Berman, to head the well-funded National Endowment for the Humanities.

enlist civilians as . . . defenders of bridges, tunnels and airports, while others are charged with maintaining the supply of food and water. We should find out how many arms we have available and how many more we would need to fight a long siege. In short . . . New York will fight. If he sends his soldiers, there will be a lot of tough 'wops' and 'Jew boys' and Irishmen and blacks and Puerto Ricans waiting for them with machine guns.

The Judiciary Committee was not the only committee guilty of engaging in trial by leaks. The Senate Watergate Committee, which seemed to be finding it impossible to get off the stage, continued to leak like a sieve.

On June 11, 1974, Archibald Cox denounced the tactics of the committee as similar to those used by the late Senator McCarthy. Cox accused intellectuals and the press of deliberately failing to point out and to denounce these similarities. "Should not the same objections be raised when the staff or possibly some members of the Ervin Committee leaks the result of incomplete investigations, gives out the accusatory inferences it draws from secret testimony and even releases proposed findings of guilt upon men under indictment and awaiting trial?" he asked.

Almost from the beginning a group of majority staff members led by (who else?) Carmine Bellino began looking into the $100,000 that Howard Hughes had turned over to Rebozo for transmission to the Nixon campaign. According to Rebozo, he kept the money in a safe deposit box at his Key Biscayne bank. And the reason he didn't turn it over to the Nixon committee was because of the internecine battle raging within the Hughes empire. "I didn't want to risk even the remotest embarrassment of Hughes' connection with Nixon," he said. He was convinced, he added, that the Hughes loan to the President's brother Donald had cost Nixon the 1960 election and "didn't help him in 1962 in California" when he ran for governor. In June 1973 Rebozo returned the money intact to Hughes. An examination by the committee bore out Rebozo's contention that he had returned the very same bills he had placed in his deposit box three years before. But the finding was difficult for the anti-Nixonites to accept. They just knew, deep down in their bones, that some sort of chicanery must have been involved. The fact that there was no such proof did not curb their tongues or their typewriters.

The investigations into Rebozo's financial affairs broadened. As a consequence enormous amounts of taxpayers' money were expended on what turned out to be fruitless efforts to "get"

Rebozo. As Fred Thompson reported in his book,* "Members of the majority staff became highly competitive, because the one who achieved the breakthrough might be able to question witnesses at a public hearing. The same desire for glory . . . required that the hearings be prolonged. So staff members passed the word to the press and to Senators on the Committee that a breakthrough, like prosperity in the Great Depression, was just around the corner.

"During this process of staff politicking, the elements of fairness and respect for individual rights frequently suffered," wrote Thompson. "Rebozo was a particular target and an easy one. By the time the staff concentrated on him, Nixon had been severely wounded, and no one stepped forward to defend the rights of Nixon's best friend for fear that he might be accused of being soft on Nixon."

Rarely had such a witch-hunt been conducted against a single individual. According to Thompson, staff members were constantly flying down to Key Biscayne to interview Rebozo. They traveled in pairs, sometimes in threes. "Sometimes one team would interview Rebozo for four, five, or six hours; a few days later another group would arrive and go over the same material with Rebozo, seemingly unaware of what their colleagues had done."

Rebozo cooperated completely. He gave the staff access to his records. But every time a batch of records was examined, stories would appear in the press quoting sources "close to the Committee," none of which was ever flattering to Rebozo. "One day," Thompson reported, "Carmine Bellino examined the records of all the loans Rebozo had made over a period of several years. The next morning at 9:30 the *Miami Herald* began calling each of the lending banks to verify information . . . about the loans."

Then there was the time the ABC network reported that the probers were checking into an allegation that Rebozo was running a "private investment portfolio" for the President. The fund, according to ABC, contained "more than one million dollars" in unreported political contributions from "two international corporations." Without naming ABC, the President angrily denied the charge at a press conference and claimed the network

---

*At That Point in Time, the best account thus far of the behind-the-scenes shenanigans, as well as partisanship of the Watergate Committee, this book was even praised by Sam Ervin for its honesty.

had broadcast the story "knowing it was untrue." ABC's executive vice president Bill Sheehan countered: "If we do find that we were in error, we will broadcast a correction. So far, all the facts stand up." It turned out that the facts did not stand up, but ABC never broadcast a correction.

What particularly distressed Rebozo was the harassment of members of his family as well as business acquaintances. Another target was his longtime lady friend. Their financial records over a six-year period were subpoenaed. At the same time people to whom he had written checks in that period were questioned. Most of those interrogated, bewildered by the gung-ho tactics of the young probers, were forced to hire lawyers. "At a Committee meeting," wrote Thompson, "when I asked what six-year-old business records had to do with the 1972 presidential campaign, I never received an answer. By this time, the staff members realized they were really answerable to no one."

The investigators, who had obtained the toll records for 11 telephones Rebozo had used in this six-year period, questioned him about 400 telephone numbers, asking whom he had talked to and about what. Staff members also cased his bank, seeking to determine who entered or left the premises. Unable to get the answers they wanted, two of them told a respected trust officer of the bank, "We'll see that you get immunity if you'll tell us the truth." One immediate result was a decided falling off of bank business. At the same time Rebozo gave up some of his business endeavors rather than involve his partners in his problems. Essentially a private person, Rebozo found himself the target of scurrilous articles in even respected newspapers.

And yet not one word of protest was ever uttered by any of the nation's civil libertarians. The American Civil Liberties Union said nary a word.

Fred Thompson did seek to protect Rebozo's rights. More than once Thompson raised the issue with Ervin. In view of the fact that the Senate had limited the investigation to the 1972 campaign, he asked, what gave the committee's staffers the authority to investigate a private citizen's business life? And what about the leaks to the press? According to Thompson, Ervin's usual reply was that he understood that matters would be clarified in a week or two. But they never were. The witch-hunt continued.

Eventually Rebozo was fully exonerated of all the innuendoes spread by the Ervin Committee and an only-too-willing media. The first inkling of this came from Leon Jaworski, who had just resigned as special prosecutor. In an interview Jaworski said that Rebozo had violated no laws in his handling of campaign contributions. What a blow to the dozens of newsmen who had been on Bebe's tail for nearly two years! And what a blow to the anti-Nixonites who had conjured up all sorts of fantasies regarding sinister doings down in Key Biscayne. Now it turned out that all those millions of words regarding Bebe and Nixon—as well as all those TV newscasts—were based more on wishful thinking than factual evidence. For it was obvious from Jaworski's remarks (and who should have known better than he?) that Rebozo had been telling the truth.

Jaworski's comments were contained in an exclusive interview published in the Knight newspapers on January 9, 1975. The former special prosecutor contended that there was no hard evidence on which his staff could make a case against Rebozo. The story, summarized in an AP dispatch out of Miami, quoted Rebozo as saying he was "delighted that Jaworski came to the only conclusion any fair-minded person would come to based on the facts." Though the Washington *Post* did publish a few paragraphs, that newspaper of record *The New York Times* must have lost its AP copy. The big TV network news shows, which had previously gone overboard detailing allegations against Rebozo, completely ignored the Jaworski comments. The Cronkites, Chancellors, and Reasoners now appeared never to have heard of Rebozo.

But many in the media were still hoping; for Rebozo was not yet fully out of the woods. As Jaworski said, the investigation was being continued by his successor. Some months later the Special Prosecutor's Office disclosed that, after fifteen months of its own investigation, it had failed to turn up any evidence to warrant any charges against Rebozo. But no apologies were offered Rebozo by anyone. In fact there were expressions of dismay and outrage that he had been exonerated.

The partisan character of the various investigators was reflected in the fact that they showed very little inclination to look into allegations of hanky-panky on the part of Democratic bigwigs. For example there was testimony that during his 1968 presidential campaign Hubert Humphrey accepted $50,000 as a contribution from Howard Hughes. The charge was made under oath by Robert Maheu, the former aide who had broken with Hughes. According to Maheu, he personally handed over the sum in $100 bills in an attaché case during a limousine ride on July

28, 1968, with the then Vice President in Los Angeles. Humphrey denied he had been given the money personally, adding, "He may have given the money to a campaign committee supporting me." But one witness, Lloyd Hand, a former chief of protocol who had been Humphrey's aide during the 1968 campaign, testified that they had been in the limousine when Maheu apparently handed over the attaché case. All the testimony was given in the course of a federal trial originating in Maheu's $17.3 million defamation suit against the Summa Corporation, the Hughes holding company. In the end the jury chose to believe Maheu, rendering a verdict in his favor against the reclusive billionaire.

To this day the question of what happened to the $50,000 which Maheu claimed to have handed over to Humphrey has never been resolved. And no interest was ever demonstrated by the Special Prosecutor's Office, the Senate Watergate Committee, or any of the other agencies which were so busily ferreting out evil in the Nixon camp. The media also showed a disinclination to pursue the subject, with one notable exception. Jack Anderson did report on October 17, 1973, that while Spiro T. Agnew was being sentenced for income tax evasion, the IRS had been quietly auditing the returns of his predecessor as Vice President. The IRS "raised its eyebrows over Maheu's sworn testimony," Anderson wrote, "because of evidence Humphrey did favors for Hughes. If $50,000 was paid for Humphrey's services, then the money should have been reported as income. It was Agnew's failure to pay taxes on a bribe that got him into trouble with the IRS."

Anderson produced handwritten memos from Hughes to Maheu, some of which were later placed in evidence in federal court. This was the way the eccentric billionaire communicated with his staff in the last ten years of his life. He wrote down his instructions on yellow legal pads; and the memos were delivered by trusted retainers. Several memos dealt with Hughes's crusade to halt a huge nuclear test explosion that had been scheduled to take place in Nevada in 1968. Hughes apparently was concerned that the test would do damage to the numerous properties including gambling casinos he was acquiring near the test site. But he also appeared to have legitimate environmental concerns. One memo read:

> I think that the AEC must be made to realize that I am dedicated to the minimum request made of them [to delay the test]. That if

they do not grant it, I will ally myself completely with the all-out anti-bomb faction throughout the entire U.S. That this group has only been waiting for a strong leader and I am ready to dedicate the rest of my life and every cent I possess in a complete no quarter fight to outlaw all nuclear testing of every kind and everywhere. . . .

Hughes seemed to think he could enlist Humphrey's aid in ending nuclear testing. "Bob," Hughes directed Maheu, "there is one man who can accomplish our objectives through [President] Johnson and that man is H.H.H. Why don't we get word to him on a basis of secrecy that is *really, really reliable* that we will give him immediately *full unlimited* support for his campaign to enter the White House if he will just take this one on for us? Let me know." Other memos suggested that Hughes believed Humphrey's help had been obtained. But Humphrey, whose son Bob was employed by a Hughes company, later told Anderson that he had been opposed to the Nevada tests long before he learned of Hughes's interest in the matter.*

Just as embarrassing to Humphrey was the disclosure that he had tried to keep valuable gifts that legally belonged to the government. In 1974 when columnist Maxine Cheshire began looking into the matter, Humphrey suddenly remembered the 7.9-carat diamond that had been presented to his wife in 1968 by the president of Zaire. Worth $100,000, the diamond had reposed in a Minnesota safe deposit box all that time. Humphrey returned the diamond to the State Department, explaining that he had not realized that the Foreign Gifts Act covered members of his family. At the same time the senator disclosed that a sack of valuable baby leopard skins, gifts to Mrs. Humphrey from officials of Somalia, had been sold in 1970 for $7,500 and the money given to charity. The Humphreys however had no authorization to so dispose of the skins.

Other financial irregularities continued to embarrass the senator.

---

*According to Maheu, Hughes had also tried to reach President Johnson. Maheu testified that Hughes had assigned him to offer $1 million to LBJ, provided nuclear testing in Nevada was ended. Hughes also instructed Maheu to "feel out" the President's attitude about ending the war in Vietnam. Maheu said he did meet with the President at the LBJ Ranch and that Johnson insisted that the nuclear tests were of extreme importance to national security. Maheu then said he did not make the $1 million offer.

—Like Nixon, Humphrey had obtained a tax deduction for the vice presidential papers he had given to the Minnesota Historical Society. But after the furor over the Nixon deduction, the IRS took another look at the Humphrey transaction. The IRS then decided to disallow the nearly $200,000 deduction it had granted Humphrey.

—Two of Humphrey's campaign aides, Jack Chestnut and Norman Sherman, were convicted on federal charges involving illegal campaign contributions. Sherman, the senator's former press secretary, pleaded guilty to a charge that he had participated in a scheme to launder $82,000 in corporate money to buy computer lists. Sherman said that he had accepted the corporate money on legal advice of Chestnut, a lawyer who was then Humphrey's campaign manager. When asked by minority staffers of the Watergate Committee to testify about the incident, Chestnut took the Fifth Amendment.

—The Associated Milk Producers Incorporated (AMPI) was alleged to have given Humphrey's 1968 presidential campaign $91,691 in corporate funds, his 1970 Senate campaign $22,500 out of corporate funds, and his 1972 presidential campaign $34,500 out of corporate funds. Humphrey's response was that his campaign organization handled such matters, not he, and anyway it would be difficult for a recipient to know whether the funds came from a corporate or noncorporate account.

—Dwayne Andreas, a longtime Humphrey financial backer, was charged on October 19, 1973, by Special Prosecutor Jaworski with giving Humphrey's 1968 campaign four $25,000 payments —$100,000 in all—out of the corporate funds of Andreas's First Interoceanic Corporation. The payments took place late in October 1968. And again Humphrey denied any knowledge that the payments were from corporate funds. Moreover, he said, "the campaign committee handled it."

—John Loeb, a Wall Street investment banker, was accused of contributing $48,000 to Humphrey's 1972 campaign for the presidential nomination, but concealing the contributions by ascribing them to the names of nine of his employees. Several of the charges were dropped and Loeb eventually pleaded no-contest to counts involving donations of $18,000. Here again Humphrey denied knowledge of any illegality.

—Then there was the disclosure that the Seafarers International Union had poured $100,000 into Humphrey's 1968 campaign a few days after the Johnson administration had denied a request by the Canadian government for extradition of a former union official to face a Canadian perjury charge.

Humphrey himself declined to be interviewed by the Watergate Committee after minority staffers sought to question him concerning "funny" money. In fact the senator sent a note to Ervin saying, "I see no point in inconveniencing any member of your committee to meet with me." And the chairman, who had been nearly apoplectic about White House stonewalling, let the matter pass.

The fact that so little had been made of Democratic misdeeds was noted by the Washington *Star*. "Imagine how the blood, subpoenas and leaks would have flowed had a Nixon official invoked the Fifth Amendment to keep from testifying or had sent a letter to the Committee saying he wouldn't show up because he didn't want to inconvenience the Committee. One can only wonder whether it was Democratic partisanship or Capitol Hill clubbiness that caused the Senate Watergate Committee to let Humphrey off so easily."

Humphrey's vulnerabilities could well have been one reason why the Minnesotan declined to enter the primary contests in 1976—thus affording the little-known Jimmy Carter an almost clear shot at the nomination. Humphrey was well aware that his opposition, including Carter, was prepared to dredge up his Watergate-type problems. Yet for sheer *chutzpah* Hubert had few peers. Addressing the 1976 Democratic Convention in Madison Square Garden, the senator described the Republicans as "self-appointed experts on law and order," who "have taken crime off the streets and put it in the White House." And Humphrey applauded wildly when Carter said in his acceptance speech that there was a "double standard" of justice in this country with "big shot crooks" going scot-free while poor people were being jailed. Well, that "double standard" obviously didn't do Humphrey any harm.

Also taking the Fifth Amendment against self-incrimination was the manager of Congressman Wilbur Mills's ill-fated campaign for the presidency in 1972. The chairman of the House Ways and Means Committee, considered one of the nation's most powerful men, declined even to reply to two letters sent him by Ervin asking him to appear for questioning. The questioning would have been about Mills's connections with the Associated

Milk Producers Incorporated, which contributed to his campaign and provided office help. According to Thompson, there also was sworn testimony that Mills had asked the AMPI to arrange an Iowa rally for him so he could address farmers. The bills for the rally, amounting to $45,000, were paid by the milk producers group. Apparently in return Mills had assisted the AMPI in its organized drive to persuade the administration to increase milk-price supports. In addition the minority staffers discovered that Gulf Oil had arranged to deliver $15,000 in corporate funds to a Mills fund-raiser—something which most definitely was illegal. And as Thompson later noted, "Our investigation received little attention in the press, but our findings were well known to the political figures involved. And they were not exactly coopera-tive."

And when Mills got into trouble in the famous episode involv-ing an Argentine stripper who had leaped into the Tidal Basin, he returned to Little Rock, Arkansas, for a campaign appearance before the Jaycees, most of whom—so reporters noted—ap-peared generally sympathetic.

"You are the number one Democrat the Republicans would like to get rid of," a member of the audience said to Mills. "Do you feel the jackals are after you?"

"There are still Nixon people in the federal government who might be because I declared that President Nixon might have to resign when people learned about his taxes," responded Mills. "There were reports that the driver of my car the other night at one time was in the government under the Nixon Administra-tion, but there's no proof that he had any instructions from any-body."

But such was the temper of the times that there were those in Little Rock who believed him. At least he was reelected. Of course the Tidal Basin escapade was not his last; and he was finally forced to resign.

As a noted Democrat once observed, "Money is the mother's milk of politics." Contributions of all kinds, legal and otherwise, have fueled the campaigns of politicians of both parties from time immemorial. "One remembers," Bill Rickenbacker remem-bered in the *National Review*, "Senators Kennedy and Bayh crashing on a hilltop in Massachusetts and being found in a bed of money; literally, the cash was drifting all over the mountain. It is on record that they were flying up to attend the annual banquet of the Democratic party, and one supposes that services had been rendered, and payment in full was due." But no congressional investigation ever was launched into the episode, which was quickly forgotten.

There was a belated effort to examine McGovern's campaign finances on the part of Thompson's overworked probers—this the same McGovern who has been wearing a Watergate halo over his sparse locks. Yet the record shows that McGovern transferred some $340,000 in 1972 campaign funds to his 1974 campaign for reelection to the Senate. While apparently not illegal, nevertheless this was done at a time when McGovern's 1972 campaign creditors were being asked to discount their bills at half-price. This raised a question about a violation of the spirit of the law prohibiting corporate contributions to political campaigns.

Commenting on these unethical, if not illegal, practices, former admirer Martin Peretz noted that, during the 1972 campaign,

McGovern could not resist the opportunity to talk about how open and aboveboard he and his associates were. It now seems that they were not quite as candid as they pretended. While repaying loans of some of the McGovern rich, they were still deluging the McGovern rank and file for last-minute contributions. At the same time, subsistence workers were taken off salary. At the end, however, there was a huge surplus; and some suspect that this surplus was the real goal of late October fund-raising. But what was to be done with that surplus? Hundreds of thousands of dollars contributed by thousands of citizens to a campaign to turn Nixon out of the White House was quietly shifted to keep McGovern in the Senate.

McGovern was infuriated when he heard that the draft report of the Watergate Committee had cited an "apparent violation of the spirit of the law" in regard to how he had settled his debts with some corporations. In a letter to Ervin he denounced Thompson and his minority staffers, comparing them to Haldeman and Segretti. What McGovern did not know was that the language to which he objected had actually been suggested by Dave Dorsen, one of the few Democratic staffers who was not blinded by excessive partisanship. It was, as Thompson later noted, "language with which we, of course, wholeheartedly agreed." Nevertheless, unlike Republican targets of the committee, McGovern won his battle. Ervin passed the word that the phrase to which McGovern had objected was to be deleted from the report. And it was deleted, with no outcry from a media supposedly on the lookout for "cover ups."

"Because of our limited manpower," wrote Thompson, "the minority staff was spread thin; but it seemed that everywhere we looked there was an array of campaign irregularities waiting to be discovered." Thompson's investigators, for example, found that Ed Muskie's campaign had made an arrangement with Hertz Rent-A-Car which smacked of illegality. Even more promising was an investigation into Mayor Lindsay's campaign which had to be terminated. But enough was discovered for the committee's final report to cite Lindsay's presidential bid as having accepted cash contributions from paving contractors who somehow wound up with $1.7 million in contracts to provide asphalt to New York City.

The cavalier manner in which the Democratic majority on the Ervin Committee engaged in cover ups in behalf of Democrats was further illustrated by the treatment accorded a member of the House named James R. Jones, of Tulsa, Oklahoma. Jones, who had been an aide to President Johnson, had once written a letter to the AMPI complaining that the milk producers had stopped paying a retainer begun shortly after he left the White House. The letter in effect suggested that AMPI had placed him on the retainer because he had persuaded LBJ to do certain things in behalf of the milk industry. "When our staff contacted Jones about the letter, he faced a painful decision," reported Thompson. "He had to admit either that he had improperly used his influence while serving in the White House or that, to keep the retainer, he had misled AMPI about his efforts in AMPI's behalf. He told us that the latter situation was true—that he had not really provided any of the help for AMPI that was spelled out in his letter."

Jones pleaded with Ervin and other members of the committee to keep any reference to his letter out of the report. And the Democratic majority agreed to do so. The argument was that the Jones matter did not fall within the charter of the committee to investigate matters surrounding the 1972 campaign. But, as Thompson noted, "the ruling was not consistent with the Committee's action on other matters of our investigation, including Rebozo's dealings," few of which had anything to do with the 1972 campaign. "I believed that the Democrats were using the jurisdictional issue to bail out one of their Democratic colleagues."

As it turned out, the milk producers had also taken care of Johnson when he left the White House. Through the AMPI they had entered into an agreement with the former President to lease his thirteen-passenger Beechcraft turboprop airplane at a minimum of $94,000 a year. According to the contract, the AMPI had first call on the plane, which was based at the LBJ Ranch airstrip. It was a deal which the Texas-based co-op tried to terminate. All this became known as a result of an investigation of the co-op's political dealings undertaken by Edward L. Wright, a former president of the American Bar Association. The study was initiated by the co-op's board of directors to follow up reports of illicit contributions to the Nixon campaign and other questionable expenditures by AMPI officials. Basically the findings showed that the AMPI was more heavily involved with Johnson, Humphrey, and other Democratic leaders than with Republicans.

Some interesting revelations came out of the study. The major revelation had to do with LBJ's plane. The former President was quoted as saying that he had welcomed the lease arrangement with AMPI because the payments supplemented his retirement income. LBJ had conceded in a conversation with George L. Mehren, AMPI's general manager, that the price was fairly "lush."

Mehren had gone to work for AMPI on June 1, 1968, one day after Johnson had accepted his resignation as Assistant Secretary of Agriculture. According to Mehren, he had sought LBJ's advice in October 1972 when a Nixon fund-raiser sought additional campaign contributions. He met with the former President at the ranch. "During the meeting," he said, "the President told me that the dairy people in his last campaign had agreed to give $250,000, but had not done so."

Outlining other ties between the co-op and LBJ, the Wright study reported that in 1968 the AMPI had paid $104,521 to publish a slick 241-page book as a tribute to President Johnson. Titled *No Retreat from Tomorrow*, it contained color photographs of LBJ along with two dozen of his messages to Congress. Apparently printed before LBJ's decision not to seek reelection, it was designed as a memento for campaign contributors. AMPI deducted the costs as a necessary business expense but its claim was disallowed by the IRS. Another phony bookkeeping entry was made by AMPI when it paid a printing bill for the Humphrey senatorial campaign through a New York advertising firm. The item was invoiced as "consulting fee for Minnesota." In both the Humphrey campaign and the brief 1972 campaign for the presidential nomination waged by Wilbur Mills, the co-op paid the salaries and expenses of individuals who worked fulltime on political chores—all decidedly illegal.

Another corporation which maintained a secret fund for political purposes was Minnesota Mining and Manufacturing, better known as 3M. Illegal funds were given to Senator Walter F. Mondale, Democrat of Minnesota; Hubert Humphrey; Gale McGee, Democrat of Wyoming; William Proxmire, Democrat of Wisconsin; Minority Leader Hugh Scott of Pennsylvania; and Senator Mark Hatfield, Oregon Republican, among others. In addition 3M contributed to various congressional campaigns as well as dinners in which the receipts were collected by party campaign organizations. Yet under a deal worked out with then Special Prosecutor Cox, 3M's illegal contributions were wiped clean when the company pleaded guilty to a single count—the donation of $30,000 to the 1972 Nixon campaign. So from the very beginning a record was being compiled which centered mainly on the sins of the Nixon administration.

The unwillingness of the Ervin Committee to delve into campaigns other than that of Nixon was noted by the Washington *Post* in a news story on January 6, 1975: "The staff . . . felt obliged for political purposes to stay close to their charter and out of fund raising affairs of candidates other than Richard M. Nixon." And the *Post* quoted a former staff member as observing, "Basically, the Senators were not wild about going beyond the narrowest scope of inquiry." And for good reason. Had the committee begun looking into the illegal contributions of such companies as 3M, its work would have been endless. And it also would have struck too close to home.

Former President Johnson's name cropped up again when *The New York Times* reported on depositions and documents filed in a Washington court which chronicled the distribution of millions of dollars in Gulf Oil Corporation funds to politicians of both parties over many years. According to the *Times,* the documents showed how "a Gulf lobbyist began his career with the company by delivering $50,000 to Lyndon B. Johnson, then the Vice President." This was shortly after the 1960 election. The transaction had all the hallmarks of the kind of activity that led to the forced resignation of a future Vice President—Spiro T. Agnew.

The Gulf employee was identified as Claude C. Wild, Jr., who later became the corporation's chief lobbyist in Washington. Wild's role was disclosed to SEC investigators by Thomas D. Wright, a Pittsburgh lawyer who served as outside counsel for Gulf. Wright quoted Wild as having said that David Searls, Gulf's former general counsel, gave him $50,000 in the early 1960s to deliver to LBJ. "That was his first assignment at Gulf Oil," Wright said. "He did not know where the funds came from. And, secondly, he did not know anything about the arrangement or why these funds were being delivered."

In addition to Johnson other top political figures were also paid off by Wild. In Wright's notes of an interview with Wild there was this statement: "All Senators on Watergate except Ervin." According to Wright, "this was a reference in some way (that) Wild had assisted all of the Senators" on the Watergate Committee with the exception of Ervin. Therefore it was not surprising that when the committee called Wild to testify, the senators were only interested in hearing about the terrible arm-twisting the oil lobbyist was forced to endure from Nixon fund-raisers. Overlooked in his testimony was a sentence which most certainly sent a chill through the senators questioning him. "There is a great deal of solicitation done by the legislative branch, too," said Wild. The record then shows that neither Ervin nor any of the other senators present—Baker, Inouye, Montoya, and Weicker, all of whom were basking as fighters against evil—sought amplification of Wild's allegation. Instead Ervin changed the subject.

In March 1976 Wild was indicted for having made illegal contributions in 1973 to Senators Inouye and Sam Nunn. Previously Gulf and Wild had both pleaded guilty to having given secret funds to the campaigns of President Nixon, Senator Jackson, and Congressman Mills. Other alleged recipients of Gulf cash included Hugh Scott of Pennsylvania; Senate Finance Committee Chairman Russell B. Long, Democrat of Louisiana; Senate Ethics Committee Chairman Howard W. Cannon, Democrat of Nevada; House Majority Leader Thomas P. O'Neill of Massachusetts; Senator Humphrey; and Senator Hatfield, the latter "at the request of the Kuwait Ambassador."

At Wild's trial in July 1976 Senator Inouye's administrative assistant testified that he gave his boss $1,200 of an illegal $5,000 Gulf contribution to cover out-of-pocket expenses. He said he didn't tell Inouye where the money came from and his boss didn't ask. The transaction took place in early 1973, when Inouye was serving on the Watergate Committee. It was during that period that Inouye had warmed the hearts of TV fans everywhere when, at the conclusion of John Ehrlichman's day in the dock, the Hawaiian whispered "What a liar!" into an open microphone. At the Wild trial, under cross-examination by defense counsel, the administrative assistant admitted he had committed perjury when first questioned about the Gulf contribution by a federal grand jury on September 10, 1975. "I testified untruthfully the first time," he said, "to protect the Senator." Shades of Watergate!*

An account of how Gulf money was delivered to politicians was provided to SEC lawyers by Frederick A. Myers, who had been the corporation's "coordinator of legislation" in Washington. In a sworn deposition Myers insisted repeatedly he never knew what was in the plain white envelopes that Claude Wild had asked him to deliver to various individuals around the country. Between 1961 and 1972 Myers said he made about twenty trips. Election years were usually busy times for him. In May of 1964, for example, he flew to Oklahoma City, where he said he rented a hotel room and waited for Fred Harris, then running for the Senate. "I called him and he came to the hotel," said Myers. Harris, along with his wife and perhaps two or three other men, came to collect the envelope, he said. In 1976 Harris, a self-styled populist, unsuccessfully sought the Democratic nomination for President. One of the chief planks in his platform was the breakup of the major oil companies. Obviously if the payment was made, Harris didn't stay bought.

In all at least thirty-two senators and about two dozen members of the House were cited in court depositions as possible recipients of campaign fund largesse from Claude Wild. Several of the named recipients, such as Senators Baker and Jackson, announced they were returning the money. Others, like Senators William E. Brock and Russell Long, said they had no record of receiving Gulf money. Former Senator Fred Harris denied ever "knowingly" accepting an illegal contribution. And Humphrey, when asked to return the money, said he was consulting his lawyer.

Of course it was hardly considered likely that any of those named in the court depositions would ever be prosecuted—even if it could have been established that they had knowingly ac-

---

*On a ruling by the judge Wild was freed because the alleged illegal transaction took place outside the three-year statute of limitations.

– 384 –

cepted illegal contributions. And that's because of the statute of limitations conveniently shortened in their behalf. For this they all owed a debt of gratitude to none other than Wayne Hays, the Ohio Democrat whose dalliances with Elizabeth Ray were to cost him his extraordinary power in the House. In July 1974 Hays rammed through an amendment to the pending campaign "reform" law which, in effect, gave his colleagues-in-trouble statutory immunity from prosecution. In a secret session of his House Administration Committee, members by a show of hands voted to approve Hays's proposal to reduce the time period for prosecution from five to three years after the alleged violation. The bill was reported out and then passed by the House at a time when most media attention was concentrated on the Watergate-buffeted White House. At the same time Hays was loudly demanding that Nixon be called to account.

Thus by voting for what they proudly mislabeled "reform" legislation, the lawmakers who feared prosecution literally pardoned themselves. The outcry from the Watergate-obsessed media was minimal.*

The new law had the immediate effect of letting various prominent statesmen, including Wilbur Mills, off the hook. Another who escaped prosecution was Robert Strauss, the genial chairman of the Democratic National Committee who had admitted receiving $50,000 in illegal funds from Ashland Oil in 1970 and 1971 when he was party treasurer. Strauss conceded he may have unknowingly committed a "technical" violation of the law. He claimed he had not known that the money came from the corporate treasury. "It was clearly represented to me as individual contributions," he added. But then it turned out that Strauss had never listed the contributions and the names of the donors as required for all gifts of more than $100. Instead he reported the money as "miscellaneous" contributions, i.e., those under $100. Strauss later explained he had laundered the money because he felt Ashland Oil would not want the Nixon administration to know about the contributions. "I thought it was legal at the time," he said.

But it wasn't. And the only thing that saved Strauss from prose-

---

*Arguing that there wasn't any reason to grant "special privileges" to politicians, Henry S. Ruth, Jr., then the special prosecutor, urged Congress to repeal the three-year limitation. But when the Senate passed the Watergate Reform Act of 1976, not one senator had offered an amendment to do so.

cution was the "fix" engineered in the Democratic-controlled Congress. No wonder then that on *Meet the Press* in June 1976, following the scandals enveloping Hays, Bob Strauss said he intended to support the Ohioan's reelection bid to the House. (This of course was before Hays decided to resign from Congress.) Replying to another question, Strauss said that the DNC had not yet returned the $50,000 to Ashland Oil, though this had been demanded by some people in his party. The previous November for example Stanley Sheinbaum, a California thorn in Strauss's side, had told fellow liberals: "Republicans had their Watergate. But we—for a lousy $50,000—are not clean."

Not as lucky as Strauss was his fund-raising counterpart in the Nixon camp. Maurice H. Stans, unable to get under the umbrella of the statute of limitations, was forced to plead guilty to five misdemeanor charges of violating campaign finance laws—three for failing to make accurate reports of these transactions and two for accepting corporate contributions. He was fined $5,000.

Strauss meanwhile continued to serve as chairman of the Democratic National Committee.

23

Midway through the impeachment proceedings Nicholas von Hoffman heard a congressman utter these historic words: "We're going to impeach his ass. We're going to do it." And von Hoffman agreed that impeachment was inevitable. "We're going to do it, although nobody will quite know why.... Beyond all questions of guilt or innocence, he must be impeached because we, the Super-Bowl people, have been promised the show. We're gearing up for it emotionally the way we did when the ballyhoo built up for the Billie Jean King–Bobby Riggs match."

Von Hoffman, hardly an admirer of the President, did recognize the hypocrisy of much of the campaign being waged to drive Nixon from office.

There was the example of Senator Kennedy who, in commenting on the President's refusal to turn over certain tapes subpoenaed by the Judiciary Committee, said on May 8, 1974: "I think a fundamental part of our whole tradition is not to allow the person being investigated to set the terms of the investigation." Of course five years before, the heir to the myth had done everything possible "to set the terms of the investigation" of Chappaquiddick. He had hunkered down, hung tough, and adopted a public relations posture. He had gone on nationwide television to give his equivalent of a self-edited transcript of what had happened on Dike Bridge that terrible night. Having done all this, the senator then announced that this was the last time he would ever discuss the matter—let others wallow in Chappaquiddick. And he got away with it; the cover up continues to this day.

Meanwhile the thirty-eight members of the Judiciary Committee sat behind closed doors and listened to Doar drone out the evidence. What Doar and his staff were doing was pulling together a vast amount of material from numerous sources—the Senate Watergate Committee, the Joint Committee on Internal

Revenue Taxation, the Internal Revenue Service, grand juries, and other congressional fact-finding committees. All this information was compiled in thirty-six black loose-leaf notebooks, each dealing with such specific subjects as: the cover up, "White House Surveillance Activities," the Cambodian incursion, Nixon's taxes, the ITT settlement, the 1971 milk price support decision, and the like. Less than 10 percent of the evidence was originated by the Judiciary Committee. Which is why, in the end, Doar earned the title pinned on him by a detractor—"The World's Greatest Archivist."

Even Democratic members were appalled. "If these meetings were ever televised, the country would impeach us," said one. "This isn't an investigation; it's a compilation," said another. And the Republicans agreed. "Damned dull!" said Robert McClory of Illinois.

When the executive sessions were finally over, Bill Greider reported in the Washington *Post* on July 22, 1974, that "even the most bullish Democrats conceded that their investigation did not produce a thunderous concensus that Mr. Nixon should be removed from office, the kind of compelling bipartisan agreement which would remove all doubt about the outcome."

Congressman McClory put it this way, "I kept waiting for the bombshell to appear, and it never appeared." Even Democrats agreed that not one piece of evidence had been produced—no "hand in the cookie jar" or "smoking gun"—which would show conclusively that the President was guilty of a crime, or at least a broader "impeachable offense." The impeachment forces were worried. Some worried out loud. As Ed Mezvinsky said somewhat incoherently, "This is it, this is the crunch. When we pull the package together. Are we equipped to do it? Can we pull it off? That's the question now. I'm very concerned about that."

But seeking new material would have meant the calling of witnesses; and this Rodino and company wanted to avoid at all costs. Thus none of the principal Watergate figures were interrogated by Doar or by the President's lawyer, James St. Clair. The reason was the need for haste. As John Pierson, in a *Wall Street Journal* analysis of the impeachment hearings, put it following the Nixon resignation: "The Committee didn't take more time to probe and think because the House Democratic leadership buckled under to public impatience with Watergate and to legitimate fears that a Senate trial might slop over into 1975, thus raising awkward questions about the new Congress' right to try someone the old Congress had impeached." But time could have been found. For one thing the committee could have hired more staff people and the members themselves could have worked harder. But most of the members—at least on the Democratic side— were opposed to heavier schedules. After all, their minds had been made up even before the hearings had begun. And they made no secret of their peculiar concept of justice.

The failure to do more original digging drew the fire of Charles Wiggins, the California Republican who brilliantly argued Nixon's case during the public debate. Along with Charles Sandman of New Jersey, Wiggins had been among the minority of Republicans who had voted against the unseating of Adam Clayton Powell as a member of the House. Concerning Doar's presentation, Wiggins said, "It wasn't a careful and thorough presentation of the facts. We would have had great difficulty in proving the case in the Senate. You don't start your case there by calling a transcript. You have to call witnesses."

In all of this the President's rights were being constantly violated. Fairness went by the board. As Pierson noted, "The Committee should have worried less about public relations and more about assuring due process to Mr. Nixon." Pierson incidentally could hardly be described as a Nixon apologist. He had written some tough critiques of presidential policies. And as a result the *Wall Street Journal* correspondent found himself on one of the idiotic enemy lists aimed at preventing him from being invited to any White House social affair. Which is what makes his analysis even more crucial for a proper understanding of the committee's rush to judgment.

As an example of how fairness was sacrificed to public relations, Pierson wrote: "Having heard ten weeks of evidence behind closed doors—primarily to avoid partisan bickering but also to protect the rights of Watergate defendants awaiting trial, innocent third parties and Mr. Nixon himself—the panel then did an about face and released almost all its closed-door testimony." And then, in the week between the end of the hearings and the start of the televised debate, the members weren't even given time to think about the meaning of the mass of data presented them. Instead Doar and company devoted most of that time to selling their own particular theories of the case. In this Doar was also assisted by the supposed minority counsel, Al Jenner, to the deep annoyance of even liberal Republicans. The result was that they voted to get rid of him. But Jenner refused to take a hint and go home. He remained with the committee, working directly for Doar. He insisted on remaining for the kill.

The committee's rush "directly from testimony to tube" was deplored by James Mann, the South Carolina Democrat who voted for impeachment. What he had wanted was for his colleagues to "draw our chairs into a circle" and reason together "in a thoughtful, deliberative atmosphere." But, as he said later, the committee "just sat there watching the trees march by for ten weeks and then didn't even discuss what they meant."

Of such was the highly hoked-up TV impeachment spectacular composed. "The suspicion lingers," wrote Pierson, "that . . . the Democratic majority was less intent on schooling the public about impeachment than on swaying the public toward a certain conclusion and in putting public pressure on wavering Republicans and Southern Democrats. Was the case against Richard Nixon so weak that resort had to be made to such tricks? It wasn't. And the tricks only served to cheapen somewhat an otherwise sound process."

"Getting" Nixon was the name of the game. When Doar finally dropped his mask of impartiality and stood as a self-appointed Torquemada, Rodino said proudly, "When I hired him, I always knew he eventually would do this." Since Rodino had been playing the role of a serious, fair-minded man to the hilt, this was a bone-headed thing for him to have said. But stumbling was habitual with the chairman. On June 27, 1974, in what he apparently thought to be an off-the-record session in his office, Rodino told three journalists—Jack Nelson and Paul Huston of the Los Angeles *Times* and Sam Donaldson of ABC—that he believed all twenty-one of the committee's Democrats "will vote impeachment and if five Republicans also vote for it, the full House will follow suit." When the story was published, administration spokesmen including Vice President Ford cried "partisan lynch-mob."

Rodino's reaction was as predictable. He raced to the floor. "I want to state unequivocally and categorically that this statement is not true," he said. "There is no basis in fact for it, none whatsoever." Since the three newsmen stuck by their guns, nobody really believed Rodino. The episode was soon forgotten in the rush of events. Still, as William Safire observed, though the main focus had been on Rodino's prejudgment of the case, the episode went to what presumably was the heart of Watergate: "The apparent willingness of politicians, when caught in embarrassing 'situations,' to cover up their blunders with obvious, 'categorical' lies." And lying, in the post-Watergate morality, was a crime only when indulged in by Nixon officials.

But Rodino's undiplomatic comment did point up the partisan nature of a body which ostensibly was proceeding in a judicious manner. Another example of political bias came when the committee's Democrats—all twenty-one of them—voted against issuing a subpoena to obtain the records of dairy contributions to House members before April 7, 1972, when the public reporting law for such contributions took effect. The Republicans—all seventeen of them—voted in favor. Iowa Republican Wiley Mayne said that since the committee was investigating whether Nixon had raised milk price supports in exchange for a campaign contribution, it had the duty of examining dairy contributions to House members or lay itself open to criticism for setting a double standard and a "cover up." But Rodino contended that the committee had no authority to make such an inquiry. All of which led White House spokesman Ken Clawson to maintain that this meant that the Democrats did not want to be judged by the same standards to which they would subject the President.

Then suddenly the milk issue evaporated as a possible impeachable offense, as did other matters which for many long months had made big, black headlines—the bombing of Cambodia, ITT, illegal corporate contributions, public expenditures on San Clemente and Key Biscayne, impoundment, the President's taxes. The reason why most of the committee members agreed to drop them was explained by Hamilton Fish. "Many Congressmen had received illegal corporate contributions," said the New York Republican. "The milk thing was out because sixteen members of the Committee had received money from the milk trusts. The President had lied to us about Cambodia, but we couldn't shoulder him with responsibility for a war many Congressmen had supported. And it was hard to show any direct quid pro quo on ITT. . . ."

In other words, in terms of impeachment all these various allegations added up to nothing. But not before they had done grave damage to Nixon. For they had most certainly been used by his critics and particularly by the media to fuel the atmosphere of crisis. Now suddenly they were gone. "We went fishing," Harold Froehlich, the Wisconsin Republican who voted for impeachment, told Greider. "And we played every issue we could for whatever it was worth. Part of it was creating an atmosphere for impeachment." In other words all the issues were used to provide thunder-and-lightning—if no rain.

A good example was the insistence of such Democrats as Mezvinsky that the President's alleged income tax dodges be discussed, even though there was no likelihood that the subject would make its way into an article of impeachment. With Rodino's blessing the subject was brought up on prime-time television, thus assuring a maximum audience for all kinds of unsubstantiated allegations. This aroused the ire of Charles Sandman, who turned his scorn on his Democratic colleagues. "This bunch of baloney was supposed to have been taken up in the afternoon but it's taken up tonight because there's a larger audience." On one tax issue, the one involving the First Lady's use of Air Force One on her travels, Sandman noted correctly that the matter had never been brought up when Jackie Kennedy and Lady Bird Johnson were flying around at government expense. And even Railsback of Illinois, a moderate Republican who favored impeachment, accused the committee of "overkill" and "impeachmentitus." Not all of the media was entranced by the committee's performance either. James Reston admittedly was in a dissenting minority of commentators when he sourly accused its members of "making recitations before the TV cameras," adding that the whole exercise produced "bad law and boring television."

Most of the press however was of a different mind. So much so that Alabama Democrat Walter Flowers, a pro-impeachment vote, felt compelled to tell reporters: "I simply ask that each of you look inward and decide for yourself if each of you has treated fairly with the President. I feel the perspective of Middle America has not received equal time from you."

Remarkably *The Village Voice* thought Flowers could be right, pointing out that

reporters regularly snicker at Presidential defenders, and act as p.r. agents for "agonizing," "anguished," "courageous" Republicans who vote against Nixon. No one bothers to point out how slovenly and vague the original Committee's staff's draft articles for impeachment were, few point out how little real investigation the Committee did, how suppositional and circumstantial much of the Doar case is. Stupid Republicans are ridiculed. Slow-witted Democrats like Joshua Eilberg (who claims that Nixon throwing an ashtray across a room at Key Biscayne after learning of Watergate is proof positive of guilty prior knowledge) escaped well deserved ridicule.

Some idea of the atmosphere inside the hearing room was also provided by the *Voice* correspondent. He reported that two reporters who hadn't seen each other for some time had met for what to them must have been a joyous occasion.

"This is like the McGovern campaign," one said.

"It is the McGovern campaign," the other replied. "He just peaked too late."

Or as Richard Reeves reported in *New York*, "You only had to spend five minutes in Rayburn House Office Building 2101, the press room, to know that it was us against them—and 'them' is Nixon and the boys still on the burning deck."

But it wasn't all easy sailing for the impeachment forces. The Nixon loyalists mounted a campaign demanding "specificity"— that is, dates, times, and events to support each and every allegation in the first article of impeachment. The article accused Nixon of having violated his constitutional oath in having "prevented, obstructed and impeded the administration of justice, in that . . . using the powers of his high office, engaged personally and through his subordinates and agents, in a course of action or plan designed to delay, impede, and obstruct the investigation of (the Watergate break-in); to cover up, conceal and protect those responsible; and to conceal the existence and scope of other unlawful covert activities. . . . In all of this, Richard M. Nixon has acted in a manner contrary to his trust as President and subversive of constitutional government, to the great prejudice of the cause of law and justice and to the manifest injury of the people of the United States. Wherefore, Richard M. Nixon, by such conduct, warrants impeachment and trial, and removal from office."

It was Charles Wiggins who took the lead in attacking Article I, which had become known as the "Sarbanes substitute," because Maryland Democrat Paul S. Sarbanes had a major hand in drafting it.

WIGGINS: Now, the heart of this matter is that the President made it his policy to obstruct justice and to interfere with investigations. Would you please explain to this member of the committee and to the other members, when, and in what respect, and how did the President declare that policy? And I wish the gentleman would be rather specific, since it is the heart of the allegation.

SARBANES: Well, of course, the means by which this policy has been done are the ones that are set out subsequent to the second paragraph.

WIGGINS: If the gentleman could confine himself to the question, when was the policy declared?

SARBANES: . . . Well, the policy relates back to June 17, 1972, and prior thereto, agents of the committee committed illegal entry, and it then goes on and says subsequent thereto, Richard M. Nixon, using the powers of his high office, made it his policy, and in furtherance of such policy did act directly—

WIGGINS: I can read the article, but I think it is rather important to all of us that we know from you, as the author of the article, exactly when this policy was declared, and I hope you will tell us.

But Sarbanes was unable to do so. And this was due, as *The Village Voice* noted, "to the staff's failure to prepare the Democratic majority with the specifics it did have." Then Sandman took over, hitting hard at his Democratic opponents and nearly toppling their defenses.

SANDMAN: Do you not believe that under the due-process clause of the Constitution that [sic] every individual, including the President, is entitled to due notice of what he is charged for? Do you believe that?

SARBANES: I think this article does provide due notice.

SANDMAN: You are not answering my question.

SARBANES: Well, I think I am answering your question.

SANDMAN: Well, let me ask you this, then. As I see this, you have about twenty different charges here, all on one piece of paper, and not one of them specific. . . . How does he answer such a charge? This is not due process. Due process—

SARBANES: I would point out to the gentleman from New Jersey that the President's counsel entered this committee room at the very moment that members of this committee entered the room and began to receive the presentation of information, and that he stayed in the room—

SANDMAN: I do not yield any further.

SARBANES:—Throughout that process.

SANDMAN: I do not yield any further for those kinds of speeches. I want answers, and this is what I am entitled to. This is a charge against the President of the United States, why he should be tried to be thrown out of office, and that is what it

- 394 -

is for. For him to be duly noticed of what you are charging him, in my judgment, he is entitled to know specifically what he did wrong, and how does he gather that from what you say here?

Still other Republicans joined the counterattack, demanding "specificity" from the President's accusers. Said Del Latta: "A common jaywalker charged with jaywalking any place in the United States is entitled to know when and where the alleged offense is supposed to have occurred. Is the President of the United States entitled to less?" The impeachment spokesmen had no ready replies. They were being completely routed under the glare of the television lights. Some tried to fight back with the argument that the problem was they had too much evidence, not too little. "Isn't it amazing?" Sandman hit back. "They are willing to do anything except make these articles specific. It is the same old story, you know, when you don't have the law on your side, you talk about the facts. If you don't have the facts on your side, you just talk, and that is what a lot of people have been doing today."

But it was all too late. Under pressure of a media which had suddenly discovered their "anguish" and "courage," six of the more liberal Republicans broke ranks to vote with all the Democrats in favor of Article I. The vote to impeach for obstructing justice was 27 to 11. And though it was generally applauded, there were voices of dissent. One was that of the Washington correspondent of *Le Figaro*, France's leading newspaper. According to Jacques Jacquet-Francillon, "the eleven faithful Republicans who vainly pleaded the President's cause during the last four days before the Judiciary Committee" had underlined "that none of the points of Article I approved by the majority is really backed by precise facts. . . . They are denying Nixon the most elementary right of any accused man: to know precisely for what he will have to defend himself." And earlier in the week, the London *Daily Express* said the televised debate was "a political version of Peyton Place, a continuing story played up, or hammed up, by politicians chasing the limelight and using every twist and turn of the sad, messy saga for their own ends." At the same time the London *Daily Mail* accused some sections of the American media of "lynch-mob behavior."

On Article II, which concerned allegations of abuses of power, the vote was 28 to 10. Article III had less support. By a vote of 21 to 17 the President was to be summoned to trial for defying the committee's subpoenas.

But the real blows to Nixon's cause came from elsewhere. One of his top aides, John Ehrlichman, was convicted in the Ellsberg break-in case. Had he been found innocent, that would have bolstered Nixon's case enormously. Instead when a jury in Watergate-obsessed Washington found Ehrlichman guilty, a lot of people appeared to transfer his guilt to the President. And even while the committee was debating the articles of impeachment came another sledgehammer blow: John B. Connally, who had been Secretary of the Treasury and the man Nixon had hoped would succeed him as President, was indicted by the grand jury. The charge was taking a $10,000 bribe from the dairy interests. And its disclosure also had a profound effect on the impeachment proceedings.*

The major accusations against the President, as contained in Articles I and II, were framed in very broad and general terms. For one thing it was difficult to determine the precise extent to which he was being held to blame for his own actions rather than those of his subordinates. Moreover many of the conclusions reached by the committee were based largely on hearsay, guilt by association, suspicion, and opinion hung together with free-wheeling inferences. As editor C. L. Dancey observed in the Peoria *Journal-Star*, "The hard evidence isn't there that actually links the President as a participant in illegal acts. You have to juggle it around in a pretty complicated manner to weave him into something in some way *connected* to some illegal act. What *evidence* does exist offers clues, only, that have to be interpreted and manipulated and which can be interpreted, therefore, in different ways." In other words the charges were not spelled out with the "specificity" or the detail which would have been required, say, in any ordinary indictment. In addition much of the case against the President appeared to be based on testimony given to grand juries and legislative investigators who, in turn, had never sought to resolve various contradictions of fact or challenge surmises, of which there was a superfluity. One thing

---

*Eventually a District of Columbia jury voted to acquit Connally, who had produced a dazzling array of character witnesses to testify that he was a man of "honor and integrity." The witnesses, mostly Democrats, included Congresswoman Barbara Jordan, Lady Bird Johnson, Robert McNamara, Democratic Chairman Bob Strauss, and former Secretary of State Dean Rusk.

was certain: Doar and company simply were not interested in obtaining exculpatory material of any kind, a fact made obvious by their reluctance to call major witnesses who could be subjected to cross-examination on past statements and assertions.*

Instead the committee unloaded a mountain of material, the sheer weight of which was bound to have an effect, for it consisted mainly of a one-sided presentation of information taken from previous investigations, deliberately slanted to make President Nixon appear to be evil incarnate. All of which, to a few observers at least, seemed a bit much. As Crosby S. Noyes put it in the Washington *Star:* "It is hard to avoid the impression that if a truly evil man set out consciously to abuse the formidable powers of the presidency, he would have raised a great deal more hell than Nixon has managed to do and would have been a great deal harder to stop." And it could also have been argued that the impeachment charges involving the alleged misuse of government agencies—the FBI, CIA, IRS, and the like—could just as readily have been brought against almost every President from Franklin Roosevelt on, and most particularly against John Kennedy and Lyndon Johnson.

Of course this was no time for reason. Few really cared what was contained in the articles. A bandwagon psychology had gripped Washington and the move toward impeachment was feeding on its own momentum. The media was in a frenzy. The Nixon-haters, who had seized on Watergate as lifeblood, smelled victory in the offing. They were finally going to "get" the man who had so galled them with his big win in 1972. All eyes were trained on the embattled White House.

After the deed was done, after Nixon raised his arms in the familiar double victory sign, stepped into the helicopter, and disappeared into the sky, Congressman Conyers told an interviewer: "But for the tapes, there would never have been an impeachment. Richard Nixon literally caused himself to be impeached."**

---

*For a reasoned but devastating critique of the articles of impeachment, see the minority views expressed in the *Report on the Impeachment of Richard M. Nixon, President of the United States* of the Judiciary Committee, as published August 22, 1974, in the *Congressional Record,* pp. H-9059 to H-9101. These were the views of Messrs. Hutchinson, Smith, Sandman, Wiggins, Dennis, Mayne, Lott, Moorhead, Maraziti, and Latta.
**As it turned out, neither the House of Representatives nor the United States Senate had the opportunity to vote on impeachment.

And Leon Jaworski agreed. Interviewed shortly after the President's resignation, the Watergate special prosecutor said that had it not been for the tapes, "Mr. Nixon would still be in the White House."

Then why, if he had been engaged in a conspiracy to obstruct justice, as alleged in Article I, had he turned over the tapes which led to his downfall? Why hadn't he gone ahead and obstructed justice? Why, at the very beginning, hadn't he taken all the tapes and put the torch to them on the White House lawn—as John Connally and Pat Buchanan, among others, had recommended? These are questions historians are going to be asking themselves. And their answers may well be different from those of most observers in recent years. For say what you will about Nixon, the preservation of the tapes was hardly the act of a man who knew in his heart he was guilty of crimes. Of course there is the argument that, being too lawyerly and believing in the law, Nixon didn't have the heart to destroy evidence. The problem with this theory, as Nicholas von Hoffman has noted, is that it runs counter to "the utterly shameless devil-man hypothesis," as propounded by many Nixon-baiters. Therefore, as von Hoffman pursued the subject, "if Richard Nixon is not purely evil, the question of why and how he was removed ceases to be an unalloyed struggle between the forces of darkness and light." In other words not all the Good Guys were necessarily "good" or the Bad Guys necessarily "bad." Human frailties were more than abundant on both sides.

By this time the dwindling Nixon forces were in disarray, unable to stem the irreversible tide. They could take faint comfort in some of the praise accorded Nixon by avowed enemies. Thus prior to the resignation Philip L. Geyelin, editorial page editor of the Washington *Post,* had this to say in a speech before (of all places) the Women's National Democratic Club:

"The supreme irony of it is that there is in fact much to be said for the Nixon foreign policy—it has *worked* in some instances rather conspicuously well. You can argue that the evolution with China was coming anyway; but President Nixon made it happen, at a political risk which a Democratic President might not have been willing to take. You can argue that we should have gotten out of Vietnam much faster than we did—that it cost us as much under Nixon in lives and treasure, while getting out, as it did for Lyndon Johnson to get us in. But Johnson and preceding Presidents did get us in. Nixon did get us out. The same thing may be said for the Mid-east. President Nixon's celebrated structure for peace didn't save Israel from its fourth war with the Arabs—and its costliest. But you can argue that there had to be that war and that cruel near-defeat of Israel—that plain showing of Arab military capability—before you could negotiate today's disengagement, and open up the first genuine opportunity for honest negotiations toward a lasting settlement. We had also to create with considerable skill and effort the breakthrough with the Arabs in general and Egypt in particular that made the trip possible. And Nixon and Kissinger did it."

Few of the critics were as objective in their appraisals of Nixon's undoubted achievements. And most of them roared with disapproval when a compassionate Gerald Ford pardoned his predecessor. Dr. Hunter S. Thompson of *Rolling Stone* was jolted out of a sweat-soaked coma that black Sunday by a frantic telephone call from Dick Tuck. "Ford *pardoned* the bastard!" the trickster screamed. "I warned you, didn't I? I buried him twice, and he came back from the dead both times. . . . Now he's done it again; he's running around loose on some private golf course in Palm Desert." The hysteria spread across the land. There were cries of "sellout" and "a deal." The integrity of the new President was called into question. Once again Washington was out of joint. Shades of the Inquisition and Oliver Cromwell. The witch-hunters were at it again, filling the air with righteousness and virtuous declamation.

"The tone of this attack," wrote Richard Wilson,

> clearly seeks to establish the historical base that Nixon's offenses were so enormous that they threatened the continuance of free government, for which he should have been made to pay by public trial, conviction and sentence to prison even if he never served a day.
>
> More mature consideration may focus on the hysterical exaggeration of such conclusions, taking into consideration that the chief impeachable offense, Article I of the Bill of Impeachment, grew from a ludicrous act about which Nixon knew nothing in advance . . .

The cry for the last drop of blood continued even when it became known that the former President was suffering from a flareup of his phlebitis. Much of the media expressed doubt about the illness, implying it was all a ruse designed to keep Nixon from testifying in Sirica's courtroom. There was the cartoon by Oliphant, for example, showing Nixon propped up under a veranda, faithful dog King Timahoe by his side. Nixon was pictured telling his doctor that his condition was aggravated by his inability to get his tapes and records from Washington, and could he write him a prescription? The omnipresent Punk the Penguin, in an aside, says, "Somebody tell him he has the wrong foot up."

Even when Nixon was rushed to the hospital for an emergency operation on his leg, few of his critics could summon compassion. Some, in fact, hoped for the worst. "I don't care if Nixon dies," a PBS commentator muttered. "If he does, I hope he twists slowly in the wind as he goes." And it galled the humanitarians of the left that President Ford would ignore the potential political damage to visit Nixon's bedside and wish him well. Also annoying was the mountain of letters and telegrams, mostly from ordinary citizens, which descended on San Clemente. Then there were the phone messages with "get well" wishes from Kissinger; Secretary of the Treasury Simon; Betty Ford; the shah and empress of Iran; Chinese Premier Chou En-lai; former prime minister of Japan, Nobusuke Kishi; Romanian President Nicolae Ceausescu; and—perhaps more significantly—scores of returned prisoners of war released the previous year from Hanoi prisons. For these former PWs felt that if it hadn't been for Nixon they would still be languishing in North Vietnam.

Nixon of course came out of the hospital, ready to use his unquestioned talents not only to rehabilitate himself but to encourage the nascent belief that he was, indeed, hounded out of office by cruel and implacable foes who had no regard for the long-range interests of the nation. Which is why his enemies let loose a barrage of ferocious comments when he signed to write his memoirs and to respond to questions from David Frost in exclusive television interviews. The paranoid fear that Nixon might rise from the ashes, first voiced by Dick Tuck, began to haunt his critics.

When the long-awaited report of the Watergate special prosecutor finally was issued in October 1975, its several hundred pages also proved to be a downer for the critics who had been hoping for new revelations about the dark doings of the Nixon administration. "If the report evokes a sense of disappointment," commented *The New York Times*, somewhat balefully, "it is because the Special Prosecutor evidently saw no fruitful way of reaching the end of the trail."

But that's precisely what did happen. The outgoing prosecutor, Henry Ruth, had indeed come to the end of the trail and found that most of the Watergate-related issues, though sensationally damning when they had appeared in the headlines, had come to nothing. Thus at the end the special prosecutor had to acknowledge that he and his staff could come up with no new bombshells and that, in fact, the old bombshells had proved to be duds.

And the biggest dud of all was the case of Bebe Rebozo, whose only "crime," as it turned out, was his close friendship with the former President. After two years of well-publicized investigations by the Senate Watergate Committee, the Internal Revenue Service, assorted gumshoes of the media, and the Watergate Special Prosecution Force itself, Henry Ruth was forced to concede that there was no evidence of wrongdoing by Rebozo. In all the various federal investigations into Rebozo's affairs cost the American taxpayer a minimum of $3 million.

On issue after issue, allegation after allegation, the special prosecutor reported that after intensive investigations he and his staff could come up with no evidence that would warrant action in the courts. Thus "although a large number of allegations about possible misuses of the IRS were investigated"—including the alleged efforts to influence the agency to audit various political "enemies"—the prosecutor reported that nothing was uncovered that could have resulted in criminal charges. About White House-ordered wiretaps directed at a number of government officials and newsmen, the prosecutor found most of them to be justified within the law. As for two questionable taps, there was "insufficient evidence to bring criminal charges." Nixon and his lawyers moreover were not shown to have been guilty of fraud in connection with the former President's tax returns. And so on and so forth.

Thanks largely to a media lusting for blood, all of these issues and allegations had been used to inflame the atmosphere of Nixon's final days and facilitate his removal from office. Yet, as the special prosecutor's report made clear, none of them amounted to very much. And with the passage of time even Nixon's guilt in the so-called obstruction of justice charge as contained in Article I of the Bill of Impeachment was coming under skeptical examination. As for the White House tapes of June 23, 1972, the disclosure of which prompted Nixon's departure from Washington, those "smoking gun" transcripts are subject to varying interpretations regarding motive, context, knowledge of fact on the part of the participants, and even exactly what the conversation was all about.

What did happen that fateful day of June 23, 1972—six days after the bungled burglary at the Watergate? A preoccupied President was scheduled to take off later that Friday for a weekend at Camp David. He was tired and he wanted a few days of solitude to think about the forthcoming Republican Convention as well as the campaign itself. But first there were a number of chores to be taken care of. And his chief of staff, Haldeman, usual notebook in hand, began to enumerate them. The time was shortly after 10:00 A.M.; the place the Oval Office.

The conversation was rambling, jumping from subject to subject. According to the transcript,* much of which is garbled with "unintelligibles," it began with a reference to photography.

PRESIDENT: (Unintelligible) . . . they've got a magnificent place—
HALDEMAN: No, they don't. See, that was all hand-held cameras without lighting—lousy place. It's good in content, it's terrible in film quality.
PRESIDENT: (Unintelligible) Rose, she ought to be in here.
HALDEMAN: No, we'll let her in if you want to, sure—
PRESIDENT: That's right. Got so goddamned much (scratching noises).
HALDEMAN: Goddamned.
PRESIDENT: I understand, I just thought (unintelligible). The one thing they haven't got in there is the thing we mentioned with regard to the armed services.
HALDEMAN: I covered that with Ehrlichman who says that can be done and he's moving. Not only armed services, but the whole government.
PRESIDENT: GSA? All government?
HALDEMAN: All government procurement, yeah. And, I talked to John about that and he thought that was a good idea. So Henry [Kissinger] gets back at 3:45.
PRESIDENT: I told Haig today that I'd see [State Secretary] Rogers at 4:30.
HALDEMAN: Oh, good, O.K.
PRESIDENT: Well, if he gets back at 3:45, he won't be here until 4:00 or 4:30.
HALDEMAN: It'll be a little after 4:00 (unintelligible) 5:00.
PRESIDENT: Well, I have to, I'm supposed to go to Camp David. Rogers doesn't need a lot of time, does he?

---

*Transcript released by the White House, August 5, 1974.

HALDEMAN: No sir.

PRESIDENT: Just a picture?

HALDEMAN: That's all. He called me about it yesterday afternoon and said I don't want to be in the meeting with Henry. I understand that but there may be a couple of points Henry wants me to be aware of.

PRESIDENT: Sure. (Unintelligible) call him and tell him we'll call him as soon as Henry gets here, between 4:30 and 5:00 (unintelligible). Good.

HALDEMAN: O.K., that's fine.

And then without pausing for breath—"his voice flat, unconcerned, familiar, curiously disengaged, filled with Bob Newhart upward inflections," according to a reporter who heard the tape in court—Haldeman brought up a subject, the disclosure of which two years later was to lead to the toppling of a President. The background was this. By June 23 the FBI had been conducting a week-long investigation of the break-in. The Bureau was leaning to the notion that, considering the number of former personnel involved, the whole affair might have been a "CIA operation." Or so Acting Director Gray had informed Dean the night before. Haldeman in turn had learned this, and more, from Dean before he went in to see the President.

As of that moment neither Haldeman nor the President had any real knowledge of the events leading up to the break-in. And, if we are to believe Haldeman, they didn't particularly want to know. Which, in retrospect, probably was Nixon's major blunder. "Our greatest mistake," wrote Haldeman in June 1976,

> was in not getting ahead of the game at the outset, finding out who were culpable and bringing them to justice. The President and I, together with John Ehrlichman, never quite made enough tough moves. We were all afraid to find out. Afraid that what we suspected might be the case, would, in fact, turn out to be the case —that it went very high up, to Jeb Magruder and even to John Mitchell. . . . It is significant, however, that despite all the investigations and revelations, Mitchell has never been indicted in connection with the break-in.

And as the record also shows, it was not until March 21, 1973, when Dean, saying, "I have the impression that you don't know everything I know," told the President everything he knew about the origins of Watergate.

But on June 23, 1972, what did concern the President and his chief of staff was not Watergate as such, but the sources of campaign contributions. The FBI was then closing in on the money sources and both Haldeman and Nixon clearly wanted to side-track the investigation. In their eyes it would have been embarrassing for major contributors who had been promised anonymity.

One such contributor was Dwayne Andreas, a longtime Humphrey supporter who figured the senator had no chance of being nominated that year and therefore preferred Nixon to McGovern. On April 5, 1972, Andreas had called Ken Dahlberg, a Nixon fund-raiser in the Midwest, to tell him he wanted to contribute $25,000 in cash. And he wanted to turn the money over before April 7, the legal cutoff date for contributions which did not have to be publicly reported. Andreas, who then was in Florida, suggested that Dahlberg fly in to pick up the money. While awaiting Dahlberg's arrival, Andreas placed the cash in a safe deposit box at his hotel. When Dahlberg finally arrived on the night of April 7, the hotel's vaults were closed. The next day Andreas handed the money over on the golf course. And because he didn't want to carry all that cash with him, Dahlberg had a cashier's check made out to himself at a bank in Boca Raton. It was dated April 9.

Two days later Dahlberg gave the check to Maurice Stans, Nixon's finance chairman, in Washington. Stans in turn handed the check over to Hugh Sloan, treasurer of the finance committee. Sloan said he would check with the committee's counsel on how to handle the check as well as four Mexican checks totaling $89,000 which had come from Texas donors who had also wished to remain anonymous by contributing before April 7—the deadline before new reporting requirements took effect. The counsel, G. Gordon Liddy, said there would be no problem. After consulting with Howard Hunt, Liddy flew to Miami where he gave the checks to Bernard Barker, who then deposited them to the account of his real estate firm. Then, in a period of three weeks, Barker withdrew $114,000 in cash. Liddy in turn handed it back to Sloan—minus $2,500 for "expenses."

All of which was on the minds of Maurice Stans and John Mitchell when Dean met with them on June 21, 1972. Of that meeting Dean later told the Ervin hearings, "Stans was concerned about the Dahlberg check. I was informed because it was in fact a contribution from Mr. Dwayne Andreas, whom I did not know, but I was told was a long-time backer of Senator Hubert Humphrey. Neither Stans nor Mitchell wanted Mr. Andreas to be embarrassed by disclosure of the [$25,000] contribution." And, as he later testified at the cover-up trial, Haldeman was fully aware on June 23, 1972, when he saw the President, that the $25,000 was from Andreas. "The understanding I had that morning was that there was concern reported to me by Mr. Dean on the part of the people at the Re-election Committee that the FBI investigation was in fact going to uncover the fact that Mr. Andreas, through Mr. Dahlberg, had given $25,000."

This then was the background for the crucial portions of the "smoking gun" tape.

HALDEMAN: Now, on the investigation, you know the Democratic break-in thing, we're back in the problem area because the FBI is not under control, because Gray doesn't exactly know how to control it and they have—their investigation is now leading into some productive areas—because they've been able to trace the money—not through the money itself—but through the bank sources—the banker. And, and it goes in some directions we don't want it to go. Ah, also there have been some things—like an informant came in off the street to the FBI in Miami who was a photographer or has a friend who is a photographer who developed some films through this guy Barker and the films had pictures of Democratic National Committee letterhead documents and things. So it's things like that that are filtering in. Mitchell came up with yesterday, and John Dean analyzed very carefully last night and concludes, concurs now with Mitchell's recommendation that the only way to solve this, and we're set up beautifully to do it, ah, in that and that—the only network that paid any attention to it last night was NBC—they did a massive story on the Cuban thing.

PRESIDENT: That's right.

HALDEMAN: That the way to handle this now is for us to have Walters call Pat Gray and just say, "Stay to hell out of this— this is ah, business here we don't want you to go any further on it." That's not an unusual development, and ah, that would take care of it.

PRESIDENT: What about Pat Gray—you mean Pat Gray doesn't want to?

HALDEMAN: Pat does want to. He doesn't know how to, and he doesn't have, he doesn't have any basis for doing it. Given this, he will then have the basis. He'll call [Associate Director] Mark Felt in, and the two of them—and Mark Felt wants to cooperate because he's ambitious—

PRESIDENT: Yeah.

HALDEMAN: He'll call him in and say, "We've got the signal from across the river to put the hold on this." And that will fit rather well because the FBI agents who are working the case, at this point, feel that's what it is.

PRESIDENT: This is CIA? They've traced the money? Who'd they trace it to?

HALDEMAN: Well they've traced it to a name, but they haven't gotten to the guy yet.

PRESIDENT: Would it be somebody here?

HALDEMAN: Ken Dahlberg.

PRESIDENT: Who the hell is Ken Dahlberg?

HALDEMAN: He gave $25,000 in Minnesota and, ah, the check went directly to this guy Barker.

PRESIDENT: It isn't from the committee, though, from Stans?

HALDEMAN: Yeah. It is. It's directly traceable and there's some more through some Texas people that went to the Mexican Bank which can also be traced to the Mexican Bank—they'll get their names today—and (pause)—

PRESIDENT: Well, I mean, there's no way—I'm just thinking if they don't cooperate, what do they say? That they were approached by the Cubans. That's what Dahlberg has to say, the Texans too, that they—

HALDEMAN: Well, if they will. But then we're relying on more and more people all the time. That's the problem and they'll stop if we could take this other route.

PRESIDENT: All right.

HALDEMAN: And you seem to think the thing to do is get them to stop?

PRESIDENT: Right, fine.

HALDEMAN: They say the only way to do that is from White House instructions. And it's got to be to Helms and to—ah, what's his name—? Walters.

PRESIDENT: [Deputy CIA Director Vernon] Walters.

HALDEMAN: And the proposal would be that Ehrlichman and I call them in, and say, ah—

PRESIDENT: All right, fine. How do you call him in—I mean you just—well, we protected Helms from one hell of a lot of things.

HALDEMAN: That's what Ehrlichman says.

PRESIDENT: Of course, this Hunt, that will uncover a lot of things. You open that scab there's a hell of a lot of things and we just feel that it would be very detrimental to have this thing go any further. This involves these Cubans, Hunt and a lot of hanky-panky that we have nothing to do with ourselves. Well what the hell, did Mitchell know about this?

HALDEMAN: I think so, I don't think he knew the details, but I think he knew.

PRESIDENT: He didn't know how it was going to be handled though—with Dahlberg and the Texans and so forth? Well who was the asshole that did? Is it Liddy? Is that the fellow? He must be a little nuts.

HALDEMAN: He is.

PRESIDENT: I mean he just isn't well screwed on is he? Is that the problem?

HALDEMAN: No, but he was under pressure, apparently, to get more information and as he got more pressure, he pushed the people harder to move harder—

PRESIDENT: Pressure from Mitchell?

HALDEMAN: Apparently.

PRESIDENT: Oh, Mitchell—Mitchell was at the point (unintelligible).

HALDEMAN: Yea.

PRESIDENT: All right, fine, I understand it all. We won't second-guess Mitchell and the rest. Thank God it wasn't Colson.

HALDEMAN: The FBI interviewed Colson yesterday. They determined that would be a good thing to do. To have him take an interrogation, which he did, and that—the FBI guys working the case concluded that there were one or two possibilities—one, that this is a White House—they don't think that there is anything at the election committee—they think it was either a White House operation and they had some obscure reasons for it—nonpolitical, or it was a Cuban and the CIA. And after their interrogation of Colson yesterday, they concluded it was not the White House, but are now convinced it is a CIA thing, so the CIA turnoff would—

PRESIDENT: Well, not sure of their analysis, I'm not going to get that involved. I'm (unintelligible).

HALDEMAN: No, sir, we don't want you to.

PRESIDENT: You call them in.

HALDEMAN: Good deal.

PRESIDENT: Play it tough. That's the way they play it and that's the way we are going to play it.

HALDEMAN: O.K.

PRESIDENT: When I saw that news summary, I questioned whether it's a bunch of crap, I thought, er, well it's good to have them off us awhile, because when they start bugging us, which they have, our little boys will not know how to handle it. I hope they will though.

HALDEMAN: You never know.

PRESIDENT: Good.

HALDEMAN: [Protocol chief Emil] Mosbacher has resigned.

PRESIDENT: Oh yeah?

HALDEMAN: As we expected he would.

PRESIDENT: Yeah.

HALDEMAN: He's going back to private life (unintelligible). Do you want to sign this or should I send it to Rose?

PRESIDENT: (scratching noise)

HALDEMAN: Do you want to release it?

PRESIDENT: O.K. Great. Good job, Bob.

HALDEMAN: Kissinger?

PRESIDENT: Huh? That's a joke.

HALDEMAN: Is it?

PRESIDENT: Whenever Mosbacher came for dinners, you see he'd have to be out escorting the person in and when they came through the receiving line, Henry was always with Mrs. Mosbacher and she'd turn and they would say this is Mrs. Kissinger. He made a little joke.

HALDEMAN: I see. Very good. O.K.

PRESIDENT: Well, good.

Then there ensued a somewhat disjointed discussion of various unrelated topics. The topics included social security, revenue sharing, the debt ceiling, the downward gyrations of the British pound and the Italian lira, foreign problems which didn't particularly interest the President that morning.

"Okay," said the President. "What else have you got that's amusing today?"

"That's it," said Haldeman.

But it wasn't it. There was the issue of school busing, and the President wanted to know whether John Ehrlichman thought "everybody is going to understand the busing?"

HALDEMAN: That's right.

PRESIDENT: And, ah, well (unintelligible) says no.

HALDEMAN: Well, the fact is somewhere in between, I think, because I think that (unintelligible) is missing some.

PRESIDENT: Well, if the fact is somewhere in between, we better do it.

HALDEMAN: Yeah, I think Mitchell says, "Hell yes. Anything we can hit on at anytime we get the chance—and we've got a reason for doing it—do it."

PRESIDENT: When you get in—when you get in (unintelligible) people, say, "Look the problem is that this will open the whole, the whole Bay of Pigs thing, and the President just feels that ah, without going into the details—don't, don't lie to them to the extent to say there is no involvement, but just say this is a comedy of errors, without getting into it, the President believes that it is going to open the whole Bay of Pigs thing up again. And, ah, because the people are plugging for (unintelligible) and that they should call the FBI in and (unintelligible), don't go any further into this case, period! (Inaudible) our cause—

HALDEMAN: Get more done for our cause by the opposition than by us?

PRESIDENT: Well, can you get it done?

HALDEMAN: I think so.

Then for about fifty minutes the President and his chief of staff discussed the forthcoming campaign, and particularly the convention at Miami Beach. Nixon also said he had been thumbing through his book *Six Crises*, and found it such "fascinating reading" that "I want you to re-read it, and I want Colson to read it, and anybody else" in the campaign. And next, with Ron Ziegler entering the office, followed a discussion of public relations matters. The session ended at 11:39 A.M. Shortly after 1:00 P.M., Haldeman returned to the Oval Office.

PRESIDENT: O.K., just postpone (scratching noises) (unintelligible) just say (unintelligible) very bad to have this fellow Hunt, ah, he knows too damned much, he was involved—you happen to know that? If it gets out that this is all involved, the Cuba thing it would be a fiasco. It would make the CIA look bad, and it is likely to blow the whole Bay of Pigs thing which we think would be very unfortunate—both for CIA, and for the country, at this time, and for American foreign policy. Just tell him to lay off. Don't you?

HALDEMAN: Yep, that's the basis to do it on. Just leave it at that.

PRESIDENT: I don't want them to get any ideas we're doing it because our concern is political.

HALDEMAN: Right.

PRESIDENT: And at the same time, I wouldn't tell them it is not political . . .

HALDEMAN: Right.

Later that same afternoon in the President's office in the Executive Office Building:

HALDEMAN: No problem.

PRESIDENT: (Unintelligible)

HALDEMAN: Well, it was kind of interesting. Walters made the point and I didn't mention Hunt, I just said that the thing was leading into directions that were going to create potential problems because they were exploring leads that led back into areas that would be harmful to the CIA and harmful to the government (unintelligible) didn't have anything to do (unintelligible).

At this point the telephone rang. It was Colson. The President asked "Chuck" to telephone John Connally to fill him in "about this quota thing," adding, "I don't want him to read it in the paper before Monday. . . . Good, fine."

HALDEMAN: Gray called and said, yesterday, and said that he thought—

PRESIDENT: Who did? Gray?

HALDEMAN: Gray called Helms and said I think we've run right into the middle of a CIA covert operation.

PRESIDENT: Gray said that?

HALDEMAN: Yeah. And (unintelligible) said nothing we've done at this point and ah (unintelligible) says well it sure looks to me like it is (unintelligible) and ah, that was the end of that conversation (unintelligible) the problem is it tracks back to the Bay of Pigs and it tracks back to some other leads run out to people who had no involvement in this, except by contacts and connection, but it gets to areas that are liable to be raised? The whole problem (unintelligible) Hunt. So at that point he kind of got the picture. He said, he said we'll be very happy to be helpful (unintelligible) handle anything you want. I would like to know the reason for being helpful, and I made it clear to him he wasn't going to get explicit (unintelligible) generality, and he said fine. And Walters (unintelligible). Walters is going to make a call to Gray. That's the way we put it and that's the way it was left.

PRESIDENT: How does that work though, how, they've got to (unintelligible) somebody from the Miami bank.

HALDEMAN: (Unintelligible). The point John makes—the bureau is going on this because they don't know what they are uncovering (unintelligible) continue to pursue it. They don't need to because they already have their case as far as the charges against these men (unintelligible) and ah as they pursue it (unintelligible) exactly, but we didn't in any way say we (unintelligible). One thing Helms did raise. He said Gray—he asked Gray why they thought they had run into a CIA thing and Gray said because of the characters involved and the amount of money involved, a lot of dough. (Unintelligible) and ah (unintelligible).

PRESIDENT: (Unintelligible).

HALDEMAN: Well, I think they will.

PRESIDENT: If it runs (unintelligible) what the hell who knows (unintelligible) contributed CIA.

HALDEMAN: Ya, it's money CIA gets money (unintelligible) I mean their money moves in a lot of different ways, too.

PRESIDENT: Ya. How are (unintelligible)—a lot of good.

HALDEMAN: (Unintelligible).

PRESIDENT: Well you remember what the SOB did on my book? When I brought out the fact, you know.

HALDEMAN: Ya.

PRESIDENT: That he knew all about Dulles? (Expletive deleted) Dulles knew. Dulles told me, I know, I mean (unintelligible) had the telephone call. Remember had a call put in—Dulles just blandly said and knew why.*

HALDEMAN: Ya.

PRESIDENT: Now, what the hell! Who told him to do it? The President? (Unintelligible).

HALDEMAN: Dulles was no more Kennedy's man than (unintelligible) was your man (unintelligible).

PRESIDENT: (Unintelligible) covert operation—do anything else (unintelligible).

The rest of the twenty-five minute conversation dealt primarily with campaign matters.

It is obvious from all this that it was Haldeman, not Nixon, who initiated the suggestion that the FBI be asked to limit the scope of its inquiries. And, contrary to the generally held assumption, the primary concern in the Oval Office was not about the break-in itself but rather the five telltale campaign checks which had incredibly been laundered—not illegally, incidentally—through Bernard Barker's bank account in order to safeguard the identities of the donors. As Haldeman later put it, "The June 23 tape does turn out to be the most damaging evidence available because it shows a political motivation in bringing the CIA and FBI

---

*The reference was to Allen Dulles, who headed the CIA in the Eisenhower and early Kennedy years. In *Six Crises* Nixon complained how Kennedy had taken advantage of CIA briefings he had received as a presidential candidate. According to Nixon, Kennedy had been informed of the covert operation being planned to topple Castro. Under the circumstances Nixon felt it was unfair for Kennedy to have urged more militant U.S. action. As a consequence, Nixon wrote, he had been unable to reply publicly because to do so would surely have disclosed secret plans. When *Six Crises* was published in 1962, Dulles issued a press release saying he had not discussed CIA "plans or programs for action, overt or covert" with the Democratic candidate. Obviously Nixon felt he had been led to believe otherwise by Dulles himself.

together. But it did not represent an obstruction of justice in the Watergate case, and that's what I was indicted for. It was purely a question of trying to prevent a source of campaign donations from being disclosed. And that was political. So maybe we used the CIA and FBI politically—but not in terms of obstructing justice."

And it was Nixon who kept raising the issue of national security —the possibility that FBI inquiries might extend into Mexico and interfere with CIA covert activities unrelated to Watergate. Similarly the President voiced concern that further investigation of the activities of former CIA agent Hunt, whose name had been linked publicly with the break-in several days earlier, would "blow the whole Bay of Pigs thing which we think would be very unfortunate—both for CIA, and for the country. . . ." Thus whether the CIA was a reason or an excuse for White House meddling in the FBI investigation is open to question, particularly in view of later testimony by L. Patrick Gray before the Senate Watergate Committee.

Gray, as acting FBI director, testified that, responding to the request of White House aides, he had contacted CIA Director Helms to determine whether any of the Agency's covert activities, especially in Mexico, could be compromised by a full FBI investigation. Gray said his finding was negative.

But Gray also testified that two weeks after the break-in, after he had expressed concern to Nixon that members of the White House staff were about to "mortally wound you," the President replied as follows:

"Pat, you just continue your aggressive and thorough investigation."

Asked later what kind of defense he had been planning had the impeachment process reached the Senate, presidential lawyer St. Clair said: "It would have been appropriate to argue that whatever was done was not of the magnitude to justify impeaching a President. Secondly, in fact, the FBI was not impaired in its investigation, that within a matter of two weeks they were instructed to carry on their investigation without interruption and that there was some reason to believe that maybe the FBI investigation was in fact impinging on CIA prerogatives. . . ."

Several weeks before the "smoking gun" transcripts were released, the President's chief of staff Al Haig unexpectedly telephoned his predecessor, "Bob" Haldeman, and asked whether he recalled anything about his June 23, 1972, meeting with the President.

"Think carefully," said Haig. "Do you recall any problems with it?"

"Absolutely not," replied Haldeman, who felt that at most the conversations were an embarrassment, rather than a problem, to the President.

The President, however, felt the conversations did constitute a problem as well as an embarrassment. Curiously, for a man who was alleged to have engineered one of history's greatest conspiracies, Nixon had only a dim recollection of the June 23, 1972, conversations. It was only when he listened to the controversial tape two years later that his memory was refreshed. And for the life of him he couldn't see anything in it that could conceivably point to an obstruction of justice. In any event nothing came of Haldeman's proposed curtailment and a full FBI investigation proceeded with the expressed approval of the President. Embarrassing the tape was, but hardly fatal, in the President's view. And so he tried to reassure his staff, most of whom by now were too shaken by the relentless media barrage and the certainty of impeachment to think very clearly. Panic overtook the President's closest advisers. For them the tapes appeared to be the "smoking gun" that the President's enemies had been feverishly seeking to prove Nixon's infamy conclusively. And the irony was —as one of those advisers, Patrick Buchanan, later conceded— that had the tapes been released earlier with the others, the impact probably would have been minimal. But standing alone at that late hour, they took on an ominous significance, particularly since Nixon had previously stated that he had disclosed everything pertinent to the House inquiry. As the President admitted, they were "at variance with certain of my previous statements." In other words the President in effect conceded that he had lied. And that probably was more damaging to his cause than what was recorded on the tapes.

One would have thought from the consequent uproar that previous presidents had never lied; that what Nixon had done was peculiarly Nixonian. The fact is, however, that mendacity is intrinsic in the government process. Franklin Roosevelt lied about not getting involved in foreign wars; Eisenhower lied about the U-2 flight; Kennedy lied about the Bay of Pigs; and Johnson lied about Vietnam. And in each of those cases far more was at stake than a third-rate political burglary. For, as the slogan had it at the time, "No one died at the Watergate."

Lying is not uncommon among media folk either. There was the case of Daniel Schorr, the CBS correspondent who won numerous kudos for his Watergate coverage. In early 1976 Schorr arranged to sell a copy of a secret congressional report on the CIA to *The Village Voice*. In a highly questionable transaction he also arranged for the proceeds to go to the Reporters Committee for Freedom of the Press. But when the report was published, Schorr flatly denied having anything to do with it. He told fellow newsmen: "I have no knowledge of how *The Village Voice* acquired its copy. I had no connection with it. . . ." And he also denied having made any approach to the Reporters Committee about the assignment of the profits. At the same time he did not level with his superiors at CBS News, letting suspicion fall on one of his colleagues, Lesley Stahl. Later Schorr confessed his duplicity. But instead of being disgraced he became a media hero. Among other things he was honored with a National Headliners Award. And though suspended from broadcasting, he still collected his full pay for a time from CBS News. He was lionized. Even Secretary Kissinger told a reporter that Schorr "had gotten a bum rap." In other words it all depends who does the lying.

On the evening of August 8, 1974, one hour before he went on national television to announce his resignation, Nixon met with forty-six of his staunchest congressional supporters—twenty senators and twenty-six representatives—to say good-bye. These were old comrades-in-arms, mainly from the Chowder and Marching Club which Nixon, as a young congressman from California, had helped form with other youthful Republicans back in 1949. Some Democrats, largely from the South, were also present. All had rallied behind the President in the past and most, if not all, were willing to rally behind him in his hour of greatest need.

The President arrived shortly after 8:00 P.M. and was greeted with a standing ovation. "It was," a Midwest congressman recalled, "a lengthy greeting that I am sure moved the President." After a few tense moments the President spoke of his family, who had stood by him so steadfastly throughout his troubles. But, he went on, he had made his decision to resign "on the premise that the presidency is bigger than any man. Yes, even bigger than your personal loyalty." Of course, too, it was obvious to him that a vote against him in the House was inevitable and that the number of votes he would need for acquittal in the Senate was probably more than he could muster. There were those who had counseled him to "fight it all through," but he said what seemed to him most important was that this "long, debilitating thing called Watergate should come to an end and a lengthy trial in the Senate would be just too much for the country." And the problems facing the nation, both domestically and abroad, required the services of a "full-time President." He went on: "As much as I would have preferred to fight it out, the country cannot afford a half-time President and a half-time Senate.

"Watergate," said the President, "divides our country . . . it gnaws particularly among men of good will right here in the Congress. One needs Congressional support to be credible abroad and I don't have it anymore. Therefore I will resign effective at noon tomorrow. I shall leave the White House around 10:00 A.M. and Vice President Ford will be sworn in at noon in the Oval Office, as I am winging my way back to California. I will still have the little black box aboard the plane up to the moment of transition. Jerry Ford is a good man, but no matter how good a man, how clever . . . he needs your support, your affection and your prayers. . . .

"This is my last meeting in this room," he went on. "I will not be back here. But without you—believe me, boys—gentlemen— I couldn't have made these tough calls without you. I particularly appreciate your calls of comfort . . . I want to say most of all I appreciate your friendship more than ever and I hope you won't feel I have let you down."

At which point the President lost his composure. Some of his friends sought to comfort him. Barry Goldwater, his eyes running with tears, hugged him. Then the President quickly left the room. For he had only fifteen minutes before he was to address the nation on television.

And as the Midwest congressman later recorded the scene, "The room was filled with tears, for each of these men had a really deep-seated affection, respect and feeling for Richard Nixon, the man, and probably felt closer to him at that moment than at any time before. I surely did and shall remember it for the rest of my life."

At 9:00 P.M., fully composed, the President began his thirty-seventh and last speech to the American people from the Oval Office. "I would have preferred to carry through to the finish," he said, "whatever the personal agony it would have involved, and my family unanimously urged me to do so. But the interests of the nation must always come before any personal considerations. . . . I have never been a quitter. To leave office before my term is completed is opposed to every instinct in my body. But as President I must put the interests of America first. . . . Therefore I shall resign the Presidency effective at noon tomorrow."

The President walked back alone to the residence. There he had dinner with his family. Then he and Mrs. Nixon took a last sentimental walk around the White House.

The next day the President bade farewell to his staff and members of his cabinet in the East Room. He received a standing ovation. And standing behind him, David Eisenhower thought how hard his father-in-law had worked to become President and how much he wanted to do a good job, and now "it was like watching a man die." The President expressed his thanks to those who had served him and closed with this admonition:

"Never be petty. Always remember: others may hate you. Those who hate you don't win unless you hate them. And then you destroy yourself."

Then he was gone.

SOURCES

CHAPTER 1
Waldie on Nixon pardon: Court Gifford, *Federal Times,* Jan. 8, 1975; Wallis on reaction to Watergate: speech, Roberts Wesleyan College, June 10, 1973; Solzhenitsyn quoted: *N.Y. Times,* Sept. 15, 1973.

CHAPTER 2
Replies to *New Yorker:* May 20, 1974; Royster quoted: *Wall Street Journal,* Jan. 8, 1975; Alsop on felony: Wash. *Post,* July 2, 1973; Mankiewicz rebuttal: Wash. *Post,* June 9, 1975; Schlesinger quoted: *Wall Street Journal,* July 2, 1975; Bartlett quoted: Wash. *Star,* Nov. 23, 1975; JFK quoted on Wilson: Benjamin C. Bradlee, *Conversations with Kennedy* (N.Y.: Norton, 1975), p. 135; JFK on Ohio: *ibid.,* p. 18; JFK on Baker: *ibid.,* p. 215; JFK on Krock, *ibid.,* p. 141; JFK on Rocky, McCormack, and Humphrey war records: *ibid.,* pp. 68, 74–75; *New Republic* on JFK-press: June 28, 1975; Exner on JFK: *N.Y. Times,* Jan. 15, 1976; Roberts in *National Observer:* Jan. 17, 1976; Truitt background: *Human Events,* Dec. 7, 1974; Oberdorfer on JFK-Meyer: Wash. *Post,* Feb. 23, 1976; *New Times* quoted: July 9, 1976; Bradlee on JFK re Meyer: *op. cit.,* p. 54.

CHAPTER 3
W. Va. primary: Lasky, *JFK: The Man and the Myth* (N.Y.: Macmillan, 1963), p. 346; FDR, Jr., quoted: *ibid.,* p. 344; Tallmer in *N.Y. Post:* Sept. 10, 1966; Ike threat: Drew Pearson, Wash. *Post,* Aug. 9, 1960; Hoffa in primary: Lasky, *op. cit.,* p. 332; RFK-Robinson episode: Lasky, *Robert F. Kennedy: The Myth and the Man* (N.Y.: Trident, 1968), pp. 157, 131–132; Roche quoted: Philadelphia *Bulletin,* Sept. 9, 1972; Childs quoted: *N.Y. Post,* March 28, 1960; *National Review* on Corbin: Dec. 16, 1961; Dr. Cohen quoted: *N.Y. Times,* May 4, 1973; JFK's Addison's Disease: Lasky, *JFK,* pp. 375–378; Lundgren break-in: Long Beach *Independent-Press Telegram,* May 4, 1973; Hogan records stolen: *N.Y. Times,* Sept. 30, 1973.

CHAPTER 4
Garth quoted: Jack Newfield, *New York,* Oct. 19, 1970, pp. 28–31; JFK quoted: Lasky, *JFK,* p. 467; JFK on Hoffa: *The Joint Appearances of Senator John F. Kennedy and Vice President Richard M. Nixon, Presidential Campaign 1960,* p. 74; *Commonweal* quoted: July 22, 1960;

Greenville (S.C.) *News* quoted: Sept. 27, 1960; Roper in *Saturday Review:* Nov. 26, 1960; Nixon a "racist" and NAACP member: *National Observer,* Oct. 27, 1972; Charges against Bellino: *Congressional Record,* July 28, 1973, pp. S-14944–14946; Investigation of charges: *Senate Select Committee on Presidential Campaign Activities* (Pursuant to S. Res. 60, 93d Congress), Sept. 11, 1973; Bellino cleared: *Congressional Record,* Nov. 19, 1973, pp. S-20817–20821.

CHAPTER 5
JFK-Daley call: Bradlee, *op. cit.,* p. 33; Childs on vote frauds: Wash. *Post,* July 21, 1973; Giancana-JFK: Memoirs of Judith Campbell Exner, *National Enquirer,* Aug. 19, 1976; Chicago *Tribune* on 1960 frauds: Dec. 11, 1960; *N.Y. Herald-Tribune* on Texas frauds: Dec. 5, 1960; *Look* on stealing election: Feb. 14, 1961; Sorensen quoted: *Kennedy* (N.Y.: Harper & Row, 1965), pp. 231–232; Vanocur question: *The Joint Appearances . . . Presidential Campaign 1960,* p. 81; Nixon's later reply: *Six Crises* (Garden City, N.Y.: Doubleday, 1962), p. 339; Wash. *Star* on JFK preparations: Nov. 13, 1960; Sorensen on USIA polls: *op. cit.,* pp. 203–204.

CHAPTER 6
JFK on firing IRS Republican: *N.Y. Times,* Jan. 6, 1974; Bradlee on JFK information from IRS: *op. cit.,* p. 218; V. Reuther memo: M. Stanton Evans, *Human Events,* Nov. 17, 1973; W. F. Buckley quoted: Wash. *Star,* April 4, 1975.

CHAPTER 7
Bradlee on JFK-steel: *op. cit.,* p. 77; JFK memo on press: Wash. *Post,* Oct. 26, 1975; JFK gaps in logs: W. Safire, *N.Y. Times,* Jan. 29, 1976; David Wise on JFK re Huntley-Brinkley: *The Politics of Lying* (N.Y.: Random House, 1973), p. 254; JFK on Fischetti cartoon: *ibid.,* pp. 326–327; R. G. Spivack quoted: *N.Y. Herald-Tribune,* June 10, 1962; F. Knebel in *Look:* Aug. 28, 1962; Bradlee banished: *op. cit.,* pp. 23–26; Bradlee on Kennedy's joke re steel: *op. cit.,* pp. 111–112; JFK on FBI-Baldwin: Bradlee, *op. cit.,* p. 154; Wiretaps: Staff Memorandum of Senate Intelligence Committee, "Political Abuse and the FBI," Dec. 3, 1975, and Wash. *Post,* Dec. 6 and 8, 1975; JFK-Halberstam episode: Lasky, *Robert F. Kennedy,* p. 176; McHugh phone bugged: Baltimore *Sun,* May 27, 1973; RFK-Mazo episode: Lasky, *JFK,* p. 536; Rep. Wilson quoted: *Congressional Record,* April 11, 1962, p. H-5884; Bishop IRS audits: *N.Y. World-Journal-Tribune,* March 24, 1967; Sidey quoted: Denis Brian, *Murderers and Other Friendly People* (N.Y.: McGraw-Hill, 1973), p. 247; Wiretap of press at Newport: Paul S. Meskil and Gerard M. Callahan, *Cheesebox* (Englewood Cliffs, N.J.: Prentice-Hall, 1974), pp. 254–256; Keating surveillance: *N.Y. Post,* May 19, 1973.

CHAPTER 8

Church quoted: Lasky, NANA, July 2, 1975; McGrory quoted: Wash. *Star,* July 14, 1975, and Chicago *Tribune,* June 16, 1975; RFK-Bowles: *Time,* Feb. 16, 1962; Hoover memo re Mafia-CIA: *N.Y. Times,* May 30, 1975; Houston briefed RFK: *Time,* Aug. 4, 1975; Lansdale quoted: Wash. *Star,* May 31, 1975, and *N.Y. Times,* June 1, 1975; Operation Mongoose: *Alleged Assassination Plots Involving Foreign Leaders, An Interim Report of the Select Committee to Study Governmental Operations with Respect to Intelligence Activities,* U.S. Senate, Nov. 20, 1975, Report No. 94-465, 94th Cong., 1st Session, pp. 148–170; Smathers quoted: Wash. *Star,* July 24, 1975; Rockefeller quoted: Wash. *Post,* June 16, 1975; Osborne comment: *New Republic,* June 28, 1975; Harker interview: J. Anderson, Wash. *Post,* July 27, 1975; Cubela connection: *Alleged Assassination Plots Involving Foreign Leaders . . . ,* pp. 86–90; Anderson on RFK: *op. cit.;* LBJ Smith interview: Wash. *Star,* June 25, 1976; LBJ on Trujillo and Diem assassinations: David Wise, *N.Y. Times Magazine,* Nov. 3, 1968; Trujillo endorsed JFK: Lasky, *JFK,* p. 448; Shannon recollection: *N.Y. Times,* Aug. 8, 1975; U.S. Criminal Code on Dealing with Foreign Countries: Nicholas Horrock, *N.Y. Times,* June 13, 1975; Ydigoras on JFK: *N.Y. Times,* April 18, 1974; *Wall Street Journal* on mistake: March 12, 1975; LBJ on Diem assassination: Wash. *Post,* June 23, 1974; Senate study on Vietnam: Chicago *Tribune,* March 20, 1972; Diem assassination: *Pentagon Papers* (N.Y.: Bantam, 1971); Lodge quoted in 1975: Wash. *Post,* July 25, 1975; Lodge's last talk with Diem: *Pentagon Papers,* p. 232; "Assassination Report" of Senate Intelligence Committee: *Alleged Assassination Plots Involving Foreign Leaders . . . ,* Walton on Op-Ed of *N.Y. Times:* Dec. 10, 1975; Eisenhower officials' denials: Evans & Novak, Wash. *Post,* Dec. 3, 1975; McCone remarks to Murphy: *Fortune,* June 1975; Safire on Church Committee cover up: *N.Y. Times,* Dec. 15, 1975; Von Hoffman on cover up: *N.Y. Post,* Dec. 23, 1975.

CHAPTER 9

Freedman in *Georgetown Law Journal:* Vol. 55, No. 6 (May 1967), p. 1035; C. Shaffer on RFK-Hoffa: Victor Navasky, *Kennedy Justice* (N.Y.: Atheneum, 1971), p. 406; Starnes column: *N.Y. World Telegram & Sun,* Jan. 26, 1961; Hentoff on RFK: *Village Voice,* Dec. 9, 1974; Sheridan quoted: Navasky, *op. cit.,* p. 409; Warren dissent: *ibid.,* p. 420–421; Hoffa comment: ABC documentary "Close-Up," Nov. 1974; Navasky comment: *op. cit.,* p. 432; Sen. Long comment: Lasky, *Robert F. Kennedy,* p. 244; Chicago *Tribune* comment: *ibid.,* p. 246; Salinger memoir: *With Kennedy* (Garden City, N.Y.: Doubleday, 1966), pp. 20–21; Trohan comment: Chicago *Tribune,* June 30, 1969; Hoover letter: Lasky, *Robert F. Kennedy,* pp. 351–352; RFK wiretapping: *ibid.,* pp. 348–358; Von Hoffman in Wash. *Post:* May 28, 1973; Mollenhoff on Rusk: Richmond *Times-*

Dispatch, May 26, 1974; Press hypocrisy on Otepka-Ellsberg: *Human Events,* June 16, 1973.

CHAPTER 10

LBJ 1948 race: Alfred Steinberg, *Sam Johnson's Boy* (N.Y.: Macmillan, 1968), pp. 260–265; C. Stevenson on Democrats: Wash. *Star,* June 24, 1975; Kohlmeier in *Wall Street Journal:* March 23 and 24, 1964; Wheeler and Lambert in *Life:* Aug. 21, 1964; JFK on LBJ: Bradlee, *op. cit.,* p. 216.

CHAPTER 11

Beichman on LBJ: *New York (N.Y. Herald-Tribune),* Jan. 17, 1965; LBJ on Baker a "son": Eric F. Goldman, *The Tragedy of Lyndon Johnson* (N.Y.: Dell, 1969), p. 98; Mrs. Lincoln on JFK-LBJ: *Kennedy and Johnson* (N.Y.: Holt, Rinehart & Winston, 1968), p. 205; Bradlee on JFK-LBJ: *op. cit.,* pp. 217–218; Goldman on LBJ-Baker: *op. cit.,* p. 29; Reynolds-Baker episode: *Responses of the Presidents to Charges of Misconduct,* edited by C. Vann Woodward (N.Y.: Dell, 1974), pp. 329–334; Goldman, *op. cit.,* pp. 96–100, and Rowland Evans & Robert Novak, *Lyndon B. Johnson: The Exercise of Power* (N.Y.: New American Library, 1966), pp. 413–415; Sen. Curtis on Democratic hypocrisy: *Congressional Record,* Nov. 7, 1973, p. S-20080; LBJ TV interview on March 15, 1964: Evans & Novak, *op. cit.,* p. 415; Reedy on LBJ: *Newsweek,* Jan. 20, 1975; Crane on Democrats' cover up: *Congressional Record,* July 27, 1973, pp. E-5158–5159; LBJ asked FBI to check staff: *Time,* Dec. 22, 1975; LBJ-RFK meeting: Theodore White, *The Making of the President 1964* (N.Y.: Atheneum, 1965), p. 265; Treasury wire episode: *Hearings before the Select Committee to Study Governmental Operations with Respect to Intelligence Activities,* U.S. Senate, 94th Cong., 1st Session, Vol. 6, Federal Bureau of Investigation, Nov. 18, 19, Dec. 2, 3, 9, 10, and 11, 1975, pp. 728–729.

CHAPTER 12

LBJ on Lady Bird: *Time,* Feb. 10, 1975; Sullivan memo to Dean: Fred D. Thompson, *At That Point in Time* (N.Y.: Quadrangle, 1975), pp. 126–144; FDR-J. P. Kennedy conversation: Arthur Krock, *Memoirs: Sixty Years on the Firing Line* (N.Y.: Funk & Wagnalls, 1968), p. 399; Boston *Globe* interview: Joseph F. Dinneen, *The Kennedy Family* (Boston: Little, Brown, 1959), pp. 80–87; Sullivan letter to Cambridge Conference: *Privacy in a Free Society, Final Report, Annual Justice Earl Warren Conference on Advocacy in the U.S., June 7–8, 1974,* Roscoe Pound-American Trial Lawyers Foundation, Cambridge, Mass., pp. 92–99; Truman anti-Semitic remark: *Newsweek,* Dec. 1, 1975; FDR and Jewish refugees: Gordon Thomas and Max Witts, *Voyage of the Damned* (N.Y.: Stein & Day, 1974); Lindbergh's travails: Walter S. Ross, *The Last Hero* (N.Y.: Harper & Row, 1964); John Roosevelt quoted: Bob Considine,

Boston *Herald-American,* May 25, 1973; FDR packing Supreme Court: *National Review,* Nov. 23, 1973; FDR favors for sons: Alva Johnston, *Saturday Evening Post,* July 2, 1938; Elliott's financial problems: Finis Farr, *FDR* (New Rochelle, N.Y.: Arlington House, 1972), pp. 271–275; John T. Flynn quote: *The Roosevelt Myth,* p. 272, as quoted in Farr, *ibid.,* p. 275; Prof. Kurland quoted: Wash. *Post,* Dec. 22, 1974; FDR bugging in 1936 campaign: *National Observer,* Oct. 27, 1972; H. Fish harassed by FDR: *N.Y. Times,* July 18, 1973; FDR taps on advisers: *Time,* Dec. 22, 1975, *Political Abuse and the FBI,* Staff Report, Senate Intelligence Committee, April 1976, and Wash. *Post,* May 10, 1976.

CHAPTER 13
Sullivan memo to Dean: Fred D. Thompson, *op. cit.;* LBJ use of FBI on Democratic senators: *Time,* Aug. 27, 1973; LBJ use of FBI at conventions: Sullivan memo, *op. cit.,* and *Hearings before the Select Committee to Study Governmental Operations with Respect to Intelligence Activities,* U.S. Senate, Vol. 6, pp. 503–510; Hobson-FBI connection: Wash. *Post,* Feb. 15, 1975; Wicker comment: *N.Y. Times,* Dec. 5, 1975; LBJ and Mississippi delegation: Steinberg, *op. cit.,* pp. 681–682; *N.Y. Times* on L. Clark: Jan. 29, 1975; Goldwater on press: Wash. *Post,* June 22, 1973; Roche on Goldwater speeches: Philadelphia *Bulletin,* Sept. 29, 1972; Hunt a spy for LBJ: Wash. *Post,* Dec. 20, 1973; *N.Y. Times,* Dec. 21, 1973, and Dec. 31, 1974; Schorr episode: Lionel Lokos, *Hysteria 1964, the Fear Campaign Against Goldwater* (New Rochelle, N.Y.: Arlington House, 1967), pp. 123–124; *N.Y. Times* smear: *ibid.,* p. 126; Knight comment: *ibid.*

CHAPTER 14
Moyers on White House: "An Essay on Watergate," transcript; Moyers note to DeLoach: *Hearings before the Select Committee to Study Governmental Operations with Respect to Intelligence Activities,* U.S. Senate, Vol. 6, p. 510; FBI inquiries re Goldwater staffers: Goldman, *op. cit.,* p. 299, and Steinberg, *op. cit.,* p. 689; Moyers explanation: *Newsweek,* March 10, 1975; LBJ on Moyers: Steinberg, *op. cit.,* p. 633; Goldman on Moyers: *op. cit.,* p.129; LBJ campaign commercial: *N.Y. Times,* Sept. 15, 1964; Thimmesch column: Baltimore *Sun,* May 7, 1974; "Five O'Clock Club": Evans & Novak, *op. cit.,* pp. 468–469; Democrats on Goldwater: W. F. Buckley, *National Review,* Nov. 9, 1973; LBJ resolution on Vietnam: Steinberg, *op. cit.,* p. 767; Tuck's spy on Goldwater train: Vic Gold, *Potomac* (Wash. *Post*), Sept. 7, 1975; and *Newsweek,* Oct. 12, 1964; *Village Voice* on Tuck: Nov. 23, 1972; Sayre episode: Goldman, *op. cit.,* pp. 270–271; Jenkins memo: Chicago *Tribune,* Sept. 29, 1964; Jenkins episode: *Responses of Presidents to Charges of Misconduct,* pp. 335–336; Evans & Novak, *op. cit.,* pp. 479–480; Goldman, *op. cit.,* pp. 295–299;

Sen. Curtis on records disappeared: *Congressional Record*, Nov. 7, 1973, p. S-20080; Greider in Wash. *Post:* Dec. 2, 1973; LBJ's Presidents Club: *Washington Monthly*, Sept. 1974.

CHAPTER 15

King tapes: *N.Y. Times*, March 9, 1975; LBJ and King tapes: Hugh Sidey, *Time*, Feb. 10, 1975; Patterson on FBI re King: Wash. *Post*, May 18, 1976; Katzenbach on reporter re tapes: *Supplementary Detailed Staff Reports on Intelligence Activities and the Rights of Americans*, Book III, *Final Report of the Select Committee to Study Governmental Operations with Respect to Intelligence Activities*, U.S. Senate, Report No. 94–755, 94th Cong., 2nd Session, April 23, 1976, pp. 152–153; DeLoach memorandum: *ibid.*, p. 153; Moyers on episode: *ibid.*, p. 154; *Newsweek*, March 10, 1975; Katzenbach on authorizing King wiretap: *Hearings before the Select Committee to Study Governmental Operations with Respect to Intelligence Activities*, U.S. Senate, Vol. 6, pp. 225–250; Hoover fed LBJ sex information: *Newsweek*, Feb. 17, 1975; Rowan on LBJ: Wash. *Star*, March 19, 1976; LBJ "name checks": Staff Report, *Select Committee to Study Governmental Operations with Respect to Intelligence Activities*, U.S. Senate; *N.Y. Times* on LBJ-RFK: Wash. *Star*, Oct. 12, 1975; Moyers on LBJ-Kearns: Wash. *Star*, Sept. 11, 1975; Alsop on LBJ's White House: *N.Y. Herald-Tribune*, Jan. 17, 1966; A. McCarthy on LBJ: *Private Faces, Public Places* (N.Y.: Curtis, 1972), p. 284; LBJ and Dominican Republic: Steinberg, *op. cit.*, p. 737; Thomasson on LBJ: Wash. *Star*, Aug. 15, 1973; Kitt episode: Wash. *Post*, Feb. 12, 1973; CIA and dissidents: Text of William Colby's Report to Senate Appropriations Committee, *N.Y. Times*, Jan. 16, 1975; Hersh in *N.Y. Times:* Dec. 22, 1974; Rusk quoted: *N.Y. Times*, Jan. 18, 1975; Two Clarks: Richard Wilson, Wash. *Star*, Oct. 21, 1974; Rockefeller Commission report on Clark and Doar: *Report to the President by the Commission on CIA Activities within the United States*, June 1975, pp. 116–118; Doar's memo to Clark: Wash. *Star*, Jan. 22, 1975; Greider in Wash. *Post:* Dec. 2, 1973; Kilpatrick on '68 campaign: Wash. *Star*, May 14, 1974; FBI use on Agnew in '68: *Hearings before the Select Committee to Study Governmental Operations with Respect to Intelligence Activities*, U.S. Senate, Vol. 6, p. 193; Wiretaps on Chennault: *ibid.*, pp. 195–196; Humphrey aware of illegal activities: *ibid.*, pp. 756–760; Humphrey warning to S. Vietnam: Jack Anderson, Wash. *Post*, Aug. 11, 1973; CIA in '68 campaign: William Safire, *Before the Fall* (Garden City, N.Y.: Doubleday, 1975), p. 90; and *N.Y. Times*, April 1, 1975; Chomsky and Von Hoffman quoted: W. Safire, *N.Y. Times*, Dec. 8, 1975.

CHAPTER 16

Cater quoted: *Newsweek*, Sept. 16, 1968; LBJ to Agnew: John R. Coyne, Jr., *The Impudent Snobs: Agnew vs. the Intellectual Establish-*

ment (New Rochelle, N.Y.: Arlington House, 1972), p. 16; Humphrey aide quoted: *Newsweek*, Sept. 16, 1968; NBC bug: *N.Y. Times*, Sept. 7, 1968; Anderson caught bugging: *Drew Pearson Diaries, 1949–1959*, edited by Tyler Abell (N.Y.: Holt, Rinehart & Winston, 1974), pp. 460–461; C. Phillips on '52 bugging: *The Truman Presidency* (N.Y.: Macmillan, 1966), p. 421; British journalists quoted: Lewis Chester, Godfrey & Bruce Page, *An American Melodrama* (N.Y.: Dell, 1969), p. 515; Kissinger on Nixon: *N.Y. Times*, Oct. 17, 1975.

CHAPTER 17

Thompson on advance knowledge: *At That Point in Time*, pp. 207–230; Advance knowledge: Minority Staff Report, *Investigation of Advance Knowledge of Illegal Political Espionage, Senate Select Committee on Presidential Campaign Activities;* Jack Anderson on advance knowledge: *Parade*, July 22, 1973; Wash. *Post*, July 25, 1973; Helms destroyed tapes: Thompson, *op. cit.*, p. 152; CIA connection: Thompson, *ibid.*, pp. 145–182; Baker report on CIA-Watergate: Minority Staff Report on CIA Involvement in Watergate.

CHAPTER 18

Neal quoted: *Time*, Jan. 13, 1975; Nixon-Dean conversation of Feb. 28, 1973: *Submission of Recorded Presidential Conversations to the Committee on the Judiciary of the House of Representatives by Richard M. Nixon*, April 30, 1974, pp. 108–109; Nixon-Dean conversation of March 21, 1973: *ibid.*, pp. 172–183; Rosenbaum in *Village Voice:* Aug. 8, 1974; Hughes hired Democratic lawyers: Philadelphia *Inquirer*, republished in *Congressional Record*, March 17, 1976, p. E-1350; March 18, 1976, p. E-1402; McCord and bombing incidents: *A Piece of Tape* (Rockville, Md.: Washington Media Services, 1974), pp. 15–16; Martinez article: *Harper's*, October 1974; Weicker meeting with Miamians: Wash. *Post*, Oct. 14, 1973.

CHAPTER 19

Wallis speech: *op. cit.;* S. Alsop on liberal journalists: James Keogh, *President Nixon and the Press* (N.Y.: Funk & Wagnalls, 1972), pp. 43–44; Nixon on Hiss in *Six Crises*, pp. 3–4; Senate vote on "slush funds": Wash. *Star*, Oct. 9, 1975; Media spokesmen quoted: Keogh, *op. cit.*, pp. 6, 8–9; Broder on breaking the President: Safire, *op. cit.*, p. 171; Kissinger on leaks: Lokos, *op. cit.*, p. 44; Senate Foreign Relations Hearing: *N.Y. Times*, Sept. 8, 1973; Goldwater on leak: *Family Weekly*, Oct. 14, 1973; Nixon-Dean quote: William Shannon, *N.Y. Times*, July 23, 1974; Colson affidavit on leaks: *N.Y. Times*, April 30, 1974; Colson on Hanoi rejection of peace: Chicago *Tribune*, May 14, 1975; Carter on press: W. Safire, *N.Y. Times*, Sept. 16, 1976; Transcript of Nixon-Dean conversation: *op. cit.*, pp. 157–158; Thimmesch on Kissinger testimony: *Park East*, Jan. 31, 1974;

N.Y. Times editorial: June 11, 1974; J. Alsop on pre-Nixon taps on him: reprinted in *Congressional Record,* June 17, 1974, p. S-10696; Kraft on Kissinger: as quoted in *Human Events,* June 22, 1974.

CHAPTER 20

Salinger in *Life:* Dec. 29, 1972; McGovern on blame: Wash. *Post,* Oct. 26, 1975; Osborne in *New Republic:* Oct. 21, 1972; Mankiewicz-Novak episode: Richard Reeves, *New York,* March 11, 1974; McGovern tricks on Lindsay and Muskie: Frank Mankiewicz, *Perfectly Clear* (N.Y.: Quadrangle, 1973), pp. 10–12; Cannon review of Mankiewicz book: Wash. *Post,* Jan. 7, 1974; Van Dyk on tactics: *Newsweek,* Oct. 22, 1973; Roche on Muskie episode: *Saturday Review/World,* July 13, 1974; Background checks by Sheridan: Mankiewicz, *op. cit.,* p. 20; McGovern dirty tricks: *N.Y. Times,* Oct. 11, 1973; Wash. *Post,* Nov. 7, 1973; Haldeman on Tuck activities: from Haldeman's Opening Statement at Senate Watergate Hearings, as published in *Watergate: Chronology of a Crisis* (Washington: *Congressional Quarterly,* 1973), Vol. 1, pp. 244–245; Nixon on Segretti: *Submission of Recorded Presidential Conversations to the Committee on the Judiciary of the House of Representatives by Richard M. Nixon,* pp. 103–104; Drew interview of McGovern: Transcript, "Thirty Minutes with . . .", PBS, Channel 26, WETA-TV, Washington, D.C., June 14, 1973; Tuck scared: Wash. *Star,* Sept. 30, 1973; Mankiewicz testimony on dirty tricks: Wash. *Star,* Oct. 12, 1973; Corbett letter re Fialka article: Wash. *Star,* June 30, 1973; Rosenbaum on McGovern illegitimate child story: *Village Voice,* June 27, 1974.

CHAPTER 21

Noyes in Wash. *Star:* Sept. 21, 1972; Eagleton on spying: Visalia *Times Delta,* June 15, 1973; *Washingtonian* article: Harvey Katz, Sept. 1973; Hentoff on Sirica: *Village Voice,* June 28, 1973; Mansfield on Ervin: James M. Naughton, *N.Y. Times Magazine,* May 13, 1973; Participation by reporters: Thomas Collins, *Newsday,* republished in *Congressional Record,* Sept. 20, 1973, pp. E-5963–5964; Thompson on McGrory: *op. cit.,* p. 234; Dash background: Adrian Lee, Philadelphia *Bulletin,* Sept. 30, 1973; Dash hired convicted bugging expert: Thompson, *op. cit.,* pp. 35–36; Lenzner background: Thompson, *op. cit.,* p. 33, and *Human Events,* June 2, 1973; Wilson quoted: Wash. *Star,* Aug. 23, 1973; Lowi quoted: *N.Y. Times,* Op-Ed, Sept. 23, 1973; Lenzner-Moore episode: Thompson, *op. cit.,* pp. 69–70; Krogh on Dean: Baltimore *Sun,* Jan. 28, 1974; Buchanan testimony: *N.Y. Times,* Sept. 27, 1973; Reactions to Buchanan: Thompson, *op. cit.,* pp. 117–119; Crouse article: *Rolling Stone,* Nov. 22, 1973; Dash reaction: *N.Y. Times,* Nov. 20, 1973; Armstrong suspension: *New York,* May 20, 1974; Simonds in *The Alternative:* Nov. 1973; Weicker as leaker: Bill Anderson, Chicago *Tribune,* July 11, 1973; Colson-Weicker encounter: Charles W. Colson, *Born Again* (Old Tappan, N.J.: Chosen Books, 1976), pp. 105–107; Weicker and IRS audits: *Wall Street Journal*, April 17, 1974; Haldeman on hiring Dean: *Wash. Star*, June 23, 1976; Huston quoted: *N.Y. Times*, May 24, 1973; FBI illegal entries: *N.Y. Times*, Sept. 24, 1975; Case on "enemy list": Gould Lincoln, *Wash. Star*, July 14, 1973; Dean list of McGovern supporters: *Wash. Post*, Dec. 22, 1973; DeBakey comment: *N.Y. Times*, July 7, 1973; Mills-Long report: Chicago *Tribune*, Aug. 30, 1974; *Wash. Star* quoted: Aug. 2, 1973; *Wall Street Journal* on critics: Aug. 9, 1973; Cox background: *Human Events*, Aug. 4, 1973; Chicago *Tribune*, Oct. 13, 1968; *Wash. Post*, May 26, 1973; Cox staff: *Washingtonian*, December 1974; Merrill background: James Dickenson, *National Observer*, Aug. 18, 1973; Kennedy quoted: *Wash. Post*, Oct. 21, 1973; *Wash. Star* quoted: Oct. 28, 1973; Cox leak episode: *Wash. Post*, Oct. 31, 1973; *N.Y. Times*, Oct. 31, 1973; Jaworski and staff: *Newsweek*, Nov. 12, 1973; *Time*, Dec. 3, 1973; Saxbe-Jaworski conversations: *Wash. Star*, March 13, 1974; Dean shredded documents: W. Safire, *N.Y. Times*, Feb. 7, 1974; Greider on reversed roles: *Wash. Post*, June 9, 1974; Warren-press episode: *Wash. Star*, Dec. 2, 1973; Von Hoffman quoted: *New Times*, March 8, 1974; Cohn in *Newsday*: reprinted in *Newsweek*, June 4, 1973; E. McCarthy quoted: *Village Voice*, Nov. 22, 1973; Dobrovir episode: Nick Thimmesch, Baltimore *Sun*, July 11, 1974; *Wash. Post*, Dec. 20, 1973; *Wash. Star* quoted: Dec. 20, 1973; Schorr speech: Bruce Herschensohn, *The Gods of Antenna* (New Rochelle, N.Y.: Arlington House, 1976), p. 141.

CHAPTER 22

Rodino book episode: *N.Y. Times*, March 25, 1974; Doar quoted: Arnold Forster and Benjamin R. Epstein, *The New Anti-Semitism* (N.Y.: McGraw-Hill, 1974), p. 68; Jenner background: *N.Y. Times*, Jan. 25, 1974; Jenner on TV: *N.Y. Times*, Jan. 16, 1974; *Wash. Star*, Jan. 15, 1974; Rodino labor contributions: *Wash. Post*, Jan. 21, 1974; Judiciary members' bias: *Time*, Feb. 18, 1974; *N.Y. Times Magazine*, April 28, 1974; *Wash. Star*, March 17, 1974; Schlesinger quoted: *Wall Street Journal*, Feb. 28, 1974; Thimmesch on hysteria: *Newsday*, Feb. 2, 1974; C. Morgan quoted: *Wash. Post*, Jan. 21, 1974; Kempton and Viorst quoted: Thimmesch, *op. cit.*; Welch quoted: Philadelphia *Bulletin*, Dec. 9, 1973; *Newsweek*, Dec. 16, 1974; Judiciary leaks: *N.Y. Times*, June 20, 1974; *Wash. Star*, June 21, 1974; Weicker quoted: Thimmesch, Baltimore *Sun*, July 4, 1975; Dixon memos: Chicago *Tribune*, June 19, 1974, and Wash. *Star*, June 18, 1974; Nixon quoted: W. Safire, *N.Y. Times*, May 2, 1974; Bartlett quoted: *Wash. Star*, May 25, 1974; Bridge quoted: *National Observer*, March 30, 1974; Luce quoted: *Time*, April 8, 1974; Cox quoted: *National Observer*, March 30, 1974; Ervin quoted: *Wash. Star*, March 11, 1974; W. Safire, *N.Y. Times*, July 11, 1974; Haldeman quoted: *N.Y. Times*, March 30, 1975; Buckley quoted: *Wash. Star*, July 26, 1973; Nixon quoted: *Wash. Post*,

July 2, 1975; Haldeman quoted: *N.Y. Times*, March 23, 1975; Nixon-Haldeman transcript: *op. cit.*, p. 224; Nixon-Dean transcript: *ibid.*, p. 62; Haldeman quoted: *ibid.*, p. 238; Nixon-Kleindienst transcript: *ibid.*, p. 726; *National Review* quoted: May 24, 1974; Transcripts compared: *Comparison of Passages from Transcripts of Eight Recorded Presidential Conversations*, Committee on the Judiciary, House of Representatives, July 9, 1974, p. 104; Finding Nash: *Congressional Record*, July 31, 1974, p. H-7453; Nixon quoted: *Wall Street Journal*, July 17, 1974; Anderson "assassination": Wash. *Post*, Sept. 21, 1975; *Supplementary Detailed Staff Reports on Foreign and Military Intelligence*, Book IV, *Final Report of the Select Committee to Study Governmental Operations with Respect to Intelligence Activities*, U.S. Senate, April 23, 1976, 94th Congress, 2nd Session, Report No. 94–755, pp. 133–138; Woodward-Bernstein criticized: Max Kampelman, "The Arrogance of the Press," *Washingtonian*, October 1974; Lester Markel, *N.Y. Times*, June 15, 1974; Nicholas von Hoffman, Wash. *Post*, March 5, 1976; Edward J. Epstein, *Commentary*, July 1974; Roche quoted: *Saturday Review/World*, July 13, 1974; Shanahan quoted: William Rusher, *Human Events*, July 3, 1976; Hamill quoted: *N.Y. Post*, May 13, 1974; Cox quoted: *N.Y. Times*, June 12, 1974; Boston *Herald-American*, June 12, 1974; McGovern funds: Nick Thimmesch, *Human Events*, Oct. 12, 1974; Peretz quoted: *Rolling Stone*, Dec. 19, 1974; McGovern letter: Thompson, *op. cit.*, p. 200; Muskie and Lindsay irregularities: Thompson, *op. cit.*, p. 197, and *Final Report of the Select Committee on Presidential Campaign Activities*, U.S. Senate, pursuant to S. Res. 60, Feb. 7, 1973, 93rd Congress, 2nd Session, Report No. 93–981, June 1974, pp. 558–563; Thompson on Jones: *op. cit.*, p. 201; LBJ-milk producers episode: *N.Y. Times*, May 8, 1974, Wash. *Post*, March 27, 1974; *N.Y. Times* on LBJ-Gulf: Nov. 26, 1975; Wild-senators connections: W. Safire, *N.Y. Times*, June 21, 1976, *N.Y. Times*, Jan. 13, 1976, *National Review*, Feb. 6, 1976, and Wash. *Post*, March 20, 1976; Wild's trial: Wash. *Post*, July 27, 1976; Myers-Harris connection: *N.Y. Times*, Nov. 26, 1975; Wash. *Star*, Nov. 20, 1975; ABC quoted: *Newsweek*, Sept. 5, 1973; Thompson quoted on Rebozo: *op. cit.*, pp. 184–194; Jaworski interview: Miami *Herald*, Jan. 9, 1975; Humphrey-Hughes connection: Jack Anderson, Wash. *Post*, Oct. 17, 1973, *Time*, April 19, 1976, *N.Y. Times*, April 6, April 17, and May 18, 1974; Humphrey gifts: W. Safire, *N.Y. Times*, March 11, 1976; C. Mollenhoff, *Human Events*, Jan. 31, 1976; Humphrey financial irregularities: *N.Y. Times*, Aug. 13, 1974, Chicago *Tribune*, Aug. 3, 1974, Wash. *Post*, May 28, 1974, and *N.Y. Times Magazine*, Sept. 1, 1974; Humphrey quoted: *N.Y. Times*, June 27, 1974; Thompson on Mills: *op. cit.*, pp. 199–200; Mills quoted: Wash. *Star*, Oct. 12, 1974; *National Review* quoted: June 7, 1974; Statute of limitations: Wash. *Post*, June 8, 1976; *Wall Street Journal*, Sept. 17, 1976; Strauss-

Ashland connection: Wash. *Post,* Jan. 10, 1975; Stans fined: Wash. *Post,* March 13, 1975.

CHAPTER 23
Von Hoffman quoted: Wash. *Post,* April 19, 1974; Kennedy quoted: Baltimore *Sun,* March 9, 1974; Pierson quoted: *Wall Street Journal,* Sept. 3, 1974; Rodino off-the-record: W. Safire, *N.Y. Times,* July 11, 1974; Judiciary Committee partisanship: Wash. *Post,* June 26, 1974; Greider in Wash. *Post:* July 27, 1974; Democrats on TV: Kay Gardella, *N.Y. News,* Aug. 1, 1974; *Village Voice* quoted: Aug. 1, 1974; Articles of Impeachment: *Congressional Record,* Aug. 22, 1974, pp. H-8967–8968; Wiggins-Sarbanes and Sandman-Sarbanes quoted: as reprinted in J. Anthony Lukas, *Nightmare* (N.Y.: Viking, 1976), pp. 532–533; Peoria *Journal-Star* quoted: *Congressional Record,* Aug. 2, 1974, p. E-5238; Noyes quoted: Wash. *Star,* July 23, 1974; Conyers quoted: *Wall Street Journal,* Sept. 3, 1974; Jaworski quoted: Martin Agronsky's Evening Edition, WETA-TV, Washington, D.C.; Von Hoffman quoted: Wash. *Post,* March 3, 1976; Geyelin quoted: Wash. *Post,* June 17, 1974; Hunter Thompson quoted: *Rolling Stone,* Oct. 10, 1974; PBS commentator quoted: Nick Thimmesch, Baltimore *Sun,* Nov. 5, 1974; *N.Y. Times* editorial: Oct. 20, 1975; Reporter quoted: Tom Dowling, Wash. *Star,* Nov. 12, 1974; Haldeman article: Wash. *Star,* June 20, 1976; St. Clair quoted: Wash. *Post,* Nov. 24, 1974; Haig-Haldeman quoted: Haldeman article, Wash. *Star,* June 20, 1976; Nixon meeting night of resignation announcement: Contemporaneous notes made by a Midwest GOP Congressman, Wash. *Star,* Aug. 20, 1974.

INDEX

Fairness doctrine, 62–63, 66
Fall, Bernard, 73
Farmer, James, 165, 166
Federal Bureau of Investigation
    (FBI), 111–112, 134, 143–145, 148,
    154, 161, 163–171, 178–179, 196–
    203, 206–209, 405–407
Federal Communications Com-
    mission (FCC), 62–63, 66–67,
    123–124
Feldman, Myer, 61, 181
Felknor, Bruce, 187
Felt, Mark, 331, 405
Fensterwald, Bernard, 45, 271,
    272
Fialka, John, 309
Fielding, Fred, 341
Fielding, Lewis J., 249, 287–288
Finch, Robert H., 55
Fish, Hamilton, 160–161
Fish, Hamilton, Jr., 262, 391
Fitzgerald, Desmond, 89
Flaherty, Joe, 69
Flax, Louis, 187–188
Fleeson, Doris, 228
Flowers, Walter, 392
Flug, James, 317, 336
Flynn, John T., 151, 156
Folliard, Edward T., 228
Folsom, Marion B., 64
Ford, Betty, 400
Ford, Gerald R., 1, 88, 194, 237,
    284, 346, 350, 390, 399, 400, 415
Forster, Arnold, 348
Fortas, Abe, 121, 122, 130–132, 135,
    138, 169, 180, 190, 191, 264
Fowler, Henry, 61
Frank, John Joseph, 38, 40
Frank, Reuven, 225
Freedman, Monroe, 106
Friendly, Alfred, 230, 233, 236
Friendly, Fred W., 62–67
Friendly, Henry, 336–337
Fritchey, Clayton, 230, 231, 233–
    234, 236
Froehlich, Harold, 391
Fulbright, J. William, 3, 93–94,
    183, 184, 206

Gall, Norman, 91
Gallagher, Christine, 73

Gallup, George, 37
Gandhi, Indira, 290n
Garth, David, 34–35
Geismar, Maxwell, 183
Geller, Henry, 67
Geraty, Franklin R., 219
Getty, John Paul, 39, 58
Geyelin, Philip L., 398–399
Giancana, Sam ("Momo"), 17, 38n,
    48–49, 85, 86, 103
Gilligan, Jack, 35
Gold, Victor, 173, 185
Goldfine, Bernard, 227
Goldman, Eric, 180
Goldwater, Barry, 59, 138, 164,
    170–175, 180–183, 187–189, 280,
    330, 415
Goldwater, Barry, Jr., 330
Gonzalez, Virgilio, 246, 268, 270
Goodell, Charles, 194
Goodman, Julian, 168n
Goodpaster, Andrew J., 102
Goodwin, Richard, 137
Gorey, Hays, 255
Graham, Fred, 344
Graham, Katherine, 202, 277, 286,
    367
Graham, Philip, 230
Gray, Gordon, 102
Gray, L. Patrick, 341, 403, 405,
    410, 412
Greenspun, Hank, 250, 264
Gregory, Tom, 250
Greider, William, 193, 214, 342,
    388, 391
Grenier, John, 188
Griegg, Stanley L., 242
Griswold, Erwin, 64
Gronouski, John, 182
Gulf Oil Corporation, 382–384
Gurney, Edward J., 44, 221, 324

Haddad, William F., 239–245
Haig, Al, 338, 412–413
Halberstam, David, 75, 186
Haldeman, H. R. (Bob), 255, 256,
    258–260, 283, 305–306, 312, 318,
    329, 330, 333, 356, 358, 359,
    367, 379, 402–413
Hall, Leonard W., 51

112, 127, 134, 137, 138, 141, 165, 167; Kennedy assassination and, 89–90, 208–209; King, surveillance of, 196–199, 200; military spying, 215; Moyers and, 179–180; presidential campaign (1960), 30, 33, 49; presidential campaign (1964), 164–173, 178–192, 218; presidential campaign (1968), 215–217, 219–220; as Senate Majority Leader, 205–206; senatorial campaign (1948), 119–123; as Vice President, 123; Vietnam and, 93, 96, 183–184; wealth of, 123–125; wiretapping, 112, 165–166, 196, 215–216; women, relationships with, 203

Johnson, Robert H., 102
Jones, Edward Murray, 38, 40–45
Jones, James R., 216, 380
Jones, Jesse, 155
Jones, William B., 345
Jordan, Barbara, 396n
Jordan, Everett, 138

Kastenmeier, Robert W., 352
Katzenbach, Nicholas D., 73, 90, 192, 199–202
Kearns, Doris, 203
Keating, Kenneth, 77, 81–82, 86
Kelley, Susie, 287
Kelly, Martin, 307
Kempster, Norman, 343
Kempton, Murray, 174, 284, 351
Kennedy, Edward M., 39, 88, 104, 317, 336, 338, 339, 378; Chappaquiddick, 20–21, 26, 387
Kennedy, Ethel, 336
Kennedy, Jackie, 7, 392
Kennedy, John F.: assassination of, 89–90, 208–209; assassination of foreign leaders, discussion of, 8–9, 83–92, 94–99, 101; Baker, Bobby and, 14; Bay of Pigs invasion, 84, 86, 92, 93; Chile and, 103; Cuban missile crisis, 81; Diem and, 92, 94–99; fairness doctrine and, 62–63; health, 29–30; Hoffa and, 105; Hoover and, 12; IRS and, 1, 39, 56–58, 60–61; Johnson, L. B.

and, 123, 125, 127–129; Katanga secession issue, 74; Mafia, link to, 17, 48–49, 103–104; presidential campaign (1960), 23–30, 33–40, 44–45, 47–54; press and, 13, 16, 69–72, 75–77, 274; private language of, 12–14, 69; Rockefeller and, 14–15; steel crisis (1962), 69, 72, 75; Trujillo and, 90–92; Vietnam and, 92–98; in wartime, 15, 23; wiretapping, 1, 71–74, 81; women, relationships with, 7, 16–20

Kennedy, Joseph P., 26, 48, 56, 145–147, 151
Kennedy, Robert F.: assassination of foreign leaders, discussion of, 83–90; Cohn and, 109–110; Hoffa and, 105–110; IRS and, 61, 62; Johnson, L. B. and, 112, 127, 134, 137, 138, 141, 165, 167; King, surveillance of, 195, 197, 199; Monroe and, 19–20; Otepka case, 114–117; presidential campaign (1960), 23–28, 35, 37, 38, 44, 45; press and, 75–77, 79; wiretapping, 10–11, 72, 73, 79–81, 110–116
Kerner, Otto, 210
Kessler, Ronald, 166
Kilpatrick, James J., 215, 354
King, Coretta, 195–196
King, Martin Luther, Jr., 10–11, 112, 113, 141, 165–167, 182, 195–202, 348, 363
Kishi, Nobusuke, 400
Kissinger, Henry, 237–238, 279–283, 286–287, 290–293, 399, 400, 414
Kitt, Eartha, 209–210
Kleindienst, Richard, 339, 360
Knebel, Fletcher, 29, 71
Knight, John S., 175
Kohlmeier, Louis, 123
Kopechne, Mary Jo, 20–21
Kopkind, Andrew, 284
Kraft, Joseph, 203, 292
Krock, Arthur, 14, 146, 154, 277
Krogh, Egil M. ("Bud"), Jr., 247, 257, 262, 285–286, 288–289, 322
Kurland, Philip, 157